The Misremembered Man

Books by the author

My Mother Wore a Yellow Dress (memoir)

The Dark Sacrament (non-fiction)

Christina McKenna

The Misremembered Man

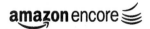

The characters and events portrayed in this book are fictitious.
Any similarity to real persons, living or dead, is coincidental and
not intended by the author.

Published by AmazonEncore
P.O. Box 400818
Las Vegas, NV 89140

ISBN-13: 9781935597766
ISBN-10: 1935597760

To Mr. Kiely as ever

Everyone has conscience enough to hate;
few have religion enough to love.

Henry Ward Beecher,
Proverbs from Plymouth Pulpit, 1887

Chapter one

Jamie McCloone rose from his bed, hotly dazed and stiff with undiagnosed lumbago.

Jamie was not an elegant sight first thing of a morning, most especially after a night of drink and embittered sleeplessness; a night in which he'd tossed and wept and brought the name of Jesus down and cursed his mother, in fact all women in general—nuns in particular—and wished a plague on all children under ten-and-a-half months (this being the age at which his mother had abandoned him, in a Curley's Discount shopping bag, on the stone steps of the St. Agnes Little Sisters of Charity convent, in the city of Derry, one cold November morning in 1934).

From that day on he'd always feared waking up in the claustrophobic darkness of some colossal pouch; feared being slapped on his bare bottom by a female hand; feared jangling keys and rosary beads, being locked inside boxes and lavatories, being fed thin gruel from a wooden bowl and cod-liver oil from a spoon. Such were the effects of those seminal events that, over the years, had carved deep pathways into the lumpy geography of his brain, rendering him incapable of forgetting the injury that had been done to him, making him wary of people and anxious of change, and forcing him to live a lesser life, full of empty dreams and broken hope, without much joy, without much meaning, without much love.

Jamie yawned extravagantly, ran a hand over his stubbly cheeks and tweaked his right ear. It stood up slightly higher than the other, giving him the look of being yanked forever heavenward by a celestial hand. This minor deformity had encouraged bullying in the schoolroom and funny stares on the street. When other boys fantasized about train sets and blazing cowboy guns, Jamie had dreamed of owning a perfect set of ears.

Sitting now on the edge of the bed, he stared down at his rough, forty-one-year-old feet, wondering idly about their uses; saw them, in that moment, as instruments of brute abuse, for stomping out the vision of the bitch that his mother must surely have been. Jamie was not a violent man, but on this particular morning—perhaps because his hangover seemed more severe than usual—he sat for longer, simply looking down, taking pleasure in the fanciful vengeance that was his, while outside the birds chirped, the rooster crowed, the dog barked, the cows roared (to be fed) and the day broke, sending a blush of hazy sunshine through the window.

The clock in the hall struck seven, jerking him free of the reverie. He rose carefully and proceeded to dress himself.

First, the red plaid shirt. Next, his army surplus trousers, zipped and buttoned over his expanding stomach, and needlessly secured by a set of brown suspenders, which he hoisted and snapped into place with a satisfied grunt. Then his Wellington boots, caked and frilled in last winter's mud, from their station behind the bedroom door.

In the back scullery he filled the pock-marked kettle, put a match to the gas ring, retrieved a chipped mug from under a pile of dishes in the greasy sink and proceeded to make tea.

He moved about the cramped quarters with exaggerated caution, as if balancing a hundredweight sack of coal on his head. As if delicate antennae protruded from every part of his body, sensitive to the touch, as if he were made of breakable stuff that needed careful tending and he were a man treading a tightrope made of twisted, shattered glass.

Jamie McCloone's limestone cottage in the townland of Duntybutt was a two-up, two-down structure, which he'd inherited from his adoptive aunt and uncle, Alice and Mick. It had changed little in its one-hundred-and-five-year history. No woman had lasted long enough under its broken roof to clean and polish its roughness; no man of a sensitive nature had ever entered it without catching his breath. Father Brannigan, the parish priest, on his monthly mission to collect his stipend, would often falter on the threshold, flourish a handkerchief and make a show of blowing his nose noisily so as not to cause offense. "It's the bronchitis, Jamie. Never leaves me, so it doesn't. The little cross I have to bear."

Jamie poured the tea with a quivering hand and carried the mug and his aching carcass to his armchair by the banked hearth fire. He reached for a Valium and swallowed it. The medication was his defense against too much reality, too much reflection on the past. Since his uncle's death, he'd been forced again and again to wade through the quicksand of his childhood. The pills helped him keep his head above the mire.

The demanding voices of the farmyard came to him in a muffled discordance; each one demanding feeding, each one reminding him of the work that lay ahead.

"I'll be out in one wee minute!" he shouted. "You'll be fed soon enough, all right."

He leaned over to poke the slack-filled fire into life. It responded with a slow hissing—the divil rousing hisself, thought Jamie. Without warning it spat out a chip of coal, which flew across the floor, ricocheted off a table leg and bounced under Jamie's armchair, where it joined a slew of others, adding to the accumulated detritus that was his home. He replaced the poker on the hearth, sat back in the chair and stared down at his lap.

There was a tear in the left knee of his trousers. Two weeks earlier he'd snagged it on a spur of barbed wire while tethering the goat to a post in a hillside field. Every morning since this small accident Jamie would sit, study the rent fabric, put his forefinger into the hole, wiggle it about a bit and think that maybe he'd need to put a stitch or two in it before it got any bigger. His eyes would then drift guiltily to the glass case where, propped against a green-rimmed plate, stood a fan of sewing needles in a gaudy packet cut to the shape of a flower-filled basket. He remembered buying them from a tinker woman, who'd gripped his arm after pocketing his penny and said: "God'll reward yeh, son. Dere's darkness round you but dere's brightness if you look for it." Her gypsy eyes glittered in the noonday sun and a gold tooth winked in a cavernous mouth.

Jamie pondered the image of the old woman for a minute and concluded that since it was a good while ago maybe the needles would be rusted by now. Even if they weren't rusted, where would a body get a bit of thread? And at the end of the day, sure, wouldn't it only be the two cows and the pig that would be seeing him anyway?

Thus mollified, he sighed and smiled to himself, the matter of the torn trousers and the needles and the tinker woman bundled back into that "It'll-wait-another-wee-while" box that sat tightly fastened at the back of his mind. A box that grew weightier with neglected jobs and weak intentions carried along by the wifeless Jamie, a man possessed of a thousand petty deferments.

He would have deferred the farm work too, but since Uncle Mick was no longer around to tighten the fences, scutch the corn, fill the troughs with J.J. Bibby Farmfeed, and switch an ashplant off of a cow rump when required, the work fell to him. He saw the onerous toil of the day stretch out before him. And, as was his wont, he believed in the efficacy of having a good wee rest before he got going. However, the longer he sat, the more urgent the notes from the farmyard animals grew.

After ten minutes he rose abruptly, drained the last of his tea, gave the mug a hasty lick under the tap, returned it to the sink and shuffled back to the bedroom to groom himself.

Jamie's ablutions consisted of fixing his hair—his oh-so-unsuccessful hair—and giving his face a rub (quite literally with his hand as opposed to a damp cloth). He lowered his eyes to the pockmarked piece of mirror that sat on the tallboy and looked at himself in dismay. His comb-over fell down on his left shoulder like a she-ass's tail. A deep scar ran from under his right eye to the jawline, as if all the pain of his life had been cried and cut there. His long nose and morose mouth stopped him from being handsome, but his blameless green eyes made one forgive the imperfections of his face.

He sighed at the image that stared back at him; an ancient prophet with a scalp condition. Every morning he experienced a pang of regret for his lost locks, followed by a sharp admonishing voice— *"Jezsis, look at the state of ye!"*—before fixing his hair.

Thus deflated and thoroughly depressed, he hurriedly arranged the precious strands over his balding crown, held them carefully at one side, and shoved on his cap to anchor all in place. With that distasteful act accomplished, this son of the soil was ready to face the day.

Personal hygiene did not feature in his weekday routine, which took Jamie from bedroom to barn in five minutes flat. On Sunday mornings, though, he made a special effort with a razor, comb and a basin of soapy water, before facing his Maker at Mass.

He was not to realize, however, on this fine summer morning, that he, Jamie McCloone, would soon be making such an effort with his appearance that even his Maker would have to be content with second place.

Chapter two

Lydia Devine folded her slate-gray, V-necked sweater (50% angora, 33% wool and 17% polyamide/acrylic) into a tidy rectangle and laid it in the bottom drawer of her chiffonier with an air of cautious contentment.

With the school year finally finished and summer wafting warmly through the bedroom window, she felt it was high time to put her winter wardrobe to bed. This realization, this moment which marked the transition from cool days to warm, gray skies to blue, from work to well-earned leisure, was the highlight of Lydia's year. It wasn't that she did not enjoy her job; she did. It wasn't really that she adored the sun; in fact, she hated getting sunburned. It was simply that her summer holiday afforded her some time to herself, to indulge her passion for reading novels, writing letters and taking long walks in the country lanes.

She sighed with pleasure at the prospect. With a light heart and a head full of joyous ideas, she danced to the mahogany closet, and—like a magician's assistant—flung the doors wide open. Inside, lay a stack of neatly labeled boxes containing the much more attractive lightweight blouses and frocks which signaled the insouciant nature of the next two months.

Nothing pleased Lydia more than an orderly environment with everything in its proper place. Too many years in the classroom instructing children to be clean, orderly, to sit up straight and keep their desks tidy had, of necessity, forced her into being a diligent practitioner of correctitude.

She dressed herself carefully at the cheval mirror, pleased that her figure still allowed her to zip herself effortlessly into the shift-dress. At forty and still unmarried, she felt a certain obligation to retain a youthful silhouette. Men, she knew, who could not find a beautiful face, often settled for a beautiful figure instead.

Pleased with herself, she sat before her dressing-table mirror, only to experience an all-too-familiar twinge of annoyance on seeing her face. There was little to admire. Her nose was too long, the mouth and eyes too small. An ever-deepening crease between her eyebrows bespoke years spent listening to her young pupils' problems and dilemmas. The cheeks were too red, the winter wind having much the same effect on them as the summer sun. No matter: She could remedy this flaw, as always, with a liberal dusting of Max Factor Sheer Beige face powder.

Her make-up routine did not take long. She had read once in the Dorothy Dibbit's beauty column of *Woman's Realm* that lipstick and eye shadow should only be used to accentuate the beauty of one's lips and eyes, not underscore their defects. She had wisely taken the advice. A carefully powdered face and well-groomed hair then became her priorities—and really the only improvements she felt she could make.

She rose satisfied, smoothed down her dress, neatly replaced the satin stool in the bay of the dressing table, and left the bedroom. The preparation of her mother's breakfast was already a priority.

When Lydia pushed into her mother's room with the breakfast tray all of twenty minutes later, she was surprised to find the old lady already sitting up in bed, furiously knitting at the cuff of a Fair Isle sweater.

"My, you are early this morning, Mother!" She tended to tune her voice to its brightest note first thing in the morning, in order to leaven the atmosphere. She felt it necessary, because, like facing her pupils, facing her mother always carried with it the same faint twinge of dread. She placed the tray before her on the bed.

"Thank you, dear."

Elizabeth Devine removed her eyeglasses and stowed the knitting in a tapestry bag by her side. She was a plucky seventy-six-year-old, still very much aware of her position as matriarch. Like her daughter, she was careful about appearances.

Sitting up in the bed she resembled a geriatric doll, an elaborate, baby-pink bed jacket, festooned with satin ribbons and crocheted rosettes, adding to this impression. The bright blue eyes that followed the daughter's every move remained focused, alert and cataract free, despite her years.

Only the aquiline nose—a feature prominent in the maternal family line which Lydia was grateful she had not inherited—spoiled the childlike effect. In her younger days, seen face-on, Elizabeth was a princess; in profile, she was the pantomime ugly sister.

"Did you have a bad night, did you?" the daughter asked, concerned.

"The sun woke me up." She looked up accusingly at Lydia. "You didn't draw my curtains properly last night."

"Oh really, Mother? I *am* sorry. Still, it's a nice morning to be up, isn't it?"

She planted herself as usual in the Jonas chair by the bed and waited for her mother to complain about some aspect of the breakfast or her daughter's appearance. Both women had become so used to this ritual—the one accusing, the other defending—that their first meeting of the day had come to resemble a lively session in the local courthouse.

Today, however, it was not the breakfast that was at fault, but Lydia's glamorous apparel.

"What are you all dolled up like a dog's dinner for? Are you seeing someone or what? That headmaster is a married man, you know." She noted the daughter's cheeks redden visibly, even through the protective layer of face powder.

Mrs. Devine's greatest fear was that Lydia might find herself a husband and abandon her. Her own dear husband had died a year earlier, and this tragedy, coupled with her advancing age, had caused her to loosen her grip on reality. She sensed that, freed finally from her father's stern grasp, the daughter might assert herself and seek her independence.

Reminding Lydia of the evils of men seemed the only weapon she had left in the battle for her daughter's affections. At every available opportunity, she wielded her sharp views on the weaknesses of the male species and the unfavorable estate of marriage.

"Men, married or single, only have one thing on their minds, anyway. You mark my words."

She whacked the top of the egg with her James Eaton teaspoon, part of a prized silver set given to her as a wedding gift by the Ballinascuddy Ladies Friendship Club and Circle.

"The only reason I married your father was because he wasn't much interested in all that bedroom unpleasantness."

She scooped out some egg and held it aloft.

"The only reason we had relations was because—"

"Yes, I know: to bring me into the world…" Lydia knew the script well and got there before her.

"Now don't be bold with your mother!"

"Really, Mother. I'm forty, hardly a child, and anyway isn't it time you stopped making me feel guilty for existing?"

She got up and went to the window, her arms folded tightly across her chest.

"This egg's hard! You know I can't eat anything hard with my digestion." The air crackled with the static of Elizabeth's sudden anger. "Dr. Moody says I have to be very careful."

"It can't be hard." Lydia concentrated on a tiny bunting that had just landed on a garden post. "I gave it the usual four minutes with Lettie McClean's egg timer."

Every heirloom and antique in Mrs. Devine's home bore the previous owner's name, a custom which Elizabeth had picked up from her mother and unwittingly passed on to her own daughter. Lydia had been raised among a ghostly crowd of relatives and friends who still lived among a clutter of crockery and bric-a-brac.

"Ah, Lettie McClean, now *there* was a woman; so good with her hands." Elizabeth lapsed into one of her spiels about her old, departed friend, the egg quite forgotten. "Could turn her hand to anything, so she could. Her flaky pastry was the talk of the parish and…"

The bunting suddenly rose up and circled the garden before swooping back to light on the same post, its russet breast athrob. Lydia marveled at its beauty, quite lost to her mother's ramblings.

"…it was the butter, you see. She once told me that her secret was the Kerry Gold. Never any of that nasty lard everyone else used. Her apple tarts won the Harvest Thanksgiving three years running, you know."

Without warning, the bird took flight and Lydia took her own cue. She turned, annoyed to see the toast and egg barely touched.

"Mother, I know all about Lettie McClean's tarts. I've heard about them often enough. Now eat your breakfast before it goes cold. I've got to get *on*."

She had almost shouted the final word, but just managed to retain her composure.

"Don't want any more breakfast," Elizabeth said defiantly, pushing the tray away.

"Really, Mother, you've eaten nothing. All that good food going to waste."

Elizabeth did her best to dismiss the patronizing reprimand. How times have changed, she thought, and her eyes began to well with tears. The mature woman by the window was no longer the child she had doted on. Lydia had grown free of her grasp, had outgrown the ponytails and ankle socks, the dolls and coloring books, and those bedtime stories that had transported her into sleep. Oh, how her mother wanted those times back again! When she alone was the fairy queen who could open doors and create magic in the little girl's world. When she had the power to make her daughter believe in dreams.

She struggled to remain stoical, still conscious of the importance of staying in control, and fumbled in the little tapestry bag for her glasses.

"You still haven't told me why you're all dressed up," she said, in no time at all back to her old battling self.

"Mother, it's the first day of my summer holidays. Did you forget? I dressed up because I felt like it. Because I'm free." She turned back to the window. "Well, nearly," she added ruefully.

"Oh good, then you can take me to the hairdresser's. I have the Women's Institute trip on Thursday and I promised Beatrice Bohilly that I'd make the effort, if only for your dear father's sake."

She patted her hair with both hands, as if checking that it was still part of her.

"He always liked me to look my best," she continued. "And he probably would not approve of my purple-pansy rinses. But you know sometimes he could be very strict, your father could, especially when it came to a woman's adornment; lipstick was for the harlots of Rome and jewelry for the traveling classes and—'

"In that case I expect you'll be wanting to be up and ready soon. I'll be back in a minute."

Lydia hastened to remove the tray, fearful she might get trapped in yet another tangled web of her mother's reminiscences.

Chapter three

After his midday meal, Jamie McCloone dozed content-edly by the fire. At his feet, Shep, the collie, was wrestling with the remains of his master's lunch: a chicken leg, a charred sausage and a length of bacon rind.

Suddenly, the dog barked on hearing a familiar sound. Jamie roused himself; a motorcar was struggling up the far side of the hill beyond the house.

Through the window he saw a welcome sight; the buffcolored Morris Minor was nosing into view. He heard the throaty rasp of an errant gearshift, as the vehicle sputtered and rocked down the incline. Presently it shuddered to a halt by the front gate. Jamie shifted in his chair, and prepared to greet his friend and neighbor Paddy McFadden.

Paddy's arrival was accompanied by a series of squeaks and rattles that Jamie had come to know well. First the horn was sounded in warning, then the car door creaked open on its rusted hinges. A short silence ensued while Paddy heaved his arthritic hips from the seat, banged the door shut and secured it to the trunk handle with a length of baler twine. Finally, a few crunches across the graveled yard and there he was in the doorway.

"Fine class of a day a say, Jamie."

Paddy hovered on the threshold before removing his cap. He was a mild-mannered little man, badly put together—legs too short, arms too long, ears too big, as if he were being pulled in both directions by phantom bullies. He smoked fifteen cigarettes a day and drank his whiskey neat. He went through life not wondering much about anything, but he knew for sure that God had a beard and the devil had horns, and that his guardian angel had been flapping alongside him from the day he was born.

"Not a bad one atall, Paddy," Jamie said. "Sit yourself down there."

"Rose sent a couple a them pancakes." He placed a brown paper bag on the table and made his way to the other armchair, taking a few short steps.

"Aye so. Keeping all right, is she?"

"Oh, the best, Jamie, the best."

Paddy hung his cap on the armrest and gazed about him, taking in the slack-strewn floor and dust-furred furniture: incontrovertible evidence of his friend's failure as a housekeeper. He wondered how Jamie could live in such squalor and shuddered at the thought of what Rose might say if she saw it. His wife's life seemed to revolve around a rigorous routine of cleaning and tending. Paddy was of the opinion that their twenty-three-year marriage had survived for the most part because early on he'd acquiesced to Rose's desire for order and tidiness.

When he looked at Jamie's home, he thought that if his friend were to find himself a wife, she would need to be a woman who was very fond of housework. He was not to know, however, that there was a very good reason for Jamie's fondness for disorder. It represented an unspoken rebellion against the enforced cleaning rituals of his childhood. Jamie would never discuss that period of his life with anyone. Not even with his closest friend.

"She worries about you, so she does."

Paddy seemed uneasy. Jamie wondered what was wrong.

"Who?" he asked confused. Both men, not having perfected the art of conversation, were apt to leave long silences between comments and queries so that they often forgot what they'd been talking about.

"*Rose* is worried about you, Jamie." Paddy scratched his eyebrow and studied the roaring fire. "Aye, Rose is worried about you, so she is."

Jamie did not know how to respond. "Aye, I s'ppose…" He trailed off.

Since his uncle's death, the McFaddens, being good neighbors and friends, had become increasingly concerned about Jamie. There was a woeful silence which he waited for Paddy to break.

"Y'know, Jamie, she said to give you…she said to give you…" He looked about him, confused. "To give you… Begod, now what was it she said to give you?"

"To give me a call?"

"Naw, it wasn't that."

"To give me the pancakes?"

"No, it wasn't that either—well she did tell me to give you the pancakes—but there was something else she told me to tell you *after* she talked about the pancakes." Paddy shot a look at Jamie's smoke-stained ceiling, hoping to find illumination there. "What was it now?"

"Maybe to give me a lift somewhere?"

Jamie was fast running out of ideas. But finally Paddy's brain tripped its memory switch.

"Och, now I remember. She told me to give you a bit of advice."

"Lordy me, advice?" Jamie sat back on his chair and wondered where all this might be leading. He thought Rose a very wise woman and was eager to know what message she had for him. "Advice about what?"

"Aye, well now, that's the thing…it's about, about maybe…well it's what Rose told me to tell you. It's about…" Paddy was clearly embarrassed. Jamie saw him look about his untidy room.

"About cleanin' the place up?"

"Naw, not about that. Well, what she told me to tell you is that… is that…" He took his cap from the armrest and started to examine it. "Well what she said was that maybe you should start lookin' to get...to get yourself a..."

"A car?"

"Naw, not a car, to get yourself...well, what she said was, that maybe you should...you should get yourself a woman."

Jamie winced visibly. It was as if Paddy had dealt him a blow to his private parts. No one had ever broached the subject of a wife. Not even his Uncle Mick as he lay on his deathbed, when he would have had good reason to.

Paddy coughed noisily with relief. "Aye a woman...that's what she said...and she said that you wouldn't be on your own if you got yourself one."

Shep raised his chin off the floor and gazed up at Jamie, who was now focusing on the fire, his brow furrowed, as if he were attempting to solve a mathematical puzzle of some complexity.

Get yourself a woman.

The utterance hung in the air like a cartoon speech bubble. Paddy, aware of his friend's discomfort, reached into his back pocket. He took out a packet of John Player's cigarettes and extracted two, each curved to the contour of his buttock. He straightened one out and handed it to Jamie, who automatically struck a match and lit both cigarettes with an unsteady hand.

"Och now, nobody would look at the like of me," he said finally.

"Well y'know, Rose drew me attention to something...to something...to something that might be a help to you. She sez to me yesterday, she sez: 'Y'know, Paddy, that's the very thing Jamie needs.'"

Paddy hesitated, puffed several times on the cigarette. He was nervous, realizing that he was on the verge of announcing what might prove to be a life-changing idea to his friend. The problem was: how to phrase it.

"And what was that?" asked Jamie.

"What was what?"

"The thing that Rose said would be 'the thing' for me?"

"Aye, well now, that's the thing, she said...she said that you... she said that you wouldn't have to go out and find one...in a pub, or whatever, because she said, well, what she said was that you could find a woman in the paper."

"Boys o!" was all Jamie could say. He had never heard the like of it before.

Paddy pressed on. "Y'know there's them that's puttin'…that's puttin' them advertymints in the paper these days for to, for to get men, Jamie." He saw his friend's amazement. "Aye, it's true. They say only a letter or two does it…." He paused and looked at Jamie's tea-spattered table. "Which isn't much to get your tea made…and your house cleaned up, and your, your bits and pieces washed and whatever else…" There was a weighted pause as Paddy searched for the right word that might cover the taboo subject of sexual congress. He gave up, embarrassed. "Aye, and whatever else you'd be lookin'."

Jamie was fiddling with the tear in his trousers as he listened, his heart beginning to warm to the idea, His glance swept the room—about all that ever swept it—as he tried to imagine a woman being part of his life. He thought back to a much happier time when Aunt Alice's fragrant presence had spoken to him in shining windowpanes, spotless floors, and in flowers that bloomed in pots on every sill. Yes, he decided, yes, it could only be a good thing. Rose McFadden often said that a house needed a woman's touch to make it a home. And she was right.

He looked across at Paddy sitting in the armchair where his future wife might sit. He thought of his lonely bed where a future wife might lie, and suddenly the scene darkened, and all the old fears reared up to fell him: fear of change, of circumstances, of other people, of women, of intimacy. In short, fear of all that might make his life better.

"I couldn't do it," he blurted out, more to himself than Paddy.

Paddy flinched. "Couldn't do what?"

"God, I couldn't bring any woman in here."

"But you wouldn't have to bring her here right away," Paddy persisted, oblivious to the turmoil in his friend's head. His wife had advised him to be forceful, and he knew if he didn't carry home a positive response, he'd get an earful. "You could meet her…you could meet her in a hotel…or a, or a pub or whatever first. Rose and me would help you tidy up anyway—that's if you…that's if you…if you decided she was right for you and you wanted to show her your home, like."

"And what kinda paper did you say these women were in?" Jamie tried to sound casual. He knew he could not confide his true feelings to Paddy.

"What kinda what?"

"Paper, Paddy."

"Aw, the paper. I believe she said it was the *Mid-Ulster*…the *Mid-Ulster Vindi*-something…"

"*Vindicator?*"

"Aye, that's the one: *The Mid-Ulster Vindicator.* You'll get it down in Minnie Sproule's on a Thursday."

A long ash had formed on Jamie's cigarette as he listened. The smoke issued up from it in a thin column and dissipated toward the ceiling, staining it a little more.

"I see," he said, powdering the floor with ash. "Y'know, I might take a wee look at it if I mind."

The combined smoke from the cigarettes, hearth and recent cooking had commingled to fill the small space, like a medium's ectoplasm at a séance. So muggy was it that Paddy had difficulty seeing Jamie's expression, but he sensed it to be favorable.

"Aye, no harm in lookin', Jamie." Paddy was relieved that he'd got the awkward news delivered and was also pleased that Jamie seemed to be amenable to the idea. He couldn't wait to report back to Rose. "Naw, no harm in lookin' atall, atall. And Rose sez…Rose sez, you're a fine lookin' fella, Jamie, an' she sez…she sez it'd be a shame if you'd to spend your whole life lookin' at the…lookin' at the…at the…"

"The fire?" Jamie said, while looking at the fire.

"Aye, the fire."

There was another slack silence. Shep, sensing that the conversation had finished, labored up onto his paws and wandered out the door.

"Rose is right about that," Jamie said thoughtfully, from behind his wall of pained repression. The wall from which Paddy had just removed the first brick, leaving a chink through which Rose could reach to help build for Jamie a whole, hitherto unimagined future.

Chapter four

The doctor will see you now, Mr. McCloone."

Jamie, head buried in the back pages of the *Mid-Ulster Vindicator*, failed to hear the summons. For the past few minutes he'd been dissolving the remains of a cinnamon lozenge, while his eyes roamed the "Lonely Hearts" column in wonder and amazement. So many faceless women demanded his attention; so many pleading ladies waited behind the newsprint to be claimed. He had never come across the like of it before.

"Mr. McCloone!"

Jamie jumped, tried to fumble the paper shut, but it fell to the floor in a heap. Florid-faced and flustered, he got down on his knees to retrieve it, aware that Miss Mulligan, the receptionist, was advancing across the floor. He'd barely got the last of the pages in order when he saw her black patent toes and thick ankles come into view. He squinted up and met eyes that glared above a pair of half-moon spectacles.

"Dr. Brewster Will See You Now." She amplified each word and bent unnecessarily low toward his left ear as if addressing a child, a senior citizen—or, indeed, an idiot.

"Right ho, Miss Mulligan, right ho."

He rolled the paper into a thick baton and stuck it into his jacket pocket before shuffling into the doctor's office.

Dr. Humphrey Brewster, a large man with bluish jowls and the eyes of a Clumber spaniel, did not look up when the door opened, but continued to scribble in his notebook. Jamie sat down in the vacant chair, put his hands on his knees and studied the doctor's bald crown as he waited.

He experienced a sensation similar to that which usually gripped him when he waited at the confessional grille, rehearsing his oft-repeated list of sins, a list that rarely varied from one month to the next. It was a feeling of foreboding that would make him want to bolt out of the box as Father Brannigan, bored listening to the same rigmarole and eager to get home to his slippers and supper of boxty and beef stewed in Guinness, called a halt to the penitential mumbling on the other side. Jamie wondered now about all sorts of cancerous warts and tumors, as he considered the sparse scattering of hair on the doctor's poll, and waited for the "grille" to slide back and the doctor to meet his eye.

Presently, the dreaded moment arrived; the scratching fountain pen was capped and the glasses removed. Dr. Brewster sat back in his leather swivel chair and laced his fingers across his pullover-ed paunch.

"So, James, what can I do for you this morning?"

"Well, you see, doctor, I've had this back for a while now. Can't seem to get rid of it."

"Where exactly is the pain?"

"Ehh, in me back, doctor."

"Yes, I know that! But could you be more specific?" The doctor replaced his glasses and canted forward. "Where exactly...upper, lower, middle?"

"Oh, aye, now I'm with you. The lower bit; aye, the lower bit. Gets me in the morning something fearful. 'Deed begod, there are times when I can hardly get outta the bed atall, atall."

"Quite so. Worse in the morning then, is it?"

"Oh...far worse."

Dr. Brewster, slightly hung over, dyspeptic, and weary of listening to the grunts and groans of the culchies and bogmen of Tailorstown, studied Jamie, saw a man who drank like a sea trout and smoked like a stovepipe, and decided, against his better judgment, not to rise and exert himself with any kind of invasive prodding.

"Sounds as if you have a touch of lumbago," he said, reaching for his prescription pad and pen. "Nothing to worry about."

"Lamb what, doctor?"

"*Lum*, James, *lum*bago. Comes from lifting heavy objects and lack of exercise." He narrowed his eyes in an accusatory manner. "Which I can see, with the farm and your lifestyle, probably fits the bill."

He began to write. "Any stiffness in the buttocks or genital area?"

"In the...in the where, doctor?"

"Backside, private parts, man." The doctor indicated Jamie's groin with a few swift circular motions of his pen.

"Oh, down there. Naw, never any stiffness there...not that I know of anyway," he added thoughtfully.

The doctor considered him over the rims of his glasses. "Yes, indeed. What age are you now, James?"

"I was the forty-one this May past, so a was."

"Still a young man, James. You should get out more. Take a break at the seaside. Good food, sea air... Do you the world of good."

"But who would look after things? Y'know I can't leave the cows and the hay and stuff."

"Nonsense! Doesn't Paddy McFadden live down the road? Paddy's a very obliging sort.... Portaluce, that's the place."

Dr. Brewster wrote extravagantly in his pad, his great chins quivering with the effort. "Still taking the Valium, I trust?"

"Yes, doctor."

"Helping, is it?"

"Helpin' a bit, doctor." Jamie consulted the floor, at once sad. "But they'll not bring Mick back."

The doctor, sensitive to the sudden mood shift, stopped writing and laid down the pen. "I know, James. It must be very difficult without your uncle," he said gently. "But y'know, time's a great healer. The medication will help you. How long's it been now?"

"Ten months, two weeks and five days, doctor. God I never thought he'd die. That mornin' I found him dead, I wanted to die, too." He began twisting his cap in his hands. "Still do sometimes."

"Come now, James, that's no way to talk. It's been hard for you, I know. But you're a tough one and you're making good progress."

"But I miss havin' nobody to talk to, doctor. It's just me and wee Shep...Mick was always there and we talked 'bout everything."

Dr. Brewster drew a handkerchief from his top pocket and began polishing his glasses slowly and ruminatively. "Hmm...that's why I'm suggesting you take that little break by the seaside. It'll take your mind off yourself and you never know who you might meet." He returned the hankie and replaced his glasses. "Y'know, James, there are lots of people in your position, but especially women of your age, who've dedicated their lives to caring for parents only to discover that when they die they've no one to turn to. You're only forty-one after all. A woman like that would be very glad to meet a man like you."

"God, d'you think so, doctor?" Jamie brightened slightly. "Y'know Paddy and Rose told me I should maybe try and meet someone, too. But I don't know if any woman would look at the like-a me...a wouldn't know what to say to them."

"D'you know, James, that fact alone would make you the ideal husband. There's nothing a woman likes more than a silent man; most of them could talk for Ireland anyway, my wife included."

Dr. Brewster let out a laugh and Jamie smiled.

"That's the spirit, James. Now promise me you'll have that break?"

"I will indeed, doctor."

"Good man!" The doctor took up his pen again and continued to write. "Now, I'm prescribing painkillers. Two, last thing at night; should ease things in the morning."

He tore off the page and handed it over.

"Me back's not too serious then, doctor, is it?"

"No, not serious. Gladys Millman. The Ocean Spray guest-house."

"What?"

"On the promenade. They say it's hard to beat."

"Oh, I see. Thank you, doctor."

Jamie got up, grateful that the ordeal was over, and thankful that the doctor had not examined him or inquired about his fag and booze habits.

"I'll go now, doctor," he said, relieved. "Ocean Spray, you say."

"That's the spirit, James!" Dr. Brewster got up and ushered him to the door. "Now keep taking your medication. It'll stop you from brooding too much. It's very important that you don't come off them until I say so." He patted his arm, "And after you take that break in Portaluce, call in and tell me all about it. Will you do that, James?"

"I will indeed, doctor. Right ye be. Thank you, doctor. Cheerio now!"

Lydia parked her Fiat 850 two-door car outside the Cut 'n Curl hairdressing salon on Killoran's high street, and helped her mother out of the passenger seat. This was a complicated business—the unfolding of Mrs. Devine—what with her rheumatism, arthritis, and general reluctance to being helped by anyone. A good five minutes was taken up, with Lydia grappling and the elderly woman resisting, before finally both stood upright, the car door was banged shut, and they made their way slowly and carefully into the salon.

Susan, the young assistant, was immediately in attendance with her cheery greetings, eager to get Mrs. Devine out of her coat and her head into the washbasin as soon as possible. In Susan's business, time was money, and Elizabeth could be quite a handful at times, "could keep a nation back" with her long-winded stories and remembrances of times past; stories in which the opinions of her late husband, the Reverend Perseus Cuthbert, and the foibles of the young always figured large.

With her mother safely installed, Lydia reminded her of the arrangement. "I'll pick you up in two hours' time, Mother, at..." She pulled back the cuff of her jacket and checked her watch, "...at half-past three exactly. That would be correct, Susan, for the rollers *and* rinse?"

"Yes, that would be about it, Lydia," the hairdresser said over her shoulder, already steering Elizabeth toward the washbasins. "A half-hour extra for the color to take."

"And where are *you* going?" Mrs. Devine demanded of her daughter. "Why can't you stay here with me?"

"Mother, I told you: I have things to do." And with that she made her escape.

Lydia drove back home, relieved to have some time to herself. It was only in those interludes of absence, when her mother was not about, that she could fully appreciate solitude and silence. Often, she longed for a life of freedom and independence, would dream of living in a quiet place, answerable to no one but herself. At the same time, she drew a veil over such a future, was reluctant to picture it too clearly because of the harsh reality that would precede it. Deep down, she dreaded the day when her mother's voice would not call out her name, when she'd not be needed to help her find "the dark way through her dress," when a breakfast tray would not be required in the elderly lady's bedroom.

Her mother's needs always came first, and Lydia rarely questioned why this should be so. Such allegiance and daughterly docility had been planted in her long ago by her strict Presbyterian father. Even in death his uncompromising spirit persisted. His thunderous sermons still echoed down the days, and the fearsome image of him in the pulpit, nostrils flared, great hands gripping the Bible stand, remained as defined and real as the Vermeer print that hung in the drawing room. She being an only child, the fourth commandment—the one about honoring parents forever and always—carried an excessive potency for Lydia. In no time at all, the helpless, obedient little girl had grown into a selfless, loyal servant, taking on the functions of nurse, cook, maid, gardener, cleaner, caretaker—and whatever other roles her demanding parents decreed needed filling. What a gift she was! The malleable, dutiful daughter to the righteous, controlling couple.

She maneuvered the car into the driveway of Elmwood House and cut the engine. She sat for a time massaging her temples against a headache, and gazed up at the respectable, ivy-clad vicarage where she'd been raised. It held memories of everything she knew: her infancy, girlhood, womanhood. She thought of the child she had been, inching her way toward maturity; so naive, facing the great and as yet walled-in future that had been so carefully planned for her by her parents. What chance did she have in the face of all that authority and good sense? It had been decreed that teaching was an honorable profession, and Lydia had willingly acquiesced. What else could she do? In her heart she had wanted to be a beautician, a hairdresser even, but could hardly have dared voice this desire. Her father would have considered her vain and frivolous and certainly no daughter of his.

Yes, her father: her intractable, inflexible father. For more years than she cared to contemplate, she'd lived according to his exacting standards. He'd constructed the rigid little box into which he'd fitted her life, his beliefs and opinions screwed tightly in place, and had hammered down the lid with his righteous reasoning. All her life she'd felt constricted. Now that he was gone, she wanted to stretch herself, collapse the sides of all that restraint, and break free.

She continued to stare up at the house, the prison, the box in which she'd grown up, and wondered at what point the child had become an adult. Because for Lydia there had been no defining moment, no chalk line crossed nor touch tape broken. She had lived forever, it seemed, under a disciplining hail of "no's" and "never's"; often she felt she was still a minor with little experience of the real world.

She was forty and had never had sexual intercourse, had never drunk alcohol, had never flown in a plane or traveled in a fast car. She often wondered, too, how far her upbringing had colored her likes and dislikes. She had no desire to swim in the sea or sunbathe on a beach or by a pool; did not like sleeveless dresses or a hemline above the knee. She retained an aversion to dogs, and still carried a scar on her left ankle where the neighbor's wire-haired terrier had sprung into the yard and bitten her when she was just a toddler. She hated being photographed in direct sunlight, could not go out without her sunglasses, an umbrella and a freshly laundered hankie tucked into her right sleeve. She had never danced to live music (but in her bedroom had shuffled her feet to Andy Williams, the volume turned to a low hum so her father would not hear, pop music being considered "the devil's refrain").

She had a dislike of certain foodstuffs: shop-bought bread, corn on the cob, tomatoes and cheese—such things having a tendency to make her feel unwell. She never ate between meals or standing up, hence her steady, unfluctuating weight. She hated crowds and went shopping in the early morning to avoid them. She was obsessed with time, was never late for an appointment and looked with disfavor on those who kept her waiting. She believed in the guiding power of the Lord, attended service every Sunday, could sing most hymns without straining her voice and could recite all twenty-seven chapters of Leviticus by heart.

In short, she was her father's daughter, and it took his death and his absence from her life to confirm for her that she had become a walking contradiction. Perhaps now that he was gone, she could finally be the person she wished to be. She pushed open the car door with a fresh resolve. It's time to change, she thought, and slammed it shut, causing a flock of ravens to bluster free of the garden elm.

In the kitchen she prepared the breakfast she'd postponed in deference to her mother. She had the best part of two hours to herself while Elizabeth got primped. She guessed that the hairdresser could do for her mother what drink, or other indulgences, could do for others. The styling of her hair was one of the few pleasures she had left.

Lydia sat down at the table, spread her napkin wide, poured tea, and smeared her toast with a film of Golden Bee honey from a frilly-topped pot. All at once she became conscious of the solitude, and how it was not a negative quality but one that gave her strength in the calm, bright room. She noted the hush that swelled between the random sounds: the traffic hissing past on the road outside, a child crying faintly in the house next door, the clicking of stiletto heels on a nearby sidewalk. And, nearer still, the thinning whine of the kettle cooling on the stove, the clink of her cup on the china saucer, the thrum of the fridge in the corner, her own sips and swallows.

She became aware also of her mother's cluttered kitchen and the emblems it contained, snagging for a moment on the nail of a childhood she wished she could forget. It seemed that all the bric-a-brac on walls and shelves hauled her back to the episodes that had put them there. Those things Lydia knew could not be removed until her mother died. Those connections. Those reminders.

The risen Christ looked fondly down upon her from a gilt-edged print on the far wall; an anniversary gift which she'd bought her parents in The Good Shepherd bookstore when she was twelve. The man behind the counter had frightened her. She remembered his hooded eyes and the long white beard, his purple mouth, like a buried bruise. He might himself have been the risen Christ. He had counted the change into her palm with long pale fingers and rasped "Praised be the Lord, my child," causing her to run for the door.

She remembered her parents' smiling approval as they unwrapped the picture. Her father had conjured a hammer and nail as if from nowhere and secured it to the wall. And there it had hung, unmoved, for twenty-eight years. She guessed that the portrait of a smiling Queen Elizabeth below it might have hung there just as long, and the fan of souvenir spoons from trips to the coast, and the faded tapestry of birds gliding on their smudged reflections over a pond— its age, whom it had belonged to, she did not know, but she believed it might have been another precious wedding gift.

It seemed that every room in the house had the power to entrap her with some form of sentimental pull.

The sound of the postman at the front door brought her back to the present. She went immediately into the hall and collected the letters lying on the *Bless This House* mat.

There was a bill from the electricity company, a circular from Gallagher's furniture store ("20% off all Draylon suites") and a stiff vellum envelope which looked like a greetings card. She trashed the furniture flyer, stuck the invoice in Uncle Sinclair's wooden cat on the kitchen windowsill, and sat down again at the table to open the letter. It was addressed to her.

It was a card with a gilded edge, a wedding invitation. Lydia saw that it was from an old college friend: Heather Price. Gosh, she hadn't seen or spoken to her in years.

Herbert and Henrietta Price
Have great pleasure in requesting the company of
Lydia Devine & Partner
On the occasion of the marriage of their daughter
Heather
to Mr. Simon Taylor
on August 28th 1974 in St. Hilda's Parish Church
& afterwards at the Ross Park Hotel,
Main Street, Killoran

Lydia reread the invitation with a mounting sense of unease. It was that word "partner" which caused her the most discomfort. All her old girlfriends seemed to be married now, and she was not. She had attended too many of those weddings, knew all too well the embarrassment of being seen in the company of her fractious mother, and the attendant smirks and sly looks that went with the questions: "Any word of you, Lydia? When are you going to give us another big day?"

She returned the card to the envelope, angry at the very thought. Yes, she would go to the blasted wedding, and she would find a man to accompany her—even if she had to hire one for the day! After all, her father was no longer around to censor her every move. And as for her mother: She was not her partner, and was therefore not invited. And, by heavens, she would no longer stand in her way!

Lydia knew what she had to do. She'd look up Daphne at the library and ask her advice. Daphne always knew what to do in such circumstances. She rose, galvanized into action, checked her watch, saw that she had most of an hour left, grabbed her purse and left the house.

Chapter five

Tailorstown, a small village in County Derry, had started out with Flynn the grocer, O'Shea the bar owner, Duffy the undertaker, a smattering of dwellings and the obligatory parish church. Over the decades it expanded its buildings and population through the committed efforts of the above-mentioned stalwarts, alongside a steady influx of traders and urban speculators. So the ladies from the shirt factory met the bricklayers from the council estates, and in time the school and every church pew were filled with the by-products of their passions. Tailorstown was a success.

To the outsider, the village was nothing more than a one-horse town leading nowhere, ringed by the peaks of the Slievegerrin mountains, which neither sightseer nor adventurer yearned much to see. Like most small villages, Tailorstown remained unremarkable, of interest only to its townsfolk and the local historical society. A society which had been formed, out of frustration, by a retired school principal, who, after a lifetime of hammering the daylights out of pupils, needed a displacement activity to keep bitterness at bay.

Jamie McCloone unchained his bike from the railings outside the doctor's office and began pushing it up the main street, the spokes a-glitter and wheels ticking like crickets as he walked. Few people were out and about that fine sunny morning. The mothers were in their kitchens, the fathers at their trades or in the fields, while their offspring ran loose in yards and gardens, enjoying their first few days of freedom from school.

Jamie felt at peace, content for the most part, living in the vicinity of this tranquil place. There were times when he felt like a twig in a river—broken off and insignificant perhaps, sometimes getting caught and tossed in the rough rapids, but eventually breaking free again to be carried along by the great force and flow that told him he belonged. Tailorstown was home.

The morning's events had lifted his spirits—what with the discovery of the "Lonely Hearts" column, the doctor's good news, and the prospect of his break at the seaside taking shape—a celebration was called for in the nearest pub. But which one? They were all within spitting distance. He had to think hard since he'd run up tabs in Hickie's, Doolan's and O'Shea's, yet had difficulty deciding which bar had the steepest tally and, as a consequence, might be the least welcoming at that hour of the morning. After a few minutes of brow-puckering uncertainty, he decided on O'Shea's, because it was nearest and he had a few bob on him anyway, and Slope wasn't the worst, and…

"Slope" O'Shea—bartender, janitor, cleaner and long-suffering spouse of Peggy—had a disposition to annoy, and could, with drink taken, let slip ill-considered observations on his fellow men. He was in the process of opening the premises, having overslept because of a late night. He was none too pleased at the sight of Jamie in the doorway. His head ached and his stomach heaved every time he righted a bar stool or returned a chair to one of the many tables in the lounge of his establishment.

"Morning, Slope," Jamie called out. "A fine one, isn't it?"

He struggled up onto one of the high stools at the counter, hooked his feet under the foot rail, rested his elbows on the blue-veined Formica counter and settled himself.

"Aye, Jamie, not a bad one atall," sighed Slope.

Due to his calling, Slope had, over the years, mastered the art of initiating and prolonging the mindless conversation. On this occasion, however, he was in no mood for talk. He reluctantly left off the unstacking and pushed open the half-door behind the bar counter. He had earned his nickname from his slouching gait and slow manner, had the stunned, vacant look of a man prematurely released from a mental institution, a man still coming to terms with the fact that a doctor had been crazy enough to let him out; his raised eyebrows and wall-eyed stare seemed permanently focused on some preternatural mishap a little ways ahead.

"Usual, is it?" he asked Jamie's left ear.

"Aye, and a wee drop of that port wine as well, if you have it."

Jamie half-rose off the stool to fish the money from his trousers pocket. A few fumbling moments later he slapped down a heap of loose coinage—along with a fistful of hayseeds, a bus ticket, a rusty wing nut, a spent match, the remains of a custard cream—and began to sort through it.

"You didn't, be any chance, see that Barn Conway about, did you?"

"Well, I did and I didn't," said Slope evasively. "Were you lookin' him, were ye?"

He placed the Black Bush whiskey in front of Jamie, taking care not to catch his eye—which wasn't difficult, given his strabismus—slid a jug of water into place beside the tumbler and proceeded to pour the glass of port wine.

"Aye, the bugger owes me three pound...borra-ed it off me a couple a months back." Jamie trembled an inch of water into the whiskey and took a gulp. "So, ye said there that y'seen him, did ye?"

"Aye, I did but at the same time I didn't, if you unnerstand me, Jamie?"

"Naw, I don't!"

Jamie wiped a hand across his mouth and stared at Slope. If there was one thing he disliked it was being made to look foolish. Slope read the disquieting signs and reveled in the knowledge that he was provoking the farmer. Since McCloone's appearance, his hangover, just about bearable, had begun to throb with a dogged intensity.

"Well, it's like this," Slope explained, "a boy came in here the other night and I thought it was him…had the same head on him as Potts. But, when I got up on him, begod, it wasn't him atall."

"So ye didn't see him then?"

"Well, you know, Jamie, when you put it like that, a suppose a didn't." He then added casually: "But if a *do* see him, I'll tell him you were lookin' him, so a will."

There followed a sore silence in which Slope celebrated his tiny victory and Jamie sat with feathers ruffled, unable to let go.

"Why didn't you say that at the start, then?" he demanded.

"Say what at the start?"

"Say that you hadn't seen Conway atall atall!"

"Well, a *didn't*, because as I told you before, I *thought I'd seen him, didn't I?*"

Jamie would have left it at that had Slope not grinned in that triumphal, point-scoring way which so incensed him. He desperately wanted to say, "Well, maybe you should get yourself a pair of glasses, you squinty-eyed frigger." But he knew that voicing such an observation would most likely land him outside on the street. Since he really did want another drink, he decided to change tack and irritate Slope by talking about his planned vacation by the sea.

He took another gulp of the whiskey while the barman's skewed logic and crazy eyes roamed about looking for a purchase on what his customer might say next.

"Could be doin' with it now," Jamie said, as if their convoluted exchange had never taken place.

"Could be doin' with *what* now?"

"The three pound Conway borra-ed off me."

"And what's the big hurry with the three pound? Christ, it isn't as if you're gonna starve if you don't get it."

"Well now, the doctor sez that I need to rest meself by the sea-side with me sore back, and the three pound would be useful, so it would, for the wee holiday."

Jamie's statement had the desired effect.

"What? *You* need a holiday? God, your whole bloody life's a holiday." Slope gave out an adenoidal snort and returned to his chores.

"If you had a bloody bar to run and kegs to haul about all day, you'd know about backs."

"I've got lambago," Jamie protested, "and the doctor sez I have tae rest."

"Lambago me arse! That's the big drum the Prods bate the bejayzis outta on the Twelfth, isn't it?"

Jamie ignored the weak joke and continued his attempt to win a sympathetic ear.

"It's true a man of my time a day needs to be takin' things easy," he said, pushing the empty whiskey glass aside and reaching for the port wine. "And you know I'd need-a be givin' up this stuff too." He stared into the glass, trying—and failing—to work up a sense of guilt for this indispensable, daily indulgence. "But sure what would a body do with hisself if he didn't have it, like?"

He threw back the wine in one fiery gulp, thumped the glass down and belched. A hot glow flushed his neck and face and he experienced a rush of pure bliss for one heady minute. He swayed slightly on the stool and wiped his mouth.

"Another wee one a them, Slope, if you please."

The pub owner, wanting desperately to be rid of him whilst simultaneously wishing to remain reasonably civil, finished his tidying and went back behind the counter.

"Only if you have the money for it, Jamie."

He slapped a dishcloth on the counter and began to wipe it with slow circular motions while Jamie fiddled like a shove-halfpenny player with the slew of coins before him. To Slope's disappointment, he came up with the correct sum, and another glass of port wine was duly placed before him.

Slope shook a cigarette from a crumpled pack and lit it. He was aware that the farmer wanted one too, but thought he'd make him suffer the indignity of having to ask for one.

Jamie shifted uneasily on the seat. He had purposely left his cigarettes at home, lest Dr. Brewster find them on his person. Now he was dying for one.

"Y'wouldn't have another wee one a them on you, would ye, Slope?"

A tense silence followed as the two sucked greedily on the cigarettes and released lungfuls of smoke into the air. This was an uneasy silence that stretched like a rope between them, held taut through years of resentment and remembered injury. But each needed the other: Slope needed the custom and Jamie needed the drink. On this frayed logic their relationship somehow worked.

The sun struck hotly through the large, flyspecked window, making Jamie's eyes water and revealing Slope's slapdash ministrations with mop and cloth. Outside, a truck roared past on its way to Killoran. Jamie felt the vibration of its velocity under his elbows; Slope felt a similar sensation in his crepe-soled feet. In its aftermath, someone wolf-whistled loudly, and on the heels of its quivering end-note, the door opened and in shuffled Miss Maisie Ryan in her orthopedic sandals, come to collect her money from the Padre Pio charity box Slope kept on the counter.

"That son a Minnie Sproule's is gettin' to be a awful cheeky ruffian," she complained, shutting the door and giving off wafts of camphor balls and peppermint. She placed a gingham pegbag on the counter.

"How are ye, Maisie?" Slope placed his smoke in an ashtray.

"Not so good, Mr. O'Shea, between me hips and me bunions I'm nearly kilt, but sure I offer them up at Mass every morning. That's all a body can do." She turned her attention to Jamie.

"And how are you, Jamie? Didn't see you at Mass lately."

"Naw, I was in bed with me back, Maisie. The doctor says it's lambago and I have a heap-a tablets to take."

Slope upended the box and began to count out the money, building careful towers of nickel and copper like a croupier at the gaming table, while Maisie looked on and Jamie eyed Maisie. What he saw was a bull terrier in a tweed coat, wearing a pair of highly reflective double-sighted eyeglasses. The glasses made her eyes look huge in her pillowy face, and her small mouth spent most of the day pursed in scorn. On her head was the inevitable knitted cap, pulled well over her ears despite the summer heat.

She was a dedicated churchgoer, devoted do-gooder, and throbbing artery of village gossip. She sharpened her tongue on the loose lives of others and judged each member of the community by the dazzling light of her own unattainable standards. Slope rarely attended church, but was excused because he was a married businessman with money, which in Maisie's book was equated with respectability. Jamie, being a poor bachelor with a drink problem, was a target.

"Maybe if ye spent more time in church than the pub, Jamie, then God wouldn't give ye the sore back to start with," she piped triumphantly.

"Aye so…" He pretended to ponder this with a serious air, thinking to himself what a nosy oul' bitch she was.

All at once their attention was diverted by a rap on the window, and the trio turned to see the disagreeable face of local bad-boy Chuck Sproule grinning in at them.

"Hey'ya Maisie?" he hollered. "Hey'ya, Jamie. Be givin' the oul' accordjin a squeeze on Sa'rday night, will ye?"

"Get down-a that window, Sproule, or I'll come out an' knock ye off it!" Slope warned.

"Hey'ya, Slope!" Sproule's head disappeared momentarily from view and then shot back up again. "Hey, Slope," he shouted, "blessed are the squinty-eyed for they shall see God twice!"

Slope dashed to the door and yanked it open, but by then young Sproule had taken off like a whippet down the main street.

The bartender banged the door shut and returned behind the counter, his face flaming. Jamie put a hand to his mouth, stifling a grin.

"There's nothin' funny about it, McCloone!" Slope glared in his general direction.

"I'm gonna 'ave a word with that rascal's mother," said Maisie, casting a hostile eye at Jamie. "But then his father spent most of his days in the pub, and a wild dog never reared a tame pup, as you well know, Mr. O'Shea."

"You're right there, Maisie!" Slope deposited the money into the pegbag, "There ye go: six pounds and four pence."

"Thank you very much, Mr. O'Shea."

"Tell ye what would fix Jamie's bad back, Maisie," he added, addressing a spot north of Maisie's eyebrows, "a good rub-down with one a your relics. Have him leapin' about like a billy goat. Have you got one a them handy?" He grinned, exposing a fence of broken teeth, the legacy of a customer he'd insulted some months before.

"I'll thank you not to be coarse, Mr. O'Shea."

She turned her back and stooped to stuff the collection money into a plastic shopping bag. Jamie had a sudden urge to flex his left leg and kick her big, tweed arse. But it was only a thought.

"Cheerio then," she said, turning to face him. "And I hope to see you at Mass when your back's mended, Jamie."

"Oh, I'll be there right enough, Maisie." Jamie observed her and for an instant saw her big eyes change through the lenses to a jungle of beer bottles and some blue sky as she made for the door.

"Right ye be then," she said, satisfied with her mission.

"Right ye be, Maisie," both men chorused.

The door clanged shut and the bar returned once more to its restive, smoky silence.

The public library was enjoying a lull when Lydia pushed through the main doors. Sean, the part-time junior—young, handsome and aware of it—was sprawled over the desk, chewing the end of a Biro and engrossed in the sports section of the *Derry Democrat*. He did not register Lydia's approach and she had to cough to get his attention.

"Oh hello, Miss Devine." He looked up but didn't bother to stand. "She's having her break. You can go on in if you want to," he said to the open page, once again engrossed.

"Good day to you too, Sean. See you're working hard as usual."

She walked away, gratified that the insult had hit its target, and sensed him straighten up and glare at her retreating back as she knocked and went through the door marked "Private" at the far end of the room.

Daphne was glad to see her friend as always.

"What a coincidence: I was just thinking about you, Lydia. Haven't seen you in ages," she said, embracing Lydia warmly. "I expect you could do with a nice cup of tea."

"Oh, no thanks, dear. I've just had some." Lydia set her purse on the floor and sank down into the canvas Parker-Knoll chair.

"Sure? Just freshly made." She held up the teapot.

This relaxed attitude was the quality Lydia prized most in her friend. Daphne never seemed distracted or pulled off balance by anything. She was solid, dependable; was not afraid to shine a light into the darkest corners and offer solutions to problems Lydia believed insoluble.

"No, really. I have to collect Mother from the Cut 'n Curl shortly. Just wanted to ask your advice about something." She hesitated. "That's if you have the time?"

Daphne settled herself in the chair opposite. "All the time in the world. His lordship is very underworked, as you probably noticed." She nodded in the direction of the door.

Lydia considered her friend with an approving eye. She was wearing a coral twinset and matching cotton skirt. The color suited her, offsetting her honey-colored boyish bob and healthy, outdoor complexion. Only the gold-rimmed spectacles on the chain around her neck ruined the girlish impression. She had a perpetual air of enthusiasm about her which Lydia envied. Every time they met, she was reminded of a child on the brink of opening yet another birthday gift, of a child who would forever be the adventurer in a game of hide and seek, always looking and exploring while she, Lydia, remained in hiding, not wanting to be found.

They had been firm friends since their high-school days, after which, they had gone their separate ways for a time: Lydia to teacher-training college in Belfast, Daphne to the local technical college to follow a secretarial course which, a year later, had resulted in her securing a position at the library where she'd been ever since.

Their friendship was founded on a mutual respect and understanding of the other's circumstances and aspirations. They shared their problems and celebrated their achievements in a spirit of empathy and genuine goodwill.

Like Lydia, Daphne was unmarried. She did, however, have a fiancé, a farmer named John whom she'd been going out with for at least ten years. John refused to get married until his mother died, and there was no sign of that happening just yet. At seventy-three, his mother was as robust and active as someone half her age, and had no intention of sharing her only son, *her* home—and indeed *his* inheritance—with another woman, even if that other woman was as amiable and good-natured as Daphne.

The idea of marriage was simply unthinkable.

"Do you remember Heather Price from school?" Lydia said. "Tallish, brunette, quite plain. We trained together."

"You mean Ettie and Herbie's daughter?"

"Well, you'll never guess what I got this morning."

She took the invitation from the envelope and handed it over. "She's getting married."

"Really? How nice." Daphne unfolded her glasses and inspected the card.

"I expect you'll be getting one too, Daphne."

"Oh, I hope so! It's been so long since I had a nice day out. Give me an excuse to buy a new outfit, too." She removed the glasses, at once deep in thought. "Now, I'll have to warn John well in advance so he can prime his mother. She can be very difficult, you know…" She looked up from the card. "Oh, Lydia, forgive me for thinking of myself. This is great news. Aren't you looking forward to it?"

"Well, that's just it, Daphne. I can't face another wedding with my mother. I have to find someone else to accompany me. Otherwise I just won't go." She leaned back in the chair, deflated.

"You mean a man."

"Yes, of course I mean a man! One of those alien creatures whom my father disapproved of and my mother thinks objectionable." She sighed and looked out the window. "Oh, I do get so depressed with my life, Daphne. All my school friends are either married or engaged and I'm still alone, like some kind of reject at a jumble sale." At that moment, the engagement ring on Daphne's finger winked playfully as the sun bloomed in the window. The coincidence was not lost on Lydia. "No, I'll just have to find someone to go with. And how on earth can I manage that in the next eight weeks? Something I haven't been able to manage in the past twenty years."

"Nonsense, Lydia, that's easy. I've got the answer at the main desk." She got up and went to the door.

Lydia looked up, alarmed. "Daphne, really! Sean's a child, for heaven's sake."

"Please, give me some credit. Just wait here; be back in a jiff."

Daphne amazed her, always seeming to have an answer at hand. The reassuring part of it all was that she was usually right about most things, too. Lydia thought her wasted in her monotonous job, stamping and shelving books, greeting the same people all day long. She should have been a hotel manager, or perhaps a hospital matron; the sort of position that would match her practical, problem-solving nature. But what could she have meant by "the answer?" What on earth could it be?

Lydia didn't have to puzzle for long. In a couple of minutes Daphne was back, thrusting a copy of the *Mid-Ulster Vindicator* into her hands and urging her to turn to the second-last page.

"Lonely Hearts?" asked Lydia incredulously. "Honestly, Daphne!"

"Why not? I just noticed it the other day. There's nothing wrong with it. You're a lonely heart and you want to meet another lonely heart. Put an ad in and see what happens. Can't do any harm. And you never know who you might meet."

Lydia toyed with the idea. Daphne was challenging her to do something audacious for a change. It was an exciting prospect: stepping into the light of this new possibility. But still she hesitated, throwing up a protective arm against the glare.

"But it's all so tawdry…not natural somehow."

"Nonsense! When you're living in a backwater like Killoran and you want results quickly, sometimes practical measures are needed. Besides, it'll be a bit of fun and you just never know who you might meet. Go on, be a devil."

There was a knock.

"Can I have my lunch break now?" Sean looked from Daphne to Lydia. They both chuckled.

"Yes, of course you can."

"Oh God, is that the time? Mother's hair! I've got to dash." Lydia waved the newspaper. "Can I hold on to this?"

"That's the spirit. You know, that humble paper could be the start of a whole new life for you."

Lydia smiled. "We shall see, Daphne. We shall see."

Chapter six

ome here, Eighty-Six."

The voice, orotund, heavy with menace and dark design, rolled like thunder above the boy. He dared not look up but stared down glumly at his bare, dirt-caked feet, and shuffled forward. He could hear the rain streeling the mullioned window and the snapping, muttering flames in the grate behind him. The dreaded command tensed his stomach muscles tight against the blow that was bound to follow at some point.

He made his way to the voice's source as slowly as possible, over the rug of sun-faded hummingbirds and peacocks.

He knew the room well, had been dragged into its musty confines too often; knew the position of all its gloomy appointments: the somber, claw-footed sideboard with the silver service that chittered every time the door was shut; the lumpy, velour sofa with the balding armrests; the copper-potted fern on the windowsill.

But he knew, better than anything else, the bed in the far corner behind the velvet drapes. He had felt every dip and swell of its mattress, could count every ridge in the blue chenille quilt, knew the suffocating stench of the striped bolster that reeked of sweat and night hair, so often had his face been pushed into it.

"Closer."

The voice had raised itself a notch higher, just a notch—and the boy knew, even then in his innocence, that this was all part of the adult's cruel game. He was the cornered mouse for the cat to paw and play with for a while. He inched his feet onto the second peacock's head. Still a whole bird and a half to go.

"I hear you've been wicked again, Eighty-Six. And after all that the good Sisters of this school have done for you."

The boy began to cry. The peacock dissolved into a wash of blue and began swirling round and round as his weeping became more intense. He coughed out great salty sobs and hoped that this pathetic display might wring some pity, and perhaps a rare reprieve, from the owner of the voice. He cried on and on, trying desperately to communicate his pain, until he had no tears left, until his throat was hoarse. But still nothing happened; the voice remained silent. The room shook with his grief and there was no one listening but him. It was useless, he knew.

After a time he stopped, wiped his eyes with the over-stretched cuff of his jersey and resigned himself to his fate. He was guilty of the crime. But he'd been hungry and the turnip had simply been there, about to fall from the sack.

"A turnip, a whole turnip this time, you greedy pig!" The voice rose on the last two words and lashed about the child like a savage wave.

"Come over here, *now*."

He went quickly to the final peacock, a mere foot now from his accuser, but remained staring down, the tears still tightening on his cheeks. The man's breath smelled of sour milk and fish heads; he could feel the rotten gusts waft across his face. He thought that if he looked up he might faint.

"Anything to say for yourself, boy?"

He attempted to raise his head but it was painful. He'd discovered that keeping his head bowed was the safest way to protect himself from the stinging stares, and the slaps that an upturned face could bring. So far the orphanage, with its flagged floors, its gravel-strewn yards and grassy gardens, had afforded him some safety, but not so the aging carpet with its faded birds. He knew he was in deep trouble when he was staring down at it.

"I was hungry, sir," he blurted out in his defense, at last lifting his tear-stained face, and meeting the blood-veined eyes of his tormentor. He knew the lines of the face well; it was a practical lesson in the bogeymen of his nightmares.

The nose was pointed, and porous like a wedge of stone; a crooked mouth of ruined teeth half-grinned like a rip in a grain sack. The pallid, lumpy flesh called to mind the skin on his breakfast gruel. It fell away from his cheekbones, to crouch in a series of slack folds at the man's neck. The white hair was surprisingly lush, yellowed and oiled back, showing the tooth tracks of a recent combing; his large withered ears stuck out like the waxy handles of a toby jug.

"You don't deny it then, Eighty-Six?"

"No, sir."

The boy was trembling. Fear tore at his insides, flinging everything this way and that. The black cane leered at him from the far corner. He prayed that the ordeal would be quick.

But then there came a sudden rapping on the door: loud, ominous, urgent. The room thrummed in its aftermath. The boy caught his breath.

"Yes? What is it?" The man hurled the words at the door. The sideboard silver shivered. The door opened.

"Master Keaney, can you come? We have an incident in the yard. Thirty-Two again."

Mother Vincent stood in the doorway, bristling in her black robes, her stern face like the queen of spades, framed in its starched casing. She looked from Keaney to the boy, then back to Keaney again. Something cold and cruel reared up and twisted between them, then slumped and fell low.

Keaney rose.

The woman had spoiled his game, had flipped over a card she was not supposed to see. The boy thanked God, and the master cursed Him.

"I'll be there presently, Mother Superior. Meanwhile, can you see that Eighty-Six here scrubs the refectory floor after supper—for the next five evenings."

He shot out a fist and punched Eighty-Six full in the face. The boy doubled up as blood poured from his nose. Keaney pushed him toward the nun.

"Get out, you useless beggar!"

Eighty-six could not believe he'd been saved from the savagery of the cane; he wanted to scrub a hundred floors for a hundred nights in thanksgiving.

Chapter seven

Aweek after his visit to the doctor, Jamie bought the latest issue of the *Mid-Ulster Vindicator*. Last week's had already gone up in smoke as fire kindling, the "Lonely Hearts" column having yielded a succession of candidates that were either too young (twenty-five to thirty), too experienced (widowed or separated), too eager (willing to travel any distance), or too righteous (Christian, teetotal, non-smokers).

Jamie, for the first time since his uncle's death, was becoming excited at the great new vista that was opening up for him. Life was bearable again. The prospect of meeting someone gave him a fresh focus; he could see a light shining on a far hill, urging him on.

He didn't have much of an idea of the kind of woman he wished to meet. All his life he'd felt exiled from the game of courtship and marriage. He had never felt himself worthy of that union, which somehow seemed the natural preserve of all other men but him. Marriage was for men who were not afraid. Men who could walk life's tightrope and not allow each wobble and tremor to hold them back from their goal.

But, perhaps now was the right time. Uncle Mick's passing had left a gap that needed filling. Rose and Paddy thought so, and even Dr. Brewster.

But what kind of woman would want me? Jamie tried to unpick the snarls to the knotty question as he cycled home from town, bumping over the hills and dales of the road he knew so well. He sat slouched over the handlebars of Uncle Mick's ancient bicycle, chewing a Bassets fruit bonbon, staring down at the road flying beneath the shrieking wheels.

Maybe she'd like a bit of cawntry-and-western music, he mused—the Clancy Brothers and Jim Reeves were his heroes—and enjoy and encourage his "accordjin" playing. He sometimes took it along to Slope's of a Saturday night, to relieve Declan Colt & The Silver Bullets when they needed a rest and the toilet. Up there on Declan's vacated stool, Jamie would squeeze out "The Fields of Athenry" or "The Boston Burglar". And if there wasn't a stranger on the premises—someone whose unfamiliarity might mark him out as a Protestant—he'd risk a bar or two of "Roddy McCorley" or "Sean South of Garryowen", both Republican songs having the same melody anyway.

Hopefully she wouldn't mind the farm and the noise of the animals, and smell, and so forth. But she wouldn't have to help outside if she didn't want to, Jamie reflected. Rose McFadden didn't do much outside except the bit of gardening, cooking being her major interest. So, above all, this imagined woman would be a good cook. Someone who'd have his fry-up ready and on the table when he returned from doing his chores. And wouldn't it be great if she would wash his shirts and underwear now and again, without always having to take them down to Rose and the embarrassment of it?

Jamie sped down the hill toward his home, smiling to himself. He felt content that he had more of an idea now of what he was looking for.

In the yard he dismounted from his creaky conveyance and wheeled it over the raddled ground, scattering the brown-speckled hens, rousing the dog from its doze by the barn door and causing the two Ayrshires in the near field to lurch toward the gate and gaze hopefully at the customary source of their sustenance.

A so-far rainless June had baked the ground into a crazy cross-hatching of bicycle and tractor tires. Here and there, an assortment of deceased machinery—the innards of a cultivator, the limbs of a hay shaker, the body of a grain spreader—lay bogged down in the earth, trapped for ever.

The yard lay to the left of the house, sheltered by a ragged ring of sheds and barns. Those timeworn structures sagged forlornly in their ancient foundations; they had been erected many decades earlier with the meager profits from the ten-acre farm and by the callused hands of Uncle Mick's great-great-grandfather. Mick had wisely kept quiet about his colorful ancestor, but Jamie had heard the stories.

It was said that Turlough McCloone was a lunatic with a passion for grog and loose women. He had begotten a string of children through a vigorous, lust-crazed violence, scattering his seed and deserting his women, before finally settling down. The Duntybutt farm was tangible evidence that he might have finally gathered sense. But unfortunately he did not live to find out. One day an enemy in a silk hat unseated him from his dappled cob with a five-shot Paterson-Colt, a gun that had proved notoriously inaccurate, until that day.

By the time Uncle Mick had come along, the fiery blood of his dissolute ancestor had been cut and thinned, to such a degree that only a weak trickle of lunacy remained.

If there was madness in Mick, Jamie never saw it.

The bicycle was propped by the gable, in the shade away from the saddle-cracking sun. From the bag that hung at its rear, Jamie extracted his shopping: first the newspaper, followed by a pot of lemon jam, a currant loaf, a tin of Andrews Liver Salts, and a white grease-stained bag containing an apple turnover and a cream slice. He cradled the goods in his left arm and rebuckled the saddlebag into place, a precaution he'd been forced to employ since the previous March, when a couple of mice had adopted it as their home and started a family.

On rounding the front of the house, he stood for a time contemplating the scene before him. His eyes traveled out across the fields and homesteads that stretched away in the distance, to meet the Slievegerrin mountains. In the hazy sunlight they appeared vague, obscure, as if seen through breathed-on glass. Above them, a vast blue sky was building clouds in rumpled masses of dove-flocked grays and whites.

What did Jamie see when he observed this tranquil scene, with its clumps of whitewashed dwellings and scatterings of short-shadowed cattle? In truth, he saw very little of it. The scene had become so familiar that all its rich beauty had faded, had been bled out to frame a mere backdrop to Jamie's colorless musings.

The time he stood there gazing out across the fields was time torn from the present and fed to the murky past that trailed like sludge behind him; the past that messed him up and slowed him down to despair and indecision. For with Mick's death, the memories of that child who'd answered to a number and not a name had risen again. That lonely, frightened boy standing in the wind-torn darkness of the past had come back to haunt him both day and night.

It was why, now more than ever, he reached for the drink and the lung-rotting smokes, the sweet cake in the greasy bag, the accordion in its musky case; all those fleeting pleasures to anesthetize his pain. Such joys lit the darkness, burned away the memories for a time, so that he could see all the way to "the sunlit clearing," to that hallowed place where the future hadn't shaped itself yet—a future which he knew to be one hundred times better than the present.

All he wanted was to somehow get there, and taste that joy which everyone but him seemed to be experiencing. And at that point in his beleaguered life, with middle age upon him and his loved ones gone, he felt that sharing his thoughts and few possessions with a woman might be the answer. He looked down at the newspaper and his armful of shopping and, with a wan smile, turned and went into the house.

After wetting the tea, he spread out the newspaper on the table, plonked his mug beside it and ripped open the pastry bag. The torn bag would do duty as a plate.

The cream slice had collided with the pot of jam in transit and emerged from the bag looking like a bull had sat on one end of it: a soggy, half-flattened rectangle with a frill of cream bursting out over the apple turnover and mapping the paper with greasy blots. Jamie was not too bothered at the sight of the ruined slice. Sure wouldn't it get crushed in his mouth anyway, and who was about to see the state of it, only himself?

He ate with his right arm curled round the bag. In the orphanage he had learned to guard his meager rations from the other inmates in this way, his forearm becoming at once a barrier and a weapon which helped him survive.

When he'd finished eating, he wiped the crumbs from the newspaper and started reading the entries slowly, using his index finger as a guide. He stopped under each word as if stitching a series of short rows along the page. He'd learned this reading technique in the schoolroom, and had never forgotten it. When, in the course of perusing the classifieds, he came across words such as "professional," "intelligent," or "adventurous," some inner guiding force would snap a blind down, stall the roving finger and move it automatically to the ad below.

This laborious task—reading, considering and reading some more—took time. Jamie had finished the tea and buns, smoked two cigarettes, used the outside privy, and rejected fifteen women before he finally came upon what he believed he was looking for.

He read it a second time aloud just to be sure it was real, and not his imagination playing tricks.

> **MATURE LADY**, enjoys cooking, gardening, reading, music and animals, would like to meet a like-minded gentleman with a view to friendship and outings. BOX Nr.: 218

It was just the thing. He fetched his blue ballpoint from the broken ear of the ceramic cat in the glass case, and drew a careful circle round the ad. Now came the difficult part: writing a letter of introduction to the lady in question.

He had to find notepaper and knew he'd seen a fairly decent pad in the house at some stage. But when that was and where it might be—now that was another thing. There was a suitcase of Aunt Alice's in the upstairs bedroom, where Uncle Mick had locked her effects after her committal. And she, being a woman, might have had writing paper, and it might still be in the case, going to waste. Mick had cleared the house of his wife's presence soon after her departure, knowing she would not be returning. He could not bear to be reminded of what had been. And the young Jamie had somehow understood that.

He climbed the stairs two at a time and pushed into the dusty bedroom. He could not remember the last time he'd been in there, but it was probably just after Mick's death; he'd no reason or desire to visit it since. The place held too many recollections of his ailing uncle in the big bed. He could still see Mick's stricken face sunk into the fat bolster, like a wizened pear in a gift box, and could hear the rasping voice, vainly battling with the throat cancer that would finally claim him.

Jamie stood in the doorway, subdued by the memories of that awful time, somehow afraid to tread the unwalked floor, breathe the unshared air. This was *Mick's* room, and it seemed that even in death he was still here.

Everything was as it had been left: the stripped bed in the corner, the dark dresser with its cloudy mirror, a cracked bowl and pitcher on the small table by the window. Then, all at once, as he stood there, a shaft of cloud-freed sun threw a bandage of light across the floorboards, as if in warning, as if to thwart his trespass.

Jamie could see the shabby suitcase under the bed, its secrets secure behind the rusted hasps, and he knew with mounting apprehension that he could not cross the floor to open it. Out of respect for his uncle, he changed his mind. He'd buy a pad of writing paper of his own. Sure he'd probably be needing a fair few pages, because he felt certain that he'd make some mistakes, him not being used to the writing down of things and all.

He shut the door quietly and turned the key. He'd go out straightaway to Doris Crink at the post office and get some.

"The post's rather late," Lydia murmured to herself and checked her watch against Cousin Ethel's clock on the far wall. "Quarter past one…Probably no delivery now at this time."

Elizabeth Devine, sitting at the other end of the table, in a Naples yellow sweater dress, left off eating her apple crumble and custard, and looked up suspiciously at her daughter.

"Why are you so interested in the postman all of a sudden? He's a married man too, you know…and I should hope you wouldn't even be *considering* anyone from the common classes—not even in your dreams."

She resumed eating. Her purple-pansy rinse had turned out a deeper shade than expected. She'd blamed Susan for neglecting her. But the fact of the matter was that Susan could not get Elizabeth to come out from under the dryer until she'd finished reading an article in *Cosmopolitan* entitled, "Does He Only Want You for Your Breasts? 10 Ways to Tell."

"Mother, please…" Lydia continued to eat her pudding, sitting straight-backed in the bentwood chair, chewing each mouthful slowly and thoroughly, her silver spoon dipping in and out of the bowl at regular intervals.

"You haven't told me much about your Women's Institute outing. Ballymena can't have been that uninteresting." Lydia was steering the subject away from the post. Her mother could be a proper old Miss Marple when she applied herself—a tendency which, to Lydia's dismay, seemed to grow stronger with age.

"What's any town like these days: only full of shops and vulgar pubs? And Beatrice couldn't walk too far with her corns, so we had to sit down most of the time in tea rooms. And you know most of these places don't know how to make a proper cup of tea. They don't warm the pot first. Beattie and me, we could always tell right away after the first sip."

"Didn't you complain?"

"We did the first time, and the manager came out. Oh, you know the type: not long out of short trousers…a young galoot in a ready-made suit and rubber slip-ons. And he looked at Beattie and me as if we were crazy and said: 'Ladies, where d'you think we are,

Victorian England? This is a cafeteria and d'you see that big five-gallon steel vat over there that's boilin' and bubblin' away? That's the twentieth-century version of the teapot, and that big teapot serves everyone who comes in here, and I've never *hey* any complaints till now.' (You know how they have trouble with their vowel sounds in County Antrim). And it was terrible because his voice was rising and his face was getting red and people started looking. Beattie and me were mortified."

"How awful." Lydia reached for her napkin. "So what did you do?"

"Well, I thought I'm not going to let the young pup away with that, so I said, 'I'll thank you to mind your manners, young man.'"

"Good for you! And what did he say to that?"

"Oh, he got worse. He said: 'May I suggest that if you don't like my tea you take your custom elsewhere, because I *hey* a business to run and no time to stand around here discussin' the virtues of tea-making with a couple of oul' buzzards like you.'"

"The cheek of him!"

"Exactly: the cheek of him. So we got up, and poor Beattie with her corns and all could hardly walk, and she said: 'Don't worry, we're going. You're badly brought up and I don't mind saying it, and if you were a son of mine, I'd box the ears off you!' And d'you know what, the people in the café gave us a round of applause as we left, and he was livid, so he was." Elizabeth pushed the dessert bowl aside. "Is there any tea?"

"Of course there is. I'll make it now and I promise to heat the pot," said Lydia, smiling. "I am sorry, Mother. That doesn't sound as though you had such a good day after all."

"Oh, we got over it soon enough. We weren't going to let that young rascal spoil the rest of our day. We treated ourselves to a few wee things. Beattie got a nice paint-by-numbers set called *Horse and Foal by Lake* and I bought that cottage tapestry and that pair of elastic stockings, the Wolford ones with the reinforced toes. The ones I showed you. And then later on we had a nice spread in the Lakeside Hotel. Oh, they know how to do things there…"

Lydia got up to prepare the tea.

"…Georg Jensen silver and that Blushing Rose china your Aunt Hattie adored. You know, she took a liking for it in Belgium when she was there in nineteen thirty-one. She went to work as an au pair to the Vansittart family. Oh, they were very grand you know, aristocratic I believe…"

"Really…?" Lydia scarcely listened. She was used to her mother's ramblings, and as she reached for the teapot and the tea caddy, gazed out the window to remind herself of how beautiful the garden looked. She was proud of her vegetable patch, where the rows of carrots, potatoes, cauliflowers and sprouts expressed her unstinting devotion to the soil, and her confidence in the power of Mother Nature to provide all goodness. Because for Lydia, order and neatness did not stop at the boundaries of one's home; they extended to the scrubbed paving, trimmed hedges and carefully cropped lawns that lay beyond it.

"…and after that we did pass-the-parcel, and then Mrs. Leslie Lloyd-Peacock showed us slides from her trip to Canada. Oh, Mrs. Lloyd-Peacock is *such* a lady! She would be connected to the Rickman-Ritchies, you know, the linen people. Oh, very grand, very well off and such good friends of your father's.…"

"Mmm…," murmured Lydia. She noticed a scattering of naughty dandelions between the rows of vegetables, nodding their little heads in the noon breeze, and wondered how on earth she could have missed them thus far. She made a mental note to pluck them immediately after tea.

She carried the teapot to the table and stole a quick glance down the hallway, but there was no mail as yet. She could not afford to have her mother collect any letters, because her ad had already appeared and she hoped and expected an envelope of replies soon, even though it was very early days.

Elizabeth was examining the cabled cuffs of her sweater dress. "…oh terrible good with her hands, could tackle any Aran stitch put in front of her; cables, garters, fagots, twists, the chunky bead, fisherman ribs, and y'know her bunny bobbles were the talk of the country. You name it and she could do it…"

She left off the examination and studied Lydia, who, having placed the teapot on the table was fetching Auntie Dot's tea cozy, a wondrous item crocheted in the shape of a purple strawberry.

"You know, Mrs. Leslie Lloyd-Peacock's slides put me in mind of the sea."

"Oh really," said Lydia, half listening. "How's that?"

"Made me long to go on holiday. Portaluce, that's where I want to go. Why don't we go and stay with Gladys next week?"

"Really!" Lydia was suddenly alert. She'd no wish to go anywhere until she'd received that all-important letter. "Gosh, Mother, if memory serves, you and Gladys always end up fighting."

"Gladys is the one who starts it! But then she never was anything but impetuous." Mrs. Devine addressed the sugar bowl, suddenly thoughtful. "Takes after her Aunt Millicent." Lydia could see another reminiscence coming on.

"Look, I'll tell you what, Mother: We'll go the week after next. How's that?"

"Why not next week?"

"Well…" Lydia didn't know what to say. "I'm just not ready yet. I'm…tired."

"I thought that was the reason one went on holiday: because one was tired." Elizabeth's eyes narrowed. "You're up to something."

"No, Mother, I'm not up to anything, and anyway Auntie Gladys would need a week's notice. It's high season, you know." Lydia proffered a plate of cherry slices. "Now, some cake."

Doris Crink, the postmistress, was an attractive widow in her early fifties—petite, slim, well groomed—who still felt it necessary to make an effort, especially with her appearance. Her dear husband's death had been premature. They'd only been married four years when he was hit by a delivery van, driven by a shortsighted retiree, whose attention had been momentarily diverted whilst wresting a barley-sugar from its wrapper. Since that fateful occurrence, the mere sight of the said sweets could trigger in Doris an immeasurable panic. Such a catastrophe had not put her off, however, and as the years passed she never lost hope of marrying again. By tending to her looks she kept that flame of hope alive. You just never knew when the right man might come along and fan the flame into a roaring fire.

Doris was surprised to see Jamie McCloone coming through her door. He had little reason to visit her establishment because he rarely sent or received letters. He did have a savings account, however, which, she was glad to see, was seldom debited (or for that matter credited). It held quite a healthy sum, too: £3,129 and fippence to be exact, which had been lodged soon after his uncle's death.

Ms. Crink had inherited the business from her parents and had run it for as long as anyone could remember. Consequently, she knew the intimate goings-on of most members of that small community. As the shrewd clairvoyant can determine a person's future from the clothes they wear and the things they say, so Doris could judge the state of a marriage or a person's circumstances through the mail they received and the transactions they conducted over her woodwormed counter.

"Another red reminder from the gas board for the Kennedys at number nine, I see," she'd say. "Thomas must be hitting the bottle."

"That daughter of Betsy Bap's out of work again," she'd observe on another occasion. "That's the third welfare check she's cashed this month. Oh, she takes after her mother, that one: a strumpet, the temper of a billy goat. The Lord himself couldn't work with *her*."

All such speculations and slanders about the people of Tailorstown would be relayed to Mildred, her sister, who worked in the clothing store next door: Harvey's, Purveyors of Ladies and Gentlemen's Fashions. At supper in the evenings, in the cramped kitchen behind the post office, the ladies would mull over the day's events, sifting through the evidence of what was said, done and bought by their customers, in order to build a case against them. Sometimes the purchase of a pair of silk stockings and a withdrawal from a savings account on the same day—*and* by the same person—could fire their imaginations with the fury of a Cape Canaveral rocket, before returning them to earth like a damp squib.

"Oh, she couldn't be having an affair. She's only just married," a Crink sister might observe. To which the other would respond with: "Well, I can't see a hellion like Mickey McCourt allowing his wife to buy, let alone notice, she was wearing a pair a them, can you? Oh, something's going on there, you can be sure."

As Jamie McCloone approached her counter, Doris Crink removed her spectacles, believing she looked better without them.

"Jamie, haven't seen you in a long while. How've you been keepin'?"

"I'm not so bad atall, Doris. But me back's givin' me a bit of bother, so it is."

"Ach, I'm sorry to hear that. Y'know that back's goin' round. Aggie Coyle is nearly kilt with it." Doris was studying Jamie sympathetically. He might not be an oil painting but he was a civil enough creature, and he did have £3,129 and fippence in his savings book, and no wife to be whittling away at it...or, Doris mused idly, not yet anyway. "Is it the rheumatism, is it?"

"No, Doris, it's the lambago, the doctor says. And he give me tablets to take and wants me to take a rest by the seaside, so he does."

"Well, so you should, Jamie. That's very good advice. You're liftin' too many heavy things on the farm, no doubt." She placed her elbows on the counter and leaned confidentially toward him. "Y'know I had a bit a bother with me ears last winter, and Dr. Brewster told me the exact same thing. He said: 'Doris d'you know what you need?'"

"God-oh, did he tell you the same thing, did he?"

"He did indeed. He said: 'Doris, you need a good rest by the sea in Portaluce with them ears of yours.' And you know, I took his advice and went for a week and came back," Doris gave the counter a triumphant slap, "as right as rain with no ears atall."

Jamie pushed up the bill of his cap to air his scalp a bit, both flustered and flattered that a woman of Doris's sensibilities would confide as much in him.

"Boys-o, that's a good one—he told you the same thing. Oh, he's a smart man, Dr. Brewster. He knows what's wrong with you by just lookin' at you, so he does."

"Oh, a gentleman." Doris inhaled deeply and shook her head. "None of that pokin' and proddin' at a person. Oh, a very decent man...couldn't get the better of him, so you couldn't."

"Aye, yes, you couldn't get the better of him, that's right. I know what you're sayin' right enough." Jamie pulled on his ear and righted his cap again.

"Was it the stamps you were lookin', Jamie?" she asked, opening her book, suddenly officious. Another customer had just entered the premises and she didn't want to be seen to be getting too friendly with Jamie, lest rumors started circulating.

"Yes, Doris, a coupla stamps and a coupla them envelopes. And a need a pad a that Basildon Bond over there."

Doris lifted an eyebrow at such a list, wondered what Jamie McCloone might be up to, and quickly filed away the tantalizing snippet for discussion with Mildred later on.

She began totting up the cost with her pencil. Jamie lowered his face to Doris's left ear.

"And I'll be needin' to take out a wee bit a money for the wee trip y'know," he whispered.

"Certainly, Jamie. If you'd just fill this wee form out, and while you're doing that, I'll let this customer away." Doris looked up expectantly at the waiting youth behind him, all thoughts of romance shelved for the time being.

Chapter eight

He scrubbed the floor on his bony knees; his purpled hands clamped on the wire-bristled brush. He was doing four big tiles at a time, his body shuttling back and forth, machine-like, mopping up the sludge with a greasy rag that he'd rinse out in the bucket. Four hundred and fifty tiles in the cold refectory; only a hundred more to go.

Every five minutes he'd stop and move to the next set, hauling the bucket with a screech farther along the speckled terrazzo, positioning his knees on the sodden towel, rinsing and wringing and scrubbing—scrubbing, scrubbing until the gray flecks flashed white under his determined strokes, until his heart beat too rapidly and his arms went numb.

Mother Vincent timed him with her fob watch, appearing sporadically at the open door, either withdrawing satisfied or advancing enraged. He dreaded her coming, the hard heels cracking across the empty room, a hail of hammer blows to his heart.

"Not good enough, Eighty-Six! I told you five minutes exactly per section." Her words struck the walls like rifle shots, and made the floor beneath him sway.

He knelt before her with his face upraised, his swollen hands crossed in a penitential pose: *Saint Francis Beholding the Afflicted.*

"S-sorry, Sister," he stammered.

"How old are you now, Eighty-Six?"

He did not know his age, but knew that such an admission would earn him a ringing slap; maybe just one, maybe several, depending on how Mother Vincent felt. He thought hard. He remembered the time he'd entered the refectory, 7.30 P.M. He shifted his knees on the soggy cloth, kept looking up, seeking out her face so as not to linger at the tooled leather belt that swung at her waist, the cane in her hand.

"Seven and a half, Sister."

"Quite," she said, sneering at the inaccuracy of the guess. She'd noted him from the day he'd arrived on her step five years earlier, but why should she tell him his real age? These sons of whores deserved nothing.

"Do you see that clock down there?" and she pointed needlessly at the far wall. "That clock is there so you can time yourself. Now reverse three sections and start again." She drove the last words down, bending low to level with him. The air vibrated with her anger. Fear crushed his throat. Her eyes locked with his.

"Remind me why you're here, Eighty-six?"

"Because...' He swallowed back the tears. "Because I'm bad and me mammy d-didn't want me...and she put me h-here because...'

He stopped, terrified. Her unblinking eyes and doughy face made him think of hooded figures in the forest, death and buried bones, a headstone-crowded darkness.

"Stop that at once!" She slapped him across the face, grabbed him by the shoulder and trailed him to a bench set along the wall. He immediately scrambled up onto it.

"Stand up!" They were at eye level. "Do you know why your sister is *not* here, Eighty-Six?"

He shut his eyes tight. He did not want to say the word. But another blow to his cheek brought the answer she required.

"Di...died, Sister."

"She died. That's right: she *died*." She spat the awful word into his face. "Your mother put the pair of you in a shopping bag and dumped you on our doorstep. Your sister was already dead. *We saved you.*" The boy was looking down at his feet, the tears falling freely now. "Only for *us* you would have died too, you ungrateful, greedy, thieving little devil."

She pulled him off the bench and flung him across the floor. He collided with the bucket, sending the water everywhere. He ended up sprawled on his knees in the dirty puddle, unable to right himself.

"Now look what you've done." She unhooked the strap at her side.

He screamed and doubled up under the lashing leather, believing that the tighter he held himself, the less pain he'd feel, an instinctive yet useless tactic he'd used many times before.

Then she stopped. He heard her rapid breathing and slowly uncurled himself into the full, throbbing aftermath. He retrieved the damp cloth and attempted to soak up the "sin" he'd just been found guilty of.

"I'm not finished with you *yet*, Eighty-Six." She hauled him to his feet again. "I'm waiting, Eighty-Six. Your mother put you here because *what*?"

"Because she want...id, w-w-wantid you...y-y-y-you to make me...make me good, Sister?" His whole body shook as his words slid everywhere. He stopped and swallowed deeply.

"And if you're not good and you don't do your work, what will happen?" Her face was a mask of disdain. Sweat misted her brow. She grinned, lips peeling back from dingy teeth.

"God will puniss...punish me, and me ma...me mammy won't come for me."

"Correct, little man." She straightened up. "Now get to it or there'll be no bed tonight and no breakfast in the morning."

She marched to the door, then halted. He set immediately to work, fearful she might come back to beat him again.

"Eighty-Six, change the water when it gets dirty. Do you hear? If you can't see to the bottom of the bucket it needs to be changed. You understand?"

"Yes, Sister."

And with that she left him in the joyless hall with the bucket, the brush and his small heart pounding, a trail of dread and danger battering in her wake.

Two hours later, he was finished and lay in the darkness in the crowded dormitory, three rows, ninety-six beds in all. Ninety-six hungry boys, hungry for love and hungry for nourishment, and their sleep disrupted for lack of both. Ninety-six rejects with no gifts or grace, on whom a cloudless sun would never shine.

They were all under ten years, yet none of them knew their age, or what birthdays meant, or what presents were for, or that Santa Claus came at Christmas. In their long years in the orphanage, they'd never been hugged, never been smiled at, never eaten meat or used a knife and fork; they did not know the pleasure of bathing in warm water, or the feel of cotton sheets against the skin.

Their only crime was that their mothers had died, or been too poor to keep them, or too frightened to resist the forces of power and authority that deemed them unfit for the maternal role. Each child was paying for the "love" that had brought him into being: a love that in the "holy" eyes of the children's "carers" was tainted, because it had come from lesser beings—poor people.

Eighty-Six lay curled up tight like a tiny leveret in a tiny nest, his blanket pulled over his head. The aching in his back, his knees, his hands could not be eased. In his mind he was still down there in the deserted hall, scrubbing the unending floor. He could not sleep.

All around him, his comrades writhed and moaned in their sleep, the thin blankets that covered them rising and falling to the fearful rhythms of their dream worlds. The wind whistled in the loose window frames. He lowered the cover and peeped out, suddenly afraid. Somewhere, a door was banging. He thought it might be the door of the outside shed where the cleaning things were kept.

Immediately alert, he rose up on his elbows in a frisson of disquiet, straining hard to identify the sound and the direction from which it came. He remembered stowing the bucket and brush, but had he fastened the door again? He could not remember and, as his thoughts churned round and round, the consequences of his oversight took shape and struck him with a terrible force. There would be fifteen on the backside with the tooled belt. He would have to go down and bolt it.

He flung back the blanket, straightened his sore legs and eased himself onto the floor. It was strictly forbidden for a child to leave his bed after 10 P.M. So he was committing one transgression to escape the consequences of having committed another.

His sockless feet whispered across the cold cement as he made his way to the heavy door, past the rows of restive sleepers. Someone whimpered, a thin mournful note sliding out from under a cover as if to pull him back. He did not stop, but carried on, quietly heaved the door shut behind him and turned to face the darkness of the corridor.

He could see the newels of the staircase in the pre-dawn light from the landing window. Conscious of the risk he was running, he made for it on tiptoe, groping at the helpless air; past the adjacent dormitory, past Mother Superior's quarters, Master Keaney's room. A floorboard creaked in betrayal and he stopped, frozen by the hideous notion that he'd been heard. He held his breath for a moment, his foot poised above the traitorous board. He heard the shed door slam again as if in warning, as if urging him on. He quickened his pace and flew soundlessly down the stairs, all dread falling behind him in his eagerness to be gone.

Outside, the wind battled him for control of the raging door, like a demon in the face of an exorcising priest, his nightshirt by turns ballooning out and plastering itself against his body. He was too small and his strength too weak. His bare feet slithered out from under him on the slick grass. He fell on his belly and lay there, feeling the damp grass through his shirt, his cheek to the earth, hearing all the way down beneath, where, he was assured almost daily, hell's fires raged at its baleful core.

But he could not waste time and got up quickly. He pitted his painful back and all his weight against the door until eventually it yielded. The rusty bolt he hammered home with his little fist, the huge relief of his achievement at once releasing him to run back the way he had come.

At the top of the stairs he faltered, lassoed by a dreadful sight. The door to Keaney's room stood open. In the darkness he felt a presence and smelled the fetid breath. Fear flared and choked him. In his mind, a curtain fell and a light went out. He yelled silently for the mother he never knew and the God who never listened as a heavy hand gripped his shoulder and propelled him forcibly into the room.

Chapter nine

Dearest Lady...
Dear Madam...
My Dearest Lady...
Dear Lady...
Dear Miss...

Jamie McCloone was in despair as to how to address the anonymous woman behind the ad. Having already used and discarded four pages on the salutation, he worried that the whole writing pad might be in the grate and up in smoke before he'd manage to get the first sentence down.

He leaned back on the kitchen chair and sighed heavily. There was nothing else for it but to cycle down to Rose McFadden and ask her to write it for him. Because although Jamie's handwriting was reasonably legible, he wasn't so great at the spelling and punctuation and the like.

Of course, this would mean that Rose would know his business. But since she was on intimate terms with his underwear anyway, sure what did it matter? And wasn't it Rose who had suggested the idea to Paddy in the first place, after all? And, at the end of the day,

Rose was a very decent woman and not one to go spreading rumors or smearing gossip about—unlike Maisie Ryan and her sort.

Rose understood at once. "No trouble at all," she said. "You just sit yourself down there, Jamie, and we'll see what we can do."

She pulled out a chair from the cluttered table, straightened and patted a plump cushion.

The kitchen was hung about with the aromas of baking bread commingling with past and future meals: the breakfast fry-up, the lunchtime casserole, a pot of broth a-bubble on the stove. She appeared like a dust-blown mason in a quarry; flour coated her strong forearms and powdered her ginger hair, unwisely permed in a nimbus of loopy curls. Her cheeks were forever reddened from heightened blood pressure, broken veins, and the heat from oven and stovetop.

She was an industrious housewife and capable cook, had conquered most recipes in her *Raeburn Royal Cookbook* with varying measures of success, could knit and sew, produce and fashion most things from instruction sheet or pattern.

Every chair and window and surface in the house expressed Rose's devotion to creative crafts and a liking for thrift-store tat. Drapes: swagged, tailed, pleated and flounced. Cushions: ruffled and ribbed. Antimacassars and runners: laced, crocheted, appliquéd, embroidered, tatted and frilled. Items of basketry: a bowl and matching stool wrought in a postnatal occupational therapy class when she'd felt depressed. A papier-mâché rooster made over six Friday nights at the local parish hall, whilst Paddy competed in the Duntybutt Championship Darts Tournament in Murphy's pub. Items with shells and ideas from Portaluce beach: a wine-bottle lamp with a fringed shade; a postcard plate of a whale; a card table trimmed with cockles and scallops; a collage of a fish with milk-bottle-top gills, a Fanta cap eye and a seagull's primary wing feather, stiffened with glue for a tail.

"Ye know," Rose told him, "I drew them ads to my Paddy's attention for you. I sez: 'Ye know poor Jamie could be doin' with a woman about the place, to help him out now that Mick isn't about no more, and here's the very thing,' sez I, and I showed him the paper and he sez: 'Ye know, Rose, you're right,' sez he."

She won some space on the messy tabletop, pushed the rolling pin and mixing bowl to one side, wiped the area clean with a damp cloth. The plastic tablecloth showed a repeat pattern of piglets hopping over gates in a green field, their tails spaghetti twists against a blurred, blue sky.

"God, that was very good of you, Rose."

Jamie settled himself, took the ballpoint from his inside pocket, fumbled out the notepad and envelopes from his string bag.

"Now, Jamie, I'll just get me glasses. I'm as blind as a mole without them, so a am." She plucked the spectacles from the gaping lips of a china guppy on the mantelpiece, and held the ad at arm's length, murmuring over the wording. "Oh, she sounds like a fine lady, right enough."

"Maybe she's *too* fine, Rose, to be havin' anything to do with the like of me." Jamie was studying the plastic pigs in the plastic field, growing depressed at the thought of rejection before the project had even got underway.

"Nonsense, Jamie! There's many's the woman would give their back teeth to have you as a husband. And I'm not just sayin' that. It's the God's honest truth, so it is."

Jamie wondered what back teeth had to do with anything, but had the idea that Rose was paying him a compliment all the same. It was a rare thing to inspire, or indeed hear such praise from another, especially a woman. He was nonetheless confused, and had a vision of a half set of dentures that he'd found at the back of a drawer in Mick's bedroom. He tried now to reconcile the set of yellowed grinders with the beauteous creature this woman might prove to be.

After a minute or two he gave up, fondled his ear and fairly glowed with embarrassment. He wanted to thank Rose for the compliment but thought that if he did, it might seem as though he were agreeing with her. So instead he coughed and said, "aw, now," looking away to the picture on the wood-chipped wall: an image of the Virgin Mary crushing a writhing serpent beneath her perfect, blessed feet.

Rose took up the pen.

"Now I'll do a wee rough one, Jamie, first. Then you can copy it out—or if you like I can write it for you. Either way, it's all right by me."

"Naw, Rose, if you write it, I'll copy it out. Wouldn't want to be puttin' you to any more trouble than was called for, like."

"Good enough, Jamie, good enough." Rose began to write. "Now, first after your address I'm gonna say 'dear lady'." Rose peered over her glasses. "'Cause y'know, Jamie, a woman always likes to be called a lady even if she isn't one. Not that I'm sayin' this lady you're gonna meet isn't gonna turn out to be a lady, 'cause I'm sure she will be, but y'know it's always better to be on the safe side."

After several minutes of Rose writing—stopping every now and then to shoot a look heavenward for inspiration—and Jamie following the words that flowed from the pen in her exuberant hand, the task was done. Rose read it aloud to Jamie's nodding approval. When she'd finished he scratched his head in amazement.

"That's the best I ever heard, Rose! Just the thing, so it is. God, but you're powerful good at the writin'. Y'know I'd a been sittin' at the table from now to Christmas, begod, tryin' to get the like a that writ."

"Deed ye might-a been, Jamie."

Rose beamed and handed the page over. "Well, it's great that you like it, and if there's anything you want added or changed just let me know and I'll do it." And she stood up. "Now, Jamie, I'll get us a wee cuppa tea while you're at the copyin' out-a it, so I will."

"Good enough, Rose."

"Oh, and Jamie, it might be an idea to give your hands a wee rub before you start, because you don't want to be soilin' the page, mightn't look so good."

Jamie looked at his hands, ingrained as they were with several days' dirt from cowshed and barn, conceded that Rose was right, and immediately set to with soap and brush at the kitchen sink. When he finally got round to the writing task, he applied himself with great deliberation and care.

The Farmhouse,
Duntybutt,
Tailorstown

Dear Lady,

I saw your advertmint in the Mid
Ulster Vindicator of 14th day of July, 1974
and was immediately taken by it, because I
think you and me have a lot in common
and for this reason would maybe get on well
together.

I will now tell you a bit about myself
so you can decide for yourself.

I am a forty one year old farmer
and I live two miles from the town of
Tailorstown in the townland of Duntybutt. My
farm is not too big, but not too wee either. I
have ten or so acres where I grow spuds and
some corn.

I have some animals, one pig, two
Ayrshire cows, five sheep which I graze on the
Slievegerrin mountains along with the goat
and some hens for eggs and the like.

I like cooking and reading just like
you and I like music especially cawntry and
western stuff. I can play the accordion well
and sometimes play it in the public house
of an evening. I like going out for the
evening to the public house for music and
conversation.

I also have a nice garden to the front
of the house and I ride a bike and drive
the tractor but not the car. I would be very

pleased if you wrote back to me and told
me a little bit about yourself. You could
also ask me any questions you like for I
don't want to be writing too much about
myself just yet.

    I look forward to hearing from you soon.

Yours sincerely

James Kevin Barry Michael McCloone.

The complicated task finally finished, Rose poured more tea
for Jamie, and pushed a plate of drop scones lathered with butter
and jam in his direction.

"Well done, Jamie! I'll just run me eye over it to make sure
all's in order."

She replaced her bifocals and held the page up to the light for
inspection. He hoped she'd find no mistakes.

"No, that's fine, Jamie. That's very good writin' too. Well done.
Happy enough with it yourself, are you?" She folded the page into
a neat rectangle and slipped it into the envelope which Jamie had
already addressed.

"Aye, but a was just thinkin', Rose," Jamie glanced at one of
Rose's artistic endeavors on the far wall; a collage of Christ with
macaroni hair, a vermicelli beard and petit pois eyes, out of which
the Savior cried copious pearl barley tears. "Well, what a was just
thinkin' was, what if she turned out to be a Protestant, Rose? What
would a body do then?"

"That's nonsense, Jamie," said Rose. "What does it matter what
she is, so long as she has a good heart and can bake a bun or two and
keep a nice tidy house?"

In Rose McFadden's world, a woman's true worth could only
be measured by the texture of her pastry, the whiteness of her wash,
a sock heel turned on four needles without a pucker. But Jamie,
half listening, was imagining all sorts of unfortunate scenarios and
thinking up any number of unfounded reasons for the failure of this
venture.

There was a silence, while Rose sipped her tea. Her china mug showed a garish Giant's Causeway with a seagull a-flap above it. The amateur artist had rendered the bird's bill too big and given it a paint-dot eye that had missed its mark.

They sat in the warmth of the kitchen vapors, the broth bubbling contentedly, a light rain brushing the window panes like blown sand; each thinking their own thoughts. Jamie was envying Paddy all this domestic harmony. Rose was thinking: Another half hour and I'll add the chopped swede and pearl barley to that drop o' soup.

She thought also that Jamie would need to clean himself up quite a bit before meeting this woman, but she could help there, and she thought also that it was time he bought himself a decent outfit. With a good scrub and a proper suit he could look quite respectable, she decided, and not one to be ignored by a far-sighted woman with an eye to the future.

Jamie's gaze—as if he were reading Rose's thoughts—now settled on a framed photo of a more youthful Paddy holding aloft a silver cup, won for the unrivaled breeding capabilities of his Bluefaced Leicester ewe at the Balmoral Agricultural Show in 1963.

"What if she wants a photo, Rose?" he blurted out. "I haven't got one, and even if I had, I couldn't send it to her because…" He trailed off, depressed at the very thought of his hair—or rather lack of it—his skewed ears, his scar and his broken smile.

"Now, Jamie, I've just been thinkin' about that selfsame thing meself, and y'know everything in this life is fixable if a body just puts his mind to it. That's what I always sez to my Paddy when he comes to me with a problem. Y'know, he came into me only last week, when I was in the middle of a jam sponge for the Vincent de Paul Bring and Buy. And sez he to me, he sez: 'Rose I'm havin' terrible bother dippin' that Wiltshire Horn; can't seem to get him to stay still atall, atall.' And I sez, sez I: 'Well, there's only one thing you can do with a awkward bugger like that, Paddy,' and I grabbed a holt a the rollin' pin."

Jamie's astonished eye fell on the rolling pin on the floured board. It lay beside a pastry cutter in the shape of a dancing bear.

"Aye, that very one there, Jamie. Well I grabbed it and sez I to Paddy, 'This'll sort the brute out, so it will.' And we ran out the pair of us to the pen and I hit him a dunder with it, and y'know it stunned him for a minute—"

"What, you hit Paddy a dunder?" Jamie interjected, his mind still on the photo, his ear not properly tuned to Rose's long-playing tale.

"Naw, Jamie, the *ram*," shouted Rose, a wee bit annoyed that Jamie had made her gramophone needle jump its groove.

"Oh, Christ aye, the *ram*. I'm with you now."

"Aye, the *ram*, Jamie, the *ram*. Anyway I hit him a dunder with it," Rose continued, "and it give Paddy the time to dip him horns and all, and he got up again and staggered about a bit, stunned as a say, like somebody comin' late outta Slope's on a Friday night, and that was the end of it."

"Lord save us, that's a good one!" cried Jamie in amazement.

"Aye. Y'know, my Paddy said the selfsame thing, sez he: 'Lord save us, I never knew you could do that with a rollin' pin, so a didn't.'"

Rose reached for another scone.

"Now where was I, Jamie, afore I went down the side-road with the rollin' pin and the ram? Another wee drop a tea?"

She didn't wait for an answer but sloshed more into Jamie's mug.

"The photo, Rose."

"Och, I wouldn't worry about a photo just yet, Jamie, not unless she asks for one, and to my mind a serious-minded woman wouldn't be askin' for a photo. A young one might be interested in a body's looks, but a woman of your own age would have passed that stage long ago, because as I always sez to my Paddy, neither he nor me would a won any beauty contests in our day—and still wouldn't, truth be told—but me mother, God rest her, would always say that God give you the face you have on you because He thought it went with the rest of you—and better a bad-lookin' face than no face at all. Isn't that the way of it?"

She sipped more tea and finished off her scone while Jamie ingested all this. He thought Rose a tremendously wise woman and did not doubt her sincerity when it came to matters of the heart.

"And y'know, Jamie, I'm not sayin' you're a bad lookin' fella—far be it from me to be sayin' such a thing—but I would say with a nice suit and a good shirt and tie, you'd look like royallity, so you would. A good white shirt and maybe a nice red tie and a starched hankie in a breast pocket would take a man anywhere. So if I were you, I'd buy meself an outfit in Harvey's, Purveyor's of Ladies' and Gentlemen's Fashions. Mr. Harvey gives very good discount if you're not afraid of spendin' a bit. But that's time enough until you're meetin' her, like." She got up to stir the soup. "My Paddy'll go with you to pick one out if you like. Paddy knows what suits a man, so he does."

"Aye, that would be the thing, Rose." Jamie drummed his fingers on the pig-patterned tablecloth, at once excited and petrified with the speed with which Rose was conjuring up his future. There was a need in him to hold back; holding back and never taking a risk was where safety lay. Suddenly he caught sight of his grossly distorted head—a troll with the mange—in the belly of Rose's silver teapot. "But then what about me hair? I wouldn't want to be wearin' a cap when I'd be meetin' her like and without it I wouldn't look so well or—"

"Well, y'know, Jamie, there's them that wear them teepees or wigs or whatever it is you call them. I see them adverted in the *Exchange & Mart* now and again, meself. What about tryin' one a them?"

"God, Rose, I don't know. D'you think it'd be the thing?"

"Well y'know, Jamie, as I always sez to my Paddy, they wouldn't be advertin' them in the paper if they weren't successful, because if the people weren't buyin' them, there'd be no point in the advertin' and sellin' of them, so there wouldn't."

"Oh, I know what you're sayin', Rose, right enough," Jamie conceded, a trifle disquieted that Rose was lifting all the obstacles he was encountering before him on the road to marital bliss and tossing them so effortlessly over the hedge.

She now stooped to a magazine rack beside Paddy's arm-chair—a rack made from pipe-cleaners, lollipop sticks, toilet-roll tubes and ribbon—fished out a copy of the periodical in question, and thrust it into his lap.

"There you go, Jamie. Take that home with you and have a wee look. I think the wigs is between the whalebone stays and the women's briefs, if I mind right, but God-blisses-an-save-us, isn't me mind sometimes like a colander betimes, so I can't be sartin'."

Jamie took the magazine with heartfelt thanks. He was beginning to warm to the idea of the exalted vision Rose was painting. A proper suit from Harvey's. A wig from *Exchange & Mart*. One thing was for sure, he'd be looking well when he met this lady, which might be half the battle won.

He got up to go, his imagination bubbling as much as the broth in the pot.

"Well, I'll not keep you any longer, Rose." He returned the pad and envelopes to the string bag, and put the sealed letter carefully in his inside pocket—the pocket next to his heart. "Thank you very much indeed."

Rose removed her glasses and returned them to the gawping lips of the guppy, turned and smoothed down an apron that showed a flock of sheep grazing serenely over her generous bosom.

"Not atall, Jamie. Anything to help you on your way. And if you want another one a them letters writ, just you let me know."

"Right ye be, Rose," he said, making for the door.

"Right ye be, Jamie, and may the sun always rise on your pig," she said, turning back to stir the broth.

And with that, Jamie was on his bike and off up the road, a brandy-ball in his gob, bright thoughts in his head, and his heart light with the vision of maybe a happy future after all. A future in which he could see a tidy house like Rose's, a table with a nice spread, a garden filled with flowers and a woman in the bed.

Well, maybe not in the bed. In a chair by the fire, anyway.

Chapter ten

Eighty-Six could not sleep. He lay on his stomach in the grim darkness. He did not know what time it was but guessed that it would be dawn soon. He dreaded the light as much as the dark because each could hold an equal weight of terror. The burdens he carried in daytime became the demons he fought at night.

He could not turn over on his back; the agony would be extreme, and he remembered with a sudden and terrible certainty that he'd wet the bed.

Around him the other little ones snored and writhed, trapped in their anguished dreams. Soon Sister Veronica would sweep through the dormitory, agitating the big triangle with a furious ringing. Soon she'd be hauling back the blankets for signs of "inappropriate bedtime behaviors," as she called it. Soon, he knew, he'd be wearing the wet sheet for the rest of the day or washing it in the tin bath outside. It depended on her mood.

Then, all at once, he'd entered the bleak vision he'd imagined. Eighty-Six was springing to attention and standing beside his bed, his heart pounding and his throat parched. Along with the other boys he trembled with the awareness of another day dawning, a day in which the misery of every minute, every hour, would be stretched and felt and borne.

The nun was moving up the row of beds; bending over to inspect and sniff, her pointed nose twitching, her cane landing ten times on the backside of the offending boy. She paused at the bed next to his.

"You again, Eighty-Four! Third time this week. You will never learn, will you? Out here!"

With the cane she indicated a spot at the end of the bed. Eighty-Four lifted his nightshirt over his head and dutifully bent over to receive his punishment on his bare behind.

The others stood silent as the blows fell, trying not to look, staring straight ahead. Each boy counted and suffered each stroke; each boy knew the indignity of wetting his own bed and frequently endured the humiliation dealt out by the merciless nun. One morning a boy woke up on a dry, spotless sheet, relieved; the next morning he woke up wet. There was nothing he could do but pray it wouldn't happen.

"What's this, Eighty-Six?" Sister was pointing at the blood-stained sheet.

"Don't know, Sister," the boy stammered.

He kept his head down as always, his eyes fixed on his bare toes, which had turned blue on the cold floor. Outside, a raven tore at the howling wind.

"Bend over. Let me have a look." He had not expected this. Would have done anything than have her inspect him. He could already hear the name-calling laughter at the breakfast table. He wished that she'd just beat him and be done with it. Faced with this predicament, he did the only thing he could. He started to cry.

"Eighty-Six, I will not ask you again. Out here, *now.*"

She whacked the stick against the foot of the bed. He jumped to it immediately, clumsily bunched the shirt in both hands and held it up. The nun bent down to have a look. She winced on seeing the series of bloody lacerations on the child's backside. The raven cawed again as if mocking him. He shivered in his nakedness and prayed for it to end.

"All right." Her voice was no longer harsh. He automatically bent over and waited for the cane to fall, clenching his painful muscles in readiness.

But nothing happened.

"No, Eighty-Six. You got your punishment last night, I see."

He did not see the fret of pity in her eyes as he lowered the nightshirt. He did not look up with the shame of what he'd just endured.

"Now gather up your sheet for washing."

She moved to the next bed.

Of the twenty boys who had wet their beds, seventeen were made to tie their wet sheets about their waists and wear them as punishment for the rest of the day. The remaining three were more fortunate, inasmuch as they got to wash theirs. They stood by the pump in the cold backyard; their sins lay before them in a sodden heap in the tin bath.

Sister Veronica pumped the water in—a blustery gush to wash away their wickedness. They set to the task, small hands slipping the bar of carbolic soap back and forth, rubbing their knuckles raw on the coarse cloth.

The bloodstains were hard to shift, so Eighty-Six was last again; last to hoist his dripping sheet up on the barbed-wire barrier that fenced the graveyard, last in the queue for the spoon of cod-liver oil and the meager breakfast.

He did not care. He could not eat.

The cod-liver oil was dispensed from the same metal tablespoon, coating ninety-six offered tongues, each of whose owners longed to spew it back in Sister Mary's face. Eighty-Six had learned to swallow it quickly. Not to think too deeply; to proffer his bowl for the ladle of lumpy gruel and carry it directly to the nearest vacant place at the long refectory table.

He attempted to sit, lowering himself gingerly onto the wooden bench. When he made contact with the hard seat, pain shot through him; pain so brutal and burning, that it was as if he were back there in Keaney's room, sprawled over the fusty bed, suffering the same violence again. He shut his eyes tight against the torment, his head down, hunched over the bowl, his backside half raised off the seat, and struggled to eat, his tears falling into the gruel.

His fellow offender, Eighty-Four, was seated in like manner beside him. He wore the emblem of the chronic bed-wetter: the wet sheet tied around his middle. He was a small boy with large eyes, and a birthmark like a red ink spill soiling most of his pale neck. They might be the same age—who was to know?—but they had the same mannerisms, and had suffered the same punishment. Master Keaney liked them small and weak. They could not speak out. They sat locked inside their frightened selves.

Sister Mary patrolled the hall like a great crow, her black robes grazing the floor, her eyes alert for dropped food and foot-fights under the long tables. She could tell, just by looking down the serried rows of lowered heads, which of the boys had suffered Keaney's "attentions" in the night. They did not want to eat; they sobbed into their hands and swapped their bowl with the nearest little glutton, one who would see in their raw pain his own fat reward.

She spotted Eighty-Four and Eighty-Six trade their bowls with the boys opposite them, but did not intervene. Just as she did not intervene in the affairs of the men. After all, these children were the products of sin, and did they not, in a way, deserve all they got?

Chapter eleven

Lydia Devine, having ensured that the coast was clear, closed the bedroom door quietly and opened the large envelope marked "Private." For although her mother was safely out of sight, in the parlor watching *Green Acres*, she could not trust her to stay put for its half-hour duration. Sometimes the appearance of the hapless, bumbling character of Hank Kimball—whom Elizabeth felt was "a talentless gype" and lowered the show's appeal—could cause her to turn down the volume and make a cup of tea. Worse still, she might decide to switch off the set completely and go on the prowl to see what Lydia was up to.

However, at that point, Lydia could hear the burbling television down below and felt confident that she was safe for the time being at least.

The big envelope contained three smaller ones, each bearing her box number. The first letter was on yellow paper, with two pink hearts entwined before a rising sun—very forward, thought Lydia—and the writing was practically indecipherable. She tried to squint her way through it, but gave up when her head began to ache at the wobbling script and careless spelling. A man who could not manage the word "because" and who omitted his definite articles (not to mention his punctuation) was either a slow learner or a foreigner, or, God forbid, both. A resounding three out of ten, thought Lydia, and resisted the urge to take her red pen and write "Please try harder" across the bottom.

The second one she opened was a marked improvement. The handwriting was regular and legible. The envelope and paper were in matching bond with a fetching scalloped border. She was impressed.

2 Harris Green
Killycock,
Co. Derry

My Dear Madam,
        Whilst perusing the July 14th edition of the Mid-Ulster Vindicator your advertisement caught my eye.

Lydia settled back more comfortably against the pillows. Full marks already for the use of the word "perusing," and more brownie points for taking the trouble to spell out the word "advertisement." That dangling participle was, of course, something else again, but she was prepared to forgive it. Here was obviously a man who believed in doing things properly.

From what I gather, and I realize that one is limited by the space in the newspaper, I sense that you are a cultured person like myself who is creative and likes the finer things in life.

She thought he must be psychic to read such depth in such a small ad. Still, she was flattered—and the proper use of the subordinate clause was impressive.

I shall now tell you a little about myself so that you can decide for yourself and I do hope that you will decide to write back to me.

I am a retired gentleman. I used to own a shop, selling mostly household items and hardware. As well as items for the ladies. Whatever the public wanted I'm proud to say I managed to get. The lady customers used to call me ·Frank the Fixer·. A title, I have to say that I was proud to wear because I believe in fulfilling a ladies needs.

Lydia shifted uneasily. What on earth was he talking about? She looked up from the letter and studied the ceiling lamp. The TV still babbled happily down below. Thank heavens, she thought; it must be a Kimball-free episode. Now, "items for the ladies" and "fulfilling a ladies needs" sounded a bit odd. But perhaps she was overreacting. Perhaps she'd solve the puzzle by reading on.

Having said that I do not miss the shop because I have plenty of things to occupy myself with. I like taking long walks in the countryside with my dog Snoop, because I believe a gentleman should keep fit and healthy. To this end I am also a teetotal, non-smoker. The strongest drink I allow past my lips is a Fanta orange when the temperature of the day is high.

Like yourself I like to poke about in the garden in the good weather and I read extensively. Always a quality broadsheet, none of that tabloid nonsense.

And, thought Lydia, raising an eyebrow, the *Mid-Ulster Vindicator* is a quality broadsheet?

I also like painting watercolours and photography and am a member of the Killycock Amateur Artist's and Glamour Photography Club. My music taste is classical. All in all I consider myself to be a refined gentleman with discerning tastes. I like to eat out in good restaurants.

I do hope that you will do me the honour of replying to my humble letter. And I do wish as a result we can meet.

Yours most sincerely and respectfully,
Frank Xavier McPrunty

My word! thought Lydia, returning the letter to the envelope; educated certainly, but a bit of a show-off. Let's see what number three has to offer.

She ran her silver sword letter-opener—a thank-you present from Emily Bingham on the occasion of passing her eleven-plus examination—along the crease and unfolded the single blue page. She was glad it was short and to the point. She began reading, but had barely finished the first sentence when she saw the doorknob turn. She tensed, stuffed the letters under the pillow and sat up on the edge of the bed.

"What were you doing there just now?"

Mrs. Devine stood in the doorway, pointing her malacca cane at Lydia's pillow.

"Mother, really! How dare you barge into my bedroom without knocking?"

"I don't need to knock on doors in my own home."

"Well, believe it or not, it's called manners and having respect for other people's privacy." Lydia stood up, her anger rising. "Even if that other person is *only* your daughter. Now I'd be grateful if you'd go back to *Green Acres* and leave me in peace. I was resting."

"I'm finished watching it. That idiot Kimball appeared."

"I thought as much!" Lydia snapped.

"Anyway, you weren't resting." Elizabeth eyed her daughter suspiciously, her knotty fingers gripping the panther head of the cane. "You're up to something. I can always tell, you know."

"I was not up to anything." She put a hand to her brow and sighed. "Good Lord, it's like living with a child!"

"If it's nothing, why's your face all red?" demanded Elizabeth.

"Let's have a cup of tea and a slice of Beattie's chocolate sponge, shall we?" Lydia said the first thing that came to her, hoping it would distract her mother from the pillow.

"What chocolate sponge? Beattie never gave me a sponge."

"Oh, but she did!" She took her mother's arm and led her out the door. "It must have slipped your mind. If we don't eat it soon, the birds will get it."

"Is that so?" said Elizabeth, confused, the pillow already forgotten.

Before retiring for the night, Jamie stood in his bedroom, angling the broken piece of mirror, taking a critical look at his full-bellied self. The letter had been sent. In fact, the anonymous lady would probably have already read it, and with a bit of luck, might be wanting to take a look at him very soon. Jamie realized that drastic measures would need to be taken to make himself appear more presentable. After all, Rose had said that a good suit and shirt could take a man anywhere. But be that as it may, he felt a lot more was needed to improve his chances of winning a wife.

As he stood now in the fading light, he was none too pleased with the image the glass threw back. He did appreciate that wearing bedraggled long Johns with a pair of grubby bare feet poking out of them did little to enhance his appearance. Nonetheless, the fact remained that he was a bit overweight, prematurely bald, and had a face like a seed potato left too long in the pit. But what could a man do about it?

He set the broken mirror on the windowsill and stepped back to obtain a more accurate reading. He turned from side to side, inhaled deeply, pulled in his stomach, straightened his posture—and was immediately struck by the difference the simple exercise made.

But what of it? He could hardly turn up to meet this woman holding his breath and belly in, and clenching his buttocks, for an indefinite period of time. Jamie winced at the very thought, sighed and let his shoulders drop to their habitual comfortable, slouched position. He stared at himself dejectedly.

He was a man of forty-one who, because of his lifestyle and outlook, was going on *sixty-one*. There was nothing he could do—or was there? He remembered Dr. Brewster advising him on several occasions to lose some weight.

"Your blood pressure is far too high, James, which puts undue stress on your heart, and you don't want to come down with a stroke or heart attack at your age. Cut down on the fries and cigarettes; that's my advice."

But how could he? Jamie thought of his frying pan: the weighty iron-bottomed pan that had been passed down the generations; thought of how he loved to see the sausages and bacon shrivel to a curl in the sizzling lard. He was unaware, however, of how many spluttering, fat-soaked feasts had been served up from that very utensil, or indeed of how many lives it had claimed. A whole line of male McCloones with furred arteries and slowed hearts had fallen into early graves with strokes and aneurisms, oblivious to the fact that the humble pan had put them there.

Dr. Brewster had passed a paper across to him. "Here's a diet sheet and some guidelines. Three weeks on that and you'll be a new man."

Jamie had taken the diet sheet but not the advice it contained. Sure a man who had nothing much in his life didn't have much incentive for prolonging it. And if you took away the fries and the smokes and the wee drop of drink, sure what would be the point of getting outta the bed of a morning atall, atall?

"*Ah, but now there is a point,*" a little voice whispered in Jamie's ear. "*Your whole life could change for the better. But it's up to you.*"

At that moment he regretted not having taken the good doctor's counsel. But maybe there was still time.

Inspired, he rushed to the drawer of the glass case in the kitchen and unearthed the diet sheet from beneath a pile of bills, coupons, tax returns, parish bulletins and St. Brigid's Church monthly stipend envelopes. He lit the oil lamp and proceeded to read through the formidable list.

Breakfast

One boiled egg, two slices of toast lightly buttered, one cup of tea with milk and one spoonful of sugar (if you must).

Lunch

Chicken, fish or red meat, preferably grilled, boiled or steamed with fresh vegetables. One potato (no butter). No pudding.

Dinner

As lunch, followed by fresh fruit. Alcohol in severe moderation.

No buns, biscuits, cakes or items of a sugary nature.

Follow for three weeks and lose a stone or a stone and a half depending on your dedication and depth of commitment.

And Dr. Brewster had added, humorously, in his own hand:

Only the weak, lazy and flabby-minded person could not stick to this diet and succeed. So ask yourself: Am I a man / woman or a mouse? (delete as appropriate)

Jamie turned out the lamp, lay down on his bed and thought: Well, no man is gonna call *me* a mouse. Not even Dr. Brewster—and there and then he decided to change himself.

That night, as he drifted into sleep, this desire for betterment took an almighty hold and began burning in him with a passionate force, as a banked fire, suddenly poked, might glow red and flame under the sucking roar of a violent chimney updraft. Yes, he'd cut down on the fries, give up the drink—or maybe take a wee drop less—take more exercise, ride his bicycle more vigorously and often into town.

And he could see the new man emerging in that new suit from Harvey's Fashions. Saw himself in a pair of knife-crease trousers that did not require suspenders, held in place by a belt of fine leather that did not demand an extra hole or two punched with the aid of a hammer and a six-inch nail. Under the suit, he saw a shirt of some whiteness, its stiff-rimmed collar making his neck feel important. To set it off, a paisley print tie in shiny red, and on his feet a pair of glossy shoes, polished to a conker's gleam.

And ultimately he envisaged himself meeting his future wife; he, James Kevin Barry Michael McCloone, a man of fine standards and high morals. A proud man with a flat-enough middle and a straight-enough back.

Chapter twelve

Lydia and Daphne studied their menus. They had met for lunch at the Golden Gate café, a place that believed in frying, frittering, and battering most of the ingredients that were delivered at its kitchen door. Of late, however, Lydia had noticed one or two healthier options nosing their way onto the menu. For this small concession she was grateful.

The friends sat opposite each other in a booth appointed with vinyl upholstery, a table laid with green-patterned oilcloth between them. All about, on walls of simulated knotty pine, hung prints of Killoran in a gentler, sepia-tinted, age.

The café was not busy. A group of youths were consuming cola and fries in a corner. At another table a lone farmer shoveled away at a fry-up, halting every so often to snorkel from a mug of tea. He ate with all the gusto of a porker at the trough. Lydia quietly noted that the place had gone down terribly, and vowed that she and Daphne would seek a more genteel establishment next time. Although she thought that this might prove difficult in Killoran.

Daphne was glad of the break from the library, and Lydia was glad to have time away from her mother. She had dropped her off at

Beatrice Bohilly's home. Beatrice had finished her paint-by-numbers picture, *Horse and Foal by Lake*, and wished to have her friend's opinion and praise. Lydia knew that when the two ladies got together, time became stretched and lost in a great labyrinth of reminiscing gossip. For this Lydia was thankful. She could spend as much time as she liked with Daphne and her mother wouldn't notice.

A young waitress approached them, bearing a notepad, a pen, a dishcloth, and an expression of terminal boredom.

"Are yous getting, are yous?"

"The quiche and salad for me, thanks," Lydia said. "And you, Daphne?"

"I think I'll try the scampi and French fries. I know I shouldn't, but oh to have your willpower, Lydia."

The glum waitress was jotting on the notepad.

"Nonsense, eat what you enjoy," Lydia said. "Life's too short. I mean to say, I'd—"

"D'yous want anything to drink with that?" the waitress interrupted.

"A pot of tea for two would be nice, please." Daphne said. "But y'know I've been very lazy about my walking," she continued to Lydia. "In the evenings I seem to have no energy and just want to collapse on the sofa with a book."

The girl stuck the pen behind her ear, tore the duplicate page from the pad and shoved it under the salt shaker. She then slapped the dishcloth down on the table and circled the surface lethargically three times. "Right ye be," she said, and slunk off in the direction of the swing kitchen doors.

"Well, you have more energy than that one." Lydia's eyes followed the girl, "and she's probably half your age. Terrible to give up and stop making an effort when one is so young. I blame the parents."

But Daphne was more concerned about Lydia's replies to her advertisement. "The letters, Lydia," she said impatiently. "I'm just dying to see them."

Her friend reached into her faux-crocodile purse. "Now, have a read of each and tell me what you think." She got up. "I'll just nip to the ladies if you don't mind."

When she returned, Daphne was immersed in the contents of McPrunty's envelope. She looked over her spectacles, a smile developing.

"'Frank the Fixer.' My word, he sounds the racy sort!"

"You know, I don't know what to make of him. But what about this one?" Lydia tapped a single page. It was the letter written so painstakingly by Jamie McCloone.

"Well now, *he* sounds terribly solid. Although…"

Daphne was looking across at the farmer who, having consumed his meal, sat picking his dentures. The table before him was littered with stray fries and scattered peas. It looked as though he'd been having a food fight instead of a meal. His eyes were locked fixedly on the ketchup bottle as if he were witnessing an apparition of the Virgin Mary put on just for him.

"Now personally, I've nothing against farmers. Goodness me, I've been going out with one for over a decade, but they can be very—"

Two plates of food were thumped down in front of them without ceremony.

"Will yous be wantin' brown sauce or ketchup or whatever with that?" the waitress demanded.

Daphne shook her head. "I will say this, though," she said to Lydia, "they can be terribly untidy. I think it comes from working with livestock and being out of doors most of the time." She speared a fry.

"Yes, I *do* see what you mean." Her companion began to saw at the quiche. The pastry case seemed as resilient as the bark of a gum tree; she gave up and scooped up some filling with her fork.

"But Daphne, I'm not intending to *marry* one of these men, just take him to Heather's wedding for the day. By the way, did you get your invitation?"

"I did, but wouldn't it be great if you met someone nice?"

Daphne wistfully considered her friend, imagining how a future husband would "complete" her.

The pot of tea arrived, and two cups and saucers were rattled into place beside their plates.

"So which one d'you think I should meet?"

"Well, why don't you cover all eventualities and meet both? Wouldn't do any harm."

"I suppose not. But I'm not really ready to meet them just yet. I need more information."

"I agree. I would write back to them both and ask some pertinent questions."

"Like what, for instance?"

Daphne picked up Mr. McPrunty's letter again. "Well, this one says he's retired, but he doesn't give his age—rather suspect, so he could be anywhere between sixty-five and ninety. Also ask if he's been married before. And our Mr. McCloone says he likes reading, so ask what he reads. And cooking; would be interesting to find out what he cooks." She pulled a face. "Because if I'm any judge, 'cooking' in bachelor-farmer speak means the 'fend-for-myself fry-up' for breakfast, dinner and supper."

The farmer in the corner rose to go, and broke wind most audibly in the process. The ladies glared at him in disgust, but he appeared unaware of the social indiscretion.

"How utterly rude!" Daphne said aloud, hoping she might be heard. Lydia flapped a hand under her nose and reached into her purse for a handkerchief.

"Gosh, I sincerely hope Mr. McCloone has more decorum than him." Daphne sat back in her seat. "Now where was I?" She referred to the letters. "Yes, now I remember: inquire as to what they look for in a woman. That should throw up some interesting insights, don't you think?"

Just then, across the square, a car horn blared. They looked out, to see an Austin Princess limousine, bedecked in ribbons, pull up outside the church.

"A wedding! How fitting, Lydia. I think that's a sign, don't you?"

"Yes, quite." Lydia's voice was laden with skepticism.

The work-shy waitress had run to the window and was gazing raptly out at the commotion. All three watched the bride, radiant on her father's arm, ascend the steps, yards of nylon tulle spilling out behind her. When they reached the church porch they turned and smiled for an array of popping flashbulbs.

"Oh, isn't she lovely!" enthused Lydia.

"I think all brides are lovely," said Daphne, swept up, like her friend, in the romance of the occasion. Because, deep down, both looked on the marriage bond as the ultimate prize for a woman's endeavor. If only for the acceptance to be gained in the eyes of society. For Daphne and Lydia the gold wedding band was a badge of honor, desired as much by their mature selves as by the young waitress who stood beside them, her girlish dreams reflected in her look of entrancement.

In Daphne's case, that longing for attachment had made her look on men as superior beings, no matter how flawed; it was an idea that corroded her judgment and rendered her infinitely flexible and tolerant. She had endured ten years of courtship by a man who showed little interest in marriage, who used his mother as an excuse for not committing. Daphne went along with this unhappy situation because to return to the manless state was unthinkable. Better to be attached and unhappy than unattached and sad—like Lydia.

Poor Lydia, she mused, because if she were honest, she *did* pity her friend. Poor Lydia; she rarely could think of her without that negative prefix. Her connection with the weak-willed John had given her a head start in the race that Poor Lydia hadn't even entered yet. How things had changed from their schooldays! Back then it was Clever Lydia, always ahead of her in every subject, the bright one who sailed through exams to claim an exalted place at teacher training college, while she, Daphne, hampered by an unhealthy home life— alcoholic father, overworked mother—had struggled with rejections and examination re-sits.

Where once Daphne had looked up to Lydia, the balance of power had shifted, and now it was Lydia who admired and wanted a little of what Daphne had. She often mused on this reversal of roles with a satisfaction not befitting the confidante and friend she gave herself out to be.

As she lost herself in the wedding taking place opposite, she reflected with a smug kind of certainty that one day she'd climb those same steps, dressed all in white, but did not think that her friend ever would.

Soon the bride and her father had disappeared into the church, followed by a multicolored retinue of guests, the ladies in flimsy frocks and wide-brimmed hats, the men suffering in suits, forced to observe decorum in spite of the warm weather. With a sigh, the waitress returned to her chores and the ladies turned back to their plates.

"I *do* love weddings." Daphne poured more tea. "I'm really looking forward to Heather's, aren't you?"

"Well, I'd feel happier about it if I knew who I was going with." Lydia held up the two letters. "Right: questions. What did you say I should ask?"

"Oh, yes. Let me see." She took the pages from Lydia and scanned them again. "Yes, now I know. Mr. McPrunty: ask his age, if he's been married before and...and Mr. McCloone, what he reads and cooks."

"That's all?"

"Yes, I think that about covers it. Anyway, I'm sure you'll think of more interesting things to ask when you're writing." Daphne looked at her watch. "Good, I've time for dessert."

Lydia smiled and returned the letters to her purse. "Do you know, dear, you should have been a sleuth or an agony aunt." She gave a mock salute.

"The pleasure is all mine. Now let's have some ice cream to celebrate, having solved that little problem."

Chapter thirteen

Sister Bernadette strode alongside her charges, through the mist of another murky morning, her habit belling out like a spinnaker in the wind. Her thoughts shut off from any softer refinements, running only the most negative footage in her head. She moved through her day like she moved through her life, keeping well within the narrow confines of her ruthless self. She dished out the cruelty and reveled in the hurt, in the mouths that screamed, the eyes that wept, seeing a small body ball up tight under her wounding lashes.

They entered a long tunnel, continued down it for a time until they came to a small square. Sister Bernadette blew the whistle once more and they halted. Before them gaped the doors of the chapel, and within its walls stood a priest waiting to say Mass.

Every day, at 6 A.M., God was served before breakfast.

They traipsed soundlessly to their appointed seats, at once kneeling down on the prie-dieux, their bony knees on the unyielding wood, their toes curled up on the stone floor. And there they would remain for the hour's duration; no standing, no sitting, no stirring that might give them a moment's reprieve. Their lips moved in prayer and their hands moved to cross themselves. No other gestures—smiling, talking, coughing—were permitted. Any sound that broke the silence would annoy the priest, and so it came with a heavy price.

Eighty-Six was running a fever. He had had little sleep because of a tearing cough, his head ached and his limbs were sore. He wanted desperately to cough now. His ribcage trembled with the pressure of keeping it in. Then a pain welled in his throat, so sharp that his will could fight against it no longer. He put his hand over his mouth and coughed and coughed and coughed.

In no time he heard the dreaded sounds: the quick, angry, frantic heels upon the tiled floor. Hard hands hauled him from the seat.

Sister Bernadette frogmarched him outside. The wind whipped at his sodden clothes as the rain lashed and pummeled him.

"Open your mouth!" she ordered, and shoved in the cake of black soap.

"Breakfast!" she snarled, and slapped him several times across the face. And he was made to stand in the rain, pondering his sin and suffering the penance it had brought him.

At 2 P.M., Sister Veronica ordered him to her lesson.

The schoolroom was a dusty, draughty place, with five long benches for the pupils. It smelled of ancient ink and chalk dust. At the front of the room, on a raised platform, sat a large blackboard on an easel, with the teacher's desk before it. On the desk was a globe that swiveled on a wooden stand. On the walls, pictures of Jesus and Mary. Pictures of animals and birds, too, and a cracked, glossy map of Ireland weighted with mahogany rods.

Sister Veronica stood by the blackboard, her cane poised below the first line of verse. This was her room. This was her world. Within its walls she drilled and taught. Where she exercised her rigid control, her commanding of attention and her steadfast refusal to ever give praise when she ought.

"Now, after the count of three, I want you all to recite the poem in chorus. One, two, three…"

Leisure
by William Henry Davies

What is this life if, full of care,
We have no time to stand and stare.

No time to stand beneath the boughs
And stare as long as sheep or cows.

No time to see, when woods we pass,
Where squirrels hide their nuts in grass.

"Good. That's enough for the present. Now take out your slates and copy it down from the board."

Something caught her eye.

"Eighty-One, did you hear me?" She hammered her desk with the cane. "Stand up. What were you doing just now?" She whisked to the back of the room, her black robes flying out behind her.

"Stand up, Eighty-One! Now, what were you doing under the desk?"

The boy, gangly, tall for his eight years, stood up awkwardly. His shaved head showed a bruise of mauve and yellow spreading from the left temple. The previous day his head had been banged against the corridor wall, punishment for having dropped his breakfast bowl. He had a cold sore on his lip, and like the rest of the boys, the sickly pallor and soulless eyes of the undernourished and uncared for.

"I dropped my slate, Sister." He held it out in his trembling hands as if to prove the point, because he did not know what else to do.

"And why did you drop it?" she snapped back. The room was hushed. The boy did not know how to answer because he knew that whatever reason he gave would be wrong.

"Well, we're all waiting. Aren't we, class?" She swept an arm in a giant arc to encompass the group.

"Yes, Sister!" the class chorused back. But Eighty-One remained silent, staring down at the bench.

"Well, since you are so stupid as to not know why you dropped it, I shall have to tell you. You dropped your slate because you were not paying attention." Her heartless words struck him like so many sharp stones. She placed the end of the cane under his chin and used it to force his head up. "How many times this month have you dropped your slate in my class, Eighty-One?"

"Two times, Sister."

"Not 'two times.' The correct answer is 'twice.' Now, can we try that again, using a complete sentence?"

The boy swallowed hard and began.

"I have…dro…drop…dropped my slate…twiced, twice this… mon…month, Sister."

"Good. And now today will be the third time, won't it?" She grabbed him by the shoulder as he struggled to get his legs over the bench, and marched him to the front of the room.

"Hands out!" she ordered.

She pulled up the sleeve of her habit and, taking careful and calculated aim, brought the cane down again and again, like a door opening and closing on trapped hands. As she thrashed him, she screamed out the words of reprimand.

"You. Dirty. Filthy. Useless. Boy. You. Will. Not. Drop. Your. Slate. In. My. Class. Again."

Fifteen words and fifteen lashes of the cane. The room quivered with her anger and the boy's fear.

When she'd finished, she ordered Eighty-One to go and stand in the corner. But, instead of obeying, he swayed, before collapsing at her feet, his bruised head and ashen face hitting the floor with a dull thud. There was a gasp from the class as Sister Veronica leaned over the supine figure.

"Get up, you lazy wretch!"

But the boy did not flinch. He was unconscious. There was a trickle of blood coming from his left ear and pooling onto the floor.

The nun ran to the door and shouted for Bartley, the caretaker. He came presently and removed Eighty-One from the room.

"Take him to the infirmary," she ordered.

Then she turned back to the class. "The rest of you, get the verse copied out *now*."

Twenty heads dropped to the task.

They had suffered and seen so much violence that their fainting comrade did not upset them unduly. Their only consolation was that, so far, they had escaped the nun's fury. Their only goal was for the situation to continue so, until they reached the close of the lesson.

Eighty-Six sat uneasily, changing his weight from one hip to the other, trying not to attract notice. The cake of soap he'd been forced to swallow earlier was exacting a scorching revenge: burning a steady path from the top of his gullet all the way down to his stomach. His whole body ached, his clothes were sodden, and the cough that had brought him so much grief threatened to betray him yet again. He wanted desperately to cry out, wanted desperately to die. But never having experienced—even for one minute—freedom from fear, he knew that even the bleakest choices were not his to make. In those agonizing circumstances he did what was demanded of him, and strove, trembling, to twist out the letters with his chalk; for now, his redemption lay in a labor of meaningless words that formed a meaningless verse.

He was on the fourth line: "And stare as long as sheep or cows." He did, however, know what sheep and cows looked like. There were pictures of them on the wall under the heading "Old MacDonald's Farm." When he grew up he wanted to be a farmer. He pictured himself like Mr. MacDonald, with a cocked hat and a crooked staff, standing out in a green field, a collie dog with muddied paws cavorting about him. He could hear the bleating and mooing animals, and see them run toward him to be fed.

"You've stopped writing, Eighty-Six. You are finished then?" The nun bent over him.

"No, Sister." He looked up.

"Then stop daydreaming and get on with it." She moved to the next boy, and then turned back to him, prodding him with the cane. "And sit like a Christian on that seat."

He sat properly, as instructed, and the pain properly beat through him, and his daydream blurred and ran. At the end of the lesson he was left with the ungraspable meaning of the chalked letters on the slate, the sight of the blood upon the floor and the vision of his comrade toppling.

None of them knew, as they filed out of the room, that they would never see Eighty-One again.

Chapter fourteen

Drinks on the house for me two friends here and your good self, Slope, please!" Jamie slapped a ten-pound note down on the bar counter.

He was celebrating the decision to straighten himself out, cut down on the booze and the fry-ups, and make a new man of himself. Tomorrow he'd be in purgatory, he reminded himself, so tonight he might as well visit heaven.

It was Saturday night, though early; O'Shea's bar was not yet thronged. Beside Jamie sat Paddy McFadden and Matty Dougan. In the back room, out of sight, a few young men were playing darts, among them Minnie Sproule's wayward son Chuck.

"Have you won the football pools or something?" Slope pressed two glasses under the Black Bush optics and busied himself with the order.

"No, I haven't won nothing but the right to enjoy meself," said Jamie, a little mournfully, "on this, my last night before I go on a diet and cut down on this stuff."

He took the glass, looked longingly into the amber liquid, turning it this way and that with reflective reverence.

"Christ, you're mental! Lent's seven bloody months away." Slope palmed the note and placed the change at Jamie's elbow. "But then you wouldn't know that, since you've been missin' Sunday Mass." He imitated Maisie Ryan's accent and glared past Jamie's ear with mock reproach.

"Aye, she's a right oul' bitch that one."

"Who's that?" Paddy and Matty asked almost in unison.

"That nosy oul' whore, Maisie Ryan." Jamie took a swig of his whiskey.

"I'd pay no attention to that one," Paddy said. "Not content unless she's givin' out about something. No man or children to look after, that's the trouble with her."

"Well, the next time she tackles me about not goin' tae Mass," said Jamie, suddenly emboldened by the booze, "I'll kick her big arse for her, so a will."

Slope was called to the back for an order, and Jamie's intention to defame Maisie's character hung in the air like a noxious gas. Matty came to the rescue and changed the subject.

"And why would you want to be goin' on a diet, Jamie? Sure there's nothing much wrong with you the way you are."

"Och now, there's a lot that could be fixed. Dr. Brewster says if I cut back on the fry-ups it'll help me heart and me back and all."

They all three stared at the blue-veined Formica and considered the wisdom of this. Matty was the first to speak.

"I wouldn't bother with all that. Sure, none of us is gettin' no younger and we're all gonna end up wearin' the wooden overcoat soon enough." Matty carried the attitude of the eternal pessimist; a man who felt badly when he felt good for fear he'd feel worse when he felt better.

He had the appearance and mannerisms of someone who'd never been young at any time. His sharp, pitted face looked as though it had come to life at the hands of a chisel-happy sculptor who'd mislaid his spectacles that day. The cheeks and eye sockets were hollowed to the bone, the nose too long and dangerously pointed; the mouth a single, daring, lopsided hammer-blow that could never be righted through smiles or talk. He was a farmer, like Jamie, unmarried, and spectacularly uninterested in most matters that did not concern the land, the weather and the rising price of things. Unlike Jamie, he had no fat to lose. His clothes hung loose from his mop-shaft frame.

"Well, there's another wee reason I want-a sort meself out," Jamie said. "Paddy here knows what it is, but I'm not at liberty to discuss it at this present moment in time." He tapped the side of his nose. "If you get my drift, Matty. No offense intended atall, atall."

"Oh, none took."

"Now, your secret's safe with me, Jamie, right enough." Paddy shifted in his seat and stifled a whiskey yawn.

"Aye, every man has a right to his privacy," said Matty, wondering deeply what Jamie might be up to, all sorts of ideas and notions flying through his head. For he looked on Jamie as a creature cut from the same cloth as himself. Of similar age, both wifeless and childless, living on inherited land, with dreams shored up in their heads like the sun-cracked peat in the bog.

"Well said, Matty," Paddy agreed. "I was just—"

He didn't get time to finish because at that moment a loud scuffling was heard outside the door—as if a bull and a sow were having a quarrel up against it. A few seconds later, the door burst open. All three turned on their stools to witness the arrival of Declan Colt & The Silver Bullets. Two of the band members, red-faced and breathless, were wrestling large amplifiers and cased instruments before them. They nodded sidelong at the trio as they passed.

Taking up the rear was the lead singer himself, his hands swinging leisurely by his sides, a cigarette dipping at the left of his mouth, a stetson on his head. He wore a purple satin shirt, its collar spread flat, like the wingspan of a peregrine falcon, a silver vest edged with gold brocade and a pair of tight white bell-bottoms with corresponding trim. About his hips, a belt of carved silver Indian squaw heads, whose plaits and feathers tinkled as he walked. On his feet a pair of rawhide Mexican boots with pointed toes, red tassels and steel-capped heels. In this garb, Declan saw himself as elegant; imagined himself as an Irish Willie Nelson, minus the braids.

"How you, boys?" He nodded at the group and strutted toward the back room. He liked the ring of his steel heels on the tiled floor announcing his arrival, and the sound of his fake Texas drawl.

The boys at the bar responded, but Declan didn't stop for small talk. His imagined fame was like a peacock's plumage rising, a waving fan he rarely saw beyond.

"Oh, Declan!" Jamie shouted after his glittering back, "I brung the wee accordjin with me just in case you want a wee filler later on, like."

Declan turned, tinkling, his thumbs stuck in his belt. His own interests were being served.

"Good man yourself, Jamie. If it gets busy we'll sure need you for sure."

He disappeared.

A great sense of wellbeing broke out in Jamie. The booze and the thought of his future performance were unleashing a rare happiness, watering his weak courage to produce a plant of some size. He returned, smiling and contented, to his conversation.

Time passed, with the three friends smoking and drinking, picking over bones of gossip and farm talk. They hardly noticed as the premises began to fill up. The door behind them rarely rested, admitting mostly couples: dedicated fans of Declan Colt and his band. The husbands: shiny-faced, freed from the fields and construction sites, eager for the drink and carousing. The wives: smiling thinly, fearful of what mayhem might lie ahead.

Jamie and his comrades knew most of the Saturday night revelers, and if a stranger appeared they would look at him slyly and speculate as to who he might be, where he might be from, and what he might be doing in those parts—and with whom, if applicable.

More time passed. More men began to thicken at the bar, some in their Sunday suits, the wifeless ones in their workaday clothes. Smoke smogged the air, voices roared out of blazing faces under the heat of the drink, the rumpus and gathering crowd. Sometimes an imagined slight brought a raised fist or a killer look; ideas and opinions formed in youth and set in stone had made inflexible men of them all.

Slope's wife Peggy joined him behind the bar. Known "affectionately" as the Bacon-Slicer, she was a no-nonsense woman, lean as a fence post, with a sharp face and a nose like a bill-hook. Her eyes darted among the crowd to target and evict trouble if she saw it. She hated the pub and the men and the drink, and kept Slope on a short leash with her vicious tongue. She had concluded long ago that he and the business were her combined penance for having slept with him before wedlock, producing a daughter, who hated them both. So she "offered it up"; a silver cross from the shrine at Knock dangled at her throat as her work-worn hands sudded and stacked the glasses.

"How do, Peggy," Jamie attempted the greeting. He was at that slack-jawed phase of the inebriation process, risking only a few words at a time, lest he might appear completely looped. The accordion sat on the floor by his feet. Jamie was oiling himself toward picking it up, to being the center of attention soon.

Peggy glanced up from the steaming sink, her pained expression breaking into a reluctant smile. "Keepin' well, are ye, Jamie?"

"Oh…the best, Peggy, the best."

"You'll give us a wee tune later on I hope."

She swept a lock of hair behind her ear and dropped her head back to the labor, building the wet glasses on the drainer dangerously high.

Jamie studied the bowed head, a straight pale line bisecting the crown in her straw-blond hair, like a harvester track in a corn field. "Give you a wee tune surely, so a will," he said.

"Give us a vodka and coke there, will ye?" a voice loud and uncouth broke in. Chuck Sproule forced his way between Jamie and Paddy. Peggy continued her chore, pretending not to have heard.

Chuck was an erratically behaved nineteen-year-old, restless and rude, a drop-out with a dead father, a hopeless mother, and four wild siblings whom he bullied to a point beyond madness. He had greasy hair and puckered skin, wore scruffy jeans which barely stayed up on his skinny arse, and a gray tee shirt that had shrunk in the wash and rode part of the way up his back.

"Did ye hear me, did ye?"

Peggy stopped what she was doing, slowly dried her hands and glared at him.

"Jamie, did you hear some unmannerly hellion ask me for something just now?"

Jamie did not want to tangle with young Chuck. He had a talent for catching on a person's flaw and pulling 'til he'd unraveled them to rage. He didn't want anything to do with the nasty wee bugger.

"I think he wants a vodkey and coat—I mean vodka and coke—Peggy," Jamie quickly corrected himself.

"Jezsis, if it isn't oul' McCloone!" Chuck elbowed Jamie in the back, flung an arm round his shoulder and stuck his face close to his. "Are you a fuckin' translator now, are ye?"

"Less of that craic in here, Sproule," Peggy warned, "or I'll bounce you out on the street. Don't think I won't."

Chuck released Jamie immediately and straightened. Paddy and Matty studied the bar counter, by turns looking into their drinks and up at the ceiling, anywhere but at Peggy. It was not through kindness that Mrs. O'Shea had earned her nickname; anyone who crossed her usually cut themselves. Her threat had the desired effect: Chuck's bravado wilted immediately.

"Och, Peggy."

"Don't 'och Peggy' me! It's 'Mrs. O'Shea' to you." She kept her eyes on him. "Now, what did you want?"

"A vodka and coke, Mrs. O'Shea, *pleeeease?*" he said in a falsetto baby voice, steepling his fingers under his chin like a pleading altar boy.

Peggy gave in, if reluctantly. She began setting up the drink. All at once there came a squeal from an amplifier, like that of a hog being hauled within sight of the butcher's cleaver. It deafened every patron for a few jaw-rattling seconds and was followed by a muffled echoing.

"One, two…one, two." Declan and the Bullets were doing a sound check. The show was about to begin.

"That's Declan gettin' her goin'," Matty made the superfluous comment. "Maybe we should head in."

Paddy took it as his cue and stumbled to the toilet. Jamie ordered another round.

The lounge, behind the public bar, was a long rectangular room with a raised platform at the far end, and below it a woodblocked dancing area, not much bigger than a generous tablecloth. In its former life the space had been a store, a toilet, and a coal shed, but Slope had seen its potential as a locus of entertainment. With a substantial loan from the Tailorstown Credit Union (which he was still paying off), he had realized his fantasy by knocking the three areas into one and naming it The Step Inside Lounge.

Secured along each wall was a row of bench seats upholstered in amber carriage cloth, salvaged from a derailed slow train from Derry to Donegal. Slope had procured the reconditioned seating at tremendous discount from a member of the traveling community. In front of each seat: a knee-high Formica table. On the floor: a carpet of clashing scarlet stripes and furious lime spots encouraged the drunker patron to believe he'd thrown up even before he had a mind to. The smoke-yellowed walls were of combed plaster. At equidistant intervals a succession of twin-pronged lamps under dusty, green shades jutted out, giving the assembled faces the look of early-stage cirrhosis—an illness that was most likely lying in wait for several of the livers present.

The lounge was crammed when Jamie and his friends took the seats reserved for them by Declan, at a top table near the band. Talk and laughter fairly bubbled, cigarette smoke and oaths poured from mouths; forests of bottles and glasses crowded every table, ashtrays spilled matches and cigarette ends onto the floor.

Mary, the O'Shea's teenage daughter—with her mother's eyes (for which she was grateful) and her father's grin—strode up and down, delivering drinks and collecting glasses. She was a tall, attractive redhead who hated Saturday nights, the unedifying mix of smoke, groping hands, sweaty men and foul language. Often she refused to help her parents out unless she got paid in advance and, being as headstrong and combative as her mother, usually got her way.

Declan Colt strutted about the small stage with hips swiveling, singing "Dixieland" in a sub-Elvis baritone, his satin collar standing up, his head down, chewing the microphone, mopping his brow frequently with a great snowy hankie. The Silver Bullets looked inert by comparison. The percussionist sat stirring a snare drum and shaking his head at some imaginary argument. The third member stood, as if in shock, thumbing a bass guitar, his eyes rooted on the far wall.

After every slow number came a fast filler to liven things up. Now Declan launched into "Blue Suede Shoes" and several couples shuffled shyly onto the dance floor. They jived and spun awkwardly, colliding with each other, the men sweating in shirt sleeves, the women dizzy and unsure. As their confidence grew, they swung and swayed more, their flowery rumps twitching, their jewelry bouncing; twisting and twirling, looking down at their shoes, as if checking for dog dirt, as if squashing insects under their feet.

The interval arrived and Declan gave Jamie the nod.

Jamie, his faculties sufficiently impaired by booze to mimic courage, was ready for it. He hoisted his Horner two-row Irish button accordion onto his front and climbed up on the stool. The crowd roared approval, sweaty hands on sticky glasses raised in a toast.

"Give her a good squeeze, Jamie!" someone shouted. "Aye, ye boy ye!"

And in seconds Jamie was away, "The Boston Burglar" roaring out in great torrents from the wheezing bellows.

Up there on the high stool, Jamie sat in a shaft of white light, brandishing the instrument like a warrior's silvery battle shield, his fingers dancing over the buttons, the room drenched in its rich droning sound. He played with his head cocked to one side, the sweat flying off him and his eyes shut against the smoke, the glare, and the undivided attention of his audience. Nothing could compare to the joy that Jamie felt in those moments in the hot room, with the eyes of seventy people upon him, their tapping feet, their clapping hands—and *he* the push, the pull and the absolute focus of it all.

He slid effortlessly from number to number in the first of his three set pieces. Half an hour's break for Declan and the Bullets was half an hour's glory for him. However, he'd just finished "The Black

Velvet Band" and was bathing in a wave of applause when a shout went up. He recognized the voice of Chuck Sproule.

"Hi, what's the difference between Jamie McCloone and a bucket of shite?"

Seventy guffaws escaped from seventy throats.

An answer flew from the back of the room and struck Jamie's ears with a vulgar force. It was young Sproule again.

"A bucket!" he yelled, and the crowd stormed with laughter.

Jamie, a rage rising in him like milk boiling up in a saucepan, decided, with a powerful self-restraint, to ignore the insult this time. He took a quick swig of Black Bush, slid the seething saucepan off the heat and began belting out "I'll Tell Me Ma" before the wee bastard had time to fling up another heckle.

The powerful, throbbing music swelled in the room as Jamie played on and on, afraid to stop in case Sproule got the chance to hit him with another broadside of abuse. Soon, however, a metallic flash in the doorway told him that Declan and the Bullets were back; his time was nearly up. Jamie finished off "Danny Boy", drawing out a deafening refrain. The crowd roared its appreciation as he vacated the bar stool and unstrapped the accordion. Then, in the murmuring lull, it came again.

"Hey, Jamie! How d'you keep an idiot in suspense?"

The hubbub lessened; the rowdier patrons sniggered in expectation. Jamie heaved off his instrument and thrust it into Paddy's hands.

"Take a hoult of that for one wee minute, Paddy," he said.

The accordion squawked like a fat infant as Paddy bundled the bellows in. When he looked up again it was to see Jamie head in the direction of the taunting voice, his hatred coming to a blaze under the most recent splash of vitriolic fuel. His accordion's music was his only way of releasing the gift he had to give. He'd been stepped on as a child but, by God, no adult was going to step on the man he strove to be.

"God, we better go after him!" cried Matty.

In a flash both men were on their feet, hauling Jamie back with an uncharacteristic swiftness.

"How d'you keep an idiot in suspense?" the shrill voice repeated. "I'll tell ye the day after the morra, Jamie!"

The crowd fell about again. Jamie freed himself with a frenzied force, elbowing his two comrades in the stomach, and in seconds he was up on young Chuck, sending the glasses and bottles flying in a glittering crash as the table was overturned. He yanked him free of his mates—none of whom was sober enough to assist—punched Chuck on the nose, doubled him up with a kick in the privates, then tore at his greasy hair, hauling him upright.

"What was that ye said, ye dirty wee bastard?" he spat. "Not so funny now, are ye?"

The crowd cheered. But Chuck shot out a fist and got Jamie smack in the belly. He fell onto his back, his arms and legs paddling the air like a capsized turtle.

Then suddenly all went quiet in the room. Jamie opened his eyes, to see Peggy the Bacon-Slicer advancing on them, her furious face set in a terrible contortion.

"Jamie McCloone, you should be ashamed of yourself! No more drink for you." She turned on Chuck, who was holding a bloody nose. "As for you: out this minute! I don't want my carpet ruined. And you're barred for a month."

"He hit me first!" Chuck wailed.

"Aye, and you insulted him first. You're nothing but a useless eejit."

And with that she led him by the ear up the floor, like a matador parading a wounded bull, as the crowd applauded. On approaching the open door, Chuck, knowing his case would not be heard, started to shout and resist, holding unto the door frame in desperation, his feet sliding all over the place in a ludicrous parody of an astronaut's moon walk.

"You're nothing but a fuckin' oul' bitch!" he cried, in a voice gritty with resentment, "and you've a face on you like a sow's arse."

"That's it, you're barred for *three* months now!" Peggy slapped him hard across the face.

Slope came from behind, planted a foot against Chuck's skinny back and heeled him out onto the street, swiftly double-locking the door behind him.

With the troublemaker well on his way, things returned to normal. Matty and Paddy helped their friend to his feet and Jamie struggled back to his seat by the podium, all too aware that his comb-over had come unstuck during the fray and that he must look a frightful sight. He attempted to rearrange his hair while apologizing to his mates.

"Och now, we know how much you wanted to get at the brute," said Paddy.

"Sure I would a done the same meself," agreed Matty, and he placed his own double brandy before Jamie to help him recover himself.

Jamie swallowed a mouthful. An otherwise grand night had been destroyed and he nearly wept at the recollection of it. How great it had all gone—and how quickly it had all been taken away by that filthy-mouthed wee get.

"That was a great bit a playin', Jamie," said Paddy, trying to salvage something from the wreckage.

"Aye, if it hadn't been for that rascal shoutin' at ye and then you havin' to get up and hit him a clout, it woulda been a grand night altogether," Matty put in, grabbing Paddy's precious piece of solace and tossing it back on the raging sea.

Declan Colt, observing the trio from the stage, and sensing Jamie's dejection, shimmered up to the mike.

"Now listen up!" he ordered the room. "I want y'all to give Jamie here a big hand. Some of the best playin' I ever did hear came from that accordjin tonight."

The crowd stood and applauded, and Jamie's face broke into a great smile as he held up his brandy glass in toast. He saw again his uncle take his awkward, twelve-year-old fingers and extend them over the ivory buttons, felt again the surging joy when he realized he could make the instrument speak another language from his tortured, silent self. The triumphant result of that entire endeavor was James

McCloone, the man, sitting on a high stool in O'Shea's bar, making hands clap and voices sing as he fed his sonorous, furious music to the room.

On seeing the cheering crowd, Jamie, for now at least, knew that he mattered, that the people of Tailorstown were behind him four-square. But he feared that the elation was fleeting and that later the nasty episode with Sproule would come back to haunt him.

Chapter fifteen

Lydia read over Frank McPrunty's letter once again in the relative privacy of her bedroom. She stood with her back against the locked door, just in case. She would be meeting him in two hours' time and needed to acquaint herself once more with his personal details.

Lydia, being a teacher, approached most things in life in an analytical manner. Frank McPrunty was a project, and his letter an examination paper. It needed revision before she set the test and decided whether his performance merited a pass or a fail.

Dear Miss Devine,

I was absolutely delighted to receive your lovely letter and deeply honoured that you would choose to be interested in a person such as myself. I hope that the answers I give to your questions will be in keeping with your expectations.

I am sixty-one years, although I am told that I look ten years younger. I retain this youthful look through a careful diet and exercise regime. I try to eat healthily and I walk a lot with my dog Snoop as I believe I mentioned in my last letter.

No, I have not been married before. Not that I did not have the opportunities mind. I realize now that I was perhaps over-cautious and a little too hard to please. I think when we are young we believe that we have all the time in the world, when in fact we have very little, as I now know to my cost.

You asked me what I look for in a woman and I will be honest and say that above all I'm looking for companionship. There is more I could write in relation to this very important question, but I think such things are better discussed face to face. Often the words set down on a glaring white page come across as impersonal and lacking warmth.

To this end Miss Devine, and pardon me if you think I'm being forward, I feel it's best that we meet. I will be at the Chestnut Inn Hotel on the main road out of Killoran between four pm and five o'clock on Thursday August 7th. I will wait for you in the lounge.

I will be wearing a navy blazer, grey slacks, a white shirt and red cravat. On the table in front of me I will place my Rolleiflex camera. My camera is expensive and used mainly by professional photographer's, [Lydia tut-tutted on seeing the grocer's apostrophe] so I think it will be a reliable marker for you. Not unless there is a function or wedding in the hotel on that day which might prove troublesome. Still I don't think a wedding photographer would be likely to leave his equipment lying about on the nearest table. So I think my camera is a good sign.

    I do hope you will decide to come. I will stay in the hotel well past five o'clock just in case for some reason you get delayed. I am very much looking forward to meeting you.

        Yours sincerely in anticipation,
          Frank Xavier McPrunty

Lydia folded the letter and returned it to her purse, satisfied that she knew what she was dealing with. She had decided to answer Mr. McPrunty first, because, of the two respondents, he seemed slightly more interesting and more in tune with her on an intellectual level. She was keeping Mr. McCloone, the farmer, in reserve for the time being, in the eventuality that Frank proved unsuitable.

She took a final look at herself in the mirror and was pleased that she cut such an elegant figure. The pink juliet dress with the white butterfly collar was, she felt, a good choice: appealing in an understated kind of way.

She checked her watch. In twenty minutes she would collect Daphne at the library. Her friend had agreed to accompany her for moral support.

"Well of course I'll come with you, dear!" Daphne had assured her. "I couldn't have you getting carried off by some mysterious stranger and never seeing you again."

Lydia smiled at the memory as she slung a white cardigan over her shoulders. She picked up her bag and a library book and left the room. The book was a decoy.

"I'm just popping along to the library to see Daphne, Mother." Lydia tried to sound as upbeat and natural as possible. "Do you need your books changed?"

Elizabeth Devine was in the parlor, her embroidery frame on her lap, a cup of tea at her elbow and the television before her showing a mute Fanny Craddock rolling out a sheet of pastry. She continued to gaze at Fanny, totally ignoring Lydia.

"I can't stand that woman's voice! Sounds as if she's chewing gravel. And why does she need to talk so much anyway? We can all see what she's doing. We're not imbeciles."

Lydia waited for her mother to finish and tried again.

"Mother, do you need your books changed?" She held up her Victoria Holt.

"And that husband of hers is an idiot. Look at him!" Johnny Craddock had just heaved into view, with a cake tin in one hand and a wooden spoon in the other.

"What way is that to dress when you're baking—a blazer and cravat? You'd think he was at the races. What happened to aprons, I wonder."

Lydia saw Johnny's blazer and cravat as an augury of imminent significance. She remembered Frank Xavier McPrunty's description of the attire he'd be wearing: "navy blazer, gray slacks, a white shirt and red cravat." As she looked at Johnny Craddock's bald head and bemonocled eye, a feeling of dread overtook her. Better to discover the truth as soon as possible, she thought.

"Mother—"

"Yes, I know: the books. I'm not finished with the Cookson, but you can take back that other piece of filth." She pointed at a book on the windowsill. "I'm not allowing Jean Plaidy back into this house. She had a woman taking her top off in front of a man. I'd never read such smut. You tell that friend of yours to put her under the counter, or better still in the dustbin, where she belongs."

Lydia picked up the item of "pornography," bent and kissed her mother goodbye as the credits for Fanny Craddock rolled.

"Why are you wearing so much scent?" Mrs. Devine demanded. She looked Lydia up and down. "And those are your Sunday shoes."

"Look, Mother, I'm going out." She saw her mother's eyes take on that all-too-familiar glint of suspicion. "To the library."

"You're up to something. Why are you wearing all that scent if you're just going to see that friend of yours?" Elizabeth touched her daughter's cheek. "And you've too much powder on your face. Yes, there's a man somewhere. I can almost smell him."

"Mother," Lydia began, her voice edged with impatience, "I'm wearing all this scent for myself, d'you hear? And the face powder, shoes, and dress—all for me." She splayed a hand on her chest and beat it several times to drive home the point. "For me, me, *me*! Not Daphne, not for any man or any woman for that matter. Just me, d'you hear?"

There was a silence. Elizabeth Devine was prepared to concede that she'd been well and truly rebuked, but still felt it necessary to throw another little poisoned dart as Lydia turned to go.

"Doesn't matter what you say. You still look like a strumpet and if your father were here he wouldn't let you out looking like that."

"See you in a couple of hours. I'm getting my hair done as well."

Lydia shouted all this over her shoulder as she made a beeline down the hallway. She had invented the hair appointment, knowing that her mother would strongly object to not having been informed earlier of something so important. Hair appointments were Elizabeth's territory.

And sure enough, as Lydia pulled the door shut, she caught the first part of her mother's objection.

"You never said anything about a—"

But Lydia was gone, and freedom beckoned.

The parking lot at the Chestnut Inn Hotel was reassuringly vacant when Lydia and Daphne pulled in. They counted only five cars.

"No wedding to contend with, it seems," Lydia said, cutting the engine and looking in the rearview mirror. "Thank heavens for that. I couldn't stand it if there were gaggles of people roaming round."

"What a lovely place," Daphne said, looking up at the white Georgian façade. "Have you been here before? God, it looks terribly posh. This Frank person has expensive tastes, I'll give him that."

But Lydia was barely listening. As her eyes swept over the clipped lawns and hedges, she was contemplating the nature of what she was about to do. This act was a defining one.

"What?" she asked absentmindedly. Daphne was still giving forth. "Oh yes, it is rather grand, isn't it?"

"Are you nervous?" Daphne gave her friend's arm a gentle squeeze. "What a silly question. Of course you're nervous. I'd be too."

"Oh, I'm okay, but…" She hesitated. "What if he turns out to be an absolute ogre, Daphne?"

"Of course he won't! Here, let me see his letter again."

Lydia passed it over without a word. Her attention was elsewhere. She was staring ahead of her, at the heavy cedar doors with their inlaid glass panels, trying to focus on what she was about to do. Was she insane?

She had never done anything rash in her life. From an early age her father had instilled in her a sense of duty and responsibility. Any venture must be mulled over and planned, viewed from all angles and weighed with the utmost consideration; that way, the outcome one expected was all but guaranteed. That way, life held no unpleasant surprises. Disappointment lay in careless thinking and an incautious attitude. And happiness? There was no such state, in her father's estimation. The trials of life must be borne with a stout faith and fortitude. The reward was the happiness of eternal life in the heavenly realms.

Lydia steeled herself against the thought of the Reverend Perseus Cuthbert gazing down on her now—as he surely must be—from those same heavenly realms. If he were alive, he would most certainly be lecturing her on the weakness of the flesh and the dangers of rash adventuring. But he wasn't alive, she reminded herself. He was dead and she was free.

"He doesn't seem like an ogre to me," said Daphne, interrupting her reverie. She folded the letter. "In fact he seems like a very nice gentleman."

"*What?*" she almost shouted, believing for a confused moment that Daphne was referring to her father. Daphne looked at her strangely. "Oh, Frank. Yes, of course. Good. Shall we go in then?"

"We should. The longer we sit here, the longer you'll worry, and that's not good."

"Do I look all right?" Lydia snapped open her Max Factor compact and checked herself.

"You look lovely," Daphne lied. She could see that her friend had applied too much powder to her nose. It looked as though it had been dipped in a bag of Early Riser flour. "And the pink really suits your coloring."

Lydia stowed the compact and shut the purse. "Thank you, Daphne. What would I do without you, dear?"

Daphne set her face in a determined smile. They left the car and strode purposefully toward the hotel entrance.

A brass arrow and carpeted steps beyond the lobby guided them down to the place of rendezvous. They descended and found themselves facing the lounge doors. Lydia grabbed Daphne's arm.

"Wait," she whispered. "Let's see if I can pick him out from here."

She opened the stained-glass doors a crack and peeked in, unobtrusively scanning the lounge interior for man-with-camera.

There was a couple at one table having a drink: a woman with a beehive hairdo and a man who looked half her age; at another table a young family was having a late lunch. A youth seated at the bar was staring fixedly up at a football game being shown on a suspended television set.

Where was he? Perhaps he hadn't arrived yet. She was about to venture in when her eye fell on a solitary figure seated by the window, looking out in what seemed like expectation.

Her heart sank.

The camera and glass of Fanta soda before him confirmed her worst fears. He was small and totally bald, with a turtle-like neck rising out of an extravagant, mulberry-red cravat. If she still had doubts, then his navy blazer with outsize shoulder pads, buttoned brassily over his front, and his gray slacks, so accurately described in the letter, verified his identity. Mr. McPrunty had come to life painfully before her eyes.

Sixty-one? He looked closer to *eighty*-one. She absorbed the scene in a few heart-stopping moments. She wanted to flee.

Daphne, sensing her disappointment, caught her arm.

"What is it, Lydia? Have you seen him?"

Lydia could not speak and simply pointed.

"Is that him?" Daphne asked. "Are you sure?"

"Yes, I'm sure," Lydia said in a desperate whisper. "Of *course* I'm sure. There's the camera he spoke about, and he's wearing exactly what he described in the letter." She put her hand over her mouth. "Oh my God, I can't meet him, Daphne! I just can't. He's an old-age pensioner. He could be my *grandfather*."

"Now, Lydia, come into the ladies and we'll discuss this. You just can't leave him there like that. It wouldn't be right."

She yanked Lydia back out through the door, and found the bathroom a little way to the right of the lounge entrance. She nudged the door shut.

"Now look, you must go and meet him. It's only proper. It would be very rude to let him down after all this."

They stood in the faux-marble enclosure under the thrum of a strip light. Lydia looked undecided. Then she went to the mirror, held her face in her hands and peered into the smoked glass.

"Yes, and I suppose it's not very rude of him to lie to me that he's sixty-one when he looks like Methuselah? Oh my God," she asked the mirror, "how did I get here?"

Daphne tried to console. "Look Lydia, it's only a meeting. And he can't be that bad." She addressed her friend's reflection. "Looks," she said, "aren't everything, you know." Lydia glared and Daphne realized her error.

"Oh, for heaven's sake, Daphne! Would *you* be seen with him?" She turned from the mirror. "Now be honest."

"Well…"

"Come on—be honest."

"Well, I'd give him a chance by talking to him…."

"But would you take him along to Heather's wedding? Remember, that's the object of this exercise."

"Well, to be honest…" She hesitated, mobilizing her thoughts. "You want the truth, do you?"

"Yes, the God's-honest truth."

"I wouldn't be caught dead with him."

They howled with laughter. When they'd recovered themselves, Daphne made a suggestion.

"Let's get out of here," she said. "We'll have tea at the Copper Kettle."

"Splendid idea."

They wiped away their tears of mirth and adjusted themselves in the mirror. Presently Daphne held open the inner door.

"After you, my dear."

"Thank you, my liege."

Lydia flung back the outer door—and halted with a gasp. There, on the checkered Axminster, stood a balding little man with a mighty camera pointing accusingly at her from his double-breasted front. Frank Xavier McPrunty.

Lydia gave a small cry. Daphne collided with her back, nearly propelling her into him.

He raised a knotty forefinger.

"You wouldn't be—?"

"Good heavens, no!" Lydia blurted out, and she reversed into the restroom, pulling Daphne with her. The door shut automatically. They threw themselves against the row of washbasins, Daphne in fits of laughter, Lydia in shock.

"Shush..."

She shook Daphne's shoulder. They heard the outer door of the powder room opening.

"Oh my God, he's coming *in*. Quick!"

And they both dashed for the stalls. But it was the woman with the beehive hairdo—one half of the drinking couple she'd spotted earlier—now with a glazed-over, unsteady look about her and Lydia noticed that part of the beehive had come unstuck. She eyed the two ladies suspiciously.

"Is one a yous a *Lid*-something *Day-vine*, are yous?" she said.

Lydia stared at her. "Why, who wants to know?"

"There's a wee man out there astin' after ye. Sez he's a Savior Mick-Brontee." She jerked her thumb in the direction of the lobby and staggered—like a newborn calf—on into the stall, grasping the door frame for support.

Lydia opened her mouth to speak, but Daphne put a warning finger to her lips and rolled her eyes at the stall.

"Wait," she mouthed, and busied herself washing her hands. Her friend followed suit and waited for the woman to finish and leave.

By and by they heard a heavy sigh followed by a noisy flushing sound, and out came Miss Beehive. She wobbled to the door, seemingly unaware that she was not alone.

"God, did you see that? She didn't wash her hands."

"Look, Lydia, there's only one way out of this." Daphne went to the sash window and began heaving it up.

"What, are you crazy? We can't do that."

"Well, it's either this, option one, or stand about here for another hour hoping he'll go away. That's option two." Lydia opened her mouth to protest again but Daphne ignored her. "Or, the third option." Her voice strained under the weight of the resisting window, but within moments she'd managed it. She turned proudly. "Good, there we are."

"And the third option?" Lydia asked expectantly.

"Yes, the third option is for you to go out there now, introduce yourself to Mr. McPrunty, and have him explain the inner workings of his life and his mighty camera." She gave her friend a challenging look.

Lydia dashed to the window and, with as much of her dignity as she could retain in the circumstances, started climbing out.

Chapter sixteen

The autumn months of every year were particularly cruel for the little inmates of the orphanage. Every morning at eight a bus clattered into the yard, and the boys would line up and climb aboard. They took their places on bare iron seats, their pale, sad faces lost beneath outsized caps, their frail bodies in ragged, grubby, hand-me-downs. They swayed and collided and wordlessly righted themselves as the bus drove across the city's suburbs, bumping and bouncing over the cobblestones, dodging the steaming horses and the chattering traps they pulled. They passed shawled women and weary workmen; rising heavenward, the smoking factory chimneys mapped the sky in monstrous yellow blots.

No one wanted to go to the fields. No one wanted to wrest the muddy potatoes from their muddy pits and load them into the baskets. No one wanted to suffer the ache in his back or the wounding splinters in his frail little hands. They prayed that it would not rain and that they would not provoke the farmer to anger.

The bus driver, Bartley, was a hard man with a pitiless face and hands made for destruction and murder. A raw man, born of pain and violence and raised on both. He despised the children he shuttled to and fro, his vehicle clanking its way through the grimy streets, as the louring sky moved above him and a sludge of fearsome thoughts foamed in his head.

He talked to himself, directing a rapid, broken discourse at the windshield, bending over the big wheel to round a corner at speed, laughing loudly when, in the mirror, he saw his charges fall out of their seats and stumble to retrieve their caps. He roared and shouted in his strange language; he made misery for others, and in so doing, warped the peace that could never be his own.

Before long, the city had fallen behind them: a gray tattered veil in the cracked rear window of the bus. Grassy swards opened up on either side of them, and a weak sun stroked the fields and raised their spirits. Mountains lay in the distance, soft and still, like sleek, sleeping deer.

Each boy observed and sought solace in this beauty, escaping for a while the graceless, lumpen nature of the life he led. Happiness for the time being was that peaceful place, always moving out of reach through the grimy glass of the window, something beyond the implacable band of nuns and men who peopled the present and the future. Each knew there was something more, when released like this on the rattling bus, with the insane driver; released from the harsh, unstable world of the orphanage with its draughty rooms and flailing voices, into this gentler world. There was peace in the unpopulated countryside under the bird-blown skies.

Eighty-Six sat with his forehead pressed against the glass, his fingers gripping the rubber ledge of the window frame. He felt every hump and hollow of the road in his throbbing brow and trembling hands. He wanted the tender violence of the journey to last. His small body thrown this way and that, whilst he dreamed his little dreams.

Sometimes he glimpsed white-and-brown cattle in a field, heard the bleat of sheep as they rushed toward the barbed wire fence at the sound of the rackety vehicle. He dreamed one day of befriending such animals, thought they would understand him as no human could. He imagined stroking their rough coats and speaking to them in their own language—their stuttering baa's and moo's. His little heart beat faster when he thought of this; it quelled his fear and put it to rest, replaced it with an emotion he did not recognize yet as passion. Later in life he would never be able to recapture—or describe—what he felt in those moments.

They all leaned instinctively to the left as the bus approached the final bend. Each boy grasped the horizontal bar of the seat in front, bracing himself in readiness for the sudden, jolting violence of Bartley's stop. As they stumbled out, he raved and spat and cuffed any boy who dared to look his way. It was said that Bartley had been an inmate of the orphanage, too. He was a sorry reminder of what they could become, the essential nature of him stripped away so that only a few raw wires and a high-pitched madness remained.

A sharp, dry wind was cutting across the landscape and driving down the open field as they braved the early morning chill. They shivered in their thin clothes, their bare knees revealed like birch saplings where their pants ended and their Wellington boots began.

The field was a vast, ribbed expanse of flowering potato heads. By nightfall a quarter of it would be turned over, the orphans having scrabbled deep and rooted out the sustenance that would keep the bellies of the Doyle family filled for a year. Farmer Doyle drove his tractor up and down the drills, spraying out potatoes from under the spinning disks of the digger. A cloud of hungry gulls flapped in his wake, swooping and diving on the exposed earth.

The boys broke into pairs as Bartley threw out the baskets. Eighty-Six and Eighty-Four stuck together. They did not speak to one another but bent immediately to the task. The reward, five hours later, would be a mug of tea and a hunk of bread.

If it were judged that anyone had been slack or if they'd talked on the job, the food was withheld and the culprit went hungry.

Soon all twenty were immersed in the torturous rhythm of bending and harvesting, their bodies a frieze of hooped shapes inching up the field. Bartley walked behind them, kicking at the ground, attentive for missed potatoes, feeling the necessity to lash out or drive his boot into a backside if he felt so inclined.

Eighty-Six and his partner worked in unison, wordlessly sharing their burdens. Their eyes scanned the mucky soil, where the worms squirmed and the bugs crawled, as their hands dug and tore and dropped the bitter harvest into the basket, their cargo growing heavier the farther they advanced down the row.

At one o'clock, a glorious sight: the tea. Mrs. Doyle at the gate in her wide, floral apron, struggling with two enormous bags. She'd set her burden down and holler at the men both big and small. The boys would rush toward her, wiping their hands on their clothes as they ran, clamoring for their hard-earned reward.

She'd unstopper the soggy newspaper plugs from several bottles of tea and fill a clatter of tin mugs laid out on the grass. Then she'd unwrap a batch of fresh-baked bread rolls and hand them round, each thick scone glued together with homemade butter and jam. Such a treat! So far removed from the stale bread and dripping which was their daily fare.

On the rattling bus back, and later on as they slept, it was not so much on the painful labors of the day that the orphans dwelt, but on the smile Mrs. Doyle had bestowed upon them as they ate.

One smiling adult in the long, grim day—a rarity indeed, a gift.

Chapter seventeen

J amie returned to consciousness on the morning following his unfortunate bout with the bold Chuck in O'Shea's bar. He was heavily hungover and mightily depressed.

He lay still in the rumpled bed, staring up at a damp patch of ceiling, while a reel of the previous night's events twisted sluggishly through his head. He saw himself once again up there on the high stool, driving the rich, sweet music into the room—"A brilliant performance," Declan had said. And then suddenly the scene had darkened: sullied and stained by the piercing shouts of the wee bastard at the back. "Jezsis!" Jamie swore aloud at the very thought of it.

He tried to imagine how great the night would have been if he hadn't been maddened to violence by the filthy words that poured from young Sproule's mouth. But he couldn't somehow picture it; the damage had been done, like an ink drop clouding clear water, the brightness could not be retrieved. The night had been ruined.

He shut off the dark thoughts and eased himself carefully out from under the covers, sat for a while on the edge of the bed, staring down at his feet, planted now on the red linoleum. The area beneath them had faded to pink from years of wear and from Jamie's habit of simply sitting there in contemplation.

That morning, he sat for a lengthier spell, dwelling on the nature of his being: his very lonely being, now that his dear Uncle Mick had passed away. Mick's death had cut him loose from life's easy groove and thrown him back within sight of a terrible solitude where the wind forever blew, the snow forever fell, and the devil blackened the night and the daytime hours. Ten months of heartache so far, and every day very much the same.

Dr. Brewster called it "depression" and was treating it accordingly, but Jamie knew deep down that he needed more than pills. Life was cruelly demanding that he finally take responsibility for himself and, in short, become a "man." But how could the child who had never been allowed to be a child somehow suddenly become that "man"? He'd have to leap across a gorge of emotions and scale an awesome height.

The future was waiting for Jamie, skulking in a dark forest with no way out. He tried not to brood on it and looked to the past instead; to that part of the past which shimmered bright with his uncle's memory and the only happiness he'd known.

His gaze fell on a St. Brigid's cross, now gathering dust to the right of the window. His uncle had painfully fashioned that cross with his unsteady fingers shortly before he died. Below it hung a photo of a youthful, pain-free Mick, smiling broadly on his wedding day, the toothy grin, stiff-winged collar and breast-pocket hankie all now deeply yellowed through years of smoke from hearth and pipe. And his beautiful bride, Alice, her delicate features dwarfed beneath a surging flourish of peacock feathers and plastic fruit; an extravagant bunch of lace sprouting at her throat.

Tragic Alice had tripped over a bucket of chicken feed and struck her head on the doorstep. Some days later it became apparent that the accident had released a toxin into her aggrieved synapses that disposed her to suffer agonies of prolonged disquiet. Dear Alice would never be the same again. Mick nursed her as best he could, but had to admit defeat when she came at him one day with a bread knife in the hen house, mistaking him for the Sunday dinner. Mick, heartbroken, had sobbed mightily at this great misfortune, and with a heavy heart and trembling hand, had reluctantly signed her over into the care of the St. Peregrine Institute for the Mentally Deranged, Disturbed & Those of a Nervous & Anxious Disposition.

She died there soon after.

Jamie's eyes began to well up when he thought of that misfortune; he reached for his wallet on the bedside table. Inside, folded into a neat square, was a handkerchief, yellowed with age and edged with a delicate border of tiny shamrocks. He dabbed his eyes with the cherished fabric, and with great reverence returned it to the wallet. He immediately felt better.

After some moments his eye fell on his most treasured possession: his uncle's silver, two-row accordion in its walnut case. Playing with the pleasure of such memories helped Jamie to face the reality of yet another day.

He heard the animals in the yard crying out for breakfast, but ignored them. His head felt like a rock trembling on a stick, his legs and arms toothpicks that might break under the weight of him. Slowly he rose, trying not to look down, seeking for support, as he scrabbled into his work clothes. Finally belted and buttoned up, he stumbled to the scullery for his first, sobering, brew of tea.

It took him longer than usual. Every sound—the clanking of the mug as he retrieved it from the crammed sink, the gushing and spitting of the water from the tap, the teaspoon stirred in the mug— all contrived to assault his fragile senses. As he sank into the tattered armchair, nursing the mug on the armrest, fishing in his pocket for the first cigarette of the day, he vowed never to drink again. But it was only a thought and it would pass.

The sun struck hotly through the window, a great shaft of mote-rich light, giving a cruel wash of clarity to the room. A blue-bottle madly buzzed. Jamie watched it settle on the armrest, knitting its frantic legs, its metallic engine throbbing. He thought he might touch it, but knew his merest shift would send it off immediately. He wondered idly how a fly always knew when it was about to be touched—or killed. Could they tell the future, feel the air from a raised hand, or maybe they had an extra pair of wee eyes on the top of their wee heads. Who was to say?

He drew on the cigarette and reached for the poker, could hear the fly stitching its way desperately up and down the windowpane. A flame shot up from the banked coal and at once the fire leaped into life. He returned the poker to its place by the crane crook and reached automatically for the bottle of Valium. These actions, these mindless moves, Jamie performed every morning with the sureness of an acrobat tumbling through the air to land, as always, dizzy and dazed on the same spot. But on this particular morning, as he unscrewed the tablet bottle and shook the pill into his hand, a thought struck him that made him falter.

What if it's like this for a body all the time? He posed the question to his open palm. What if I've to take these pills for the rest of my life? Wake up always to this empty house with only Shep for company. What if…?

He gazed about the shabby room as the tears began to flow again and he plunged into the vast terror of the question he'd been avoiding since his uncle died.

"What if it's like this always?" His appeal rang out in the hollow silence, but only the ticking clock and the madly buzzing fly responded.

Reluctantly, Jamie began to push down all the dark alleys he'd been afraid to tread. What's the point in looking for a woman, he thought. Rose and Paddy and Dr. Brewster think it'd be a good thing, but they don't know how shocking hard that would be for me. They don't know about the orphanage or what was done to me. They know nothing about all that. Besides, he pondered, he'd posted the letter to the mysterious woman well over two weeks ago and still she hadn't answered. There'd be no sign of it now.

He stared down at the Valium tablet again, then flung it into the fire, finished the tea in one hot glutch, and made for the door.

Shep leapt up to greet him as he stepped out into the sunshine. Jamie smiled and ruffled the dog, then crossed with determination to the barn with Shep on his heels. Inside he stood in the dusty silence contemplating the high rafters. He saw the last joist Mick had hammered into place all those years before when Jamie was just a boy, and thought it might be the appropriate one for the job. He studied the rafter, the hank of baler twine that hung near the door, then the rafter once more. Yes, it would be so easy to do, he reasoned. That rope and rafter could take me away from all this. Could take me to paradise in no time at all, to be with Mick and Alice again. Just a breath away, he thought. Just a breath.

"Hi, Jamie, are ye in there, are ye?" Someone was shouting from outside.

Shep was barking at a rare sight: Scrunty Branny, the postman, cycling into the yard. Jamie's heart lifted as he went to greet him. But he didn't dare hope.

"How ye, Scrunty? Not often I see ye here."

Scrunty Branny, a Breughelian peasant with a wart on his left eyelid and chipmunk cheeks, heaved his fat frame off the bike, wheezing and puffing. "Aye and it's well ye…it's well ye…it's well ye don't get many letters, Jamie…" He maneuvered his weighty satchel unto his ample front and sighed deeply, "for that hill a yours would 'ave me damn-near kilt, begod!"

"She's a steep boy, right enough, when you're not used to her," Jamie agreed.

He and Shep watched with interest as Scrunty rooted in the satchel and unearthed an elastic-bound bundle of mail. He licked a chubby finger and peeled off an envelope.

"Very grand writin', Jamie. A wonder who it's from."

Jamie studied his own address, elegantly rendered in what could only be a female hand. He believed he knew who it might be from. But Scrunty Branny, he vowed, would be the last to know.

"Could be Mick's sister in Amerikey," Jamie lied, avoiding Scrunty's tiny, prying eyes.

"But then there'd be an airborne stamp on it. That letter's from here."

"God, you're right. Well, be seein' ye, Scrunty." Jamie hurried into the house, leaving postman Branny in a state of beetle-browed perplexity as he readied his bike for departure.

In the scullery he found a knife clotted with day-old lemon curd. He wiped it off on the sole of his boot, slit open the envelope, sat down in the armchair again, unfolded the pristine pages, and proceeded to read.

> Elmwood House
> River Road
> Killoran

Dear Mr. McCloone,

Thank you for taking the time to answer my advertisement which appeared in the Mid-Ulster Vindicator, of July 17th.

I would like to meet you, but before that happens I think it fair to let you know something about myself. I would also like to ask you a number of things, so I can get a better picture of you. I apologize in advance if you think my questions intrusive. But you see I am essentially an honest person. Experience has taught me that anything less will not only waste my time, but yours as well.

Jamie scratched his head in puzzlement, wondering what she could mean. Maybe he'd find out soon enough.

I am around the same age as yourself. I teach at a primary school in Killoran and have done so for some years. I enjoy my work with the children and like the challenge of moulding young minds.

The word "teacher" frightened Jamie somewhat, his memories of such individuals being less than happy.

> In my spare time I like reading, particularly romantic fiction and historical biographies, although I can only fully indulge this passion at holiday time. During term time I am usually too busy. You mentioned in your letter that you too enjoyed reading, perhaps you could tell me the kind of books you like.

Jamie looked up from the page. The fly still buzzed madly round the window frame. On the sill stood the only two books in the house, old possessions of Uncle Mick's, which Jamie had barely opened, let alone read: *Old Moore's Almanac* and a worm-eaten copy of *Great Expectations*, which had been purloined from an ancient school by Mick's Uncle Fergal. A fearless young man with a thirst for knowledge and an eye for profit, he'd escaped a bitter boyhood by losing his religion and boarding a coffin ship to the Americas in 1849. Once there, according to Mick, Fergal had got himself an education. He became a bank clerk of some importance, only to be felled at thirty-two by a single bullet meant for Fred "The Fats" McSweeney in a New York gangster shoot-out. Fergal had been emerging from The Thirsty Bull liquor store at the time. "So it was the drink that kilt him," Mick used to wryly say.

Jamie thought that his curlicued signature, "Fergal J. McCloone," on the inside cover of the novel, indicated a man who was "terrible clever" and who knew a thing or two about something. He continued reading the letter.

> I'm afraid I do not know much about farming, but I do like animals. I would love to own a small cat, but since my mother is allergic to fur I have to forego this pleasantry.

You mentioned that you liked cooking which interested me a lot. I have not met many men who enjoy this art. What dishes do you like making most? What aspect of the culinary process interests you most?

Eating, thought Jamie immediately, but knew in his heart that that would probably be the wrong answer.

I am glad that you like music. I cannot play an instrument like you, but I enjoy singing, especially the hymns at Sunday service. I like Andy Williams and James Last.

That phrase "Sunday service" bothered him. A Catholic would have written "Sunday Mass." So she was maybe "the other sort." But then he remembered that Rose had said that religion didn't matter much and Rose, being a wise woman, was usually right about most things, so she was.

Well I think this is all I can tell you about myself at the present. I look forward to your letter and learning more about you.
By the way, you have beautiful handwriting. Are you artistic?
Yours faithfully,
Lydia Devine

"Ly-dee-a Devine, Ly-dee-a Devine." Jamie said the name over and over to himself, not quite believing what he'd just read. He looked through the letter again, the episode in the barn all but forgotten. Suddenly a new, exciting pathway had opened up in his life. She had written back—that was the magical bit. She had acknowledged him.

She had even admired his handwriting! All at once he felt invigorated. But he'd have to be very careful with his reply. Rose McFadden's letter-writing skills would have to be called upon once more.

The rest of Jamie's day was spent in a rapture of anticipation. His chores got done without his being conscious of doing them. His hangover lifted without his being conscious of its passing. He had no desire to eat, and remembered with a surge of joy that this was the first day of his diet. Well, wasn't it just as well anyway? Now he had more to think about than food. The letter had transformed the predictable monotony of his day, had made him realize that the distance between himself and happiness was getting shorter; the "sunlit clearing" was within reach. He believed now that he could accomplish anything; could maybe scale tall trees without a handhold; could make the pig sing "Muirsheen Durkin" in a John McCormack voice; even pluck the sun out of the sky and make it spin.

As he floated away on all this fantasy, he decided that now would be the time to put Dr. Brewster's advice into action. He'd mark the dawn of this new beginning by taking that wee break by the seaside the following week.

He found Rose McFadden busy in her kitchen as usual, spooning cake mixture into a bun tin; a tray of jam tarts stood ready for the oven. Paddy was seated in an armchair by the stove, the upper half of him obscured by a copy of the *Mid-Ulster Vindicator*. A kettle fizzled on the stove, and in the corner a wireless muttered at a reduced volume in anticipation of the evening news. Rose stopped her spooning and Paddy lowered the paper at the sound of Jamie's knock.

"Ye know, me and my Paddy were just talkin' about you, Jamie! Sit yourself down there." She looked to her husband for confirmation. "Isn't that right, Paddy?"

"Oh aye, that's right," Paddy confirmed.

"Sez I: 'I wonder if Jamie ever got a letter back from that lady,' and wasn't it awful that that young eejit of a Sproule ruined the great night yous was havin' at Slope's? Paddy was tellin' me that you hit him a dunder and you know, Jamie, if I'd been in your position I would a hit him a dunder meself 'cause y'know what they say: If a man keeps his tongue in his mouth and his hands in his pockets, he'll never get his nose broke, and Paddy told me that the ruffian was gropin' and pokin' at you beforehand, so he got what was comin' to him, so he did."

Rose stopped to draw breath. She pulled on a set of self-crafted oven gloves, their mitts showing two whiskered cats with orange button-eyes and pairs of unevenly positioned fur ears. This minor defect was occasioned by the fact that, during their fashioning, Rose had been in post-operative recovery from a detached retina in her left eye, brought about when, in the January of the previous year, she'd hit herself a "dunder" while setting a mousetrap (with a lump of Killymacoo vintage cheddar) in a corner of a cupboard under the sink.

"Och now, these things happen," she said, thinking of the Sproule incident, "and there's not much a body can do about it, so there isn't."

Jamie lowered himself into the plump, cushioned chair at the pig-patterned table. Rose slid the trays of buns and tarts into the roasting oven, eased the door shut and set the timer.

"Now, that's the thing." She creaked to her feet, satisfied with another job well done. "And Paddy here sez to me when he came into me last night, he sez: 'Jamie's accordjin playing was partickirly good, terrible good, so it was.' Isn't that right, Paddy?"

"Aye, that's right, Rose. That's just what I was sayin'." Paddy folded the paper and handed it to Jamie.

"Did y'hear about…did y'hear about poor Doris Crink? The post office was—"

"Was robbed yesterday." Rose couldn't abide her husband being the sole bearer of such earth-shattering news.

"God oh, I've got all me savin's with Doris!"

Jamie grabbed the paper, shocked, and found the headline: *Tailorstown Post Office Raid. No suspects yet.* He read the accompanying report.

"Now Jamie, your money's safe enough," Paddy assured him, "because, because it sez there…it sez there that the…that the bugger—"

"That the bugger only got away with a fiver," Rose called out. She lifted the teacups out of the cupboard. Every time she saw

Jamie, the circuitry of her brain fizzled and crackled and sent out the three-letter command: TEA. "Poor Doris didn't need that," she declared in a final curtain voice. "Must a been a terrible shock for the wee creatur."

"Sez here a gun was used," said Jamie, as he continued to peruse the article. He was relieved by the knowledge that his nest egg was safe. "Lord save us, but that must-a been an ordeal."

"Aye, a terrible ordeal for any man, let alone...let alone a woman," Paddy agreed. "But you know it coulda...it coulda been one a them watter-pistols. They say they can make them now to look like a...look like a..."

"A hammer?" Jamie offered.

"Naw, not a hammer...to look like..." Paddy couldn't think straight. "Christ, what was it I was gonna say...to look like a..."

"A rifle?" put in Rose.

"Aye, but wee-er than that."

"A gun?" shouted Jamie.

"Aye, that's the very thing," Paddy said relieved. "Aye, they say they can make them watter-pistols to look like a gun these days."

"I don't know what the world's comin' to," said Rose. She poured the tea and handed the mugs round. "A wee rock bun, Jamie? Fresh made, so they are." She pushed a plate under his nose. It was only at the sight of the buns that he realized he hadn't eaten anything all day and was, as they say, as hungry as a homeless tapeworm.

Jamie pulled the letter from his pocket and placed it reverentially on the table.

"She's a Ly-dee-a Devine, so she is."

"Well, what d'you know? Isn't that a good one. D'you see that, Paddy?"

Paddy couldn't comment, since his dentures were struggling with an entire rock bun. So he nodded and raised an affirming hand instead.

Rose wiped her hands on her apron and fetched her glasses from the pouting lips of the guppy on the mantelpiece. Paddy understood that matchmaking was Rose's terrain and decided to leave her to it. He got up.

"I'll go on here and get this bit-a paintin' finished," he announced to the cuckoo clock above the stove, sensing his presence would not be missed.

"Yes, you do that Paddy," said Rose, "and mind ye don't dribble on me clematis!" she shouted after him as he retreated down the hallway to continue ruining the front door with a tin of Dublin Bay Green gloss.

"Are them the wee purple boys ye have climbin' about the door, Rose?"

"They are indeed, Jamie, but Paddy would have an unsteady hand on him betimes when he's doin' an important job like paintin', and ye know—"

"Oh, I know what you're sayin' right enough," Jamie cut in, aware of Rose's spectacular ability to wander off the point and eager to get her opinion on Miss Devine's letter.

"God-blisses-an-save-us, what grand handwritin', Jamie!" Rose read the letter, quietly nodding and sighing her approval, whilst Jamie slurped the tea and demolished his rock bun in two mouthfuls.

"Well!" Rose removed her glasses. "A very fine, well-rounded lady indeed, Jamie." Since a depleted teacup and an empty side plate in front of a man signaled neglect on her part, she automatically replenished Jamie's mug and pushed more buns toward him.

"But it looks like she's a Protestant, Rose. That Sunday service bit."

"Now, I saw that, Jamie, too meself, and that doesn't matter atall as I told you before. We all worship the same God, do we not."

She broke a rock bun into pieces and slipped morsels into her mouth. It was a mouth that rarely experienced any notable periods of respite between eating and speaking, and often—as now—engaged itself in both activities at the same time.

"And this religion thing: it's only a wee blot on the horizon, if a body chooses to see it that way. And between you and me, Jamie," she leaned conspiratorially toward him, "me and my Paddy have never had anything against the other sort. Truth be told, they're more hardworkin' and not as lazy as our own lot, who can stand about in a field for hours, scratchin' their arses and not gettin' nothing done. Now I'm not sayin' you and my Paddy come into that caty-gory, but you know, Jamie, there's many's the one that does."

"Aye, I s'ppose you're right about that, Rose."

"'Deed I am, Jamie, 'deed I am. God, I had an Uncle Eustace, but y'know he got called Useless for short, 'cause he set about so much he wore the arse outta all the trousers he had. Me mother, God rest her soul, was never done patchin' and darnin' and footerin' for him. I wouldn't a been surprised if he'd bedsores on him when he was a nipper. So ye know, a hardworkin' Protestant woman isn't to be sniffed at, because she could end up being more useful to you than a lazy oul' clat of a Fenian, that would lie around all day with a fag in her gob, paintin' her toenails. And you know just when I mention fags, most a them Protestant women neither smoke nor drink, because they're so busy workin', so they are—terrible well doing—and for that reason, Jamie, would be very easy to run."

"God-oh," was all Jamie could say, the thought of a Protestant wife becoming more attractive by the minute.

"Now, let's look at all the good things about this lady."

Rose spread the letter out in front of her and, using the fingers of her left hand as counters, rehearsed what she saw as Lydia Devine's undoubted attributes.

"Now, Jamie, one: She's around the same age as yourself, which means she's sensible and not no fibberty-gibbit of a thing that would go turnin' a man's head with stuff not of a serious nature. And even though at that age she probably wouldn't tear at the pluckin', God-blisses-an-save-us—sure none of us would, because none of us is gettin' no younger, but that's just the way of it, so it is."

Jamie nodded and reached for another bun, his diet quite forgotten.

"Two: She's got a good job, and God knows there's few a them about these days, and she must like children because she wouldn't be working with them if she didn't like them, and I sez that's always a good sign in a woman because it means that maybe you and she could start a family, might it not." She took a long draught of tea.

Jamie's eyes widened. He had never even thought of children, never mind envisioning the intimate process by which they came into being.

"Now don't look so surprised, Jamie. You're the forty-one yourself, a grown man, and if she's about the same age as she sez here, well, she still has time. My cousin Martha give birth to triplets at the forty-two, eighteen months ago. And even though wee Mary has a squint, wee Molly a harelip, and wee Martin a head on him the size of a turnip, heaven's-above, God musta been in a terrible hurry at the makin' a them, but if you put all that aside there's not a bother on them. Because you know a woman over the forty can expect a wee bit of retardment, because she mighta left things a bit late, like."

Rose halted her racing discourse and reached for another bun.

"There's them that sez it was a miracle they lived atall, atall, my Paddy included, but it was no miracle, sez I, because if a woman wants a child, it'll come to her no matter the age, for God never closes one door but he bangs another one shut, if you unnerstand me, Jamie?"

Rose raised her Giant's Causeway mug to her lips once more, while Jamie sat in embarrassment, not knowing what to say, letting his eyes drift between the gamboling pigs on the tablecloth and a set of ceramic geese flapping their way up the wood-chipped wall toward the ceiling.

"Now where was I?" She looked down at the page again, hooked the index finger of her right hand round the middle finger of her left and continued.

"Yes, number three. She likes animals—which is a terrible good sign altogether, because it means she wouldn't be afeard of feedin' a pig or milkin' a cow or two if you were not able, for whatever reason, Jamie, to do it yourself. And I'm not sayin' anything's gonna happen you or the like—far be it from me to be sayin' a thing like that—but you did have that lambago and maybe still have, truth be told."

"Oh aye, I still have a wee touch of it now an' again, Rose."

"There you are then! If you couldn't get outta the bed of a cold morning—and God knows they'll be getting colder soon enough—sure wouldn't she be there to take over for you and the like?" Rose was pleased; Jamie's eager nodding to all she said meant that he'd understood her completely.

"That reminds me, Rose, just when you say it. I'll be takin' that wee day or two in Portaluce next Monday and Tuesday, with me back and all..."

"I unnerstand you completely, Jamie. You want my Paddy to feed the things, and that's no bother atall, as you well know."

"Well, y'know Dr. Brewster said that gettin' away for a coupla days would take me outta meself. And now that I'm gonna be meetin' this woman, I'm a bit un-aisey, so maybe it'd help me to get outta bit beforehand and meet some different people."

"Now, Jamie, there's no need for you to feel uneasy about meetin' this lady 'cause truth be told she'll maybe be as uneasy meetin' you too, her being a lonely heart like yourself. Sure for all y'know, she's maybe been sittin on her own lookin' into the fire like yourself, talkin' to nobody from one end-a the week to the other but a grumpy oul' lump of a brother or mother or whatever, and a coupla cats."

"Never thought a that, Rose, but when ye put it like that..."

Rose smiled broadly, thrilled that Jamie was appreciating her "agony aunt" wisdom.

"And may I say also, Jamie, I'm glad you're gettin' away with that back a yours, 'cause you said you were still gettin' the odd wee touch of it, did ye not?"

"Aye, the odd wee touch of it now and again, Rose."

"I know all about it, Jamie! Our Martha had a leg she couldn't get rid of after the births of the wee ones. It blew up the size of a Mullingar heifer's, so it did, and I went down and helped her out, because you know she couldn't get about atall, atall. And it's a terrible thing when a body is incapissitated in such a way. May your belly always be full and your bones enjoy their stretching, as me Great-grandmother Murphy used to say."

Rose broke up another rock bun on her side plate and looked back at the letter. "Now, Jamie, where were we with this lady?"

"I think we were coming to the books, Rose."

"Yes, Jamie, I believe you're right. That and the cookin' bit. But y'know, the cookin' being the most important thing, I'm leavin' that to the last." Rose got up. "Excuse me one wee minute, Jamie. I needa see if me buns have riz."

She pulled the cat-faced oven gloves on again and opened the stove door. A gust of hot air burst into the already sweltering room. She carried one of the steaming trays over to the table and left it on the cooling rack.

"But I haven' read no books, Rose! Maybe one or two on farming and the like." The last was a lie. In truth, Jamie's reading extended no farther than deciphering the heating instructions on a can of Campbell's chicken soup now and again. "But I think she means them novels and things, her being a teacher like." He looked longingly at the jam tarts.

"Now, they're a wee bit hot at the moment, Jamie, but I'll give you a bag o' them to take home with you, so I will."

She hung the oven gloves on a bracket above the stove: a laminated plaque of a bull's head whose protruding horns served as hooks for items of kitchen apparel.

"Now, my Paddy has some cawntry-an'-western cowboy books down here, so he has." She got down on bended knee and opened a cupboard to the right of the stove. "He doesn't bother with the readin' no more, his eyesight not being what it used to be." She spoke into the depths of the dark cupboard. "And y'know what they say, Jamie: A blind hawk will never find his nuts in the dark."

Presently she got up, her joints popping with the effort, her face as pink as the Sam McCready roses patterned across her generous bosom, and handed Jamie two shabby, yellowed paperbacks: *The Virginian* by Owen Wister and *Riders of the Purple Sage* by Zane Gray.

"Now that's the books seen to, Jamie. Maybe you should take a wee read at them before you meet her, just in case she might ask you what they were about, and you wouldn't like to be caught with your horns in the hay or your flies in the ointment, or whatever it is they say."

Jamie studied the books, flicking through the pages and wondering why meeting this woman was beginning to resemble sitting an exam.

"That's great, Rose," he said, with a touch of resignation in his voice. "Thank you very much. So, there's just the cookin' left."

"Yes, Jamie, the cookin' is the most important part of the whole letter; that's why I left it to last," Rose said, taking a palette knife from a drawer and arranging the jam tarts on a bedoilied plate. "Now I'm no scholar meself, but them fancy words 'culoon-in-ary process' I suppose might be another way of sayin' cookin' and bakin' and the like."

She offered Jamie a tart and took one herself. She replaced her glasses and retrieved the letter, frowning.

"'What dishes do you like making most?'" She read the salient sentence aloud again. "'What ass-pect of the culoon-in-ary process interests you most?'"

Rose peered over her glasses.

"Well, d'you know, Jamie, aren't you eatin' the answer to that one?"

"Huh?" He looked in bemusement at the half-eaten jam tart on his plate.

"Them wee jam tarts. Well y'know, a monkey with no eyes in the back of his head could make them! Not that I'm sayin' you're a monkey, Jamie. Far be it from me to be sayin' such a thing, if truth be told. But a jam tart and a rock bun you could make with your eyes closed and your hands tied behind your back, sitting on a lamppost in the middle of a field on a dark night, so you could. They're that simple."

She went to a cork board above the fridge and, from below a novena of a girlish-looking St. Joshua (*Patron Saint of Fruitless Endeavours*) standing in a plastic pocket, unpinned a cornflake packet coupon featuring a recipe for rock buns. She handed it to Jamie.

"There you are, you can hold on to that and study it. Now I'm gonna give my Paddy a wee drop more tea and then we'll get down to the writin' of it, so we will."

She left Jamie in the kitchen in a profound study, wondering how the faceless Lydia could involve him in such demanding feats as reading books and learning recipes, before he even had the chance to meet her and speak to her.

Life was indeed strange. One minute you were contemplating ending it all with a rafter and a length of rope, the next you were studying a recipe for rock buns with a view to meeting a lady. It was all very strange indeed.

Chapter eighteen

The Ocean Spray, a large, three-storied, detached guesthouse, was situated in a prime spot—facing the sea and catching the sun—on the main thoroughfare of the coastal resort of Portaluce.

Gladys Millman, sixty-five, glamorous widow, and younger sister of Elizabeth Devine, considered her establishment superior to others, due to its enviable location. Also on account of this, she felt justified in charging higher rates than her rivals. She prided herself on running a spotless guesthouse, demanded impeccable standards of herself and her workforce, and reserved a healthy contempt for those she considered to be of the lower, or indeed peasant, classes.

Whenever she encountered anyone she deemed a threat to this ideal—those from the farming community, factory workers, trades-men, dowdy women over thirty and still unmarried—she would raise her rates even more, to scare them off. And if this ploy didn't work, she would skimp on elements of their breakfast so as to compensate for having to endure such riffraff under her roof. So next morn-ing, Farmer Murphy and his wife would have set before them—but probably did not notice—margarine instead of butter, shop-bought jam instead of homemade preserves, thinly diluted squash instead of freshly squeezed orange juice.

Gladys had started the business with her husband Freddie (Freddie had been an accountant and she a secretary) after their daughters Bertha and Lillian had graduated, married and left home to settle in Canada and California, respectively.

Within two years, the childfree, carefree couple had built up the Ocean Spray as a successful and respectable venture; the success was due to Freddie's eye for profit and Gladys's skill in the kitchen. But the idyll was not to last. One morning at breakfast, Freddie died suddenly of a heart attack, going face-first into his Ulster fry-up (a specialty of the house) as he and Gladys squabbled over the virtues of serving French toast instead of fried potato bread, Freddie arguing more forcefully for the cheaper potato alternative, which was a personal favorite and which—in a way—had unfortunately and most acutely been the death of him.

Gladys was a vain woman, proud of her appearance and her status as a successful entrepreneur. She had an admirer whom she saw from time to time—"my secret lover"—who encouraged and appreciated the efforts she made to look her best.

For she dressed elegantly, and although a bit on the plump side, remedied this by wearing well-sculpted undergarments and retaining a haughty carriage; she held herself as erect and regally as the reigning monarch. In fact, H.R.H. Queen Elizabeth was her role model; consequently, Gladys was a firm believer in the value of a well-positioned brooch and a many-stringed set of pearls to lift an outfit and add that important finishing touch.

As she sat at her beige, laminated dressing table with its griffin feet and gilt-edged mirror, Gladys was aware that, on this occasion, she must make a special effort with her appearance. Her sister and niece were arriving later in the day.

She had not seen Elizabeth for well over a year and was ever conscious of the competition that still existed between them regarding dress and appearance. Elizabeth could be uncommonly forthright in her opinions, and Gladys knew from experience that the best way to silence her—or indeed lessen the impact of her jibes—was to present her with few causes for criticism in the first place.

For this reason she was careful that morning to apply her makeup with a judicious hand, opting for the discreet Delicate Dawn foundation, instead of her usual Café Gold, going easy with the kohl pencil on eyelids and brows, and finishing with just a touch of Pink Frost on her full, sensuous mouth. Her sister was wont to say that make-up was "for the harlots of Rome," an opinion fostered by her impossible late husband, the Reverend Perseus Cuthbert, whom Gladys had had little time for in life, and resented even more now that he'd passed over. Her sister, God help her, felt it necessary to keep his frightful spirit alive by rehearsing his tedious, chauvinistic mantras.

Her makeup completed, she swept her auburn hair into an elaborate French chignon and anchored it in place with several pins. Outside, the seagulls wheeled and dived in a blue sky above the metronomic push and pull of the Atlantic waves. Portaluce was a graceful place to live, its calm, natural beauty drawing the heart and eye to peaceful conclusions, notwithstanding the stresses of one's life.

Gladys registered few of those delights, however, as she fastened herself into a shirtdress of pistachio silk, and slipped on her stilettos. The scene from the mansard window, like the elegant, pale fabric on her walls, had become a commonplace, admired from time to time but rarely dwelt on.

Her final touch was a set of diamanté stud earrings—a birthday gift from the doting Dr. Humphrey Brewster—and a matching brooch pinned in place over her opulent bosom. She stepped back from the mirror, well satisfied. Now she felt eager and ready to face the day, her staff and her fractious sister, when she arrived.

The fifty-mile journey from Killoran to Portaluce had been a lengthy one, not least because Lydia did not believe in driving her Fiat 850 faster simply because the distance was longer. The speedometer needle had rarely crept beyond 40 mph. Her caution in this regard, together with frequent rests for tea at various hostelries, and the fact that Elizabeth's hemorrhoid cushion tended, for whatever reason, to leak air every half hour, and had to be inflated with the bicycle pump which Lydia kept in the trunk especially for that purpose, meant that the ladies did not arrive at the Ocean Spray until well after 4 P.M.

Gladys was already on the doorstep when Lydia pulled her car into the reserved bay facing the guesthouse. On seeing her glamorous sister, Elizabeth felt moved to make the first of many caustic comments.

"Has she nothing better to do but stand there," she said icily, "showing off her lungs in a dress like that? It's far too tight for a woman of her age. You know I think Freddie was lucky to get away, and if you ask me, she was probably glad to be rid of him!"

"Mother, no one is asking you anything, and I'm warning you: If you start annoying Auntie Gladys, I'll have a good mind to drive straight back home if the mood takes me."

Elizabeth had no time to respond, for already Gladys was sweeping down on the arrivals like a great seagull, anxious to aid her sister, and air-kissing her with a shower of exclamatory greetings.

"Good to see you too, Gladys dear!" Elizabeth batted the hand away. "Now there's no need for that. I'm not an invalid, you know."

Gladys sniffed and dived toward the niece.

"And little Lily! How good of you to come." She clasped Lydia in a heady embrace of clanking bracelets and wafting Opium scent. "And you look so *well*," she lied. "A bit thin perhaps, but we'll soon build you up. Now let's all have tea. I'm sure you must be famished after that long journey."

Elizabeth held fast to her malacca cane, wobbling on her patent Gabor heels as Gladys took them by the arm and steered them toward her great achievement: the Romanesque, wedding cake of an establishment that was her commercial enterprise and home.

"Oh, business is hectic as usual. Well, it is the season, I suppose, so one can't complain."

Gladys sat back on the cream damask sofa, one hand on her fine bosom, and crossed her shapely legs. She was conscious that between her and her two guests—the dowdy, cantankerous sister and the plain, flat-chested niece—there was no competition at all. She felt a flush of triumph and a stab of pity as she considered them both.

She was also aware that since her guests would be staying with her and taking up valuable rooms at no charge, the pair was at a considerable disadvantage. They'd be under an obligation to do her bidding and agree with most of what she said. Gladys liked to be in control of things and refused to have her authority eroded by either sibling or friend.

"But you know I do not have the luxury of delegating," she went on, "simply because I just can't trust anyone, and one simply can't get the help these days. They have to be trained up first. You would not *believe* how ill-prepared some of these young women are for the domestic demands of life. Heaven help the poor unsuspecting men who find themselves married to suchlike, is what I say…"

A gentle tapping on the door had brought Gladys's galloping discourse to a canter.

"Yes, come in, Sinéad," she said without missing a step. A young maid entered bearing a massive, silver tray. "Good. At last, the tea."

Gladys tapped a lacquered fingernail on the glass coffee table. "Just leave it here, please."

The thin, ginger-haired girl, no more than seventeen, peppered in freckles and nervous as a rabbit, set the tray down very carefully, and straightened.

"Is that all yous will be wantin', Miss Gladys?"

"Now, Sinéad, how many times have I said that 'ewes' are female sheep one finds in the field?" Gladys raised an Ava Gardner eyebrow. "They are not the plural pronoun one finds in a proper sentence."

The girl's face turned the hue of a boiled beetroot as she stood twisting her hands, as though wringing an invisible dishcloth.

"Sorry, I meant 'ye,' Miss."

"I beg your pardon!"

"Er, I mean 'you,' Miss."

"I should hope so. 'Ye,' indeed!"

Gladys lifted the silver teapot and proceeded to pour, whilst Elizabeth looked on perplexed and Lydia felt a searing embarrassment for the young woman, reduced now to a cringing mouse by her employer.

"Now, could we try it again?"

The girl coughed. "Is that all you will be wanting, Miss Gladys?"

"Good, that's better! And no, this looks fine for the moment." Gladys scanned the tray for stray sugar grains, finger-marked spoons, blemished napkins or slopped milk, and seemed disappointed to find everything in order on this occasion. "Thank you, Sinéad. You may go now."

The maid departed quickly and pulled the door quietly behind her.

"Do you see what I mean? Badly brought up. I not only have to teach them how to prepare food and make envelope-cornered beds, I also have to deal with poor grammar." She handed Elizabeth a cup and saucer—gold-trimmed turquoise Denby, expensive, trendy, so unlike her sister's nasty, old-fashioned Royal Doulton china. "But then I suppose, Lily dear, you would know all about that, having to deal with your pupils all day long." She flashed a perfect, pretend smile at her niece.

"Well I think, Gladys, if children don't read—"

"Now, how are you ladies going to spend your time?" Gladys asked, slicing across Lydia with the skill of a master swordsman. "Portaluce has really opened up since you were here last. We have our very own theater now: The Tudor Rose. So we could take in a play one evening, if you like."

"Never had much time for plays," said Elizabeth. "Perseus Cuthbert always said they brought the coarseness of life to the fore, and why should anyone want to celebrate such follies and put them on a stage for us to laugh and weep at anyway?"

She bit into her cucumber and Brie sandwich, pleased that she'd made her point so lucidly.

"Gosh, Elizabeth! If Perseus Cuthbert had had his way he would have outlawed entertainment altogether. Fun was a perversion in his eyes."

Elizabeth noted the combative glint in her sister's eye and opted, on this occasion, to ignore the insult to her dear husband's memory. Lydia, watching the proceedings, saw the beginnings of a verbal tennis match, full of acerbic backhanders and searing rallies, hotting up between the two. She was in no mood to play ballgirl at that moment. She had a headache from the long drive, and Gladys's perfume was making her nauseous; she wished to be released from the stifling room and from the clutches of her overbearing aunt. She got up.

"I think I really fancy a nice walk and some sea air. How about you, Mother?"

Elizabeth, to Gladys's annoyance, acquiesced all too readily to her daughter's proposal and returned her cup and saucer to the tray.

"But you haven't finished your tea yet," Gladys protested, thrusting upright on the sofa, her great bosom pushing out like the plumage of some exotic feathered creature.

Elizabeth, already on her feet, noted the abundant cleavage and thought if Perseus Cuthbert were present, he'd be throwing a blanket round her and exhorting her to "conduct" herself. She was dismayed that her sister seemed to get flightier the older she got, and wondered if there was a man on the scene. And, if there were, heaven help him!

"Why don't you come with us too, Gladys?" Lydia said, trying to sound enthusiastic as she headed for the door.

"I have work to do, Lily dear." Gladys rose from the sofa, miffed, and smoothed down her dress.

"Her name is *Lydia*, not Lily!" Elizabeth parried, determining after all to lock swords. She held her sister with a glacial, unblinking stare. There was a taut silence.

Lydia looked from the one to the other. She had rarely seen her mother so forbidding. "Look, I don't really care what I'm called, really."

"No, Lydia; *you* don't, but *I* do. Shall we go?"

As the older sister made to depart, Gladys tried to soften the injury with a conciliatory comment.

"Chef has to prepare dinner for fifteen this evening and I must be on hand to oversee things," she said. Lydia nodded but her mother ignored her.

And on that sour note they parted, Lydia wondering why her Christian name should have caused such enmity between the sisters. Perhaps this break in Portaluce, she thought, which her mother had so looked forward to, might not have been such a good idea after all.

Chapter nineteen

Jamie had given scant attention to his preparations for the sojourn on the coast. The letter had already been written and sent to Miss Devine, and his mind dwelt on not much else but the thought of meeting her. When he pictured Lydia, the image of his long-lost mother would merge with that of his dear Aunt Alice, to create the perfect woman, as radiant as a sunburst in heaven. He saw a smooth oval face, eyes as blue as robin's eggs and a dazzling, Hollywood smile.

In two hours' time Paddy would collect him and ferry him to the station in Killoran to catch the two o'clock bus. He had already fed the animals and himself; still conscious of his diet, he'd swapped the fry-up for tea and toast. Now, he reminded himself, he had to pack a case, because that's what most people did before going on vacation. His last vacation had been some fifteen years before. He and his uncle had spent a couple of days in Portaluce with Mick's sister Violet, who'd had a lovely house overlooking the promenade. But sadly she was now at her eternal rest, and her house had been turned into an ice-cream parlor called The Snowy Cone.

Back then, however, Uncle Mick had known what to do concerning the packing and suchlike. But now Jamie was at a loss as to know what to include in his case or bag (or whatever it was a body carried on these expeditions). He sat in the armchair nursing his mug of tea, smoking the end of a Woodbine and wondering whether he should mount the stairs and take along that case of Aunt Alice's that was under Mick's bed. But on second thoughts it was a bit big, and what would he need to be taking with him anyway?

He'd given himself a good scrub down the night before in the tin bath by the fire. After such a rare event, he could get a fortnight—if not a good month—out of his underwear. So Rose McFadden's bag of clean inner garments, which sat on top of the glass case, would not be needed for a while yet. He looked down at his feet, and thought: Maybe a change of socks, because he'd be walking a lot, not having access to his bicycle.

He went to his bedroom in search of a pair. He knew they were in another bag somewhere; he rummaged in the chest of drawers, found a decent looking black pair and sat them on the bed. He took his black suit from the closet—it was the only decent outfit he had—and laid it on the bed alongside the socks. The suit was a castoff of Mick's, a bit short in the leg maybe and a wee bit tight about the armpits, his uncle having been more low-set and much thinner than himself. But sure he only ever wore it for the hour of a Sunday at Mass. Two days by the ocean was maybe a different matter, he thought now. But he'd cross that river—or bridge or road or whatever—when he came to it, as Rose McFadden might say.

The black socks would match the suit right enough, but what about the shoes? His best pair was a custard yellow, bought in Harvey's sale at tremendous discount, due to their color and unusual style. The toes were pointed, and curved up like bananas, but Mr. Harvey had insisted they were the new Western style and that they were "the whole go in America." Jamie had bought them with the intention of dyeing them black, but like Procrastination's brother— "Och, I'll not bother now; time enough with that"—had never got round to it. He sighed at this small setback, but he had no time (or dye) to be footering with them now, so they would have to do. He placed them on the bed beside the socks and the suit.

His shirts were lapped on three hangers on the closet door. The white one looked decent enough; since he hadn't been to Mass for three weeks, it had suffered no wear and tear from Rose's last wash. Jamie looked at his watch and decided to dress. It took longer than expected; he had to dig for a belt and root for a tie, two items he rarely had cause to wear in the day-to-day run of things.

When he'd finished he paused, and realized that he was standing up in everything he was taking with him. So what need had a body to pack a bag atall, atall? But then there was his comb, his Brylcreem, his shaving things, and that extra pair of socks and maybe the tooth-brush and toothpaste—used only of a Sunday morning—which sat curled up in a cracked mug by the kitchen sink.

He was wandering about the house, checking if there was any-thing else he might need to take, when his eye fell on the two books on the table. Maybe he would have time to read a bit. Of the two, *Riders of the Purple Sage* looked the least battered; its spine was still intact, even if the corners were bent back a bit.

He noticed also, on the windowsill, a half-full bottle of Blue Adonis aftershave. It was Mick's and had been sitting on the sill for about a year. Now and again Jamie had considered throwing it out, but thought maybe it would come in useful at some stage. And wasn't he glad he hadn't dumped it, for now that stage had come. He wiped the cobwebs off it with the lining of his jacket.

He pitched all of these items into a Scully's Around-a-Pound shopping bag and checked himself in the broken mirror on the bureau. It only afforded him a view from the waist up, which was probably just as well. He studied his reflection, knew there was something not quite right, until it suddenly dawned on him that he was still wear-ing his cap. He had already ordered his Sandy Brown toupee from Rose's *Exchange & Mart*, but unfortunately it had not arrived in time for this particular expedition.

A man could hardly keep an oul' cap on with the good suit, he told himself. Jamie sighed at the mirror, quickly arranged his comb-over with the Brylcreem, his comb and a practiced hand, tossed the cap into the shopping bag and considered himself to be all set and ready for action. No sooner had he done so when he heard the guttural rasping of Paddy's Morris Minor as it labored up the hill.

Jamie instructed Paddy on the various jobs he had to do: fodder and milk the Ayrshires, feed the pig and the hens, collect any eggs, and give a scrap or two to Shep. Paddy understood, being a farmer himself; he nodded patiently and assured Jamie that all would be taken care of. He handed him a crumpled paper bag.

"Rose sent you down a couple a them…a couple a them rock buns for the bus."

"God, she's awful good, Paddy! Tell her thanks very much."

Jamie stole a quick look into the bag, and his eyes welled up at the thought of Rose and all the help she'd given him so far. He appreciated the deep significance of this heartfelt gesture; it was only a wee bag of buns, he told himself, but at the same time he was touched. Someone was thinking of him; someone cared. This small kindness meant so much; he'd had such rare flashes of affection in his early life.

"Time's going on, Jamie," Paddy said then, interrupting his thoughts. "Maybe…maybe we should make a…make a…"

"Move?"

"Aye, a move…maybe we should make a move."

"Aye, I suppose we should." Jamie reached down to stroke Shep, who sat looking forlornly up at his master. "You be a good boy now."

"Sure we can take the wee dog with us." Paddy scratched his ear and rubbed his chin, sensing Jamie's sadness. "It's not often…not often he gets a…gets a…"

"Wee run out?"

"Aye, a wee run out."

So Shep leaped into the back of the Minor and off they went, Jamie's cottage receding and disappearing in the rear window as they struggled up the hill in first gear.

Paddy's driving was erratic at the best of times, due in part to his poor eyesight, his inexperience—he could only drive the mile or so to and from the village, could only park safely in an area the size of a barley field—and the fact that he'd never in his life sat a driving test. His relationship with his motorcar was therefore a curiously one-sided affair. He knew how to drive it (just about) but not how to care for it. Water and oil were rarely replenished, and as for brake fluid and coolant—well, they'd maybe take care of themselves.

Every car Paddy bought came sooner rather than later to resemble a wounded warrior clinging on valiantly to life; tires bald as a baby's bottom, fenders dented from ill-judged parking maneuvers, wing-mirrors and wipers hanging on with "that-boy'll-maybe-hold-her-for-another-wee-while" duct tape. When Paddy drove off with his various revitalized purchases from J & B O'Lynchy's "Good As Nu" car lot, the dealer knew with certainty that their imminent deaths were assured. There was a God's acre of such clunkers and wrecks in the McFadden backyard. To his head-scratching bafflement, each vehicle had ground to a halt with a sudden bang, and "for no divil of a raisen" that Paddy could think of "atall atall, begod!"

The Minor in which the trio now rode was his fifth in three years. The car jerked and rocked its way over the tortuous country roads, groaning and grinding as Paddy's erratic gear-shifting produced wailing overtones. Nearing Killoran, he decided, rather unwisely, to take a shortcut down Pothole Lane, aptly named inasmuch as it hadn't seen a resurfacing since the Norman Invasion of 1169. On this final leg, both men discovered that conversation was impossible, and the dog went berserk. With every jolt their breath was taken away as they were thrown about, the words bouncing out of their mouths with a "Jezsis boys!" and "That's a fierce frigger of a—" getting lost in the suffering spasms of the car.

When finally they arrived at the bus station, Shep had collapsed and lay panting on the back seat, ears lying flat, tongue lolling. Both driver and passenger were speechless—Jamie, clutching the bag of rock buns, fearing he must have broken most of them, and Paddy promising himself that he'd never take that bugger of a shortcut again.

Lydia Devine was relaxing in the plush Ocean Spray drawing room, idly scanning an old issue of *Woman's Own* she'd found in her aunt's magazine rack. It was a lovely, tranquil afternoon and she felt at peace in the elegant room with its splendid view of endless sky, sea-leveled sands, and ocean.

It was day four of her vacation, with three more to go, and as she sat back in the velvet recliner, Lydia reflected that, despite its rocky start, this impromptu break was turning out to be very enjoyable after all. In fact, since that little difference of opinion between the sisters concerning the Reverend Perseus Cuthbert and the question of her Christian name, things had, for the most part, remained relatively calm and trouble free.

Lydia knew that it was she who had brought about this level of equilibrium, through her diplomatic maneuvers, by keeping Elizabeth and Gladys apart as much as possible. So she took walks with her mother when Gladys was busy, and had long talks with her aunt whenever her mother was napping. That way, she fulfilled her function as the dutiful daughter and attentive niece—and as such was a bridge and conduit for both.

She had also insisted on their having their main meals in the dining room with the other guests. That way, her aunt got to show off her skills as proprietor and host, a role she, like the consummate actress, reveled in so much that sister and niece were reduced to the minor parts of extras at a table in the corner, and all but forgotten. This situation seemed to suit everyone admirably: Gladys got to exhibit her charm, Elizabeth got to pass cynical comments out of earshot, and Lydia got to enjoy her meal without interruption.

Lydia smiled as she nonchalantly scanned the magazine, enjoying so much being left to her own devices. If I'd had a sister, she wondered, would our relationship have been quite so fractured and restive as that of my aunt and my mother? Perhaps, she mused, we never really stop being the children we once were. Some essential part of us remains wedded to the tantrums of the playpen and the schoolyard.

Soon Aunt Gladys would be joining her for an aperitif whilst Elizabeth had a nap before dinner. She noticed that her mother was eating rather less and sleeping rather more than she did at home;

Lydia did not know whether this was a ploy to escape her sister or whether the ocean air was to blame. Either way, the rest was doing Elizabeth good, which was really all that mattered.

The door opened, cutting short her musings. In walked Gladys, looking majestic in a tight-fitting, coffee-colored satin two-piece.

"Now, little Lily, time for our drinky-poos before things get busy."

Before her niece had time to respond, she strode to an elaborate cocktail cabinet and decanted generous measures of Cockburn's ruby port into two lead-crystal flutes. Lydia accepted one hesitantly.

"Gladys, you know I don't really drink."

"Nonsense." The aunt sat down carefully on the Grecian sofa. "It's time you started living a little, dear." She raised her own glass. "Cheers. Here's to my little niece finding herself a nice man and settling down."

"Not much chance of that now, is there, Gladys?" Lydia sipped the port and winced.

"Poppycock! You simply don't send out the right signals. Men like to know that a woman is available."

"Yes, but I'm not like you, Gladys." Lydia looked at her aunt's generous décolleté with its rich brocade trim, her silk-stockinged knees on show below the scalloped hem—and thought she looked like a woman on her way to bed, or indeed the whorehouse. "It's not in my nature to be extrovert."

Lydia set the glass on the coffee table, wondering how she could get rid of it without offending her hostess. These conversations with Gladys always made her feel uncomfortable because they invariably involved men, of whom Lydia knew so blessed little.

"Shall I be frank, dear? You need to become like a taxi."

"A *what*?"

"A taxi, dear. How do you know when a taxi's free?"

"Erm…the light is on?"

"Exactly! You need to show men that your light is on. That you're available."

"And how do I do that?" Lydia tried to sound interested. She knew that she must humor her aunt.

"Well, I'll let you in to a little secret…." Gladys paused and took a cigarette from an ebony box on the coffee table. She reached for a gem-encrusted cherub and pressed its cheeks. To Lydia's astonishment, a flame shot from the top of its silver-curled head and lit the cigarette. She waited, as her aunt puffed the cigarette into life, wondering what could be of such importance that it merited this nicotine fix preamble.

"How d'you let a man know that you're available? Simple, dear: You raise your hemline and lower your neckline." Gladys blew long flurries of smoke from her snooty nostrils. "In other words, Lily dear, you need to start being a little more *creative* with your look. That blue shift dress does nothing for your figure. Now I know you don't have much of a cleavage, so a low neckline is probably not the best thing for you." She drew heavily on the cigarette again. "I would suggest a gathered top or smocked blouse. It would give the illusion of a fuller bust." She put a hand to her own lavish bosom as if to reinforce her words, and sipped more port.

"You take after your mother with that flat chest," she went on, blithely ignoring Lydia's scowl of disapproval. "And don't ask me why, but most men are drawn to the upper part of a woman's anatomy initially. I expect it's something to do with babies and maternal bonding or whatever. But my point is: Show them what they think they might get eventually, and by the time they get around to actually getting it, they'll be so dazzled with your mind that your bust—or rather lack of it—won't be an issue."

Lydia could feel her cheeks heat up under the face powder, the port and the forthrightness of her aunt's opinions. She tried to change the subject.

"What's for dinner this evening, by the way?" She took care to sound as offhand and as casual as possible.

Gladys pulled a face. "Why, toad-in-the-hole, followed by stuffed apples or spotted dick," she said, quickly taking up her drink again, annoyed that Lydia had interrupted her. "Now, where was I? Yes, bosoms. I'd finished with those, had I not? The other thing is legs. Now, Lily, you have fine legs. You take after me in that regard. And there's nothing a man likes more than a nicely turned ankle." She raised her right leg slightly and rotated her foot several times, lost in admiration and her own self-regard.

"So you can afford a much shorter hemline," she continued. "Not too short, mind. Just above the knee. Like mine," and she stood up to demonstrate her point.

"Yes, I see what you mean," Lydia said weakly.

But when Gladys went to sit down again, her eye was caught by something beyond the window. She quickly crushed out her cigarette.

"My goodness, who is that strange little man loitering at my gate?" She peered more intently. "I do hope he isn't even *thinking* about coming in here."

Lydia could just about discern a figure at the gate, and wondered what the fuss was about. Gladys quickly fished a mirror compact from her purse and checked her face. Any man, no matter how lowly or dissolute, deserved to see her at her best.

"Oh my God, he *is* coming here." She snapped the compact shut and strode swiftly to the door. "Excuse me dear, while I get rid of this peasant."

In a flash she was gone.

Lydia, slightly bewildered, looked out the window again and saw a man of indeterminate age shambling up the avenue.

He was clad in a black suit whose trousers legs seemed inordinately short. He wore yellow shoes which resembled harem slippers and did not exactly harmonize with the rest of his ensemble. His hair, what there was of it, was being sustained on the ocean breeze, and he was holding a hand on top of his head as if to try and moor it. His other hand was clutching a Scully's Around-a-Pound shopping bag, weighed down, Lydia suspected, by his toiletries. A stranger, she thought, in search of a bed and shelter. In that instant she felt sorry for the poor man, and for what, she was certain, he was about to endure.

In the lobby, Gladys was taking up position behind the marble reception desk, a set of sharp excuses, like a quiver of arrows, at the ready, to quickly dispose of this intruder in her paradise. She watched Jamie keenly as he made his journey across the lush expanse of oriental rug with its Ottoman signature of intricate reds and golds. He was clearly overwhelmed by the grandeur, and almost knocked over a glass coffee table in his eagerness to take it all in.

"Yes, can I help you?" The proprietor nocked the first arrow on the bowstring and prepared to take aim.

"Good afternoon. Mrs. Milkman, I suppose." Jamie put down the plastic bag on the glossy surface. Gladys flinched and shut her eyes briefly.

"*Millman, Mill*-man. And you are?" She stared at him, noting a strand of what looked like hay protruding from Jamie's breast pocket. A farmer person obviously, she thought, and one who believed in bringing the wretched field in with him. Her nostrils twitched at the likelihood of manure and other disagreeable odors. To her surprise, she detected none.

"James Kevin Barry Michael McCloone." He splayed his hands on the desk and looked admiringly at the stucco sculpted ceiling. "God, this is a terrible grand place altogether!"

"Thank you, Mr. McCloone. And do you have a reservation?"

Gladys raised her triumphant eyebrows as the arrow hit its target.

"Sorry. A what?" Jamie looked confused.

"A booking, Mr. McCloone." She leaned forward and pretended to check the register, fully aware that she was affording the farmer a bounteous eyeful of cleavage. Jamie stared in amazement. Gladys looked up.

"Oh no, I didn't book. Seein' it was Monday, like, I thought I'd come on spec, like."

"Well, I'm very sorry to disappoint you on this occasion, but this guesthouse is very popular all year round, and more so at this time of year." Gladys slammed the register shut and watched Jamie wither under the force of her direct hit. "I can, however, recommend O'Neill's on the corner. Their rates are probably more in keeping with what you had in mind."

"Och now, that's too bad." Jamie pawed up the plastic bag again and got ready to depart.

Gladys tilted her head to one side in mock sympathy. "I *do* apologize."

"It's a pity," said Jamie, "because a very decent man praised this place highly. Said I should come here with me back for a couple of days."

"Quite. And who might this gentleman be, in the event I might know him?"

"He's a Dr. Brewster of Tailorstown. Great doctor. Couldn't get the better of him, so you couldn't."

Gladys immediately switched on her neon smile and lowered her bow. "Oh, but why didn't you say so before? If Humphrey—I mean Dr. Brewster—recommended us, then that's another matter entirely."

"What?" Jamie pulled on his right ear and ran a hand over his hair, just to make sure he looked all right.

Gladys leaned seductively over the reservations book again.

"In that case we'll just have to find a space for you, Mr., ah…"

"McCloone."

"Mr. McCloone. Of course." She traced a red talon down the list of names, paused and looked up.

"Yes, aren't you fortunate, Mr. McCloone! I *do* have one single room left. How long will it be for?"

"Just the two nights. Would like to stay the three, maybe even the four, but with the farm and—"

"Quite so, Mr. McCloone." Gladys was deciding how much she could overcharge him; not much, she reckoned, judging by the look of him. "If you'll just sign here." She offered him the gold Parker. "And that will be ten pounds and fifty-two pence."

Jamie looked up in alarm. Gladys held him in her sights with her great smiling eyes.

"Right ye be," he said, with a touch of resignation. He took the pen.

"In advance," she said to Jamie's balding scalp. She noted him quiver slightly at this news, before continuing with the slow process of writing out his name in full.

Chapter twenty

Yes, he's a good worker, this boy."

Master Keaney's menacing voice was edged with a baleful import.

Eighty-Six stood once again on the peacock-patterned rug, staring down at his feet. He was aware of four pairs of eyes watching him: Keaney, Mother Vincent and two strangers, a man and woman he'd never seen before.

"Look up, boy, when you're spoken to!" Keaney barked.

The boy raised his head slowly and tried to focus on the heavy wooden crucifix hanging on the bib of Mother Vincent's habit. She sat a few feet in front of him, looking imposing behind the sun-bleached desk.

Keaney was in his usual armchair by the fire. Eighty-Six longed to go and warm his hands and knees at the generous flames. It was another wish he held in check. The man in the chair could be as dangerous as the blazing coals he guarded.

The strangers were seated on the rump-sprung sofa with the balding armrests. He dared not look their way, and wondered why he had been summoned to that room and at that hour. To the best of his knowledge, he hadn't done anything wrong since the turnip incident, and that seemed a long time ago.

Presently Mother Vincent spoke.

"This is Amos and Constance Fairley," she told him. Her voice was brusque. "Mrs. Fairley is a sister of Mr. Keaney, our Master."

Eighty-Six looked at the unsmiling couple. The man bore a striking resemblance to Keaney himself. He was pale and gaunt, had the same pointed face and dead eyes. His ugly, dirt-creased hands seemed out of proportion to the rest of him as he sat gripping his kneecaps.

Constance Fairley appeared to be a female version of the two men, with similar eyes and a grim, rigid mouth. The only difference was the hair: blond, turning gray and pulled up severely from her skeletal face into a tight bun. She sat straight-backed, with her dry, hard hands crossed in her lap.

"Farmer Doyle says that you are a good worker in the potato field, Eighty-Six. Is this correct?" When Mother Vincent spoke, the stiff white wimple framing her face marked time with the words.

"Yes, Sister. I think so." The boy did his best to speak clearly. Perhaps he was about to be rewarded for his hard labor.

"My sister and brother-in-law wish to employ you for a few months." It was Keaney. "They have a large farm and many potatoes that need gathering."

This news held the menace of a raised ax blade. The boy tensed with dread as he saw his frail future fall to pieces.

"They have a son, Arnold, about your age," said the nun. The Master grinned at Amos Fairley when she said this. Something evil passed between the two men. Eighty-Six knew that look. He wanted to yell out.

"A *friend* for you, Eighty-Six," the nun enthused.

Then all eyes swung back to him again. He kept focusing on the nun's crucifix and on the window to the left of her. Outside, the wind hissed and tore at the laurels in the graveyard, and inside, the flames wavered frantically in the grate. He saw their furious reflections in the windowpane and felt a terrible dread.

"You will go today." Mother Vincent stood up; the others took their cue and did the same. "You need bring nothing with you. These good people will provide you with a bed and food. Your rosary beads are the only thing you'll need." The nun rustled her way from behind the desk and came to him. He was at eye level with the cord around her waist, and stared at it now, seeing the fat weave of the heavy fibers. "I sincerely hope they are in your pocket."

"Yes, Sister." The boy reached into the long pocket of his pants and produced the blue plastic rosary. He held them out in a trembling hand.

"Good. Very well. You may put your cap on now."

The boy obeyed, as Amos and Constance Fairley drew closer to him. He was seized with apprehension, and wanted to bolt from the room.

"And remember, boy," Keaney said, an admonishing finger raised, "if you misbehave you will be punished as my brother and sister see fit. You will be in *their* care so you will obey *their* rules.

"Yes, sir."

At the rear of the orphanage stood a dray horse and an orange-painted, four-wheeled cart. Amos Fairley pushed the boy roughly toward it. Eighty-Six scrambled up into the back, onto moldy straw which reeked of manure and dead things, his hands feeling for a dry place to sit.

Fairley climbed onto the bench-seat at the front and took the reins, his wife clambering up beside him. When they were settled, the horse, as if obeying an unspoken command, turned in a trotting semicircle and cantered out through the tall, heavy gates.

Eighty-Six sat with his back to his temporary guardians, his small hands clutching the dirt-encrusted tailboard as the cart flung him about. A sinking sun sent ruby and ocher splashes across the sky, plating the many-windowed orphanage in a golden light. He kept his eyes fixed on the mighty, granite structure until it dwindled out of sight. He was being freed from prison for a while, but he did not feel relieved at the prospect. Anyone connected with Master Keaney made the storm clouds gather and the hounds growl in warning.

For now, however, he had the freedom of the journey. Like the rattling bus, the cart afforded him a little interlude of joy. He hoped the jaunt would be a long one as he waited for the grim-walled city to be replaced by the rolling fields of the countryside, when he could see again the grazing animals he loved so well. He did not know what lay at journey's end, but for now at least, he could dream.

Chapter twenty-one

Jamie woke from a deep sleep into the sapphire-and-almond ambience of his Ocean Spray bedroom. For a moment or two he thought he was dreaming. There was no damp patch on the ceiling he was staring up at, and no complaints of animals demanding to be fed. From beyond the open window he could hear the languid wash of waves and the razoring cries of seagulls.

He raised himself up on his elbows, suddenly remembering where he was. Dr. Brewster was certainly correct. The Ocean Spray was indeed a fine place. Jamie hardly knew what to look at first. His eyes journeyed about the room, taking it all in: from the maple dressing table with its shell mirror, the matching built-in closet, the umbrella palm in the corner, the fringed standard lamps, the muslin drapes, the lush carpet and—the crowning centerpoint, which he now gazed up at with awe and wonder—a cut-glass chandelier.

He looked down at the white sheets and ran a hand over the shiny satin counterpane. He had never slept in such a bed before, wondered how a body could get sheets as white as that. His shirt, lying now over the armchair by the bed, was definitely not white but a smoky yellow by comparison.

The china clock on the locker read 8:15; even the clock was like nothing Jamie had seen before. He took it and examined it closely. A label on the back read: *Aynsley. Fine Bone China. Handmade in England.* He replaced it very carefully, anxious he might break it and then would probably have to pay for it. Since he was paying the price of a lambing sheep for the privilege of staying at the luxurious Ocean Spray, he could incur no more unnecessary expenditure.

He decided to get up and see about breakfast, the sunlit room telling him that it was too good a day for a man to be lying in his bed, even if he was on vacation. It was sinful, so it was.

Jamie dressed himself with care in front of the cheval mirror provided by Gladys Millman. As usual, he left his hair until last, and arranged it across his crown with a considered hand and a copious scoop of Brylcreem. While returning the jar to his shopping bag, he noticed the bottle of Blue Adonis aftershave. Maybe a wee drop of that too, thought Jamie. Given the day that was in it, he might as well.

He unscrewed the cap. It smelled a bit strong, but Jamie, not being a connoisseur of men's toiletries, was not to know that any scent left sitting in direct sunlight with the cap not properly secured, would go off in a matter of weeks. Mick's aftershave had been sitting idle for the best part of a year. Jamie poured a liberal puddle of rank Adonis into his palm and slapped it about his face.

The spacious, high-ceilinged dining room had received most of its quota of breakfast guests by half-past eight. All except Mr. McCloone, Gladys noted. She allowed her jacquard cuff to fall back over the delicate timepiece on her right wrist—for some reason, watches never worked on the left—and surveyed the guests.

There was Mr. Henderson, the solicitor, and his wife Judith (*such* lovely people). The Bradley-Carrs (both doctors) and their children, Minnie and Daisy (terribly respectable and such polite little girls). Mr. Cosgrove Murphy (retired judge) and his wife Hyacinth (oh, such a grand couple!). Elizabeth and Lydia (Why was Elizabeth refusing the specially prepared sage-and-onion sausages? What a costly waste. She would not be served them again.).

But besides Mr. McCloone, there was someone else missing. She went to the desk by the door and checked the book. Yes, Miss Doris Crink and her sister Mildred—from Tailorstown *as well*, she noted; same place as the farmer. She made a mental note to ask dear Humphrey to try and refer his more respectable patients in the future; the Crinks with their polyester frocks and plastic purses, and McCloone in that hideous suit, lowered the tone *ever so*. Put simply, they were bad for business. Standards had to be maintained.

She had earmarked two tables for the undesirables at the more remote perimeters of the room. Mr. McCloone's table was in a corner by the continually swinging kitchen doors. The Misses Crink were seated within the curvature of the bay window, safely obscured from view by what Gladys referred to as her "jardinière" of towering pampas grass.

Gladys had instructed Sinéad early on to substitute the creamery butter curls and homemade marmalade on both tables with the cheaper, shop-bought alternatives and she was happy to see as she checked both tables that her instructions had been carried out to the letter.

As Gladys was engaged in her little tour of inspection, she noted a sudden hush coming over the room; tinkling teaspoons, clinking china and murmuring voices fell silent. Some of the ladies pressed a discreet napkin to their noses. She turned slowly to investigate and saw, with a tiny spasm of alarm, that Mr. McCloone had entered and was making his way across the room. A cloud of rancid scent seemed to be accompanying him. And why was he wearing those ghastly curl-toed slippers in broad daylight?

Unbeknown to Jamie, with every step he took he was releasing sour wafts of Blue Adonis into the room. Gladys held a protective forefinger to her nostrils.

"Mr. McCloone! Good morning." She faked a smile, held her breath and steered him to the table by the kitchen door. "You had a good night, I trust?"

"The best night's sleep I ever had, Mrs. Milkman; the best."

"Why's that man wearing those funny shoes, Mummy?" Minnie Bradley-Carr had squirmed her frilly bottom down out of her chair and was standing, pointing down at Jamie's feet.

"That's enough now, Minnie!" her doctor-parent said in a warning tone. "Come back here this instant."

Jamie pulled out his own chair and settled himself.

"I expect it'll be the full Ulster, Mr. McCloone?" Gladys handed him the menu, standing well in front of him to obstruct the view of her audience, while taking a series of shallow breaths, lest she keel over with the odor.

"Oh, you mean the fry-up. Well d'you know I'd love the fry-up, and I'm sure, Mrs. Milkman, your fry-ups are powerful good. But I'm on a diet, so I am, because the doctor tells me I have to lose a bit and—"

"Quite so, Mr. McCloone." Gladys said the words a bit too loudly and could hear another of those curtain-up lulls descend on the room. "Cereal and toast?" she asked, rather more calmly.

"No, just the tea and the toast will be grand."

Gladys clicked her fingers at Sinéad, who had just emerged from the kitchen, balancing three Ulster Fries, the face roasted off her from standing over the furnace-like stove.

"Can you see to this gentleman, Sinéad, please?"

"Yes, Miss Gladys."

Gladys sped from the room, wishing for a headache powder and some fresh air. Sinéad served the fry-ups to the doctors and the judge, and took Jamie's order. On the opposite side of the room, Elizabeth and Lydia Devine were watching Jamie with interest.

"God, she's come down a bit, letting in riffraff like him." Mrs. Devine held up a sliver of potato bread and examined it closely before committing it to her mouth. "She must be desperate."

"Be quiet, Mother!" Lydia scolded in a cautious whisper. "The man will hear you."

"What's he doing with that napkin?"

"*Stop* it, Mother, *please!*"

Jamie was studying the starched, linen napkin, folded as it was in the shape of the Matterhorn peak, and wondering what on earth it was for. Maybe it's a handkerchief, he thought. But then, why would a body be wanting to sneeze before their breakfast?

He looked about the room to see if anyone else had a big handkerchief like his. He saw, to his surprise, that at least two had been placed on each of the unoccupied tables, and that the guests at the remaining tables were *wearing* theirs. One man had his tucked into his waistband, the woman beside him had one on her lap and another man had his tucked into the collar of his shirt.

So it was a bib for an adult then. Lordy me! He followed the last man's example, picked up his own and wedged a corner of it into his collar.

"GOD, HOW ARE YOU, JAMIE! NEVER THOUGHT I'D SEE YOU HERE."

Jamie jumped, so loud and unexpected was the woman's voice above him. He looked up from his napkin to see Doris Crink standing over him.

"God, is it you, Doris?" He half rose out off the chair in an effort at gallantry.

"NOW, DON'T STIR YOURSELF, JAMIE." Doris pulled out the chair next to him and sat down, transferring her beige patent purse to her knee. Jamie wondered why she was shouting so much, but didn't like to ask.

"I'LL SIT HERE A WEE MINUTE FOR A CHAT. MILDRED'S UP THERE WAITIN' ON ME, SO SHE IS."

Jamie turned and raised a hand to Mildred. She was peering out from behind a sheaf of pampas grass, like a botanist in a hothouse. She smiled and waved back.

"GOD, JAMIE, I'VE COME THROUGH A TERRIBLE LOT SINCE I SEEN YOU LAST." Doris fingered a miraculous medal pinned on her lapel.

"I heard that, Doris. It's a wonder you didn't get kilt."

"WHAT'S THAT, JAMIE?" Doris leaned closer. "YOU KNOW, ME EARS ARE AWAY WITH IT SINCE IT HAPPENED, WITH THE SHOCK OF IT."

"A SAY, IT'S A WONDER YOU DIDN'T GET KILT!" Jamie roared, to the astonishment of the room. The Doctors Bradley-Carr decided they were finished, and herded Minnie and Daisy out while the conversation continued at delft-rattling volume.

"Mummy, why's that man with the funny shoes shouting?" Minnie stared in terror at Jamie.

"D'YOU KNOW, JAMIE, HE PUT THE GUN UP TO ME HEAD LIKE THAT." Doris demonstrated by putting two fingers to Jamie's right ear.

"AND DID HE PULL THE TRIGGER, THE BUGGER?" Jamie shouted, getting carried away.

"GOD HELP US, JAMIE, IF HE'D PULLED THE TRIGGER I WOULDN'T BE TALKIN' TO YOU NOW."

"NAW, I SUPPOSE YOU WOULDN'T, RIGHT ENOUGH."

Doris had another loud announcement for the breakfasting guests.

"BUT WHAT I WANTED TO TELL YOU, JAMIE, IS THAT YOUR MONEY'S SAFE. ROSE MCFADDEN SAID YOU WERE A WEE BIT WORRIED, AND THAT'S UNNERSTANDABLE. BECAUSE EVERYBODY NEEDS A WEE BIT OF A NEST EGG UNDER THEM. BUT HE DIDN'T GET HIS DIRTY HANDS ON ANY OF IT! YOU STILL HAVE YOUR THREE THOUSAND, ONE HUNDRED AND TWENTY-NINE POUNDS AN' FIPPENCE, MINUS THE WEE BIT YOU TOOK OUT FOR THIS WEE BREAK."

"THAT'S GOOD TO HEAR, DORIS."

Jamie's face reddened and he touched his right ear.

"GOD, YOU KNOW, I WAS IN PIECES, JAMIE, COULDN'T HEAR A THING WITH THE SHOCK OF IT. SO DR. BREWSTER SENT ME HERE WITH ME EARS."

Doris was surveying Jamie with an appraising eye.

"GOD, JAMIE, YOU LOOK TERRIBLE WELL. THAT'S A VERY GRAND SUIT YOU'VE GOT ON."

"AYE, SO."

There was an embarrassed silence.

"AND I SUPPOSE, JAMIE, YOU'RE HERE WITH YOUR BACK?"

"AYE, SO. DR. BREWSTER DID THE RIGHT THING, DORIS, SO HE DID. THIS IS A GRAND PLACE ALTOGETHER. A NICE QUIET PLACE FOR YOUR EARS!"

At that point, several of the guests were beginning to dis-agree.

The doors to the kitchen swung open yet again and Jamie's tea and toast arrived. Doris got up to go, red-faced from the exertion of having shouted so much, and dizzy too, having inhaled lungfuls of Jamie's overpowering scent.

"RIGHT YE BE, JAMIE. I'LL LET YOU GET ON WITH YOUR TEA." She clutched her purse to her bosom. "AND A VERY FINE LOOKING TEA IT IS TOO, JAMIE!"

"RIGHT YE BE, DORIS. I'LL SEE YOU ABOUT, SO A WILL."

Doris tottered across the room to join her sister.

"GOD, JAMIE CLEANS UP VERY WELL," she declared in a high-pitched whisper, settling herself in her chair. "AND Y'KNOW, HE WAS WEARIN' LOVELY SCENT TOO! BUT HE'S LOST WITHOUT A GOOD WOMAN TO LOOK AFTER HIM, A MAN OF HIS AGE."

"I *know*," said Mildred, drawing in her chin and nodding knowingly. "And hasn't he got all that money sitting in *your* savings account?"

Through the pampas grass, both ladies looked longingly at Jamie, who at that moment was engrossed in the hasty demolition of his tea and toast.

"He doesn't look as if he's got a penny in that getup," said Elizabeth Devine, observing the spectacle with tremendous interest. "With that much money in a savings account, you'd think he could make more of an effort."

Lydia, not wanting to be further embarrassed by her mother's shameless comments, stood up and prepared to go.

"Time for our stroll, Mother."

As they left the dining room, Lydia glanced back at the strange man and discovered, to her surprise, that he was gazing at her. She smiled, but he shyly averted his face. He seems such a lost soul, thought Lydia, as she steered her mother back to the safety of their room.

Chapter twenty-two

Later that same afternoon, Lydia found herself at a loose end. Her mother had just lain down for her usual pre-dinner nap, and sleep was now overtaking her. Lydia would have liked to remain in the bedroom reading, but her mother's snores precluded that.

The alternative was to retire to the drawing room, but that held the risk of encountering Gladys, accepting an unwanted glass of port, and hearing more rhetoric about the various routes to a man's heart.

No, she would simply have to go out, find a nice quiet spot overlooking the beach, sit by herself and perhaps dip into her current novel. Now, first things first: a note for her mother. She wrote that she'd be back in an hour and set the note on the bedside locker. She folded up a plaid rug, placed it in her basket and tucked her Georgette Heyer underneath it.

She checked herself in the mirror and was, for a change, pleased with what she saw. The break from school and the ocean air were doing her good. Her eyes shone and her complexion had a healthy glow. She had taken her aunt's advice and chosen a knee-length cord skirt and chiffon blouse with a lacy jabot, instead of her standard—

and dowdy—shift dress. It was a particular shade of green that definitely suited her. Gladys was right. She resolved to buy more of that color in the future.

"Start living a bit, dear. Yes, perhaps I will," Lydia said to her reflection. Her mother stirred in the bed and she left the room as quickly and as quietly as she could.

The day was pleasantly warm, if slightly overcast, when Lydia stepped out. A fortifying breeze blew in from the Atlantic, as she negotiated the narrow promenade cutting its way round a balcony of rock leading to the beach.

She could see the sand shimmering in the distance, stretched out like a long golden shawl, a draw for the weary traveler and dedicated sunbather alike. She thought, perhaps, that she should walk all the way to it and mingle with the many beach lovers she could see disporting themselves there. But at that moment she simply wished to be alone. As she rounded the next bend she was gratified to see a sun seat. She went to it, arranged her tartan rug and sat down. Carefully she removed the leather bookmark—a Christmas present from a past star pupil, one Susan Peake—from between pages 128 and 129, and settled down to read.

Jamie stood outside the ornate gates of the Ocean Spray in his too-tight suit and spurned footwear, wondering what to do with himself. At half past four it was too early to visit a pub. He ambled down the street, thinking that he might try the movie theater, but when he arrived at the Odeon he saw that the matinee was well underway. A large poster to the right of the doors told him that *Young Frankenstein* had begun at half past two.

He turned left and proceeded down the main thoroughfare. He felt a bit melancholy, for as he passed the stores and cafés, many were all too familiar. He was recalling his last visit with his dear uncle and how happy he'd been. There was Cassidy's Confectioners, its window decked out with colorful boxes and jars of candy. He remembered Mick buying a pack of Marlboros for himself and a quarter of licorice allsorts for him. He decided, for old times' sake, that he would pay homage to his dear uncle's memory by doing the same.

The store was dark and narrow, more a hallway than actual premises. At first Jamie thought there was no one serving. He tapped the bell on the counter, heard a scuffling sound followed by a croaked, "Aye, I'm comin'." He was puzzled; he looked up and down and all about, but could see nobody. The shelves behind the counter were packed with cartons of candy and boxes of chocolate; those boxes nearest the window had suffered so much sunlight that sometimes only a ghostly image of a smiling beauty or a bunch of bleached-out flowers remained on the lids. Jamie thought he might treat himself to a box of chocolates, but changed his mind when he noticed the discoloration. Sure maybe the chocolates would be melted, and then a body would have wasted his money.

He thunked the bell again, and all at once saw a pair of gnarled, hairy hands clasping the counter's edge. Slowly a little man's head came into view. His bushy eyebrows crested wire-rimmed spectacles and his white hair stuck out in great tufts above his ears. He was so bent over that his bristly chin just about grazed the counter.

"A pound beg a them lickerish allsorts and twenty Marlbora, please."

"*What?*" the little man put a hand up to his ear, his face a rictus of puzzlement.

"A POUND BEG A THEM LICKERISH ALLSORTS A SAY," Jamie shouted, "AND TWENTY A THEM MARLBORAS."

It seemed to him as though he'd been shouting for most of the day.

The storekeeper rubbed his chin and nodded. He shuffled over to a crooked ladder and climbed up to the appropriate shelf. Jamie watched him wrestle a large jar of candy into his arms—expecting him to fall under the weight of it—and reverse unsteadily to the floor again.

The weighing and bagging of the licorice allsorts took a lamentable length of time and seemed to tire the little man unduly. He wheezed and coughed, a stubby pencil trembling over a jotter as he totted up the bill. At one stage, Jamie thought that the wee man might faint, and die from the exertion of getting his order, and he, Jamie, might be held responsible for his death. With this thought, he grabbed the candy and the smokes, thanked Mr. Cassidy and left the store quickly.

Three doors down he saw The Snowy Cone, and decided he must pay it a visit in honor of his Aunt Violet. He pushed through the glass-paneled door, and the jangle of a bell heralded his entrance. He could not quite believe that he was standing in the middle of what once had been his dear aunt's front room. He saw a droning ice-cream machine instead of the fireplace, and where the couch had been was a display case of several containers of variously colored ice creams under glass. Around the walls and set on tables were souvenirs and gifts of every description.

Jamie's eyes roved over the fare, taking in the leprechaun clocks, thatched-cottage key rings, shillelagh pens and pencils, items of jewelry *"for him and her,"* shamrock cufflinks, Claddagh rings, Connemara brooches, Celtic crosses with *"Free Silver Chain,"* items for the religiously minded, the crucified Savior on a hill of *"Genuine Irish Moss,"* plaster casts of St. Patrick: in a field with a flock of sheep, wrestling a snake on the ground with his bare hands, kneeling alone on Slemish mountain with his head bowed in prayer. There were items for the home for use and display: seashell baskets, stained-glass angels, Aran scarf gift sets, Irish tartan oven gloves, Irish linen handkerchiefs, a group of farmyard animals (*"damaged in transit"* and *"reduced to clear"*)—a pink hog with a chipped snout at half price, an Alsatian dog with no ears, a cow with three legs and no tail, a row of barbary ducklings being led down a path by a legless mother (*"Leg's behind the counter. Please ask."*)

Little Katie Madden was busy putting her doll Mindy into a ballet costume when she heard the store-bell ring. Her parents had instructed her to keep an eye on things while they were having lunch. She stood Mindy on the windowsill and went to do her duty.

There was a man, dressed in black. He had picked up a damaged duck and was examining it closely.

Jamie heard a child's voice behind him. "Are ye gettin', are ye?"

He turned to see a rather plump child of about ten. She had a round pink face of freckles and her little eyes regarded Jamie from behind pink-rimmed spectacles. Her fluffy blond hair was pulled into high pigtails and secured with two pink furry bunny bobbles. She folded her recently sunkissed arms across her chest; the color of her skin almost matched her pink sleeveless dress.

Jamie set the duck carefully back in its place, embarrassed.

"Ah, well now, aye, wait to we see." He studied a list of prices above her head, then looked down at the row of colored ice creams in the display case. "Which would be the best?"

"The pink's the best," Katie said without hesitation, blinking up hopefully at Jamie.

"Yes, the pink one, please."

She smiled and unfolded her arms. "A poke or a slider?"

Jamie scratched his head in confusion.

"The slider's the best, so it is." Katie was eager to use the big knife which her father had expressly told her not to touch. If anyone wanted a slider she was to call him.

After she'd performed the forbidden task of guillotining the block of ice cream for Jamie's wafer sandwich without being caught or cut, she felt emboldened. She remembered her mother saying that the longer you kept a customer in the shop, the more he might buy.

"D'you want to buy that wee duck?" She pushed her pink glasses up on her little pink nose and smiled at Jamie again. "I've got the wee legs of it in the drawer here."

"No, thank you, I wouldn't have much call for a duck." He saw the child's disappointment. "But y'know, I'd maybe take them oven gloves." He thought of Rose. To the little girl's delight, Jamie also bought a shillelagh lighter for Paddy and a leprechaun clock for himself.

At the close of the transaction Jamie was as happy as little Katie. He left the shop with his bag of gifts and drifted off back down the promenade, toward the beach, licking his pink slider.

During her reading, Lydia had been distracted from time to time by the comings and goings at a small wooden booth farther down the embankment. It was mostly women who seemed to be frequenting it, while their friends or partners waited on a bench outside. She wondered about it, and decided to investigate. She folded the rug, stowed it in the basket together with her novel and headed down the hill.

As she approached the booth, all became clear. She read a garishly painted sign which promised: *Expert Reading's from Madame Calinda. Genuine Romany Clarevoyant. Thirty Year's Experience. As Seen on the TV.*

Lydia was truly curious now. She thought such things had gone out with fire-eaters and two-headed midgets. As she was standing gazing at the sign (the teacher in her, still mentally tut-tutting at the appalling misspelling), she heard a rattle. A woman's head poked through a beaded curtain that hung above the half door.

"You'll be wantin' your fortune told, daughtur."

The woman spoke with a thick southern accent. She looked about sixty, and her appearance was indeed a throwback to an earlier time. She was heavily made up with an absurd soufflé of hennaed hair; a cigarette dangled from a mouth that looked as though a three-year-old had been let loose on it with a red lipstick crayon.

"My fortune?" Lydia hesitated, taken aback by the woman's gaudy appearance. "No, I don't think so."

"Oh, I see great t'ings for yeh, luv." She drew heavily on the cigarette, her bracelets clanking as she took it from her mouth and tapped its ash on the grass. Her metallic nails flashed in the sun. "I'm not expensive and you mightn't get the chance again."

Lydia thought of her father's edict, that *all soothsayers are the devil's handmaidens*, and of Gladys's words: *Start living a little, dear.* With both admonishments in mind and, hoping she wouldn't be seen, she ducked into the booth.

The air in the tiny space was laden with the odor of bacon fat, which a smoking incense stick was vainly trying to dispel. Around the walls hung lengths of chenille curtain and brightly colored scarves. She sat down opposite "Madame Calinda" and spread her hands on the velvet tablecloth.

"Now gimme your t'ree pound, luv, then gimme your hand."

Lydia handed over the notes, and the fortuneteller secreted them in the pocket of a voluminous kaftan.

"Now I'm gonna cross your palm wit' silver."

Madame reached into her large bosom and hauled out an old half-crown. She traced a cross with the coin on Lydia's left hand.

"Far be it from me to be pryin' into yer life, daughtur, but do yeh have a buy in your life right now?" She looked keenly at Lydia.

"Sorry, a what?"

"A buy, a fella, luv." Madame had so much kohl round her eyes, she looked as though she'd just climbed out of a chimney-pot.

"Oh, I see: a 'boy.'" Lydia shook her head. "No, I don't have one."

"Well you're *gonna* have a buy in your life very soon. D'you understan' me, daughtur?"

Lydia nodded.

"Now, I wouldn't be tellin' yeh a word of a loy, but would yeh take a wee drink itself, daughtur?"

"No, not really." Lydia's face reddened.

"Well, you're *gonna* be takin' a wee drink very soon. D'you understan' me, daughtur? And I see yeh at a gatherin', maybe it's a waddin', and you're there wit' a man and he's takin' a wee drink of the creatur too."

"Can you tell me a bit about the man?" Lydia asked, suddenly interested. "Have I met him already?"

"Now, I wouldn't be tellin' yeh a word of a loy, daughtur, but did yeh say there dat yeh had a buy already? Did yeh?"

"No. I haven't got a boy."

"Well, yeh *'aven't* met him already then, but that isn't ta say dat he's not about, if yeh understand me entoirely, daughtur. 'Tis he dat'll be speakin' wit' yeh soon."

Lydia nodded, confused, but decided it was best not to ask any questions at that stage.

"You're a woman dat likes ta dress well. Would I be right about dat, daughtur?" She saw Madame eye her lacy blouse.

"Yes, I suppose."

"Yeh like nice t'ings, and yeh don't mind spendin' a bit. Would I be right about dat, daughtur?"

"Hmm..."

"I see a much older man that passed over. Would it be your father, daughtur?"

Lydia looked at Madame in alarm.

"Truth be told, and I wouldn't be tellin' yeh a word of a loy, but he was shockin' strict with yeh, daughtur. Would I be right about dat? 'Twas he dat was a man of the cloth, was he not? And he passed over on the turd day of the month."

Madame lit another cigarette. Lydia could feel her heart pounding. The clairvoyant continued, her great magenta eyelids cast down as she resumed the study of her palm.

"Now, dis fella or buy that you're gonna meet is a bit rough and ready, but he has a good heart and good hearts is rare in dis world. And he likes a wee drink and a joke and a smoke and a laugh like the rest of us, daughtur, but the two of yeh will be close, whether yeh like it or not—for 'tis he I see in the hand dat you're showin' me daughtur, if yeh understan' me?"

Lydia shifted uneasily.

"Now, I see an older woman here, close to yeh, she is, and she would need ta be takin' t'ings easy, because she worries a lot and worry isn't good when yeh get to a sartin age.

"But apart from dat, dere's nothing, daughtur, dat yeh should be worryin' yourself about...because the future's bright if yeh choose to make it so yourself. D'you understand me, daughtur? And I wouldn't be tellin' yeh a word of a loy, but I wish yeh all the luck and happiness and good t'ings dat's due to yeh, because t'ings haven't been so aisey for yeh, but t'ings are gettin' aisier—'cause dat's what I seen in de hand you're after showin' me."

Madame Calinda took Lydia's hand in her own and squeezed it tight.

"Good luck to yeh, daughtur."

Lydia thanked her and got up. She had never had an experience like it and really didn't know what she was feeling. She had entered the painted booth as a test of courage—for a laugh, really—and had come out again confused and incredulous. How could Madame Calinda have known about her father, her mother? The fortune-teller had held up a mirror that she had no desire to look into.

She retraced her steps back up the hill, saw the sun seat she had vacated and decided she could not sit down there again to read. Something had altered. The experience with the clairvoyant had created a subtle shift in her perception of things, so much so that no matter how much she tried to discount her as a fraud, the accuracy concerning her father, she knew, would return again and again to haunt her.

She hurried along the path, conscious that she probably had stayed out longer than the hour she'd promised her mother in the note. The sun had come out again but there was a distinct chill in the air. She drew her cardigan tighter as she made her way round the bend that led back to the seafront.

It was then that she saw the strange man from the guesthouse again; he was walking toward her. The yellow harem-like shoes were unmistakable. He seemed to be eating something from a bag. Candy perhaps, and as he drew nearer, she saw that his eyes were red, perhaps from the wind or…Lydia had the distinct impression that he'd been weeping. All at once she felt an enormous compassion for him. She smiled and said hello.

He looked at her as if seeing her for the first time, and returned her smile.

"Cold, isn't it?" Lydia managed to say, and it was only then that she noticed the scar.

"Aye, so," he answered, holding his hair down and shoving the bag of candy into his pocket. She was suddenly conscious that she'd caught him off guard. She smiled again and continued on her way. She knew that he stood looking after her as she went.

She was aware also, as she hurried back to the Ocean Spray, that the ancient wound to the man's face bothered her. For the rest of the evening she found herself wondering, from time to time, about the story that surely lay behind it.

Chapter twenty-three

Eighty-Six was rarely allowed inside the big, gray stone house. He was not allowed to sleep there or to eat there, but was kept outside like the farm animals, to work in the fields and sleep in the barn.

Arnold Fairley turned out to be a fat, brutish boy, not much older than himself, but much stronger and taller. When he first met Arnold he thought maybe he could be his friend, but soon learned that, as in the orphanage, friendship on the Fairley farm was as unwelcome as an angel in Hades.

Each morning, Eighty-Six woke up to the crowing of the rooster. His settle bed was in the corner of a shed, separated from the rest by a partition of rusted zinc. The area was used for storing tools and parts of farm machinery. At night there was no light, but that from the moon or the stars. It was perhaps just as well. To have seen their evil faces time and time again, when they came for him, would have been unbearable.

He scrambled out from under the horse blanket, his nightmares still circling him like black ominous birds, their wings beating against any joy that tried to rise. For there was no joy in the boy's life. As the years passed, he knew this to be the terrible truth; as sharp and fierce as the faces of the Fairleys, as hard and immutable as flint.

There was no need to dress because it was often so cold that he was forced to sleep in his clothes.

He knelt by the bedside. He could not escape saying his morning prayers. Mrs. Fairley had placed a picture of the Sacred Heart above the bed. The beseeching face of Jesus looked down on him, a slender finger pointing to his open, crimson heart. Eighty-Six fumbled the blue plastic rosary from his pocket, ran the beads through his cold-stiffened fingers and mumbled the Our Father and a Hail Mary aloud into the echoing depths of the barn.

When he finished, he took his tin bowl and spoon from the shelf beneath the picture and made his way across the yard, through the quickening light of dawn. It had rained in the night. Little rivers coursed over the yard and rows of delicate rain-beads trembled on the greenery. He hated the rain, hated the thought of pulling the mucky tubers from their watery pits, hated the squelching mud and the slippery basket and the rain streeling his face and dribbling down his neck. When it rained, he could never get dry. When it rained, everything slowed and Farmer Fairley got angry.

He waited on the stone step outside the back door, peeping now and then through the amber-lit window of the kitchen. Inside he could see the Fairley family at the breakfast table. Beyond them a fire blazed in the grate. He longed to be inside in the warmth, imagined toasting his fingers at the leaping flames and seeing the vapor rising from his sodden clothes. Like everything in his young life, this was yet another unreachable dream, something held from him by the wretched world of adults, those who stood between him and the child he deserved to be.

Arnold Fairley saw him and stuck out his tongue, then resumed cutting up and gorging on his enormous fry-up, smirking to himself as he ate. Eighty-Six stood and stared, his stomach hollowed out with hunger, his feet and hands bleached blue with cold.

Then he heard the latch lift as the back door was drawn open. Constance Fairley was standing in the doorway, her hand stretched out impatiently for his vessel.

He carried the bowl of porridge back to the shed, under his jacket to shield it from the rain, and sat back on the dirty mattress to eat it. He ate quickly because he did not know when Farmer Fairley would appear and order him out to the field. Often he did not get time to finish the food, and then was accused of refusing to eat "the Lord's good sustenance." Mrs. Fairley rewarded him for such a wasteful attitude by not giving him breakfast the following morning. It was useless protesting his innocence because he'd get beaten for his insolence instead. One way or another, the Fairleys would find a reason to beat him.

When things were slack on the farm, or if Farmer Fairley had to go away on business, the mistress would make use of him in the house. This did not happen often, but the boy would pray for the shelter of the warm rooms and just a glimpse of the great hearth fire, even if he never got to sit by it.

He would scrub the floors on his hands and knees, beat the rugs, wash the windows and pound the bed linen in the tin bath at the outdoor pump. All those heavy chores he knew intimately; his identity lay in the dirt others left behind and his salvation lay in cleaning it up.

At night, lying curled up in the settle bed, the rain hammering on the corrugated roof, he prayed that they wouldn't come. He'd lie there, praying and hoping and fitfully sleeping, only to find again and again that he'd awake into the nightmare he'd tried to run from. He'd feel a hand over his mouth, the fetid breath in his face and the pressure of a man's body on top of his.

Some nights it was Fairley, some nights it was his son, and sometimes the two of them brought strangers into the darkened corner with its dead air, where they drank from the same bottle and laughed with the same mouth.

He never knew who the others were, only that their sins against him were the same. The only thing he clung to was the relief he felt when it was over. Then he would cry and wait for daylight to render clear the image of Christ's face—the holy picture above his bed, the only witness to his suffering and their terrible, evil crimes.

Chapter twenty-four

The Farmhouse
Duntybutt
Tailorstown

Dear Miss Devine,

I was truly honnered to receive your reply to my letter and to learn more about yourself. I too think that to be honest is a good way to be going on, because when a body is not them things can become mixed up, so they can?

So I will be honest with the answers I give here now to your questions. It is a good thing we are at a kind of an age, because maybe we could understand things better that maybe a younger person would not be known about.

It is also a good job that we do not live so far from each other, because since I've only got a bicycle them the distance in meeting you would not be a problem so it wouldn't. I do have a good friend who gives me a lift places so maybe if the distance was longer then it still wouldn't be a problem for me if you know what I mean.

So you are a school teacher. I think this must be a grand job and hard too to have to be doing with the young ones that are going nowadays. But you say you enjoy it and that's the main thing.

You asked me what kind of books I like reading and I have to say I like the Cawntry and Western novels partickarly. I have read Riders of The Purple Sage by Zane Gray and The Viginian by Owen Wister most recent and most enjoyed them.

You also asked what kind of things I like to cook and I can say that I like to bake the buns, especially Rock buns and Jam tarts. The aspect of the culunary process I like most is the cooking of them and seeing them coming out of the oven.

I like Andy Williams also but I do not know the songs of James Last, but he must be good too because you are a singer of the hymns yourself so you would know about the singing and such like.

Well this is all I can think of to say to you now Miss Devine. I think we can meet soon if you like. If you write back and tell me the time and place I will be there and the sooner the better I think for none of us is getting no younger and time is going on.

I eagerly await your reply.
Yours sincerely
James Kevin Barry Michael McCloone

P.S. Thank you for saying my writing was nice.

Lydia, at home again in Elmwood, returned the letter to the envelope and smiled to herself. Mr. McCloone did not sound like the sharpest knife in the block, but there was something endearing about the honesty of his reply.

She had already sent him a short answer—acknowledging the urgency of that final statement, "none of us is getting no younger and time is going on"—and had arranged to meet him in two weeks' time. Although, if she were being honest, she did not envision him as a suitable candidate for her purposes, she felt that she owed him a meeting at least.

Her experience with Frank Xavier McPrunty had colored her judgment, from a bright, sunny yellow toward a dull, ominous brown. Meeting a partner in that way was probably not a good idea. But at the same time, she appreciated the folly of judging future encounters in the light of that one huge disappointment. Yes, she would meet Mr. McCloone out of curiosity, if nothing else. And she would commandeer Daphne's services as chaperone once more.

The clock on her bedside locker told her that it had just gone 7.15, still too early to get up. She lay back on the pillows, delighting in the comfort and familiarity of her own bed and surroundings. They had returned from their week in Portaluce three days earlier, and Lydia was beginning to feel that another holiday was probably in order—to help her recover from the effects of her most recent one.

The Ocean Spray was indeed a fine establishment, but despite its opulence and grandeur there was something distinctly clinical about the whole place. One simply did not feel at home there. Perhaps it was Auntie Gladys—in fact, she knew for certain it was

Auntie Gladys. Places, of themselves, were rarely at fault, but rather the people who inhabited them.

Dear Gladys—even though she loved her dearly, Lydia was conscious of the immense chasm that existed between them. There seemed to be no common ground on which they could meet and really get to know one another.

Gladys inhabited a transient world of high fashion, cocktail parties and gentlemen, while she, Lydia, moved in the more sober world of books and duty and doing the right thing. It was plain to see that, of the two, the older woman was having more fun. She had taken the art of "living a little" to extraordinary heights, and deep down Lydia knew that she wanted to "live a little" like that as well.

While in the kitchen preparing her mother's breakfast, she pondered her situation more deeply. What would happen if she suddenly decided to collapse the walls of her tight little world and indeed "live a little?"

As she slipped an egg into the bubbling saucepan and inverted Lettie McClean's egg timer, Lydia decided no drastic changes were possible while her mother was still alive. Who would carry out those little humdrum, but necessary, tasks if she, Lydia, were not around? Who would help her to dress, fetch her magazines, tend to her when ill, ferry her to her appointments, answer her queries, listen to endless eulogies about her dear dead father?

She sat down thoughtfully to butter the toast, aware that *this* daughter was indeed the indispensable rock which her mother leaned on, and looked to for her very survival and support. But what if the rock were to suddenly roll away and slip into the full torrent of life? What might happen then?

These questions gnawed at Lydia from time to time. But lately there'd been a change. And she did not know why—perhaps it was the act of placing her ad in the newspaper, her Aunt's urging, or indeed the fortuneteller's predictions—but it was only now that she felt able to confront such issues head on and analyze what they meant.

How did other women like her mother fare, she wondered; those childless ones—childless, or indeed widows, those whose sons and daughters had married early and flown the nest? Those who had no one to tend to them. She speculated that such women had superior reserves of strength. They'd had to learn the harsher lessons of life. Such courage and independence had sprung from circumstances not necessarily of their choosing, but through such experiences they understood that to be bound by another's needs and wishes was perhaps, in essence, a far more fearful state than being on one's own.

Her mother and aunt had lost their parents in a car accident, when Gladys was still a teenager, and this tragic occurrence had forced the orphaned daughters to grow up very quickly. They did what they felt was all they could do at that tragic, vulnerable time: They had married the first men who came along, finding and securing substitutes for their dead protectors in the raw, harsh world they had so suddenly been thrust into.

Elizabeth had unfortunately met a man who would hold her back from exploring that world and, as a result, such fears of the unknown, such restriction, had been passed on to Lydia. Gladys, on the other hand, had married light-hearted and easygoing Freddie.

Lydia remembered his round, laughing face and his eagerness to play games with her when she was a child. He was so unlike her father: a free, cheerful spirit who encouraged gaiety and enjoyment, scattering great handfuls of it wherever he went.

How interesting, she mused, that we pick up and repeat the qualities of those closest to us, like walking reflections, whether they be good for us or not. But, thought Lydia, our freedom lies in being aware of this very fact and in shattering those illusions that do not suit us.

She considered the toast, gone cold now because of her musings, and decided it would do. Her mother only ever nibbled a corner of it anyway.

She mounted the stairs with the laden tray and went quietly into the bedroom. She could barely make out the shapes of the furniture in the curtained darkness, but no matter. She knew the geography of the room so well that locating the bureau by the window where she normally placed the tray presented no difficulty.

"Good morning, Mother!" she trilled, throwing open the heavy drapes. "Wakey, wakey."

There was no movement or answer from the bed.

Unusual.

Lydia frowned, then felt panic rising. She ran over and pulled back the covers.

"Oh my God, no!"

The old lady's face was a deathly green. Lydia gasped.

"Oh, please, God, *please*, I'm sorry for all those thoughts I had just now." She began to weep. "I didn't mean any of them. Please, God, please don't let my dear mother…" She could not finish the sentence, dared not say the word, lest its very utterance turn the situation into unconscionable fact.

She put out a trembling hand to her mother's throat and felt for a pulse. The skin was warm. She gasped with relief; there was a weak, throbbing beat.

"Oh, thank *God*. Thank God." She replaced the covers and dashed downstairs to the telephone in the hallway.

The receptionist's voice was sharp and businesslike. "Good morning. Dr. Lewis's office."

"Oh please! This is Lydia Devine." She started to cry again.

"Yes, now calm down. What seems to be the trouble?" There was little sympathy in the woman's tone.

"It's my mother," Lydia managed to say through her tears. "She's taken a turn. I think she's perhaps…" She broke down again.

"Is she breathing?"

"Yes, just barely."

"Right. Very well. Stay by her side. Continue talking to her. The doctor will be with you right away." She hung up.

The dial tone droned in Lydia's trembling hand. She slumped against the wall and let the receiver fall back into its cradle.

The delay between the phone call and the arrival of the doctor seemed interminable, as Lydia tried to absorb the shocking reality of what had happened.

She sat by the bedside, her mother's hand in her own, and tried to speak through her tears. Elizabeth's eyes were closed, her breathing was so shallow it seemed as though she were hovering in some kind of otherworldly realm, subject only to its alien rules and laws.

When the doorbell finally rang, she was so locked inside the darkness of her own grief that she barely registered the sound. The hollow, insistent ringing sent tremors through the house. Finally Lydia recognized it for what it was and the reason for its urgency. She hurried down the stairs. A stranger stood on the step.

"I'm Dr. O'Connor. I'm covering for Dr. Lewis." He held out a hand.

Lydia found herself staring at a tallish, terribly thin man with a lugubrious yet handsome face. It was the kind of face which had no doubt acquired its grimness through having to deal with the sick and infirm; a face used to delivering bad news and sad prognoses, and occasionally an alert to impending death.

"I'm Lydia," she said self-consciously. "Lydia Devine. My mother's upstairs."

He exuded a marked air of authority and professionalism, and mounted the stairs with a straight-backed, measured grace.

"What's her name?" he asked, bending over the bed.

"Elizabeth." Lydia stood on the other side, her hands pressed together, staring down fixedly at her mother. "Will she be all right?"

He didn't answer, but instead took a stethoscope from his bag and spent several seconds checking her pulse rate and heart, his eyes shifting between the patient and his wristwatch. He straightened, satisfied, and returned the stethoscope to the bag.

"How has she been lately?"

"Tired. We'd just got back from a week's holiday, and I noticed she was sleeping a lot and eating very little." The doctor kept his eyes on her as she spoke. Lydia took a handkerchief from her sleeve and mopped a tear, conscious of how awful she must look. It is odd, she thought idly as though another were monitoring her thought processes, that we care about appearances at the most inappropriate of times. "Sometimes she complained about being dizzy."

"I see. We'll have to get her to the hospital right away." He lifted his bag and made for the door. "I'll need to ring an ambulance."

He dialed the number from memory, said a few brusque words, hung up and turned to her.

"The ambulance will be here in fifteen minutes."

Lydia started to cry again. "She's going to die, isn't she?"

He laid a hand gently on her arm. His sensitive manner was strength-giving, at odds with his severe appearance.

"Now, nobody's going to die," he said softly. "You need to sit down, Mrs. Devine."

"Miss," she corrected him—and immediately wondered if she'd sounded too forward.

They went into the drawing room. He sat down in the armchair; Lydia chose the sofa.

"Your mother's had a stroke. The next forty-eight hours are critical in that respect."

"You mean she could die?"

She searched his face, waiting to hear the worst. He was wearing a crumpled navy-blue suit. She noticed the careless knot in his gray tie, and the creased shirt. No woman to check those things obviously, she thought—and was at once ashamed to be thinking such frivolous thoughts at such a dramatic juncture. She could feel her face growing hot.

"She *could* die, but it's too early to say." He sat forward. "My mother had something like it several years ago, but she pulled through."

Lydia brightened. "So she's still living?"

"Sadly, no. She died of a heart attack last year." Lydia stared at him. She thought he might be in his early forties. "My mother was eighty-two," he said. "Parents get old; they die. We have to face these things."

She thought him very direct and cold. He seemed to be preparing her for the worst. How could he be so dispassionate? A part of her, though, was conceding that such clinical detachment came with being a doctor; one couldn't become too emotionally involved or one's work would suffer. She decided nevertheless that she did not like Dr. O'Connor. He must have read something of this in her face; he examined his hands.

"Oh, I am sorry," she said. "About *your* mother."

"Thank you," he smiled, "but such is life." He turned to look out the window, then at his watch. "They're here. Ten minutes. Very good!" He stood up as the ambulance pulled into the driveway.

"Perhaps you should get a coat," he said. "You can travel in the back."

Three hours later Lydia found herself in the hospital waiting room, a large, cheerless place with vinyl plastic seating. A coffee table in the middle of the room was littered with scruffy, out-of-date magazines. A television, high up in one corner, was tuned to the katzenjammer of an ultra-violent children's cartoon.

Several people had come and gone in the time Lydia waited there, but she had scarcely been aware of them. She sat with her hands thrust in the pockets of her jacket, staring down at the floor. In her mind her mother was already dead, and she knew in those moments that things would never be the same again.

She was so glad that they'd had the little holiday with Gladys. How could she have known it would be their last? A tear rolled down her cheek and fell onto her blouse. She followed its blurred path, then shut her eyes tight against the prospect of her lonely future. The more she thought of it, the more freely she wept, lost to the reality of the waiting room and the people around her. That was until she felt a small, sticky hand on top of hers. She wiped her tears; a little girl of four or five was gazing at her with wide blue eyes. Lydia smiled and took her small hand in hers.

"What a lovely girl you are! What's your name?"

"Sar...ah." She pushed back her dark fringe and buried a tiny fist in her right eye, rubbing it fiercely.

"That's a lovely name. And where is your mummy, Sarah?"

"She over there." The little girl pointed to a young woman sitting on the far side of the room. Lydia returned her smile.

"You sad," Sarah said almost accusingly and pulled her hand free. Before Lydia had time to answer, she ran to the coffee table, brought back a tattered copy of *National Geographic* and plonked it on her lap.

"Thank you, Sarah."

"Miss Devine?" a voice called out.

Lydia turned in alarm. It was an earnest-looking nurse behind the reception desk.

"Mr. Bennett will see you now. Second door on the left, down the corridor."

Lydia got up, her legs numb from having sat for so long. She bent down to the little girl.

"Bye, bye Sarah. I'll read your magazine when I get back."

The child stood sucking her finger, looking up at her. Lydia patted her head.

"Bah, bah," she heard the little girl cry behind her as she rushed weeping from the room, to face whatever it was the cardiologist was about to tell her.

On her way home in the taxi she felt a little more hopeful. Mr. Bennett had diagnosed something he'd called "atrial fibrillation." He explained that it was common, particularly in old people; that the heart quivers instead of beating effectively, and so causes the blood to clot. One of those blood clots had broken off and lodged in an artery leading to the brain; hence, the stroke.

Her mother was still unconscious and in intensive care. Lydia had been allowed one brief visit; a visit where she could do little more than murmur words of encouragement and love to the comatose patient. She might be there for some time, Lydia learned, depending on how she responded to treatment. It was early days, the cardiologist warned, and he had echoed Dr. O'Connor's ominous assertion concerning the first forty-eight hours.

She had been advised to go home and wait by the phone.

Chapter twenty-five

Had a great time, Rose; a great time altogether."

Jamie was sitting once again in the McFadden kitchen, nursing a mug of tea and eating a marshmallow-and-Rice-Krispie traybake. It was late afternoon and he was waiting for Paddy to drive him into Tailorstown, to help him pick out a suit at Harvey's, Purveyors of Ladies' and Gentlemen's Fashions. Paddy was upstairs, grooming himself in preparation for the expedition.

"It was the grandest place I was ever in," Jamie enthused between mouthfuls.

"I know, Jamie. I've heard it's a grand place."

Rose was in an armchair by the stove, her feet resting on a footstool embroidered with the limestone peak of Mount Errigal. She was sewing a series of furry topaz bobbles onto an orange-and-emerald striped tea cozy, and preparing to give Jamie the benefit of her acres of profound yet confusing wisdom. He knew this because whenever Rose gave forth, she tended to knit vast rugs of thought into patches and clusters, ending up with something that made perfect sense to her but precious little to anyone else.

"God, I'd never seen the like of it, Rose! I was afeard to touch anything in case I tumbled it."

"Aye, that's the thing about being in these grand places. You're kinda uneasy you might fall a clatter and bring a lamp or a vase or a table or whatever down on top a ye."

She fetched another bobble from a crowded basket at her feet and anchored it to the tea cozy with her thumb.

"The sheets on the bed were the whitest I ever seen. As white begod as…" Jamie's eyes roamed about Rose's kitchen. When he failed to locate something of a comparable whiteness he simply said, "as white as the divil, Rose."

"A say, Jamie! She probably uses extra tablets o' that Reckitt's Blue when she's steeping them, like."

"God, is that how it's done?" Jamie said in amazement, looking down at the decidedly gray cuff of his shirt. "And d'you know who a run into at me breakfast one mornin'? Doris and Mildred, no less."

"Get away, Jamie!"

"Aye, Doris couldn't hear right after the robbery, so Dr. Brewster sent her for a week with her ears. And d'you know, Rose, she was lookin' terrible well."

"Now, Jamie, she might look well, but she's got hands for nothin', couldn't boil a-negg or sew on a button if you paid her. And just when I mention eggs, a s'pose you got some great feeds?" Rose was eager to steer Jamie away from the widowed postmistress, who, in her opinion was "used goods" and therefore unsuitable marriage material for an eligible bachelor such as he.

"Feeds, Rose? Oh, the best. But I didn't have the fry-ups in the morning with me diet an' all. But the dinners in the evening, well y'know the pope in Rome probably wouldn't get as good."

"Heavens above. Is that so?" Rose looked up in wonder.

"Aye, we had that thing with the pastry and a sausage stickin' outta the middle of it," he said. "I think it was called a frog-in-a-hole?"

"No, Jamie. That would be toad-in-the-hole."

"The very one, toad-in-the-hole and then that spotty dick, the thing with the raisins like a bread puddin', after it."

He reached for another traybake, the mere memory of Gladys Millman's meals giving him an appetite.

"Lord, Jamie, and was it all baked proper? Because there's them that leave the spotty dick too long in the steamer so that the wee raisins melt."

"Naw, the raisins were all there," Jamie assured her. "You coulda counted the wee brutes, every last one of them, Rose, so you could."

"God-blisses-an-save-us, is that so? And what did you eat it with, Jamie?"

"A spoon."

"No, Jamie. I mean: Did you have it with custard or cornflour? Because there's them that prefer the cornflour with the spotty dick but I like the custard meself." Rose fished another bobble out of the basket.

"Custard, Rose, but you know it was a wee bit wattery, not as good as yours."

"Och, away with you!" She smiled broadly, swelling with the compliment like a balloon on an ether nozzle. "And that's another grand place, Jamie, where you're gonna be meeting your lady. Where was it again?"

Jamie left his mug down on the table and fished in his inside pocket for the letter.

"Wait 'til a see now." He flattened out the page on the table. "It's called the Royal Neptune Hotel. Sounds grand, right enough."

"It is, because me and my Paddy were at a waddin' there of a Brigid Maryann Mulgrew about eight years ago. She got Biddy Maryann for short." Rose was in her stride, prepared to pick up and purl a cable twist of convoluted recollection for the benefit of Jamie's confused ears.

"She was a widda woman, so she was, because her first man, Dinny, fell into a drain one night on his way home from Stutterin' Joe McSweeny's pub and didn't they find him the next mornin' as stiff as a dunkey's hind leg for he'd froze himself to death. Now, Biddy Maryann wasn't much to look at, Jamie, and not only that, but she was terrible untidy. A bit of a lazy clat. The type that would keep a shovelful of dung on the table to keep the flies off the butter, as they say. But she came with a bitta land. So, y'know, when she got married for the second time, it was like a kind of a miracle, so it was, because Dinny had drunk all the land that she'd come with. Now, this new man that she got was a Cellastine Monroe. I can't mind if he was from up the country or down the country. God, y'know, Jamie, he could maybe even a been from across the country." She gripped a strand of topaz wool between her teeth and broke a piece off.

"He was *in* the country, anyway," said Jamie, anxious to haul Rose back to the road that would lead to the Royal Neptune hotel and her opinion thereof.

Rose threw back her head and laughed heartily. "God, that's a good one, Jamie. 'He was in the country,' but what I was gonna—"

"And what did you eat at the Royal Neptune, Rose?"

Rose took a mouthful of tea to help fuel the telling of yet another story on her favorite topic.

"I was just comin' to that, Jamie. I 'member that the dinner was powerful good. We had liver and bacon knuckle and bashed neaps with gravy."

"God-oh!" Jamie reached for another traybake. "Bashed *what?*"

"Neaps, Jamie. They're a mixture of the spud and the turnip. D'you like the turnips, Jamie?"

"Naw, never liked them, Rose." He stared at the floor, shutting his mind on the unpalatable truth of a buried wrong.

"And the puddin' was Irish jig pallalalover, or whatever you call it. But me and my Paddy didn't have that, as I recall. We had the sticky toffee, tipsy Irish whiskey layer pudding with a touch o' mint and crushed nuts. And d'you know, it was beautiful, because you know the secret in a good layer pudding, Jamie?"

Rose stopped to drink more tea, her bosom heaving with excitement.

"Naw, what's that, Rose?" Jamie said into the pause, never having learned the difference between a rhetorical and a genuine question.

"It's the sponge, Jamie."

"Is that so, Lordy-me?" He glanced at his now-empty plate and saw an elephant with pink ears staring back at him from under a slew of crumbs. However, the beast was not allowed to reveal itself for long. Rose was ready with the cake knife.

"Another caramel crispie?" Rose pushed two more cookies onto the elephant's trunk before Jamie had time to look up. "Yes, indeed, Jamie. I always make me own, as any woman worth the nose on her face should be able to do, and I should hope that this lady you're gonna meet knows her shortcrust from her puff and can make a decent Victoria sponge, because if she can't then it means that her mother didn't learn her proper. The first thing I learned my Marion, as soon as she was outta nappies, was how to bake a proper sponge."

Rose and Paddy did not often refer to their daughter. She had disappointed them greatly by marrying an alcoholic carpet-fitter from Muff. It was said that the only time you could depend on Seamus to lay a carpet straight was during the six weeks of Lent, when he gave God the nod and his liver a break.

"And any woman that's not learned proper in the way of bakin' a good sponge," Rose continued, "has not got the basic training in the way of baking, if you unnerstand what I mean, Jamie. And she'll be buyin' Lyons' fingers to make up for it, and anything that comes outta a packet is never the same."

Rose cast off the last stitches of her muddled discourse, satisfied to have had her say. "What time did you say you were meetin' this lady, Jamie?"

Jamie was still wondering what lion's fingers had to do with a sponge cake, but decided not to ask, for fear of sounding stupid. He checked the page again—needlessly, because since receiving Lydia's letter, he had the time, day and date chalked in foot-high letters on the blackboard of his brain.

"Half past three, it says here. Thursday the fourteenth."

"Well, my Paddy'll take you there, Jamie. You couldn't be ridin' your bike in a good new suit. God knows what you'd look like by the time you got there. And if it happened to be rainin'—and I'm not saying it's gonna be rainin', Jamie; far be it from me to be predickin' such a thing—but if it was, God knows what'd be splashin' up from the wheels and ruinin' your shoes and your suit and what else, God-blisses-an-save-us, and you couldn't be appearin' in front of that fine lady and you covered in muck."

She got up to replenish Jamie's mug and shout up the stairs. "What's keepin' you, Paddy? Time's goin' on. We don't want Mr. Harvey to be closed by the time yous get there."

"I'll be down in one wee minute," came Paddy's reply.

She turned. "D'you know, Jamie, God's good, but you shouldn't dance in a wee boat, all-the-same! That's why I'm sayin' that my Paddy'll give you a lift."

"That'd be great, Rose." Jamie shifted in his seat, lifted his cap to air his pate, tugged on his ear and rubbed his chin, wondering how he was going to phrase the next question.

"But y'know Rose…," he began, "I was wonderin'…I was wonderin' if you'd maybe come with me too. I'm gonna be a bit nervous meetin' her for the first time and I think if you were there as well as Paddy it wouldn't be as bad like."

Rose clapped her hands to her flushed face with the excitement of it all. "D'you know Jamie, I'd love to come! That's no bother atall. Me and my Paddy could sit in the lounge and wait on you, like. Mind you, me and my Paddy have passed a lot of watter under the bridge since we were there last, at Biddy Maryann Mulgrew's waddin', so we have, so it would be inter-resting to see if it's got any grander, like."

"Aye, I know what you're sayin' surely," Jamie responded. "It'll be a wee day out for you, Rose. And after it's over we could maybe have a bit of a feed or whatever."

"Good enough."

Rose fitted the finished bobbled tea cozy on a delft teapot and bore it to the mantelshelf. She stood back and admired her handiwork with a sigh of contentment. At that point Jamie heard Paddy's footsteps finally descending the stairs, and he got up to button his jacket in readiness for departure.

Mr. Alphonse Harvey stood behind the long polished counter of his fashion emporium, cracking his knuckles and gazing out the window. He'd been looking out on Tailorstown's main street, and dressing and shoeing its townspeople, for nearly twenty years. The shop had changed little in its ninety-two-year history. Alphonse was proud of his business and its lineage, the respect his family commanded and the community he served.

He was a stern, portly man with a florid complexion, his girth and color earned through many years of rich food, inactivity and a passion for several whiskey-sodas after his late-evening meal.

He was devoted to his business, had a reputation for giving generous discounts, and allowed those customers he supposed "decent" to pay off their purchases in installments.

Things generally ran smoothly in Mr. Harvey's shop. He had two assistants, Miss Mildred Crink and his young son, Thomas. It made him immensely proud that Thomas had needed little coaxing in following him into the family trade. He was turning out to be a dependable and trustworthy successor to his father's crown. Mr. Harvey could go away on business trips, content in the knowledge that his son would have everything under control.

Mildred was also a godsend; rarely sick and forever amenable, she was an essential asset in the Ladieswear and Lingerie departments.

"Good evening, James… Patrick." Mr. Harvey greeted the farmers as they shambled through the door.

Paddy removed his cap and Jamie took his cue.

"How you keepin', Mr. Harvey?" Paddy said.

"Can't complain, Patrick. The weather's fine, business is good and the wife's gone to stay with her sister in Wales for a week. So all in all I would say I'm a happy man." He clapped his hands and grinned, at the same time realizing that his joke would be lost on the pair of them. "Now what can I do for you this fine day?"

"Well, I'm lookin' for a suit." Jamie stood self-consciously, pulling on his ear. "Not too dear, mind you, but a good, decent one all the same."

"Certainly, James. Just follow me and I'll show you what we've got."

He led Jamie and Paddy through a succession of departments—Shoes, Childrenswear, Haberdashery, Ladieswear—that smelled of fine leather and new fabric, to the Menswear section at the back of the shop.

"How are you, Jamie?" trilled Mildred Crink, popping her head from behind a half-dressed mannequin, a bunch of pins in the corner of her mouth.

She was surprised to see him but did her best not to show it. What, she thought, would Jamie McCloone be wanting with a suit? Doris had mentioned that a mysterious package arrived for him the previous week, and when she'd poked a discreet hole in a corner of it, was surprised to see what looked like *hair* protruding. She'd dropped the package in alarm, thinking there might be some sort of small animal inside.

"Not often I see you in here." Mildred took the pins from her mouth. "Hello, Paddy. How's Rose keepin'?"

Jamie and Paddy tried not to look at the naked plastic breasts as they responded to Mildred's query. (Paddy wondered why a mannequin would need breasts; Jamie wondered why a woman would.)

Jamie was glad to let Paddy talk; that way, Miss Crink wouldn't have the opportunity to refer to the Ocean Spray incident. He still carried shameful tatters of her sister's loud pronouncements regarding his savings account. The bad memory clung to him like chewing gum to a schoolboy's sneaker.

He made some noncommittal noises, left Paddy with Mildred, and continued down the store in the wake of Mr. Harvey's herringbone-tweeded back.

"Any particular occasion, James?" Alphonse asked. "Funeral, wedding…?" He paused at a rail of cellophaned garments.

"No, just need something that would take me to Mass of a Sunday and the like," Jamie lied.

"Hmm. Any particular color?"

"Och, the darker the better, I think. Don't want anything too bright." Jamie pulled on his ear again. In the background he could hear Mildred and Paddy blathering at great length. He was glad that he was not part of it.

"Now: size, James. Thirty-eight, forty?"

"God, I wouldn't know, Mr. Harvey. I never bought a suit before." He looked down at himself. "I've lost a bit, so a have, so a wouldn't be too big. But then," he added helpfully, "I wouldn't be too wee either."

"Medium, then perhaps. I thought you looked a bit failed, James. But no harm in that." He slapped his own paunch. "Could do with losing a bit myself. I think it's best that we measure you first, just to be sure."

He whipped out a measuring tape, as a fairground magician would a length of knotted, colored handkerchiefs, and encircled Jamie's chest, waist and hips in three swift, accurate movements.

"Forty-two, I'd say. And price range: What's your limit, James?"

Jamie pondered this question deeply, not knowing what to say. He thought, however, that £30 might be the most he could afford.

"Good. Now let's see what we've got." Mr. Harvey went back to the rail, plucked out three suits—navy blue, brown and black—and stripped back the cellophane.

"Now, James, why don't you just hop into the changing room there and slip into these. See how you go. And don't worry about the price. I promise a good discount."

Just as Jamie was heading behind the curtain, Paddy returned, flushed from his confabulation with Mildred. He raised a hand to Jamie and sat down on a leather chair to await his friend's transformation.

The fitting room was small and Jamie felt like an elephant in a shoebox. His elbows knocked against the walls and he almost fell through the curtain a couple of times as he danced on one leg to get the trousers on. Paddy heard a series of grunts and groans and sighs.

"Are you all right there, Jamie?"

"Aye, be out in a wee minute, Paddy."

After a sweating struggle with each suit and a parade for Mr. Harvey and Paddy's benefit, Jamie could not decide which one he wanted most. All three looked good and all were around the same price. Finally, with Paddy's approval and Mr. Harvey's encouragement (the shopkeeper wanted to get home to his whiskey by the fire and England vs. Pakistan on the box), Jamie opted for the peat-brown one and returned to the changing room to try it one more time.

When he reemerged, his audience voiced their approval, but Jamie frowned, pulled back the flaps of the jacket and looked down at his fly.

"That was a stiff boy to get up, so it was."

"Yes, indeed," said Mr. Harvey, resisting the urge to laugh out loud. "Those zippers are a bit stiff when new, but just give it a good tug to get her going and you're away."

Jamie nodded, then went through a series of gymnastic movements, to test the suit's flexibility and the strength of its seams at armpit and crotch. He stretched out one leg in front of him, then the other.

"Yes, she's a good length in the legs, so she is," he declared.

He squatted down suddenly then shot up again.

"Aye, and she's a roomy boy as well."

Finally he threw his arms high up above his head, then flung them back down again, then up again, like an orangutan performing some kind of bizarre mating ritual.

"Well y'know," he announced from between his raised arms, "she just ketches me a wee bit in the armpits, so she does."

Mr. Harvey was expecting this. He had witnessed virtually every farmer he sold a suit to go through this monkey routine before handing over their money. He was therefore ready with a pithy riposte.

"Yes, James, and if you were planning to hurl a discus or throw a spear in that suit, I'd see your point. But since you are only going to wear it to Mass, where an aptitude for rigorous sport is not a requirement, then there's not much chance of that, now is there?"

He laughed and clapped his hands, hoping that his observation would clinch the deal.

"Yes, I s'ppose you're right," came the slow concession.

There was another hung silence while Jamie buttoned and unbuttoned the jacket, by turns advancing to the mirror then retreating from it in a puddle of indecision.

"I think it looks good and grand now, Jamie," Paddy observed from his chair. "That suit would take you anywhere—Mass or a waddin' or a funeral or whatever."

Mr. Harvey had his eye on the clock. The first innings of the cricket were getting dangerously near. He went to a shelf of boxed shirts, pulled one out and took off the lid with a flourish.

"Sunshine yellow, James! Polyester cotton, crease resistant, perfect. Five pounds, but to you: three. Couldn't do better than that."

Jamie examined the shirt. "Not a bit bright, is it?"

"Nonsense! Bright colors are the whole go in America these days. Brown and yellow go together, like bread and butter, salt and pepper, me and the missus." He laughed and rubbed his palms together, impatient with the realization that he'd have to dangle another carrot pretty swiftly if he were to get rid of the farmers.

"Tell you what, James," he said, proffering another box, "I'll let you have a pair of the latest brown slip-ons to go with the suit for half price."

Jamie mulled over the proposal. He knew that he could not be wearing the mustard yellow pair again because they attracted too much notice. The embarrassing memory of them finally decided him to go for the whole lot. Mr. Harvey sighed with relief and the deal was done.

Jamie, for his part, left Mr. Harvey's store completely satisfied. There was no doubt that in ten days' time, a Miss Lydeea Devine would be meeting Mr. James Kevin Barry Michael McCloone looking "like royallity," as Rose had predicted.

Chapter twenty-six

Lydia, like most people, hated hospitals, yet never had cause to be admitted to one. She rarely had a need to visit one either, and felt now that this run of good fortune was being wrested back from her, as though she were receiving some sort of overdue comeuppance.

Her father had died in his sleep, thus ensuring that at a rather late stage in her life she had experienced bereavement, though not the terrible preamble that often accompanies the final decline of the elderly.

Her world for the past four days had become the polished floors and sanitized wards of the County General, with its nurses in starched uniforms and its serious-faced doctors. It was a world of hopeful and anguished beings, held for a time in that most intimidating place, to be either released back to their lives, or expelled to the unimaginable beyond.

She walked the neon-lit corridors where death waited, as cold and harsh as a winter sun, and tried not to dwell on the reality of what she saw and heard: the rapid footfalls on the vinyl flooring; curtains jerked swiftly about a bed, wailing cries at a damage done; the many lives altered forever by the extinguishing of one.

Four days following the stroke, her mother was out of danger. She was removed from Intensive Care and given a small private room in the geriatric wing.

Lydia hardly recognized the woman in the bed: an inert, mute woman with eyes that looked but did not see. She would sit there for long periods, just holding her mother's hand and hoping for a response, but none was forthcoming. The stroke had paralyzed her right side. She had lost the ability to swallow, and was being fed intravenously. The disconnected world in which Lydia had found Elizabeth that fateful morning was still in attendance; the only difference now was that her mother's eyes were open and she had somehow gained the strength to keep on living.

So Lydia's days became a series of vigils which rarely varied in their routine: three hours of afternoon duty followed by three hours in the evening. Every so often during her visits, a nurse would enter and substitute an infusion bottle of medicaments on the drip stand, check the rhythmic graph on the ECG monitor, take the patient's pulse. The daughter would look with hope to the nurse after each ritual, willing her to indicate improvement of some kind, but there never was; there was only a smile from the medical staff and the assurance that the patient was "stable."

After a week, she went in search of the matron. Sister Milligan was a substantial lady in her fifties, whose manner was as clinical and starchy as the uniform she stood in. Her succinct analysis left Lydia in little doubt about the future.

"Your mother is seventy-six, Miss Devine. A full recovery from such a severe stroke at her age is unlikely." There was no give in Sister Milligan. Her businesslike smile said it all.

"The most we can do is keep her comfortable. And pray."

"She's stable, Daphne. That seems to be the best we can hope for."

Lydia stood in the hallway of the silent house, the telephone receiver in hand, trying to come to terms with the loneliness of this unthinkable situation.

Her words reached her friend down the telephone line, and Daphne could hear the fear and resignation in her voice.

"Oh, she'll pull through," Daphne said. "I know she will. Your mother's as strong as an ox."

"No, it's not going to be like that." She could feel her stoicism crumble as her words wobbled out of control.

It was the first time Daphne had heard her friend cry as an adult. "Look, I'll come over and we'll go out," she said. "It'll lift your mind. Give me ten minutes."

Before Lydia had time to protest, she had hung up.

"Now I know you don't drink," Daphne said, holding up a bottle, "but I insist you have a glass of sherry. It'll help calm you, I promise—medicine of the gods."

She smiled widely for her friend's benefit, trying to keep the atmosphere light. "Now, why don't you fetch us a couple of glasses?"

They sat in the chintz sitting room, the room that was so much Elizabeth's room. Her creative hands spoke from the embroidered peacock fire screen, the crocheted antimacassars, the lace doilies under the glass coffee table. Lydia's eyes filled up when she looked on all those things that recalled a happier, fruitful time of keen-eyed attention and nimble-fingered mastery. An art that her mother had perfected over decades had been snatched away so cruelly in one night.

Lydia had the sherry and listened to Daphne's accounts of acquaintances of *her* mother's who were around the same age, and had suffered similar strokes. Each had made a full recovery, and this news cheered her. The dire predictions of the matron were forgotten for the present.

"Oh, I meant to ask you," Daphne said. "Any word back from Mr. McCloone?"

"Oh dear! I'd totally forgotten about him."

"Well, naturally. That's understandable. You unfortunately had more important things to think about."

Lydia got up. "His letter's in the kitchen somewhere. I'll get it."

She was already scanning it as she returned.

"My heavens, it's the day after tomorrow!" She handed the letter to Daphne. "What am I going to do?"

"Well, go of course."

"But I can't. It wouldn't be right with my mother the way she is."

She sank back on the sofa, remembering how carefree she'd been when she met—or rather refused to meet—Mr. Frank Xavier McPrunty, and how so suddenly everything had changed as quickly and dramatically as a pantomime stage set.

Daphne, seeming to read her thoughts, poured her friend another glass of sherry. Lydia protested.

"Go on. It's got no alcohol to speak of." She turned her attention to Mr. McCloone's letter.

The Farmhouse
Duntybutt
Tailorstown

Dear Miss Devine,

I am happy to say that I am very happy to meet you at the Royal Neptune Hotel on Thursday the 14th August at half past three.

I suppose I would need to tell you what I look like because it would be a terrible thing if we missed each other after all this time.

I stand about five foot and seven inches high and I am of slim build and I suppose I look my age because I wouldn't lie about a thing like that because the lie would show on the face I have on me, so what would be the point of it.

I will be wearing a peat brown suit. If I arrive there before you I will sit down at a table and wait for you with a shandy in front of me, but if for some reason I am late I will carry a rolled up copy of the

Mid Ulster Vindicator under my right arm as a sign like.

I am looking forward very much to meeting you Miss Devine and will be counting the days till it happens, because I think we have a lot in common and will get on powerful well together.

Yours most sincerely
James Kevin Barry Michael McCloone.

"Oh dear," Daphne said, "you have to meet him. It would be terrible to let him down." She reached for her sherry glass.

"Daphne, how's it going to look if I'm seen running round the county after a man and my mother the way she is?"

"Now, Lydia, your mother is stable. The meeting will not take more than half an hour and you can visit the hospital afterwards. And believe me, no one could ever accuse you of running round the county after men; that's just a bizarre way to look at things." Daphne swallowed the last of her sherry and set the glass down with an air of finality.

"But I—"

"No, hear me out. The poor man says he's been counting the days, so the least you can do is meet him and tell him about your mother and how things have changed. Tell him that you simply wanted someone to accompany you to a friend's wedding and now you can't go because of your mother's illness."

"But—"

"No 'buts.' You owe Mr. McCloone an explanation at least, which is more than you gave poor old Frank Xavier McPrunty." Daphne pulled a face of mock censure which made Lydia smile in spite of herself.

"Yes, I suppose you're right, when you put it like that."

Daphne grinned. "Course I am. Now, get your coat. I'm taking you out for a nice meal." She raised her hand. "And I won't hear a word of objection."

217

"I can't eat, Daphne."

"Now, now, of course you can eat, and if you really don't wish to, you can watch me."

There seemed to be no getting out of that one.

Chapter twenty-seven

Eighty-Six lay in the cart, drifting in and out of consciousness, as it rumbled through the darkness. He could see the stars and smell the unpleasant reek of the straw, feel the raw, shooting pains in his body as the wheels bounced and shuddered over the gullied ground.

He wished he could pass out again, because then the torment would leave him, and his mind would not keep pulling itself back to the awful source of the "crime" he had committed, and the penalty he had paid.

He remembered the past hours as a patchwork of terrible fragments; the plate he'd been holding smashing on the floor of the Fairley kitchen, the woman lifting the poker from the brass frame, his feet splashing through the mud as he ran from the first blow. He could still hear her demented yells as he fled through the fields. Farmer Fairley was away; Arnold was in school. It was just him and the woman and the screaming gap between them as he made his escape.

With the house well out of sight, he'd found a drain in a far field and clambered down into it, sinking heavily to the knee. There he'd stayed, exiled in the waterlogged land, where the trees and hedges argued fiercely in the lashing of the wind, and he shivered and wept and prayed that nightfall would not come; that *they* would not come. But when the vast unwelcome grayness of the winter sky turned black, they *did* come, as he sensed they would; the flashlights shining in his face, the savage hands reaching down to drag him from the drain.

He shut his eyes tight against the memory as the cart horse plunged on through the darkness and the moon dashed on behind the clouds.

They had dumped him face down in the yard while father, mother and son took turns with the punishment. The farmer used his belt, the mistress used the poker and Arnold used a stick. The son kept his foot on the boy's head throughout, to stifle his screams. He had gagged on the gravel and mud and could still feel it in his nose and mouth. It was all he could remember, but it was enough; that was until he felt the burning pain below his right eye and reached up to feel the crusted, gaping wound on his cheek.

He saw again the leering face of Arnold. When his parents had left the victim to lick his wounds, the son had turned him over, taken a shard of the shattered plate and cut a deep, steady path down his cheek, laughing maniacally all the while.

Abruptly, the horse slowed. Eighty-Six opened his eyes. He could see the shapes of buildings open up on either side, sharpened into focus by the moonlight. He tried to sit up, but the pain of his injuries drove him back down again. Then he saw the rusted gates and knew with relief that he was back "home" again. The horse slowed more and the cart juddered to a halt. He shut his eyes as he was lifted from it and placed on the ground. He lay there, his heart beating fast, his injuries throbbing anew. He gritted his teeth and feigned sleep. He was finished with the awful Fairleys. He was free.

But hands were lifting him and a familiar voice sliced through the darkness.

"Take him to my room."

At that moment, his newfound hopes began to shake and tumble in on him as his whole world darkly swayed.

The voice belonged to Master Keaney.

Outside, snowflakes swerved at the high windows of the laundry room, dying at once on the hot glass. Inside, boiling water spluttered and gushed from the spigots. The water vapor was so dense that each of the thirty or so boys could see no farther than his work partner. Eighty-Six and Eighty-Four stood side by side, pounding and sloshing at the entwined sheets and clothes they had immersed in the vast tub. Down there swirled the habits, soutanes and vestments of the religious; all in congressional twists, in intimacies so frowned upon by the people whose garments they were—the coiling blacks, the snaking greens, the golds. Every stain and mark retreating under the fiercely scrubbing hands of the orphans of sin.

To the left of the tub stood a creel, piled high with soiled linen, and to the right a wooden crate to receive the laundered garments. Each pair of boys worked as a unit. They were so used to the task and so afraid of Sister Mary's stick across their backs that they did not dare slip out of rhythm, not even for one second.

The nun proceeded up and down each row, holding the ashplant weapon behind her back, by turns emerging and disappearing into the mist like a black phantom. She was a lean woman with a grim, angular face, who wore her habit pulled tight around her and secured with the knotted cord of her order.

She rarely spoke; the stick was her voice. If she observed something she disapproved of, she would point to it first and the boys would have to guess what was wrong.

Bitter experience had taught them to decipher the code of the cane. If she indicated the soiled linen in the creel, it meant they were not working fast enough. If she pointed to the contents of the tub, it meant they were not scrubbing hard enough. A frightful whack on the finished washing in the crate meant that they hadn't rinsed the laundry properly and the process would have to be repeated.

Eighty-Six could not risk another beating. He was three days back in the orphanage and his wounds were beginning to heal. Bending over the wash tub was punishment enough. At night in his bed he would lie on his stomach and cry into the night, hoping and praying that his mother would come soon and rescue him. He would picture her in a floral dress, her long hair streaming in the breeze as she ran toward him over a daisy-strewn field.

The longer he waited for her, the more he colored in and added to the picture, filling in the crayon-red mouth, the sweeping brows above her smiling, blue eyes. He could smell her soap-rich scent as she lifted him up, and feel the crisp crackle of the dress as she embraced him. He had never been hugged by anyone, but sometimes from the rattling bus window he had seen women carry children in their arms, and thought that it must be a fine thing to experience: hands that caressed and did not punish.

Eighty-Six and his partner hefted a heavy gray blanket from the tub and fed it through the mighty jaws of the mangle. They had to use both hands and all their strength to turn the stubborn wheels. Halfway through the labor, the boy felt a sharp tap on his shoulder. He stopped and looked up in alarm, wondering what he had done wrong.

"Mother Vincent wishes to see you in her room now." The nun held him with her cold eyes. "Run along, Eighty-Six." She motioned another boy to continue his work.

He knocked on the door of the Reverend Mother's quarters and waited, removing his cap in readiness. He wondered why he was being summoned, and prayed he would not be sent back to the Fairley farm. He was prepared to cry—and beg on his knees if he had to.

A postulant whom he'd never seen before ushered him in. Mother Vincent turned from the window; wordlessly, she directed him to a chair in front of her desk. This was a rare occurrence: being asked to sit in the presence of a nun. She resumed her seat.

The room was bare and chilly, but for the table and two chairs, a gray filing cabinet and a coat stand. On the dun-colored wall above the nun was a portrait of Pope Pius xii. To the left of her, a scarf of snow lay against the windowsill outside.

"Some good news for you, Eighty-Six. I am putting you forward for adoption." She smiled at him—another rare occurrence.

"Is my mammy coming, Sister?" His hopes rose sharply.

"No, she is *not* coming," she snapped, causing his hopes to be dashed as quickly as they had risen. "She dumped you and your sister here in a shopping bag like pieces of rubbish, remember. She's probably dead by now, like your sister." This was also delivered with a smile. It was not the benign smile of the plaster virgin in the chapel, but one set in stone, hard, cold, dangerous. "So you'd best forget all about her."

The boy started to weep.

"Now stop that at once!" She slammed a hand down on the desktop and he stopped immediately.

"They are a farming couple. Good, Catholic people." She consulted a tall register on the desk. "They want a boy who would be good at farm work. And you have proven yourself to be a good, steady worker—but a nuisance at the same time, Eighty-Six." She looked up from the page, fixing him with an eye of unblinking indictment. "I am right about that, am I not?"

"Yes, Sister."

"So I think you've earned the right to be put forward."

"Yes, Sister."

"Less bother for us and more benefit to the people who get you."

"Yes, Sister."

He stared at the muffled, white world beyond the window, and something weighty and substantial settled upon his heart. So many questions hung in the air unanswered. A great wave of sadness broke against him, as he wept and howled inside himself.

The room was silent. From somewhere came the chiming of a clock felling the seconds. He swallowed hard on his grief.

"You will come here again at three o'clock tomorrow. The farmer and his wife will speak to five of you individually."

The boy looked at Mother Vincent, not knowing how to put the question. She read his thoughts and answered for him.

"Oh no, you are not the only one. You will all be interviewed, but only one of you will be chosen."

"This time tomorrow," she said. "If you are chosen, this place will be a memory." She shut the register with an angry slap. "Now, back to work."

Chapter twenty-eight

Jamie had trouble sleeping the night before the meeting with Miss Devine. He lay awake for many restless hours, trying to guess the outcome of this future event, imagining what he would say, what he would do. He still saw Lydia as an icon of female beauty, and hoped he'd be acceptable to a woman of such grace and refinement.

He was confident that in the past weeks he had done everything in his power to improve himself. He'd lost the weight, kitted himself out in a brand-new outfit, and had succeeded in purchasing his mail-order toupee without too much trouble. So appearance-wise he would be fine; personality-wise, well now, that was another matter entirely.

When Rose advised him to just be himself, he had trouble deciding what exactly that meant. Who was he anyway? Jamie did not know. He had never been able to probe his essential nature, or see himself as worthy. His cheerless childhood had robbed him of confidence, faith, trust and all those things that allow a man to build a clear, unblemished image of who he is. As a child he'd incurred so much displeasure. As an adult he was determined never to give offense. So he moved through life on bended knees, skirting the puddles, dodging the blows, falling over himself to please. The forty-one-year-old man felt only able to catch and avenge his early suffering through a series of small victories: eating sweet food when he wanted, letting the hearth-fire burn when the sun burned high, leaving the front door open both day and night.

Winning Lydia, however, would be the ultimate victory. A woman friend would lift the lonely, hopeless refrain of his life into a soaring, thigh-slapping song.

By one o'clock he had completed the farmyard chores and retired indoors for the "robing ceremony." At two o'clock Paddy and Rose would collect him, and the trio would set out on the half-hour journey to the Royal Neptune Hotel. First, however, he needed to wash.

He was reluctant to fill the tin bath by the fire. Too much trouble, and anyway it was only a first meeting and it wasn't as if he was going to be...to be... He couldn't actually visualize the sexual connotations that followed on the heels of this thought. His earlier experiences had sanded his ideas down to the bare rudiments of what he believed the male and the female of the species represented. In Jamie's book men were, for the most part, perverts and predators. Women, on the other hand—those not swathed in black robes and serving their own version of Christ—could be very useful adjuncts to a man's life, in terms of housework and caring. That was enough for him; whatever happened after that was an amorphous and altogether unreachable thing that he felt unable to picture, let alone dwell on.

So, without further hesitation, he headed into the bedroom, stripped, and allowed a damp cloth to have a brief flirtation with his more intimate areas. He then sought out Rose's bag of clean under-wear atop the glass case, and pulled on a set of inner garments.

He eyed the pièce de resistance—his hairpiece—in its box on the tallboy and decided, wisely, that it might be best to tackle the positioning and securing of it before dressing.

He read the instruction leaflet. With a gathering sense of unease, he realized that in order to accommodate the application process, he'd have to trim his comb-over and shave the crown of his head. Very drastic, Jamie thought. He was very attached to his precious strands and wondered whether he should sacrifice most of the only real hair he had for the sake of the toupee.

He checked himself in the broken mirror once more, twisted his head this way and that, picked up his Adolfo Microfilament Poly-urethane "Tite-grip" Extended Wear toupee, and slapped it on.

Hmm.

No doubt about it: from certain angles it looked like a cowpat. But he doused all doubt by reassuring himself that he'd spent a fair bit on it, so it would be a terrible waste to reject it at this stage. And once the adhesive was applied, sure maybe it would look like what he'd been born with.

He struggled for a good twenty minutes with razor, scissors, lengths of toupee tape, and a tube of industrial-strength bonding wear acrylic-based glue. The last seemed to stick, Holy God, to everything within a two-foot radius, but finally Jamie had his sandy-brown tou-pee in place. He raised his head to the mirror to admire his artistry.

"Ah Jezsis!" he exclaimed, eyes wide with shock. He'd inadver-tently attached the instruction leaflet to his head as well.

Part of it stuck out, eave-like, over his forehead, and read, in reversed, bright red letters: *"Get Scalp Protector and Sealer Today. It Works Great."*

Jamie tugged at the leaflet, but soon discovered with an eye-watering acuteness, that he risked scalping himself, so resistant was the glue. Not even a Ukrainian weightlifter would have been a match for it. He located the scissors again and hacked at it as best he could, a confetti of paper falling onto the dresser as he attempted to trim away the offending leaflet, and not the toupee.

But finally it was done and he conceded to the mirror that, even if not exactly handsome, he did look presentable—which was just as good, right enough. He thought that perhaps the toupee sat slightly too high on his head, so he used his hand to try and clap it down a bit. It made little difference. He lathered a generous scoop of Brylcreem on, which seemed to tame it for about a minute, before it sprang back up again with a fresh defiance. His head could indeed have been that of a yellowhammer perking up his crest to impress a mate. In effect, and on consideration, the toupee was just that.

Jamie sighed. Well maybe, he thought, that was because there was still some paper lodged under it, or maybe it was just the shape of his head—and if that was how God had made his head, well there wasn't a lot a body could do about it because that was the way of it, and the end of it, so it was.

With his new hair (quite literally) in place, he turned his attention to dressing himself. First came the sunshine-yellow shirt, followed by the suit itself; then he knotted the red paisley tie into place. Finally he slipped on the shiny loafers. Thus attired, Jamie felt a whole lot better. The suit caressed his body in new ways and made him feel important. He could not view his entire self in the broken mirror, but imagined he looked like an insurance salesman or even, at a push, a lawyer.

With time to spare, he sat down in the armchair to have a smoke. He was beginning to feel nervous. The reality of meeting Miss Devine in a couple of hours' time suddenly hit him. He was no longer in the tattered armchair, but in the playground, being taunted by the school-yard bully. What if she doesn't like you? What if you don't know what to say to her? What if you make a fool of yourself? Because you're gonna make a fool of yourself—you know that, don't you?

Jamie needed a drink to steel himself, but there wasn't any in the house. He saw the Valium bottle on the shelf. He hadn't taken any for a fortnight. He knew he couldn't take one now because he'd be having a couple of drinks with Miss Devine and it wouldn't do to fall asleep in front of her. The last time he'd taken a drink on the heels of a Valium was before a particularly nerve-racking stint in the confessional. Just as he was about to confess his few Venials and that all-important big Mortal, he collapsed against the grille, disappearing from Father Brannigan's view. He came to just as the priest was about to anoint him, believing he'd had a heart attack.

Jamie was in a right dither now. He lit another smoke—then a thought struck him. I only take the Valium to kill the loneliness and the memories because Mick's not here. But now that I'm meetin' Miss Devine I won't need them anymore. He immediately felt better. Just then he heard the rips and roars of the Minor and peered out to see Rose and Paddy cresting the hill beyond the house.

Lydia and Daphne entered the plush lobby of the Royal Neptune Hotel and made their way to the lounge. Beside the entrance doors there was a sign in gold lettering. Lydia paused.

"Oh, I do hope there isn't a wedding here today."

"Doesn't look like it." Daphne put on her glasses and read. "'The Killycock Amateur Artists' and Glamour Photography Club monthly meeting, lounge at four p.m.' No, you're in luck; doesn't sound like a wedding."

"Gosh, that sounds familiar," Lydia said, thoughtful. "It's that name: Killycock. I know it from somewhere."

Daphne checked her watch. "Well, it's nearly a quarter past three. D'you want me to sit with you until he comes or—"

"Not at all, dear. You go off and have your stroll."

Daphne embraced her. "Good luck!" she said warmly. "You'll be fine. Don't look so worried."

Lydia chose a table by the window and settled down to read her copy of *The Times*. She had little enthusiasm for this encounter and, since her mother's untimely illness, looked upon it as more of a chore, rather than the social engagement it was supposed to be.

The lounge was not so busy. The remains of the carvery lunch were being cleared away and she was grateful that the last of the diners were preparing to leave.

At precisely three-thirty Lydia glanced up from the newspaper and saw a trio—two men and a woman—enter through the double doors. She knew immediately that one of the men was Mr. McCloone because he had a copy of what she assumed was the *Mid-Ulster Vindicator* lodged tightly under his arm.

The three stood for a while conversing, and Lydia had a good squint at them without being too noticeable—or so she hoped. But suddenly they all stared down in her direction and she dropped her head back to the newspaper. Her assumption was correct; Mr. McCloone had made his entrance.

When she glanced back up again, the man with the newspaper was approaching her table. She inhaled deeply. He was wearing a brown suit, a yellow shirt—and his face looked terribly familiar.

"You, eh, you…wouldn't be a Miss…a Miss…a Miss Lydeea Devine, would you?"

She got up. "Yes, indeed. And it's 'Lydia.' You must be Mr. McCloone."

"Aye…I mean, yes, that is right. James Kevin Barry Michael McCloone. I am glad to make your acquaintance, Miss Devine."

Lydia saw that he was extremely nervous. He held her hand in a sweaty grip, pumping it vigorously as he spoke. When finally he released her, he raised the same hand to his head as if to remove a cap, but instead pulled at his hair. She could not fail to see his look of dismay, as he quickly put the hand behind his back. His face reddened.

"Glad to meet you too, James," she said with a broad smile, attempting to put him at his ease. "Shall we sit?"

The farmer pulled out the chair opposite and installed himself awkwardly, depositing his rolled-up copy of the *Mid-Ulster Vindicator*. It uncurled itself to reveal the news that Killoran was about to be twinned with the town of Adra on the southern coast of Spain, and that a sizable deputation of local councilors was heading there on a fact-finding mission. The journal was joined on the table by a brown paper bag. Lydia found herself staring at the two items and wondering what to say.

Jamie averted his face, tugged at his ear and stared out the window. The air around him was throbbing with tension. Lydia at once felt sorry for him, and decided that alcohol might be the solution.

"Now, James, what would you like to drink?"

"Oh no, Miss Devine—"

"'Lydia,' please."

"Yes, Lydeea please—sorry I mean—no, let me get it… please."

But Lydia had already summoned a waiter and, after some little hesitation, the gentleman settled on a double whiskey and the lady decided she'd have a sweet sherry.

It was while the young waiter was noting down their order that Lydia noticed that the temperature in the lounge seemed to have soared.

"You haven't got the heating on, I hope?" she said. "Not in *this* weather."

"No, Miss. The air-condition's broke, so it is. I think a crow flew into one of the fans. But there's a man fixing it now." He tore a sheet from his pad and placed it under the ashtray.

Lydia returned her attention to Mr. McCloone. She noticed, for the first time, the deep scar that ran from his right eye down his cheek.

And all at once she recalled the loud guest from the Ocean Spray. She recognized his habit of touching his right ear; the hand that checked his hair. But she thought there was something different about him; his hair was not as she recollected it and his clothes were much better. This man was also a good deal thinner. Perhaps it was a brother.

"Haven't I seen you somewhere before?" she asked.

"No, I don't think so," Jamie lied, as he fiddled with a corner of the newspaper.

Of course *he* remembered *her*; how could he forget their meeting on the promenade?

He remembered her, all right: right down to the lacy blouse, the green skirt, the basket she carried on her right arm; but most of all he remembered the generosity of her smile when she spoke to him that day. He had been sauntering toward the beach, eating his candy and weeping for his lost childhood, when this stranger had acknowledged him and brought him back to the present with her smile.

Oh yes, he remembered Lydia all right. From that day on he'd often thought of the mysterious woman on the footpath. He could not quite believe that he was sitting opposite her now.

"So, how's the farming?"

Jamie was caught off guard by the question, and tried to remember what he'd said in his letter.

"Not so…not so bad atall. Cutting a bit of hay these days but that's about the height of it and then there's…there's…" He was as jittery as Judas at the Last Supper, hoped the drink would arrive soon. "Then there's…"

"The animals?"

"Aye…I mean yes, the animals, but they're to be worked with every day."

Faced with Miss Lydia Devine at last, he was overcome by shyness, and sat trapped inside his forty-one-year-old self. He did not know how to free himself, what to ask her. Then he recalled that she was a teacher.

"So, how's…how's the school?" he blurted out.

"I'm on holiday. For the summer." She wondered how much she should tell this stranger.

"Aye, so. I mean yes. Right." Jamie looked about him, confused, and was glad to see the waiter approach with the drinks.

"But when I'm in school I do like it." Lydia tried to sound relaxed. "It's good to get a holiday all the same. We all need time to ourselves."

Jamie found a ten-pound note in his wallet, and in his eagerness to pay, allowed it to flutter to the floor. In the time it took him to get down and retrieve it from under the table, Lydia had already paid and the waiter had departed.

She watched his head surface above the table again—his face redder now, not only from the added embarrassment, but from the heat as well—clutching the banknote.

"Where's the—?"

"Oh, don't worry, James. I've already got it."

She saw him open his mouth to protest but she held up her glass and heard herself say something she knew she probably should not have said, but, in those moments, she would have done anything to save James further discomfort.

"Cheers, James. To you and me."

Jamie was elated. Miss Devine could not have realized the effect her words had. They could only mean that she accepted him, in spite of his many shortcomings, and he could not quite believe that he'd heard her correctly. The only two women who'd cared for him in his life were his dear Aunt Alice and Rose McFadden.

But this stranger was different. She knew nothing about him apart from the little he'd disclosed in his two letters. He wanted to bow down before her.

Instead he held up his glass and returned her smile.

"Yes, to me and you," he said. "I mean to say: *you* and me, Lydeea."

He swallowed a generous mouthful of whiskey.

"Would you mind if I smoked, Lydeea?"

"Not at all. Go ahead."

She was trying to work up the courage to tell him how her circumstances had changed, but was waiting for the right moment. It would be insensitive to deliver the bad news and simply leave. Lydia somehow appreciated the enormous amount of courage it had taken to get Mr. James Kevin Barry Michael McCloone from the farmhouse in Duntybutt to this table in the Royal Neptune, Lisballymoe.

She would have to make the best of it.

After a few more drafts of whiskey and a few puffs of his cigarette, Jamie felt better. It was, however, still terribly hot and he could feel himself beginning to sweat. He wanted to loosen his tie, but thought that it might not be polite.

"Are your parents still alive?" Lydia asked.

She noted how his expression changed. He looked down at the table.

"No," he said. "Unfortunately they're not still living because they're dead."

"I see." She tried not to smile at the answer. "I'm sorry."

"Well, what I meant to say is that—"

"It's all right, James. I know what you meant."

She expected to be asked the same question and was preparing to lead into her well-rehearsed explanation about her mother, but oddly enough no such query was forthcoming. Instead, James asked something totally at odds with her train of thought.

"I suppose you drive a car, Lydeea."

"Yes, yes I do. And you?" She wondered where this was going.

"No, not the car…just the tractor."

"That's right; you told me that in one of your letters." She looked up the lounge. The couple who had accompanied him were deep in conversation.

"So, you got a lift with your friends."

"I did, aye. That's Rose and Paddy McFadden, me neighbors. Paddy's good about runnin' me places, so he is." The whiskey was loosening Jamie's vowels and flattening his consonants.

There was another pained silence. Jamie tried not to look too much at Lydia, his gaze falling everywhere except her face. He thought her too beautiful and sophisticated and intelligent to be having anything to do with the like of him, and was caught between wanting to make a good impression and not wanting to make a fool of himself. This was very difficult, in that he had virtually no experience of the former and too much experience of the latter. He was uncomfortable; he now knew what the expression "hot under the collar" meant.

"What kind is it?" Jamie did his best to look at Lydia as he asked the question.

"Sorry, what?"

"The wee car you have…what, what breed is it? Er, I mean, I mean to say…the make of it, like?"

"Sorry, James, I was lost there. Must be the sherry." She wished they'd get the air-conditioning sorted out. It was stifling. She made a face. "Oh, it's just a small car: a Fiat eight-fifty."

"Good enough wee car."

Jamie drained his glass and lit another cigarette. He took a puff—only to find, to his astonishment, that he still had the first one going in the ashtray. He stubbed it out immediately, and put a hand up to smooth his hair, changed his mind just as quickly, and laid the hand back down on the table again, staring at it as if it were some kind of offensive weapon.

Meanwhile, Lydia found herself beckoning the waiter again. James McCloone was sending out some strange signals; she felt that more alcohol might help calm him and found herself uncharacteristically ordering another sherry.

"Never took the test meself, never had the time," Jamie was saying. He was still staring down at his hand and throwing the odd glance at his friends' table. "But then Paddy's very obligin' that way."

Farther up the lounge, Mr. and Mrs. Paddy McFadden were installed at a table enjoying a malt whiskey and an orange juice respectively. Paddy sat nodding like a dashboard dog, and puffing on a cigarette while Rose—already hearing wedding bells and the patter of tiny feet—kept up a whispered commentary on developments at the Lonely Hearts table.

"God, they make a lovely couple, don't they, Paddy?"

"Aye, they do indeed."

"Y'know it's as if they were made for one another, because the pair a them have the same noses on them. D'you see that, Paddy?"

"God, now that you say it, and now that I'm lookin' at them, a see what you're sayin' right enough, so a do."

Lydia smiled at Rose and Paddy and Rose rewarded her with a tiny Windsor wave.

"Aye, Paddy's very obligin' that way," Jamie said again, "...and you like...you like the cookin' yourself, Lydeea."

Lydia wasn't terribly sure how driving and cooking went together in James's head, but she assured him that she enjoyed cooking very much.

"I brought you some a them buns I was talking about." He pushed the crumpled bag toward her. "The rock buns."

"How very thoughtful, James!"

"Oh, look Paddy. He's givin' her the wee rock buns."

"A see that, Rose. I'll maybe go up here for another half 'un. D'you want another one a them oranges?"

"Look: Jamie must be talkin' about them, 'cause Lydeea's lookin' into the bag." Rose caught Paddy's arm with the excitement of it all. "D'you see that, Paddy? God, a hope she doesn't ax how he made them 'cause he'll maybe not mind what a tolt him."

"Aye so," said Paddy, eager for the drink and breaking free. "Will ye take another one a them oranges, will ye?" Paddy stood patiently rattling change in his pocket.

Rose continued to gaze down at Jamie and Lydia, her face glowing with pleasure and approbation. All at once she felt a need to celebrate having masterminded this blessed meeting and Jamie's transition from lonely, bachelor farm hand to potential husband-to-be.

"*Rose—*"

"No, Paddy I'll tell you what I'll have," she said, removing an embroidered hankie from her sleeve and mopping her forehead, "I'll have one of them Hervy's Bristle cream sherries, so a will."

Mystery solved, thought Lydia. She closed the bag and smiled back at him. She noticed strange globules of sweat forming on his forehead. "Thank you so much. Did you make them yourself?"

"Aye, so," Jamie lied.

"Really!"

Jamie, emboldened by Lydia's admiration and the booze, thought he'd further impress her by explaining how he made them.

"Oh, they're easy to make, so they are. Ye just throw a bitta flour in a basin and stir it about a bit and…and…" He tried to remember back to Rose's demonstration. "Then ye fire a coupla eggs in and stir that 'bout another wee bit. And after that ye…ye…" Jamie looked up at Rose, thinking to gain inspiration, but all he got was another regal wave, whilst Lydia sat nodding encouragement.

"Aye, so…oh, now I mind. After that ye toss in a fistful of them wee brown boys, can't mind—"

"Sultanas?"

"The very ones! And stir them about for another wee bit and then they're ready to pitch in the oven, and that's them ready." Jamie took another gulp of whiskey, pleased with himself. He felt that by using such aggressive verbs as "throw, fire, pitch, and toss," he would come across as more of an expert in the culinary arts.

"How very interesting!" Lydia smiled, wondering what had become of the sugar, salt and that all-important margarine.

At that moment they were distracted by a commotion by the lounge doors. A group of gentlemen on the wrong side of middle age had entered. All were battling with different stages of hair depletion and had compensated for the loss with beards, mustaches and sideburns. They were casually attired in cravats and sports jackets, and Lydia saw to her consternation that each was carrying a camera. All at once she made the connection with the announcement board in the lobby. The camera club was having its convention here today— the Killycock camera club, the same club of which the dreadful F.X. McPrunty was a member. She looked away quickly, her heart pounding. God grant that Mr. McPrunty was not among them!

Jamie saw the fright on Lydia's face but was at a loss to understand the reason. He studied the gentlemen more closely, but saw nothing out of the ordinary.

"Och, they're just a heap a them...photo...photo-graphers. But I wouldn't think they'd be takin' our pitchers, so I wouldn't."

Lydia smiled and tried to appear calm. She, too, was perspiring now. She wondered whether to make a run for the ladies. When she cast her eyes toward the group again, she was surprised to see a busty young woman in their midst, wearing a miniskirt and wet-look boots. All the gentlemen were buzzing around her like mosquitoes round a tourist.

So that is what is meant by "glamour" photography, thought Lydia.

Later, looking back on all that was to ensue, she could only blame herself. As the young woman flicked her blond tresses about and flirted, Lydia was aware that one of the gents in the party was looking her way. She dared not look his way, for her fears were well and truly founded. She turned her attention back to Jamie.

"Gosh, it's hot in here, James, isn't it?"

"It is a bit warm, right enough."

"D'you mind if I open the window?"

"Oh, sure I'll do that, Lydeea."

He struggled up, almost overturning their drinks, and tried to fumble the window open, while Lydia looked on. It was hopeless.

"I think somebody must a painted it shut, so a do. The bugger won't budge."

He sat down again. "Or it could be one a them newly fangled boys that don't open because maybe somebody would be wantin' to throw hisself outta it."

"Oh, I see," said Lydia, even though she didn't. Since they were on the ground floor she thought it unlikely, not unless a midget wanted to do away with himself. She smiled and sneaked another look at the group.

What she saw confirmed that it was too late for escape. It was too late to run, too late to hide, because right there before her eyes, what she'd feared most was taking shape and trotting toward her. The little bald head atop the furious tortoise face, the mulberry cravat, the camera bouncing on his emblazered belly; all were unmistakable. Frank Xavier McPrunty halted at their table. He looked from Lydia to Jamie, and back again.

"I thought it was you," he said in a fussy little voice. "Well, may I say I think you have a cheek coming in here and cavorting with another man. You should be ashamed of yourself!"

Jamie stared at him and then at Lydia, who was deciding that her best ploy was to deny everything. She gave McPrunty a withering look; the sherry had made her bold.

"I don't know who you are," she said in her best teacher's voice, "but my friend and I are having a quiet drink and I would appreciate it if you left us alone."

"You're a fine one to talk about friendship!"

Lydia saw his wattles wobble hotly above the red cravat. She wasn't going to get rid of him that easily. But Jamie was on his feet, face blazing, temper coming to the boil—he was seizing his chance to be masterful.

"Ye heard what my friend said, didn't ye?" he cried. "If you don't get away from this table I'll hit you a dunder, so a will."

McPrunty's courage seemed to waver under Jamie's threat. He took a step back.

"Yes, and *you're* someone to be talking!" he admonished Jamie. "She's making a fool of you as well."

And with that he turned on his heel and marched back to the group by the bar.

"Did ye know that nosy oul' bastard, did ye?" Jamie eyes were following McPrunty's retreat. Then it dawned on him that his choice of words might have been better considered. "Pardon me, Lydeea, I meant to say—"

But he stopped because Miss Devine had started to laugh. Jamie joined in; he could hardly do otherwise. The strange little man with the camera had broken down the barrier between them.

"Oh look, Paddy, they seem to be gettin' on terrible well now," Rose said, nudging Paddy who'd nearly nodded off; the whiskey, the balmy atmosphere and Rose's ear-numbing blow-by-blow analysis of the romantic proceedings having a soporific effect. "A wonder did that wee man want to take their pitcher 'cause y'know they look terrible well together. *Paddy*, are you listenin' timmie?"

"Aye, maybe he did," said Paddy, blinking back into the reality of the situation, like a dozing hound being roused from its midday nap. "Jamie looks powerful well in that suit...peat brown, a think Mr. Harvey said it was called."

"Now, I'd say it was more of a gravy brown meself. Lord, and doesn't it match his teepee terrible well. Y'know, Paddy I think you should get one a them teepees as well, 'cause you're getting a bit thin on tap, so ye are."

Down at the Lonely Hearts table, the farmer and the teacher were conversing more freely, expanding on their chosen career paths— the one in the farmyard, the other in the classroom—while the temperature in the lounge took on a tropical quality. Jamie talked about his animals and his accordion, and Lydia spoke of her love of books and music.

Gradually, Jamie began to relax, the drink and sultry atmosphere doing their job of smoothing down the more abrasive corners of his fearful self. He could not believe how well he felt in this woman's company and was postponing an urgent need to visit the bathroom in case he missed out on anything. But after an hour he finally excused himself because, besides the need to urinate, he was experiencing a strange crawling sensation on his scalp.

Once inside the toilet, he checked himself in the mirror and wiped away what he imagined were beads of sweat. He was mistaken.

They were beads of glue—toupee glue.

He was startled, but not overly concerned. He ran some water on his fingers and, a few sticky minutes later, all traces of the adhesive had disappeared. He smiled into the mirror, pleased that everything was going so well.

Satisfied, he entered the toilet stall, locked the door and proceeded to urinate, gazing down at the bowl. As he peed merrily, he fell into his old habit, one he had had for as long as he could remember: He would read and memorize the writing on toilet bowls: *Shanks Patent "Unix" Washdown; Royal Doulton "Simplicitas".* . . He knew a half-dozen of the manufacturers' stamps by heart and the same ones seemed to crop up everywhere. He thought about how fortunate he had been in meeting this fine lady at last, and began to spin a fantasy that soon had him in its grip.

He saw himself in a white suit walking up a sun-kissed aisle with Lydia on his arm. He heard the organ music swell as they reached the altar and knelt on the tasseled cushions. He saw himself slip a wedding band onto her finger, then kiss the bride as the music started up again.

The outer door of the lavatory clicked open, bringing Jamie back to the present. He hurriedly finished up—only to discover that his zipper wouldn't budge. He remembered Mr. Harvey's advice: *They're a bit stiff when new, but just give it a good tug to get her going and you're away.* Jamie bent his head lower to examine it, sucked in his belly, squeezed his eyes shut and, with one deft movement, gave a tremendous tug. It solved the problem: He was safely zipped up again.

He discovered, however, that the force needed to free the zipper had had the unfortunate consequence of freeing something else as well.

Jamie felt a lightness, and a refreshingly cool sensation on the crown of his head. He went to flush the toilet, but his eye lit on something strange in the bowl. He crouched down for a better look.

"Ah, *Jesus*, Mary and Joseph!"

His hand flew to the top of his head—and found only a sticky, bare scalp.

"Ah, *Jesus*, Mary and Joseph!" he cried again as he lifted out the sodden, urine-soaked hairpiece, the full implication of the disaster hitting him with the force of a wet carp across the face.

"Jamie, is that you?" The voice came from the other side of the stall.

Jamie held his breath. What if it was the baldy wee bastard with the camera? But he realized then that the baldy wee bastard would not know his name.

"Aye, it's me," he said tentatively. "Who's that?"

"It's Paddy, Jamie."

"Aw Jezsis, Paddy!"

Two stall doors unlocked as one. Paddy stared at his friend, trying to come to terms with a rare sight of a crestfallen Jamie, looking as though he'd had a head-on collision with a child's cut-'n'-paste craft set. His scalp was ridged in adhesive tape and splodges of glue. Incongruously, in amongst it all, just below the crown, Paddy could make out the words *Bonding Times May Vary*, printed in red lettering.

"God oh, what happened, Jamie?" Paddy asked the superfluous question, knowing all too well the answer. Jamie held it in his right hand, and it was dripping urine onto the tiles.

"Jezsis Christ, Paddy, I never expected the like of this!" He looked dejectedly at the sodden hairpiece. "Thought I had it on good an' tight. I pulled away at it in the house, begod, to make sartin, and it wouldn't budge."

But even as he was saying those words, he was suddenly remembering the warning on the little instruction leaflet, the leaflet he'd no more than glanced at. Now, too late, he was recalling lines that read: *Excessive sweating can shorten bonding times. Do not use gel or lotion on this product.*

"Och, we'll give it a wee wash," Paddy said, "and slap it back on ye." He patted Jamie's head. "Sure it's still sticky, so should stay in place right enough."

"But it's gonna be wet!" Jamie wailed. "What am I gonna say to her when she sees me with a soakin' wet head?"

"Leave it to me, Jamie." Paddy took the wig and started to wash it under the tap with soap. "Ye could say you went out for a wee walk and it rained." Paddy was thinking on his feet, something he rarely had cause to do.

"But Paddy, the sun's blazin' down outside and I can hardly say it was rainin' in the toilet."

Jamie stared into the mirror and almost wept, looking as inconsolable and desperate as a convict on his way to the hangman's noose.

"God, it's a terrible thing," he cried. "Me and her were gettin' on powerful well, so we were, and now it's all spoilt."

Paddy was nodding in commiseration while drying off the hairpiece with a towel. He held it up to the light, and was satisfied.

"There ye go now, Jamie. Try that."

Jamie repositioned the toupee as best he could. But the soaking in the urine had had its effect, and this, coupled with the fact that Paddy had not properly rinsed off the soap, had caused the synthetic fibers to shoot up. The wig now resembled an electrocuted water rat.

"That's looks grand now right enough," Paddy observed, but knowing as he said it that he was stretching the truth to screeching point. "Sure it'll take you back to the table for another wee while. Me and Rose can wait as long as ye like, Jamie."

Glumly Jamie studied his reflection. But maybe Paddy was right, he thought; when he turned his head from side to side, it maybe could pass at a push. But only just.

"Och now, is it not fearful bad lookin'?" he asked the mirror, knowing it was, but leaving it to Paddy to reassure him, or not.

"Not a bit of it," Paddy said smoothly. "It looks a wee bit wet, Jamie, but it'll dry with the heat a your head soon enough."

"Well, maybe you're right." Jamie looked long and hard in the mirror. "And how's the rest of me?"

"You look grand, Jamie. Me and Rose were just sayin' we never seen you lookin' as well." He patted Jamie on the back. "And we were just sayin' that you and Miss Devine look very well together. She's a fair, well-lookin' lassie. Ye know, Rose was just sayin' you look like yous were made for each other, for the pair of yous have the same noses, so ye have."

"God, did Rose say that, did she?"

"She did indeed. Now I think that you should go out first, Jamie, because it might look a bit strange the pair of us comin' out at the same time. We've been in here a good bit and you wouldn't want people to be talkin', like."

Jamie nodded.

"You wouldn't want to be keepin' that lady waitin' any longer."

"No, I s'pose you're right, Paddy."

Jamie prepared to go, checked himself in the mirror again, rebuttoned his jacket—but made the mistake of looking down at his feet. The action had the unfortunate consequence of dislodging the wig again. It struck one of his glossy, brown toecaps and slid across the floor like a fleeing rodent.

"Jezsis Christ, Paddy, that's the end of it! It's all up now. Naw, I can't go back out. The bugger just won't stay on."

Paddy stooped to pick it up.

"Now, Jamie," he said gently, "could ye not try? You could keep your head good and steady and not look up nor down, then it'd stay on, like."

"Naw, Paddy, I couldn't risk that."

"Are you...are you sartin now, Jamie?"

"Y'know I'd rather be put up agin a wall and shot, begod, than have me hair fall off in front of her. That's as true as God put breath in me."

Paddy scratched his head, in a quandary. "Aye, I s'pose you're sartin right enough." There would be no dissuading Jamie on this one. His mind was made up.

Both men stood in a muddle of indecision. Then Paddy's eyes lit up.

"I'll tell you what, Jamie. I'll go and ask Rose what we should do."

Jamie brightened.

"That would be the thing, Paddy. Rose'll know what to do. Why didn't we think of it sooner?"

And with that, Paddy left. Jamie stuffed the toupee into his pocket and sat down in one of the toilet stalls. He would await Rose's undoubted wisdom, and her solution to this monumental problem.

Lydia checked her wristwatch. James had gone to the gents some twenty minutes earlier and she was beginning to feel uneasy. The photographers were now settled at several tables in a cordoned-off area, enjoying plates of sandwiches. Every time Lydia looked their way she would catch the menacing flash of McPrunty's bifocals as he looked *her* way. She picked up *The Times* again and pretended to read it.

What on earth, she wondered, had happened to James? She resolved to approach his friends and ask the man to go and check the bathroom.

She folded the paper and went to get up. She saw, however, that it was unnecessary. His friends had disappeared also.

"Hello, Miss Devine!" a voice behind her made her jump. She turned to see a woman holding out a hand. "I'm Jamie's—I mean James's—friend. Rose McFadden's me name."

Lydia remembered. "Oh Rose, yes! How nice to meet you. Has something happened? Is James all right?"

"No, Miss Devine—"

"Call me *Lydia*, please." She looked at her anxiously. "Do please sit down, Rose."

"Thank you, Lydeea, I will indeed!"

Rose installed herself in Jamie's chair and rested her purse on her knee.

She had dressed carefully for this very special occasion. Lydia could not have known it, but the polyester frock Rose wore had been cut on the bias by her expert hands; or that her Aran cardigan—which showed her deftness with the bunny bobble and fisherman's rib—had won first prize in the ladies' knitwear section of the Duntybutt Women's Institute Creative Christmas competition of

1972. Her hair—freshly permed at the Curl Up 'n' Dye salon—was a confection of cinnamon-tinted bubble curls. Her face was freshly dusted with Yardley Almond Surprise. At her wrist a charm bracelet clinked its twenty-three charms—each one honoring another year of a marriage survived.

"Now there's nothing to worry about, Lydeea," she said kindly. "James has just got a wee problem in the toilet which might take a while to put right—if you folly me meaning."

"No, I don't, Rose. Is he ill?" Lydia sat forward. "I have first-aid experience. Perhaps I could help."

Rose was not prepared for this, had promised Jamie that she'd "take care of everything." She had assured him that telling Lydia he had taken ill was the best ploy, but now she saw that Miss Devine was genuinely concerned and wanted to know what exactly was wrong. Rose had to think fast; it was something that she, like her husband, was not used to doing. She therefore said the first thing that came into her head.

"Well y'know, Lydeea, God-blisses-an-save-us, but it's not as serious as that. It's just that he has a problem." She glanced down quickly at her lap, then looked up again and nodded. "Down there."

Lydia continued to stare, perplexed.

"It's a *gentleman's* problem," Rose explained, her voice dropping to a whisper. "Sometimes it takes him an hour, maybe even two."

Lydia didn't know what to say. A silence ensued. Then Rose committed the cardinal sin of all inexperienced liars: She began to crochet a great frill of anecdotal "fact" to make the lie appear more plausible.

"Oh, it runs in the family, Lydeea. His uncle was the very same, if truth be told. And y'know what they say: A leper doesn't change his socks. Now me mother, God rest her soul, was different altogether: runnin' steady one week then the next nothing atall. It was the nerves, I think. She had a nervous dep-position—or whatever it is they say. Was never much of an eater anyway; would peck at things like McGinty's chicken. And y'know, when you don't eat proper it's not good for you, and James—God-save-us—was on a diet, for to meet you, like."

Rose sat back in the armchair, pleased that she'd got the awkward news delivered.

"I'm terribly sorry to hear that, Rose."

"And believe me, Lydeea, James is very sorry that he can't come out just now too." She canted forward again, clutching the purse, as if she were about to divulge the third secret of Fatima. "And he unnerstands that you don't want to be waitin' that long, so he's asked me to ask you—that's if you wouldn't mind—could you give him a phone number if you have one, because he sez he'd like to see you again because you're a real lady, and I can see that meself, Lydeea."

Lydia smiled and reached for her purse. She wrote down her number and tore the page from her diary. Rose folded it and stowed it in her purse.

"Thank you very much indeed, Lydeea. James will be very pleased that you unnerstud his wee problem."

She got up and took Lydia's hand. "And I hope you and James get to know each other better," she said, "because he's a very fine fella with a very kind heart, and there's not too many like him goin' about these days. God, y'know, since you started correspondin' with him, he's been as proud as a cock on a dunghill and as happy as a cat between two houses."

"I'm pleased to hear that, Rose. Thank you for explaining things to me. And I hope we meet again soon."

And with that Rose shot off in the direction of the toilets to impart the good news. Lydia gathered up her things—just as Daphne was coming through the lounge. She went to meet her; Daphne was frowning. She threw confused looks to where her friend had been sitting, noting the vacant table.

"Where's—?"

Lydia grasped her elbow and steered her back the way she had come.

"I'll explain in the car," she said.

"It didn't go well?"

"Yes and no. It was—"

Lydia stopped. Somebody had tapped her shoulder. She turned and caught her breath.

"Now, Miss Devine," said a little bald man, "you know what it feels like to be left in the lurch! Doeth unto others as you would have them doeth unto you. Luke six, verse thirty-one. I am a Christian gentleman myself—which is more than can be said for some!"

Frank Xavier McPrunty straightened his cravat, adjusted his spectacles and marched triumphantly out into the sunshine, leaving both ladies staring after him in astonishment.

Chapter twenty-nine

Daphne drove Lydia to the hospital, listening intently and trying to suppress a giggle as her friend related the strange story of Mr. McCloone. By the time she entered the County General, Lydia believed she had recovered sufficiently from that very odd experience to face the sobering business of her mother's condition.

Three weeks had passed since Elizabeth Devine's admittance, and in that time Lydia had become used to the routine of visiting and sitting by the bed. Although she would not admit it to herself, she felt in her heart that this ritual of vigil-keeping would, somehow, continue for a long time. The hours she sat at the bedside were very precious to her. She quickened her step down the long corridor, regretting that Mr. James McCloone and his mysterious antics had delayed her unduly.

But when she pushed open the door to her mother's room, an unexpected sight met her. The bed was empty. Someone coughed politely, and she turned to find Sister Milligan in the doorway.

"Where is she?" Dread was descending on Lydia. Her hand went to her heart, as if to slow its beating.

"I'm very sorry, Miss Devine. Your mother passed away an hour ago."

"No!" Lydia saw the stern, implacable face. She wanted to scream at the nurse for being so heartless. "She can't have! Why are you saying such a thing, such a callous thing?"

Sister Milligan took her firmly by the arm, well used to dealing with the bafflement of the bereaved, and led her to the armchair.

"We rang you several times but we couldn't reach you."

Lydia went from shocked silence to disbelief, then to despair, as she tried to absorb the stern but sympathetic words. What she'd feared the most had become a reality. The cold, hard fact was hers, and only hers, to deal with. The death of a loved one left the bereaved with no choice, no escape or hiding place—only the searing, raw pain of loss.

She floundered in this newfound knowledge, swaying back and forth, sobbing uncontrollably. The full impact of her dereliction—wasting time in that silly hotel, meeting that silly man—was taking hold of her to a high degree. The whys and reprimands rained down, as a tremendous feeling of guilt swept over her. How could she have been so foolish, so selfish?

And so she wept on and on, the room and the nurse and her whole world dissolving and drifting farther and farther away—an untethered balloon in a vast gray emptiness rising higher and higher. She heard the ambient sounds of the hospital and the world beyond the window, a seemingly random blend of lives being lived, and knew in those fearful, helpless moments that she'd reached a turning point. A point that, no matter how painful, was lit by the knowledge that she would only undergo it once. The loss of a mother is a singular and incomparable event. Such understanding gave relief. But oh so very, very little.

She did not know how long she sat in the vacant room with the indifferent nurse, or at what point she'd blacked out.

All future attempts she'd make to recollect those events—between her mother's death and burial—would remain misted over and obscured, as if seen through sun-thronged glass; blindingly real but never fully recalled or understood. Perhaps it was best that way. She was thankful for the comfort of amnesia.

The Reverend Spencer, her father's much younger successor, conducted the funeral service. He was a tall, thin man who held himself like a length of driftwood, his vestments seeming to weigh as heavily on him as his solemn office.

Lydia and Gladys sat in the front pew, and before them lay Elizabeth—wife, sister, mother—all her earthly titles stilled to that one last image: the mahogany casket.

Around them were disposed Mrs. Devine's elderly friends, spread out and brought together with their memories and tears, singing their hymns in cracked voices, their faces sagging with the knowledge that the time left to them, too, was finite.

At the graveside Lydia and Gladys stood arm in arm, watching the rain splashing down on the casket, their eyes misting with tears as Elizabeth was slowly lowered to her rest.

It was somehow appropriate that the sun did not shine, that the birds did not sing, that what should have been a bright August afternoon had given itself over to a wintry, doom-laden grayness. God himself was in sympathy. Why should the day smile when there was so much sorrow to be borne?

After the funeral, Gladys insisted on remaining for a week with Lydia at Elmwood. Even though her niece would have preferred to have faced the inevitable loneliness of her new situation by herself, and as soon as possible, she knew that to voice her true feelings would be churlish. All attempts by such well-meaning people—Daphne with her invitations to lunch, Beatrice Bohilly's offer to help her dispose of her mother's clothes, the young vicar's words of consolation—made her appreciate that she had real friends and that perhaps the empty space her mother's passing had left behind might well be the door to a less fearful place, where she was free to be herself and not just an adjunct, an accessory. After all, with her mother's death came the death of dependence and the birth of an anxious freedom. Freedom. Was it not what she'd always craved?

"Perhaps you should take time off school, Lily dear."

Gladys sat in the chintz drawing room, in Elizabeth's favorite armchair, a glass of gin and tonic—her nightcap—on the occasional table, within easy reach.

She looked like a voluptuous concubine in a shogun's palace: resplendent in a crimson kimono patterned with copper dragons and golden serpents. On her feet she wore frail mules crested with waving plumes of ostrich feather. Lydia stared down at them now as her aunt spoke.

"Take time off," she said again. "After all, they can get a replacement for a week or two, until you get back on your feet."

"I don't know if that's a good idea. Work would take my mind off things."

Lydia had one week left of her school vacation. She sat twisting a button on her cardigan, the cup of cocoa which Gladys had prepared for her going cold on the coffee table. She was caught between not wanting to appear helpless—in which case Gladys would take it upon herself to remain another week, a scenario she did not want to even imagine—and not wishing to seem ungrateful.

"You could stay a couple of weeks with me," Gladys said. "It would lift your spirits." She put the ebony cigarette holder to her lips and inhaled deeply, then laid it across the ashtray.

"Gladys, you know I couldn't do that. Our holiday with you was the last my mother and I had." She took a hankie from her sleeve as the tears started again. "The Ocean Spray would be too soon and too painful for me."

"Yes, well, I suppose you're right. But you know the sooner you come to terms with these things the better. It doesn't do to mope about. After all, you're a big girl now."

"Am I not allowed to grieve?" Lydia glared, not caring for her aunt's tone.

Gladys shrugged. "Grieve all you like, Lily dear. It won't bring her back." She took up the cigarette again.

"What a heartless thing to say. I know you and Mother didn't see eye to eye, but grief is a natural reaction to the death of someone you love. Where is your sorrow, Gladys? After all, she was your sister."

"My sorrow is my business! And yes, she was a sister in the sense that all she seemed able to do was criticize and try to dominate me. The problem was one of jealousy, I fear. Elizabeth was plain and dull and I was, well, shall we say more sophisticated."

Lydia was shocked. "What a mean, selfish thing to say!"

Gladys tightened the kimono about her, drained the remains of her glass and stubbed out the cigarette. She held Lydia with a contemptuous look.

"I wouldn't be so high and mighty—"

"*Me* high and mighty?"

"You know nothing!" Gladys snapped. "The truth is always difficult. Now that you're alone, you'll have to learn about things the hard way."

"You're cruel."

"And you're naive!" She got up. "I'm going to bed. I have a long journey ahead of me tomorrow."

Lydia looked at her aunt's feet, at the feathered mules and lacquered toenails, and decided she really could not take too seriously anything this woman said.

"I may be naive, Gladys, but at least I act my age."

"Oh, you do that all right—and look where it's got you!" Gladys's bosom rose and fell rapidly under the silk kimono. She would not be reprimanded by this flat-chested little spinster.

Lydia looked up at her, wondering suddenly how this brash, gaudy woman could ever have been her dear mother's sister.

"My mother never liked you and I understand why."

Gladys snorted. "You don't know the half of it!"

She rustled to the door, then turned.

"By the way, a man telephoned for you the other evening. I forgot to mention it. A James Something-or-other. Claimed he met you through a newspaper ad or something equally preposterous."

Lydia could feel herself blush. She decided then and there that she really detested her aunt and was on the verge of ordering her out, but knew that any such move would only serve to compound her guilt.

"I don't know what you're talking about."

"Yes, and that's exactly what I told him. I said that I could not imagine a niece of mine going to such tawdry lengths to find herself a man. So I told him he had the wrong number and to please not bother this house again."

Gladys pulled the door behind her and swept up the stairs, leaving Lydia devastated by the callousness of her timing. There was nothing left for her to do but bury her face in her hands and burst into tears.

The morning of Gladys's departure was strained but cordial. The differences aired the previous evening lay like an open wound between the two women.

Neither of them had any wish to probe or examine why the damage they'd wrought on the other still hurt so much. Apologies were not forthcoming. Time would heal, so they did not refer to their quarrel, deciding that it was best to let things be.

Elizabeth's death had brought a new set of rules into play. Lydia understood that she did not need her aunt to be a player in this new game. She, Lydia, was in control now and would conduct her life on her own terms. She had been answerable to her mother out of duty, but now she was answerable to no one. Aunt Gladys was superfluous; tolerable at the end of a telephone line, which perhaps was enough.

When she kissed her goodbye that morning, she decided that that was how she wanted things to be for the present, and Gladys knew somehow that, for the time being, her comfort and support would not be required.

Lydia turned back to the empty house and shut the front door behind her.

She stood in the hallway until the last notes of Gladys's car had died away. Then silence descended again and the whole house held an air of heavy aftermath, as if she, Lydia, were the only survivor of a nuclear catastrophe. For the first time, she truly understood how it felt to be alone; to lean on her deepest, most meaningful self. The walls of Elmwood would be of little comfort in the days to come.

She stood for a while, mustering strength, then wandered

through her "motherless" home, going from room to room, testing her courage, hoping she'd be strong enough to face the void. She felt as though she had journeyed through a darkened tunnel and had suddenly come upon this strange, bleak place, shaped to the contours of a new absence, but shimmering still with a supernatural presence: her dead mother's presence.

In the living room she struggled with the echoes Elizabeth had left behind: the partially knitted sweater in the tapestry bag, the half-read novel on the windowsill, the television shows ringed in red for what was to be her last evening's viewing.

Lydia wept again as she looked on all these things, and came to understand that grief could not be fought, only lived through. Like some Greek tragedy, it would end at some stage, but only when the gods thought fit.

She sat down in her mother's chair and looked with sadness at the knitting. She was about to pick it up when the phone rang. She took a deep breath and prepared to answer it in a steady voice.

"Good morning."

"Miss Devine? Lydia Devine?" The man's voice was brisk and businesslike.

"Yes. Who is this?"

"Charles Brown, here. Brown and Kane. I was your mother's solicitor. I'm terribly sorry for your loss, Miss Devine."

"Thank you, Mr. Brown."

"Terribly unexpected. Your mother was such a fine lady. Such a shame."

Lydia didn't quite know how to respond, so she thanked him again and waited for him to state his business.

"Perhaps you'd be kind enough to call in, Miss Devine. I have your mother's will. It's fairly straightforward. Not putting pressure on you, mind, but in my experience it's often best to get these things over with as soon as possible."

"Yes indeed. I can come at whatever time suits you, Mr. Brown," Lydia found herself saying.

"Splendid. Shall we say half past three next Friday?"

"Yes, fine." She scribbled the date and time in the desk diary.

"Good, I'll get my secretary to send you confirmation in the post."

"Thank you, Mr. Brown." Lydia prepared to hang up.

"Oh, just one more thing, Miss Devine." The solicitor hesitated. "Besides the will, there's a letter for you."

"A letter...from whom?" Lydia could not say why she suddenly felt uneasy.

"Your mother left it with me some time ago, with instructions that it was only to be passed to you on her death."

"Oh...I see."

"I'll expect to see you on Friday, then. Goodbye, Miss Devine."

With that the line went dead, and Lydia was left once more in the echoing hallway, with the image of her mother and the mysterious letter, wondering what exactly this new, untested future could hold.

Chapter thirty

Jamie lay in his crumpled bed with Paddy at the bedside. Shep was at Paddy's feet, looking hopefully up at his master.

"See that wee dog there, Paddy? He's the only friend I have." Jamie propped himself up on an elbow and looked fondly at Shep. "That wee dog and yourself and Rose."

"Och now, Jamie, me and Rose'll always help you out, so we will."

Three weeks had gone by since his encounter with Miss Devine, and twenty days had passed since he'd made that telephone call to her home. The call in which he was cruelly snubbed by that strange woman. He could only conclude that Miss Devine had not been honest with him. She had given him a wrong number in order to get rid of him.

"Jamie now, it doesn't do any good to be lyin' in the bed every day."

Paddy shook a cigarette from a crumpled pack and stuck it in the corner of his mouth. He handed another to his friend.

"There's more trout in the river, ye know. Sure maybe ye could answer another advertymint. Wouldn't do any harm, now would it?"

"Och now, Paddy, I couldn't put meself through all that again."
Jamie hoisted himself into a sitting position against the bolster and
puffed the cigarette into life. "Her and me got on so well, and a don't
think a could meet the likes of her again."

Since that call to Lydia, when he was snubbed by the rude
woman, he'd blamed the whole world for his failure. But most of all
he blamed God and the wretched toupee. He'd stopped saying his
prayers, had thrown the hairpiece on the fire and watched it melt and
shrivel, as its remains turned to ash and vanished up the chimney.

He'd lost interest in eating and had started drinking instead.
He had stopped tending to the animals, until finally Paddy had inter-
vened and rescued things.

"Rose made an appointment with Dr. Brewster for you,
Jamie."

"I'm not goin' near no doctor, Paddy."

"Now, Jamie…it's in an hour or…an hour or so. Rose sent me…
she sent me…to drive you there. And she sez…she sez if you don't
go she'll go herself and get the doctor to come to see you here."

Paddy sucked on his cigarette, noting the alarm in Jamie's
eyes.

"I know now, Jamie, that ye wouldn't want the doctor to be
comin' into your house and seein' ye in the bed an' all…"

Paddy was looking meaningfully about him, taking in the full
measure of Jamie's abhorrence of tidiness. The floor was strewn with
dust balls, chicken feathers, bread crusts and stray bones—from pre-
historic pots of soup, he supposed—which Shep had carried into the
room to gnaw on and hadn't carried out again. Under the bed there
was a cat's cradle of boots, twinless shoes, odd socks, and scattered
amongst them several Guinness cans—crushed and bent up with
the careless befuddlement of the elated drunk—two empty naggin
bottles of John Powers whiskey, and innumerable discarded Gallaher's
Green cigarette packs.

On the bedside table a bowl and saucer did double duty as
ashtrays, the table top and everything else upon it dusted in gray ash.
There was a throng of objects which Jamie considered useful: a Tate
and Lyle bag of sugar with spoon protruding, a bottle of Dr. Clegg

cough mixture, a pack of Mrs. Cullen's headache powders, a delft leprechaun whose belly doubled as a clock-face—which he'd bought in Portaluce—a cracked ceramic jug holding a monkey wrench and a spirit level; hung about the jug was a string of wooden rosary beads, and propped against it, a novena to Saint Jude, with the inscription, *Patron Saint of Hopeless Cases*, printed in heavy type across the bottom.

"Aye, a s'pose you're right," Jamie agreed reluctantly. He could see that there was no way out; he'd have to go and see the doctor.

"You've just got a wee touch a that day-pression, and it's unnerstannable because you've been badly put about by that woman."

"Aw, now. You may stop talkin', Paddy. I never thought it would turn out so bad."

Jamie put his hand up to his now-bald head, as if remembering the terrible sacrifices he'd made. His scalp was still red and scarred from the toupee adhesive, and more shaming was the fact that he could not conceal the evidence of his foolishness. His comb-over was gone. Another good reason for his not going out to face his friends in the pub. A dirty oul' cap could not be worn out on a Saturday night, when everyone else was dressed up, nor could it be worn to Mass, if indeed he'd had a mind to attend a church of a Sunday.

Paddy got to his feet.

"I'm goin' out now, Jamie, to collect the eggs and footer about a bit, so when I come back you'll be up and ready now, won't you?"

"Aye, a s'ppose I will, since there's nothing else for it." Jamie yawned widely and rubbed his eyes.

Shep followed Paddy across the bedroom floor, his paws tip-tapping on the linoleum. In the open doorway the dog turned and looked beseechingly at Jamie, willing his master back to his old self.

"Go on there now, wee Shep," Jamie said, shooing the dog away with a dismissive hand, and heaving himself out of bed. "I'll be up in a minute."

One hour later, Jamie was sitting in Dr. Brewster's waiting room. He was alone, save for a mother with a baby in a stroller. The young woman looked as tired and depressed as Jamie, though he guessed for very different reasons. The child cried every time the phone rang, setting off a howling that would only cease when the receptionist had finished the call.

The baby served as a sad reminder for Jamie, forcing him to look back through time at a younger, fragmented version of himself. It was a time he did not want to face. The screaming child in the stroller had a mother to tend it. He'd had no one. All the anger he bore toward his faceless mother came flooding back. It was because of her that he now found himself in this sorry state. All at once he wanted to strike the young woman, who was carrying the baby up and down trying to soothe it. Hit her and all she represented for all the years he'd been made to suffer, for the beatings he'd taken from the women in black, and the men who'd corrupted his innocence. But Jamie knew he could never give full voice to his anger, so he did the only thing he could do. He held his head in his hands, stared down at the floor and let the tears rain down inside himself.

"Well, James, good to see you." Dr. Brewster was seated behind his desk as usual, peering over his bifocals. "How's the form? The lumbago clear up, did it?"

Jamie sat down meekly and removed his cap. He was unsure of what to say.

"Oh, the back's fine doctor, but that's..." He stared down, twisting the cap in his hands, unable to finish what he wanted to say.

The doctor adjusted his glasses and leaned forward. "You don't look at all well, James." He was alarmed at Jamie's weight loss—not only that, but his patient seemed to be suffering from some curious scalp infection.

"Can't eat or sleep, doctor, and I have no interest in nothing."

"Sounds as if your depression is back again."

He referred to his notes. Mr. McCloone's prescription for Valium had not been renewed in a number of weeks.

"And it's no wonder, because I see that you've stopped taking your medication." He peered over his glasses.

"I thought I could do without them, doctor."

"Now, James, how many times have we had this conversation?

You can only come off your medication with my agreement and supervision. It is very dangerous to do otherwise."

"I know that." Jamie continued to stare down at his hands. He could not tell the doctor the real reason for his present malaise.

"Did you have that break by the sea that I suggested?"

The doctor remembered being reprimanded by Gladys Millman for encouraging the like of James McCloone to the Ocean Spray. He'd told her that Jamie's money was as good as anyone else's, and his comment had caused Gladys to huff and puff for hours, which Humphrey considered a triumph of sorts, because he got to watch the golf for most of that afternoon uninterrupted.

"Oh I did indeed, doctor! Had a great time at the Ocean Spray." Jamie brightened when he thought back to that carefree couple of days. "It's a very fine place."

Dr. Brewster sat back in his great leather chair and removed his spectacles.

"Well, you know, James, it wouldn't do any harm to take another break. Stay longer this time; say, a week perhaps."

"No, I couldn't do it, doctor. It isn't so good when you're on your own all the time."

Jamie sighed. He looked past the doctor's shoulder, out the window, onto the sun-splashed high street of the town. And there seemed to be no remove between the boy he'd once been and the present man. He was right back in Keaney's quarters, staring through the window at the wind-torn laurels in the cemetery. And once more sitting in Mother Vincent's office, watching the snow build up on the windowsill to the right of her black shoulder.

It seemed then to Jamie that he'd traveled no real distance at all. The scene beyond the glass might have changed, the circumstances of his life might have become more tolerable, the adult in the chair before him infinitely more compassionate, but essentially he, himself, had not really changed. He was still the fearful, solitary boy he'd always been, yearning for the mother who'd never come. He was still helplessly alone.

"I'm tired of being on me own," he said finally, and stared down at the floor. "Just tired of it."

"Nonsense! You're a young man. Think positively; you've got the best years of your life ahead of you. All you need is to have more confidence in yourself."

The doctor sat forward again and laced his fingers together as if he were about to intone an earnest prayer.

"Now, James, I know it hasn't been easy for you, but you're a good man and you'd be a prize for any woman. But you must stay on the medication. You see what happens when you stop. You lose all belief in yourself and that's not good for you. Do you understand what I'm saying, James?"

"Yes, doctor." Jamie began to feel better. He was recalling that the wise words of the good doctor had helped him over many a bad patch.

"And depression is nothing to be ashamed of," Dr. Brewster continued gently. "Everyone suffers from it to a greater or lesser degree. Life isn't easy. God knows if it was, there'd be no need for people like me, and thankfully we've got medication to get us over the rough parts."

Dr. Brewster reached for his prescription pad.

"Now, I'm going to increase your dosage." He began to scribble the cure for Jamie's ills. "And I want to see you back here in two weeks' time, to see how you're faring."

He handed over the prescription. Jamie prepared to take his leave, trying not to weep in front of the doctor. He'd remembered Richard Widmark in *Broken Lance* say that real men didn't cry. Like the heat of an insult suffered once but remembered always, those challenging words burned in him now as he turned to go.

"Not so fast, James," Dr. Brewster said. "I'd like to take a look at that nasty rash on your head."

Jamie's hand shot up to his crown. He was suddenly conscious of how awful it must look.

"Oh, that's nothing atall, doctor. I fell against the wall when I was cleanin' out the barn."

"Really?" Dr. Brewster smiled to himself. He knew the after-effects of liner tape toupee glue all too well, having battled with the evil substance himself when he was younger, and vainer—just like Jamie in fact.

"Well, in that case you'll need an antiseptic soap," he said and went to a cabinet behind his desk. "There you go, James."

"Now remember," he patted Jamie's arm and smiled, "in two weeks' time I'll see you back here and you'll be a new man."

After the door shut, the doctor stood a while, staring at the space Jamie had vacated.

It saddened him that he could not give the farmer what he most wanted: roots, a base, a family. All those essentials had been denied to him in his early life. How was it possible to erect something solid and make a life when you'd been given no building blocks to start with?

The medication he prescribed was not the answer; it simply made him forget what he never had. The only thing that would make James happy would be for his mother to appear. And there wasn't much chance of that ever happening, conceded the doctor with a sigh.

Before driving him back to the farm, Paddy insisted that Jamie have Rose make some supper for him.

He was worried about his friend since he'd discovered that most of the food he'd brought him had lain in Jamie's kitchen untouched. He had scraped it into the hog trough, tut-tutting at the waste—a wondrous mixture of his wife's cookery. What a shame, Paddy had thought, about all those lovely things: the Irish stew, the marble cake, the devils on horseback, the pork cheeks in apple sauce, rhubarb pie, leek and sausage quiche, not to mention an assortment of buns and scones. Rose was fast running out of utensils and needed her plates and vessels back. They now sat chattering on the back seat of the Morris Minor, as the two friends bumped and jounced their way over the winding lane that led to the McFadden farmhouse.

Rose's attention was on a raging pan of potato bread, eggs and bacon. She had not seen Jamie since the hotel incident and was distressed at his appearance.

"God, Jamie!" she cried in alarm. "You don't look well atall."

Jamie stood in the doorway with his cap in his hands, miserable, for he was remembering with a painful clarity that it was Rose who had done everything to help him meet the mystery woman and how, in the end, all the effort had been wasted.

There was nothing he could say, so he did something that he'd never done in front of any adult since his childhood. He broke down and wept freely.

"Och now, Jamie, dear, dear, dear!"

Rose rushed to him, took him by the arm and led him to the armchair.

"Sit down there an' I'll make you a nice wee cup of tea." She signaled to Paddy to put the kettle on, as she slid the sizzling skillet to one side of the stove.

"You just feel a bit down after being to the doctor, Jamie," she said with great understanding. "And goodness knows nobody likes goin' to see a doctor, because God knows what they might hear."

She took a hankie from her apron pocket and handed it to Jamie. He wiped his eyes but could not meet hers, the shame of his tears forcing him into the darkest place imaginable. It was a place he did not feel he could escape from anymore. With every failure in his life, he had, inch by fearful inch, been pulled toward it. Now he felt he had no resistance left.

"No, it's not the doctor, Rose," he said at last. "It's everything. I don't want to live anymore. I'm tired livin'. Nothin' ever works out for me."

"Och now, Jamie, everything's fixable, so it is."

She pulled up the embroidered footstool and sat down on the limestone peak of Mount Errigal, placing her hands on Jamie's knees. Paddy could be heard in the scullery preparing the tea things.

"Nothing's ever as bad as it seems, Jamie. And everybody gets that old day-pression betimes. But sure we've God and the tablets, thank the heavens, so we have. I mind after I miscarried in nineteen and sixty-two I coulda kilt round me. My Paddy can tell you all about it because I nearly kilt him—couldn't be lived with, so I couldn't. *Isn't that right, Paddy?"* Rose's voice gained in volume as her husband came in bearing a clattering tray of cups and whatnot.

"Aye, that's right, Jamie. She was like the divil, so she was."

Rose passed Jamie a mug of tea, her cure for all ills.

"Now you drink that up, Jamie, and you'll feel a whole lot better. And y'know, Jamie, it's not all lost with that lady. I've been puttin' me thinkin' hat to the grindstone—or whatever it is that they say—and maybe ye know that was the wrong number you dialed. You could a mixed up the numbers with the excitement and all, like. And who knows, God-blisses-an-save-us, maybe she had a whole clatter a men to look at, and misremembered you, Jamie. That's just what you could be—the misremembered man—and she's sittin' at the phone waitin' on you to ring, and wonderin' what's goin' on."

"Aye, maybe. I don't know, Rose."

"Paddy, bring in a plate a them coconut monkeys I made this mornin' for Jamie here."

Rose turned her attention back to the problem at hand.

"Now if you get me that wee number I'll ring it and see what's goin' on. Because, Jamie, Miss Devine struck me as a fine lady and I don't think she'd be doin' anything to offend you. And you know what they say, Jamie. If you put a silk frock on a nanny goat it'd still be a goat. Now Lydeea wasn't wearin' a silk frock that day—to my mind it mighta been more of a glazed cotton, truth be told—but all-the-same you could put a glazed cotton frock on a nanny goat and it'd still be a nanny goat. But I could see that day, Jamie, that Lydeea's no nanny goat. She's a real lady."

"But, Rose, I couldn't see her now with no hair." Jamie started to cry again, thinking of the time it would take to grow back his comb-over. "She wouldn't look at me like this." He bit into his coconut monkey, which began to snow down his front.

"Now, Jamie, it's the heart that matters and not the head." She patted his knees. "And anyway, a gallopin' man on a blind horse wouldn't notice anything wrong with your hair, and sure if the worse comes to the worse we can get you a new cap for the time being."

"And hair or no hair, Jamie," she continued, "you're a gift for any woman. Because, as my Great-aunt Brigid used to say, God rest her soul—I'm sure she's outta purgatory be now, because she could be fearful crabbit betimes, like a weasel with toothache, God forgive me, but she's been dead a long while so she's maybe in heaven. Anyway, I'm goin' off the point a wee bit, but what she used to say was that all any man needs is a clean shirt, a clean conscience and a pound or two in his pocket. And God save us, Jamie, but haven't you all three a them? And isn't it only the woman that's missin', so it is." Rose took a mouthful of slaking tea. "And we'll soon fix that, so we will. Now, have you got that wee phone number on you?"

Jamie rummaged in his pocket, took out his wallet and handed it to her.

"It's in there somewhere, Rose. But I wouldn't want you to be ringin' her now."

Rose responded by pressing another coconut monkey on her guest.

"No, Jamie," she said, watching in satisfaction as he made short work of her baking. "I unnerstand you completely. I'll ring her the morra or the day after, if that's all right with you?"

"Aye," Jamie sighed.

Rose found Lydia's phone number in Jamie's wallet, tucked in beside a square of worn linen edged with faded shamrocks. She wondered about its significance but knew not to pry. She handed back the wallet.

"Now, Jamie, drink up your tea and then we'll have some supper." She emphasized her intentions with friendly slaps on Jamie's knees. "And you're in no state to be goin' home to your own house tonight, so you're stayin' here with us. I'll make up the spare room and I won't hear a word of a 'no' from you. And another thing, Jamie, whenever you need a helpin' hand, well, you know where they are?"

She clapped her hands on his knees with a final flourish.

"There they are there, Jamie: on the end of my arms, Jamie, and at the end of my Paddy's, too."

Jamie dried his eyes. Rose got up and went to slide the skillet of supper back onto the sizzling heat.

As the juices from the frying began to flavor the air again, Jamie's mood brightened accordingly. The concern that Rose and Paddy were, true to form, demonstrating, embraced him with a warmth he seldom experienced, and which for now served as a remedy to pull him back from the foul darkness that threatened to overwhelm him.

Chapter thirty-one

Eighty-Six sat on a wooden bench outside Mother Superior's office, awaiting his summons. Five boys would be interviewed by the couple who had come to adopt. The boy nearest the door had been in already. There was a vacant space on the seat next to him. Eighty-Four, who was being seen at that moment, would shortly come to reclaim it. Eighty-Six would be next.

They sat in a silent row looking out the window opposite, their bare feet planted on the cold stone floor. No one dared speak because Bartley, the mad bus driver, had been put in charge of them. The air crackled with his evil presence as he paced up and down the corridor, his hands balled into fists and crossed behind his back, his feet trailing on the concrete floor as he muttered to his demons. Sometimes he'd aim a kick at the bench, frustrated that the mute, stone-still boys were giving him no reason to lash out at them.

All four continued to stare out the window, their eyes fixed on the falling snow, their minds closed boxes of agonizing thought. Would the couple in the nun's office turn out to be good people or bad? Would they be released from this present hell or simply thrust into another version of it, ruled over by two adults instead of many? Should they pray to be left alone, or pray to be set free? Or might it just be possible that finally one of their number would find the paradise of a real "home" at last, in a warm house with kind people whose eyes smiled and whose voices soothed?

A cloud of doubt hung over all of them, as dark and heavy as the sky beyond the windows. Each boy had his own way of dealing with what lay ahead.

Ninety-One, the oldest of the group, gazed vacantly at the swirling snowflakes, his face empty of reflection, his mind shorn clean of prospect or expectation. Too many times he'd sat in this position, thinking the same thoughts. There had been too many bitter disappointments for him to think otherwise; his hopes and dreams lay about him like spectral bones in a graveyard.

The boy beside Eighty-Six imagined that the woman in the nun's office might be his long-lost elder sister—the one he spoke about so often—finally come to claim him.

Eighty-nine, who had already been through the interview, knew with a painful certainty that he was not the fortunate one today. They had not detained him long enough, had shown so little interest in him. He sat now chewing his lip and trying to smother the genie of desire he had so foolishly let out of the bottle.

Eighty-Six struggled to keep his mind on the beautiful possibility that these people might be good folk and that the choice might fall on him. Whenever he felt really anxious, as he did now, he strove to calm himself by drawing and coloring in the home of his dreams. From the posters and the tattered picture books he'd seen in Sister Veronica's classroom, he had pieced together an image of what he thought a happy home might look like, and one which the couple in the head nun's office could perhaps provide him with.

He saw a whitewashed cottage roofed in thick, yellow thatch at the bottom of a winding lane. At the front of the house there was a porch with a green half-door, and a window on either side of it with red curtains, also rimmed in green. There was a black chimney pot on the right side of the roof, from which a plume of smoke curled up into a blue sky. Around the door grew bunches of pink roses, and on the front step sat a black dog—black to match the chimney pot.

Eighty-Six now started to fill in the part he most enjoyed: the animals in the yard. First, the three orange hens with their red combs and freckled feathers. Then the trough beside the green-painted pump and—

The door to Mother Superior's room suddenly opened, cutting across the fantasy. Eighty-Four stood before him telling him he must go in. Before Eighty-Six had time to think, Bartley was grabbing him by the shoulder and thrusting him through the open door.

"This is Eighty-Six," Mother Vincent informed the couple. They sat on chairs to the left of her desk. He thought they looked out of place in the spartan room.

"Take a seat, boy."

He struggled up onto the wooden chair he'd occupied only the day before. It was high and his feet barely grazed the floor. He tried not to look at the strangers, but sensed right away that they were not like the Fairleys.

"How are you, lad?"

It was the man who spoke first. Eighty-Six was obliged to look up.

"Very well, thank you, sir."

The man and woman smiled: wide honest smiles, which amazed him. The only adult who had ever genuinely smiled at him was Mrs. Doyle in her potato field. He did not know how to respond. So instead he focused on the swirling snow beyond the window, now falling between the nun's black shoulder and the woman's floral one; between the darkness and the light.

"This is Mr. and Mrs. Michael McCloone, Eighty-Six. If they like you, they might want you for their son. What do you say to that?"

Plucking up courage in Mother Vincent's intimidating presence, he managed to look at the woman, then the man, and back at the woman again. He could not believe what he was seeing; he thought that his mind was surely playing tricks on him. For in those

271

moments he believed he was looking at his mother. She was wearing the same full-skirted floral dress that he'd always imagined: white with blue forget-me-nots. Her long wavy hair framed a beautiful face with blue eyes and a smiling mouth of even, white teeth. She wore white high heels and her lace-gloved hands were clutching a matching purse which rested in her lap.

"I would like to be their son very much, Sister." He looked pleadingly at the woman, wondering how he could transmit his eagerness and sincerity. His eyes met hers across the cold expanse and his lips moved in silent prayer: Oh *please*, God, *please* let her take me away from here, please!

"What kind of farm work are you good at, lad?" The man spoke in a stern but soft voice.

"I like everything, sir. I like gathering the taters and making the hay into stooks, but I like the animals best of all, sir."

"And which animals have you worked with?" the woman asked with a smile.

The boy hung his head in shame. "I haven't worked with any, Miss—but I work with them in me head. Sheeps and cows and hens and the like."

"What nonsense, Eighty-Six!" Mother Vincent snapped, then turned her attention to the couple. "You'll have to excuse him. He's a rather simple-minded boy, I'm afraid."

"Oh, I disagree, Sister," said Mrs. McCloone. "I think his answer shows that he has imagination."

The woman's voice washed over him in one gloriously soothing wave. Eighty-Six was so grateful that he lifted his head and said "thank you" to the beautiful woman, the woman whom he wanted so desperately to be his mother.

Mother Vincent glared at him, taken aback by this uncharacteristic show of politeness.

"Indeed." She kept her eyes on him. "And Mr. McCloone, what do you think?" The nun clearly hoped for a more level-headed response from the man.

"Oh, I agree with Alice. This lad would like our farm. We've got four pigs, ten sheep, eight cows, a cat *and* a dog. How's that, Eighty-Six? D'you think you could handle all that?"

The man had beamed proudly as he listed off his livestock. He was nowhere as handsome as the woman, but his alert, brown eyes and narrow face held a friendly, genuine warmth.

"Of course, I must warn you of the offenses this boy has committed whilst in our care," the nun said sourly. "It would be dishonest of me to let him give the impression that he is some kind of saint."

She opened the register on her desk. Eighty-Six was convinced then that all was lost. He could not look at the couple but directed his gaze at the window, his eyes filling with tears. A silence ensued, as painful as held breath. He tried to ignore the incriminating rustle as the nun briskly turned the pages.

Outside, he could hear the shuffling of Bartley's feet as he dragged them up and down the corridor. Beyond the window, the graceful snow continued to fall on the graceless grounds of the orphanage. And inside, like the snow, a sadness fell on him, damp, heavy, inescapable.

A fat tear rolled down his cheek as the world clouded over. He stared down at his ruined hands and his blackened feet and waited patiently for his every sin to be driven out of hiding.

He saw himself reach once more for the forbidden turnip in the sack, felt the tearing cough that had wrecked the solemnity of the morning Mass, heard again the china plate shatter on the Fairleys' kitchen floor, woke once more in the sodden bed with his aching limbs and bloodstains, and relived again the punishment for each and every one of those infractions: in the pain of the sticks that beat him, the belts that flailed him, the hands that pushed him roughly into darkened rooms behind bolted doors.

Then, through the agony of all this remembering, he heard a voice; it had the soft, gentle cadence of a woman's voice. And it was throwing him a lifeline.

"Oh, it won't be necessary to tell us what the boy has done wrong, Sister. It's in the past, isn't it, and we all make mistakes, especially children."

Each silken word was weighted with a calm assurance. He clung to every one of them.

Before the nun had time to speak, the woman opened her purse and went to Eighty-Six, holding a white handkerchief. It was edged with tiny green and silver shamrocks. He would always remember the shamrocks.

"Now, now, don't cry, dear." As she bent over him in the faintly lisping dress, he caught the warm whisper of her scent and prayed that he'd be allowed to stay near such beauty forever.

He dried his eyes quickly and handed the hankie back.

"Thank you, Miss."

"No, no, you keep it, dear."

Then she leaned closer to him and said something that only he could hear, and which he would never, ever forget.

"I'll get it from you tomorrow, sweetheart, when we're in your new home."

Chapter thirty-two

Lydia had difficulty negotiating her way through the streets of Derry. She had not driven in a city before and made several wrong turnings before finally reaching what she was coming to see as journey's end.

The Mount Carmel Retirement Home was a somber, three-story building, clad in ivy and set on an incline at the end of a sweeping gravel driveway. A wall of lush greenery and rhododendrons fenced the property off from the outer parking lot. Lydia pulled into it.

She parked under the wide-branched shade of a chestnut tree and cut the engine. The afternoon was uncommonly hot. Even though it was mid-September, the summer showed no sign of fading. I should be in school, she thought, and immediately felt a tug of regret for that other life she'd once led; a life that had ended with her mother's death and had begun again—but so differently—with the letter.

She took the vellum envelope from her purse and turned it over and over, as though the ordinary envelope, addressed with a typewriter in need of a new ribbon, might be an apport from the spirit world. The letter connected her to the louring structure in front of her. Soon she would learn the truth that lay behind its walls. She did not know, as she sat there in the heat of the car, whether she could deal with too much more reality, too many additional facts. They'd been piling up against her, a bonfire of absurdities that might explode if she added any more fuel to what she already knew.

She opened the letter and began to read it again, a perfunctory and unnecessary exercise—she almost knew its contents by heart—but her conscience persuaded her that, in the present circumstances, it was the right thing to do. Sitting there outside her "birthplace," she felt like a penitent before a high altar; the letter in her hands served as the incontestable evidence that she had been here before, in this place.

Elmwood House
River Road,
Killoran

Dearest Lydia,

I hope that when you finally get to read these words they will not hurt you too much, although I know that what I have to disclose will come at a very great shock.

I will be at rest with your dear father at last when you get this letter and I write it with a very heavy heart. Please do not grieve for me too much. When I am gone you will be free at last to live your life, so look on the bright side and spread your wings.

Your father and I did our very best for you, always remember that. We agreed and promised each

> other that you should only learn the
> truth about the circumstances of your
> birth after our deaths.
>   You see dearest Lydia we
> adopted you when you were just a
> few weeks old on the 5th Dec 1934.

Her mother would never know how much those words stung.
Lydia looked up from the page to try and block the inevitable tears.
The bleak building seemed to mock her, and in her distress she wiped
her eyes and turned back to the page. There would be no solace for
her, so she pressed on, the sodden handkerchief at the ready.

> Please don't cry too much at this
> news my dear. Your father and I
> could not have children and I so
> wanted a little girl I could call my
> own. You were a little angel who'd
> been abandoned and we rescued you.

Indeed, thought Lydia, angry now. How many times had she
heard that her parents only had "relations" to bring her into the
world?

> I did not want to adopt locally
> so we went to Londonderry to
> the Little Sisters of Divine Love
> Orphanage. I believe that these days
> it has been turned into a retirement
> home for the clergy.
>   I was Catholic up until I
> married your father, so I did not
> think it was such a falsehood to

pretend to the nuns that I was still one and would bring you up in the faith. Because you see dearest Lydia I wanted you so much. You must understand that. And what does it matter which religion we adhere to. We all worship the one God.

How many more lies had her mother told her? It seemed that she'd built her life on a succession of them.

Oh you were such a beautiful baby Lydia. We both fell in love with you straight away. You had such beautiful chestnut curls and lovely pink cheeks and you smiled all the time, never cried. I was so proud of you. We could not have wished for a more ~~perfect~~ perfect daughter.

Lydia dried her eyes. The word "perfect" had been crossed out and rewritten. Not so perfect after all, it seemed. She thought the error significant.

I'm sorry that I cannot tell you anything about your real mother. The nuns simply said that you'd been abandoned but they did not elaborate. She left you with nothing Lydia. We gave you your name and a place in the world. We gave you a chance, so please don' t be too vexed with us. We did everything for the best.

And now dear because we love you so much we thought it only fair that, on our deaths, you should be given the opportunity to find your real mother, if you want to. I've told you everything you need to know. If anywhere retains records of her whereabouts, you can look up the above mentioned place in Londonderry.

But dear Lydia do not dig too deep for answers. If they are not forthcoming let things be. Sometimes it is better that the past does not give up its secrets.

I hope you have a happy life, dearest. Keep us in your heart and always be kind. I wish that, towards the end of my life, I could have been a better friend to you.

Always yours, my dear
Your loving mother,
Elizabeth

She stuffed the letter back into the envelope and willed herself to be strong. A week earlier, she had started weeping in Mr. Brown's office, and it seemed that since then she'd never stopped.

She opened her compact and tried to repair her face as best she could. If only she could repair the damage to her life so easily. All the roads she'd traveled since childhood had suddenly fallen into disuse. She stood at a crossroads and there was no signpost to point the way. She no longer had a mother or a father. She was an orphan, a nobody. Now she understood what Aunt Gladys meant. She saw again the glossy mouth spit out the words that had so confused her.

You know nothing. The truth is always difficult. Now that you're alone, you'll have to learn about things the hard way!

Yes, indeed: Lydia had known nothing. And Gladys had known *everything*. Gritting her teeth at the memory of those words, Lydia decided that she had no wish to see her so-called aunt for a long time to come.

She gazed up at the retirement home on the hill and felt that she should rather die than enter through its ominous doors. What truths could this building tell her that she didn't already know?

But it was best to get it over with.

With this resolve, she reluctantly locked the car and walked slowly up the avenue, through the beauty of an afternoon which was so much at odds with the turmoil of her inner self. God was about his business: in the lace cap hydrangeas, the lime-scented hedges, the sun-heated grass; and somewhere the glissando of a blackbird was unfurling its sweet song, as if to calm her. Such peace, such harmony, within reach—yet a world away.

At the portico she pressed the bell. Four times in all, and still no reply. She was about to turn away when finally the door was pulled open by a very tall monk. He wore a brown habit, secured at the waist by a length of white hemp rope. He was young, but his shaved head and joyless eyes gave the impression of a much older man. His feet were bare in thonged sandals.

"I'm Lydia Devine. I'm here to see Father Finian."

The monk's expression did not change as she spoke, a fact that she found most disconcerting. Perhaps he's taken a vow of silence, she thought; his face had the look of someone who'd chosen years of discipline and self-denial and was, for whatever reason, regretting having made such a choice.

"He's expecting me," she added, hoping it would help.

With that he nodded and stood back to admit her.

The vestibule was surprisingly bright; ivory walls, a chessboard floor, the only somber reference being a heavy sideboard—highly polished and deeply carved—which served as an altar for a three-foot plaster virgin. He indicated a chair.

Lydia seated herself as the monk disappeared down a dark corridor. All was silent except for the creaking floorboards that followed him into the depths of the house. Then the footsteps stopped and a door cried open; just as quickly it was banged shut again. Afterward she was left with nothing but the huge silence of the entrance hall.

"Miss Devine, pleased to meet you."

The young priest stretched out a hand. "I'm glad you could come. This can't be easy for you."

Father Finian, with his ready smile and easy manner, could not have been more different from the cheerless monk. He ushered her down several long corridors, then up a flight of stairs. She climbed slowly, taking everything in with forensic attention. This place, she kept telling herself, was once my home. This gray, gloomy prison with its concrete floors, chipped paintwork, high-grilled windows. There was nothing at all to lift the eye. When she reached the top of the stairs she felt faint.

"Thank God I was taken away from this."

"Sorry? Are you all right?" The priest was behind her.

"Yes...thank you..." She stopped; her hand gripped the banister. She stared down at her tautened knuckles. "Yes...I'm...fine."

The last word—thin, hollow, weightless—fell away from her and into the echoing depths of the stairwell. As she gazed down, she wondered when she'd be able to retrieve and live the full meaning of that one gentle syllable again. Fine.

"I'm fine," she said again, trying to muster courage.

Father Finian sensed her sadness. He'd seen that lost look many times before.

"We don't use this part of the building anymore. It's mostly closed off for storage."

He sped ahead of her down the corridor, resolute now, his heels like hammer blows on the stone floor. He stopped abruptly, riffled through a set of keys. He unlocked a door.

"Here we are." He stood waiting for her.

She walked slowly toward him, past what once had been the Mother Superior's office. She saw the worn nameplate on the door and, beside it, a scarred bench. For some reason she wanted to rest on it a while, as if out of respect for all the children who had sat there and suffered. Because she knew instinctively that every child who'd passed through that building had suffered, and suffered greatly.

They entered a large office-cum-sitting room; a musty, dimly lit place that escaped the afternoon sun. He directed her to a balding sofa which had a rug thrown over it, in a futile attempt to brighten it. Stretched limply on the floor between the priest's desk and the couch was a carpet of faded peacocks and humming birds. She wondered idly how many decades it must have lain there and how many pairs of feet must have trodden on it down through the years.

Father Finian read her mind. Since the building that housed the notorious orphanage had changed hands in 1968, he'd had to deal with so many Lydias. People who wanted to make sense of their lives through connecting with the mystery and secrecy of mothers who had borne them, only to abandon them.

"You'll have to excuse this room," he said, "but when the orphanage closed we kept this place more or less as it had been, to hold the filing cabinets of records. So it's a kind of storeroom which contains the past, if you like. We think it best not to tamper with the past, otherwise we might not be able to help people like yourself who come here looking for answers."

Lydia nodded slowly. She didn't know what to say. She was determined not to cry.

"I'm sorry for your loss. It is hard enough to lose someone so close without having to learn a truth kept hidden for so long."

"Thank you, Father."

An arrangement of blue lobelias had withered in the grate: They accounted for the acrid smell that pervaded the room. There was a claw-footed sideboard of heavy coffin-wood with a mirror which threw back no reflection and a worm-eaten desk. It seemed to Lydia that everything in the room had died. She felt she could neither breathe nor speak; the enormity before her was so daunting.

She looked out the window, wishing to distance herself from this nightmare, but her eye was drawn to an incline some way off, and she saw a series of lichen-coated headstones, many of them slumped down in the earth from having stood to attention for so long. No, there would be no relief here. She turned again to the young priest.

"If you'd like me to have a look at your mother's letter," he said, "it might make it easier for you." He got up from the desk and came and sat at the other end of the couch.

"Yes," she managed to say. "Thank you."

She watched his lips move over her dead mother's words and wondered why such a handsome young man should condemn himself to a life in a place as awful as this, disconnected from everything.

"Hmm…fifth of December, nineteen thirty-four. Right, let me see."

The filing cabinets were ranged along the back wall. She counted eleven. Father Finian went to one near the middle and pulled open the top drawer. He extracted a folder and carried it to the desk.

After a few minutes of study, he said: "I'm terribly sorry but I cannot give a name to your birth mother."

The priest had, in his wisdom, decided to spare Lydia the details. It was a decision he'd had to make before. He'd read that she'd been left on the steps of the Saint Agnes Orphanage, wrapped in newspaper and inside a bag, on November 4, 1934. She had been adopted one month later by Perseus Cuthbert Devine and his wife, Elizabeth.

"That's all right, Father," said Lydia, surprising him with her equanimity. "I was not expecting to get a name, but I needed to know, just to make sure."

Father Finian looked down at the folder in sadness.

"Is there anything else you can give me though?" Lydia said. She managed to keep her voice even. She wanted suddenly to be gone and knew she would never return. It was now or never.

"A sample of her handwriting. Anything?"

"There is an envelope here." It was not sealed. From it he extracted what looked like a newspaper.

"There is only this." He handed it over, but avoided her look of bewilderment. Lydia's hands trembled as she examined the flimsy, yellowed remnant. She read the masthead and date: *The Vindicator, Thursday, November 3, 1934.*

"What...what...does it mean?"

She'd forced the words out, in a voice that seemed not to belong to her. Father Finian's grave expression told her all she needed to know. She held his gaze. Waiting. But he did not answer. She saw his image blur as the tears came. Between them a silence spread, a silence that excused him explanation and forced her to confront what she could barely comprehend.

"I was...was...I was..." She held the paper out to him with trembling hands. "I was...wrapped in this, wasn't I?"

And as she uttered the words, something in her heart loosed itself and began falling, a part of her she'd always known was there, but which she'd never wished to look at or get to know—the abandoned child within. The child who had always shadowed the woman she tried to be. All at once her disconnectedness, the isolation she'd felt from her "parents," made sense. She'd entered the world to be merely discarded, like garbage, in a sheet of newspaper. How could her real mother, her birth mother, have done such a thing? Lydia's despair turned to anger and she wiped her tears.

"You mustn't blame her," Father Finian said, trying to console. "She did what she felt was best for you at the time. We do not know the circumstances she found herself in."

"Yes...I know."

But Lydia knew as she uttered the words that in fact she knew nothing.

She studied the young man's face, willing him to comprehend her need, but his mournful look confirmed for her what she'd known from the time she'd read the letter. No one could help her. She was hostage to the unfathomable decisions a young mother had made a long time ago. As she sat there in the musty room with its faded rug and dead flowers, she came to the conclusion that for the rest of her life, nothing or no one would ever release her from that knowledge, that haunting, perplexing, ungraspable knowledge.

The priest shuffled through the pages. He could not meet her eye, just kept focusing on the book. There was a prolonged silence which her voice dared not break. Then, knowing it was hopeless, she rose.

But the priest wasn't paying her any mind. He was poring over the book with a frown of consternation. He was looking at a page of numbers.

"I think you should sit down, Miss Devine."

She complied.

"When you were brought here the nuns gave you a number," he said. "All children were given numbers. You were number Eighty-Five-F. F for female. But there is another number beside yours."

"So?" Lydia's pulse began to quicken. "What does that mean, Father?"

"It means that your mother left two of you here. It means that the child given the number Eighty-Six-M was your brother."

Chapter thirty-three

I t was while he'd sat in Dr. Brewster's waiting room, with the young mother pacing the floor, that Jamie made the decision.

Thursday the twelfth would be the day, and seven o'clock in the evening would be the hour. He had been adopted by Mick and Alice on a Thursday and had arrived at their home and his new life at around 7 P.M. Appropriate, then, to mark the date again, even if he knew that what he was about to do would change nothing. It would, however, finally solve the puzzle of his being, if what they said about a life hereafter was true. He had spent so many years of his adulthood trying to fit together the pieces, trying to make everything all right, but now he had reached the conclusion that his awful childhood ensured that there would always be segments missing. Nothing or nobody could make up for the love he'd been denied as a child.

Traveling from the orphanage to the farmhouse that day, so long ago, had enabled him to experience and understand the true nature of happiness for the very first time. The memory of it still shone like a vein of precious metal in the solid darkness of his early life.

He could recall every bend and incline of that wonder-filled journey.

When Uncle Mick's car rattled off through the orphanage gates, it had carried him away from the pain and the loneliness, and on to a real home and the future he'd so often dreamed of.

There had been just one flaw in that momentous day, one wave of sadness that crashed against him for a moment and then was gone; it was the sight of the four boys he was leaving behind. As the car trundled off he saw their sad faces, hung like a row of pale moons, at the high window. He could only guess at what emotions choked and held them there, staring down forlornly on the departing vehicle.

He'd knelt up on the back seat, watching and waving eagerly, but only Eighty-Four had raised a hand. Then the high walls of the orphanage had wiped them from view, like a duster across a blackboard; they and the prison that held them were consigned to history.

He remembered sitting back down on the seat again and losing himself in the novelty of the car; that final vision of the faces of his comrades slowly fading in the feel of the vinyl upholstery, the moving, magical world waiting beyond the windshield, and the shiny, big steering wheel in the grip of his new father's hands.

Back in the orphanage he'd painted pictures in his head of the house he'd wanted to live in, the parents he longed to have and the farm he wished to be a part of. When Uncle Mick's Ford Popular had finally drawn up in the yard that day, and he glimpsed the cottage and the animals, he knew that his dreams had indeed come true. He had become part of the picture. Even the black dog on the step was his, come to life.

His new parents had given him everything, right down to his name: James Kevin Barry Michael McCloone. They had only given him "James" at first, but he begged for more. So Mick had added "Kevin Barry" and Alice "Michael," after her husband and her father. He was no longer a number. No one would ever call him Eighty-Six again.

He remembered repeating the syllables of his new names over and over, balancing each precious bead of newfound selfhood on his tongue, feeling the satisfying shape of his new identity. Until then, he had been a nobody. Mick and Alice had given him meaning, made him a real person at last.

Memories of the first day with his new parents would never fade. He could not believe the wealth of the world he'd stepped into. He was given a bedroom all to himself: a blue and white room with bluebell drapes at the window and real sheets upon the bed. He could not get used to the silence at night; no whimpering or weeping room-mates, and in the morning no clanging triangle, no punishing hands and belts, no nun inspecting if he'd wet the bed.

Alice had given him a new set of clothes: pants and a sweater that fit, socks that came up to his knees and a pair of brand-new shoes. He thought he'd never get used to the sensation of walking in them; for so many years he'd known only the feel of grass, gravel, mud and unyielding stone beneath his bare feet.

They had sat him down at a lace-covered table and during those extraordinary first days had fed him food he'd never known existed: meatballs in gravy, eggs, sausages, chicken and fresh vegetables.

For ten long years he'd been hungry. All he'd known in the orphanage was lumpy breakfast gruel, stale bread and dripping, cabbage water and potatoes with the maggots taken out. And in autumn, the crab apples from the orchard the nuns would throw to the children, and which always made him sick.

He remembered how Mick had taught him to use a knife and fork and how his untrained little fingers rebelled, the strange implements slipping from his grasp, his hands and mouth so used to the feel and fit of a spoon.

But the highlight of that first day—and the one he'd try endlessly to recapture and recreate in his adult life—was that afforded him by the cream bun and chocolate cookie Alice had given him on a willow-patterned plate, after his dinner. He would never forget the taste of this heavenly fare, the chocolate melting in his mouth, the sensation of the sweet textures on his tongue.

Oh, what joy! He was ten years old and his life had begun.

Jamie shifted uneasily as he sat there in the tattered armchair, staring into the debris of his life. It was now eleven thirty in the morning, just seven and a half hours to go. He had the first tea of the day by his elbow, the first cigarette in his hand. The sun was in the window and the dog was in the yard. This was the beginning of a day that would end with his release. He was happy it would soon be over. He was tired of interrogating a deaf-blind God. Tired of his thoughts tearing on the things he could never have. Tired of the same endless mornings that broke on the same endless days. He knew now that life only worked for the fearless and the beautiful.

He'd planned it thoroughly, had hidden a half-bottle of whiskey and a bag containing a chocolate square and a cream slice behind a bale in the hayshed. This fare, echoing as it did his first little joyful feast in the farmhouse, would be his last in the world. He wondered now where the willow-patterned plate might be—the one that dear Alice had given him with those heavenly treats all those years ago. She'd said the plate was precious; a family heirloom that had belonged to her grandmother. Wouldn't it be fitting to use it again, Jamie thought, in honor of Alice and as part of his final farewell?

He drained the tea mug and crossed to the glass case to have a look. He had not seen it in a long time, but then, he never had cause to look for it. He took out a stack of plates and went through them one by one, but the heirloom was not among them. He checked the cluttered sink in the scullery, but even as he piled the crockery on the drainer he knew it was useless. Those were dishes recently acquired. How could it be there? He stood for a while gazing out the window at a rusted trough sunk deep in the nettles, and in his mind an image stirred, then unfolded: the image of the suitcase under Mick's bed which held his aunt's belongings. It was bound to be there.

He climbed the stairs, pushed into the bedroom and pulled out the case, eager to lay his hands on the trophy. The hasps sprang open freely, sending up small coughs of dust. Jamie was surprised to discover that there was very little inside.

He took out a framed wedding picture, a match for the one that hung on the bedroom wall, a satin-covered jewelry box containing a glass rosary, strings of pearls, earrings and a gold wedding band. He closed the lid carefully and put the box back. One of the only remaining items in the case was her white purse—the one she'd carried that day in the orphanage and from which she'd extracted the shamrock handkerchief. Jamie could not bring himself to open it, but knelt upright holding the purse between his hands and said a little prayer, before returning it to the case.

There was no sign of the willow-patterned plate. The last remaining item was an old newspaper, rolled up and secured with a blue ribbon.

"An oul' newspaper," Jamie said to himself.

He slid off the ribbon, wondering why Alice would have wanted to keep such an ancient, yellowed thing. He could barely make out the title and date: *The Vindicator, Thursday, November 3, 1934.* He knew then that the paper had followed him from the orphanage and had been kept for that reason. He resolved to burn it right away. He was about to throw it aside, when his eye lighted on what looked like handwriting in the top corner of the inside back page. He peered closely at the almost illegible script.

> Thir called Jamie an Lily
> I cant keep thim Im sorry

Jamie ran his finger over what could only be his mother's handwriting and sat back on his heels. So he'd been given a name. The nuns simply would not let him keep it. The baby sister he'd never known had also had a name. He replaced the ribbon on the newspaper and returned it to the case.

"Lily!" he said the name aloud.

And as he came slowly down the stairs, he realized that he did not have the plate, but, for the first time, he did have his sister's name.

"Lily," he said again. "This evening I'll be with you, Lily, as sure as I'm standing here."

Lydia drove back from the Mount Carmel Retirement Home, torn between elation and sadness. She would go straight home first; she needed to get distance, needed time to think.

The address Father Finian had given her was terribly familiar. The surname of the people who had adopted her brother was definitely the same. How could she forget a name like McCloone? All the way home, Madame Calinda's words kept echoing in her head.

But de two of you will be close, whether you like it or not.

When she finally pulled the car into the driveway at Elmwood she was exhausted, and could hardly bring herself to open the front door and step inside.

On the mat she noticed a small white envelope. "Lydia" was scrawled across it in a hurried hand. Another condolence card, she thought wearily, and ripped it open. It was not a card, however, but a short note.

I was in the vicinity this afternoon and dropped by
to see how you were coping.
Perhaps we could have dinner one evening.
I will give you a ring tomorrow around 5 p.m.
David O'Connor

The good doctor. Lydia smiled to herself. The ring is of the telephonic kind obviously, she mused. How interesting; not the cold fish I thought he was. And dinner? Even more interesting!

She stowed the note carefully in her purse and brought her mind back to the present and that other man—the much more important man—who had written to her.

The kettle could wait. She rushed upstairs to find his letters. She only needed to look at one to confirm what she'd already suspected. The addresses were the same: *The Farmhouse, Duntybutt, Tailorstown.*

James McCloone was her very own brother. There could be no mistake.

She thought she might cry, but instead she found herself laughing—laughing uproariously.

She knew now why she'd felt a certain kinship with him, how when she had first seen him, ambling up the avenue of the Ocean Spray in those ludicrous yellow shoes, all those weeks before, she'd somehow wanted to protect him from the awful Gladys. Again on the promenade, she knew that he'd been weeping and had felt moved to console him. Then that fateful meeting in the Royal Neptune Hotel. The meeting she had regretted so much. How strange life is, she thought. In being absent from my mother's deathbed I found my brother. It was as if some divine bargain had been struck behind the scenes. A divine bargain that her father, or rather, adoptive father would have fully approved of.

She sat down on the bed and was amazed at how much she knew about James—her brother James—already. Even though she had only actually met him once. He had a dog called Shep. He played the accordion. He could drive a tractor, but not the car. He drank whiskey and smoked way too many cigarettes. He could bake rock buns without margarine, could spend two hours in the toilet, and had £3,129 and five pence in a post office savings account.

James Kevin Barry Michael McCloone was her brother. She loved the notion, and felt certain she'd love him too. She was not alone in the world after all. Dazzled by all this proof, she danced down the stairs. It was five o'clock. She would have a cup of tea, change and go to see him that very day.

The phone rang as she was filling the teapot.

"It's Rose McFadden here. Would that be Miss Lydeea Devine?"

"Yes." She did not recognize the woman's voice, although the broad accent seemed familiar. "Sorry, but do I know you?"

"Oh, thank heavens for that! I'd a feelin' James dialed the wrong number. Yes, Miss Devine, we met in the Royal Neptune Hotel not more than three weeks ago. I'm James McCloone's friend."

"Oh, *Rose*! How good to hear from you."

Lydia decided that it was best not to confess that her Aunt Gladys had rebuffed James. She also decided that the time was not right to allude to her mother's death.

"I'm ringin' on behalf of James, Lydeea. He asked me to ring you, because d'you know he's very disappointed. He rang you but he must a dialed the wrong number because some other woman answered and took the nose clean off him. And I knew, Lydeea, that a lady like yourself wouldn't be at the like a that."

Rose halted her breathless discourse and Lydia seized her chance.

"I'm very sorry to hear that, Rose. I was just about to visit James myself. I really need to see him. I've got some great news."

"My goodness, Lydeea, is that so? James'll be so pleased. He could do with a bit a good news at the minute, so he could. But would you do me a favor, Lydeea, and come to my house first? We live very close to James, because y'know I don't think James would be wantin' you to be seein' his house without notice of a day or two, so that he could tidy up a bit, if y'know what I mean, Lydeea."

Rose stopped, overcome by what sounded like a sneeze.

"God bless you," said Lydia.

"Thank you, Lydeea. God bliss me indeed. Now where was I? Oh yes, men and the cleanin' and the like. Y'know what these men are like when there isn't a woman about, to be liftin' after them. And them that doesn't make their own bed can lie to dinner time and have breakfast in the bedroom and sleep in the kitchen, if truth be told."

Lydia thought it wiser to allow Rose's talk to run its course.

"I had an uncle once who could make his breakfast from the bed, would you believe, didn't have to get up atall, atall. I came in on him one day, and there he had the gas stove and the pan and all, splutterin' away like the divil at his elbow and him still half asleep at the fryin' of it."

It occurred to Lydia that this gave a whole new meaning to the concept of "breakfast in bed." She couldn't quite follow the logic of Rose's speech but got the impression that Mrs. McFadden disapproved of James's domestic arrangements, and for this reason was inviting her to meet with him in her home.

"But ye know, Lydeea—"

"I understand completely," Lydia said. "Just give me directions and I'll be with you within the hour."

At half-past six the sun was sending amber flares across the sky. Jamie stood in the barn entrance, his face glowing in the golden light. This would be his last glimpse of a world that had been less than kind.

He gazed about him, his eyes lighting on the commonplace, the simplicity of things, for a moment holding some kind of sacred reverence. A reverence that only could be appreciated through the certainty of his imminent death.

His eyes moved over the green half-door, the garden gate, the pecking hens, his bicycle propped against the gable, the disused machinery in the yard—and never before had these mundane images held such meaning, and never before had he, Jamie, felt so "right."

A steady buzzing near his elbow caused him to glance down. A fat bumblebee was just settling down to feed on a bloom of pink wisteria that climbed and fell about the barn door. Jamie studied the bee closely as it supped on the flower, realizing that it would be his final glimpse of such a creature. He marveled at the furry throbbing back and little wings a-tremble. He had the urge to stretch out a finger and stroke its little striped jersey, but knew that such a move would scare the bee away. The sight of small, solitary creatures always moved him. He felt an affinity with them, a certain kinship.

Suddenly the bee flew off and Jamie took it as a sign.

Then, like a night worker whose immense exhaustion is pulling him toward sleep, he surrendered himself fully to the irresistible call of the afterlife.

He turned and entered the barn.

Once inside, he began to prepare the ground for his final act. There would be no slip-ups. He was going to join the only people who had loved him: Mick and Alice—and Lily of course. Yes, wee Lily. Since learning her name he'd thought of little else. The desire to see her was getting stronger as each hour passed. Would she be a baby still or would she have grown up? Did a baby grow up in heaven? He misremembered now. But no matter. He would soon find out.

He was happy, and set about each action with an unwavering zeal.

The baler twine was coiled on a nail behind the door. With his penknife he expertly snapped off a six-foot length, tied a running knot at one end and fed the remaining tail rope through it. He climbed up on the bales and secured the rope to a rafter. Mick's rafter—the last one he'd worked on. The barn roof creaked and cried under the pressure, and when he looked up through the gaps in the skeletal roof he saw a halo of wood pigeons circling in perfect accord. Jamie took it as a sign from heaven. The angels were calling him home.

"I'll be up there soon, so a will!" he declared to the sky.

Just then he heard a low whimper below him and, as he clambered down off the bales, saw Shep standing forlornly, his tail drooping, his sad eyes looking from the noose to his master's face. For an instant, Jamie's resolve—up to that moment as taut as an archer's bowstring—slackened, and he stooped down to comfort the animal.

"Now now, wee Shep, you'll be all right. Paddy'll take care of you." He ruffled the dog's coat, went straight to the far corner of the shed, and found the bag of buns and the whiskey.

He settled himself in a comfortable place amid the hay and, using a bale as a table, laid out his final feast. The bottle of whiskey first. He uncapped it and took a long swig before biting in his cream slice. The dog lay down beside him and rested his head in his lap.

There was just one final duty he had to perform: his farewell note to Rose and Paddy. It would also serve as his last will and testament.

He sat in a shaft of light from the broken roof, pen in hand like a scribe in the Old Testament, and opened his pad of Basildon Bond. He would write his last letter on the pad he'd used for Lydia.

> The Hay Shed
> Duntybutt Farmhouse
> Sept 1974

> Dear Rose and Paddy,
> I'm going away now and I'll not be comeing back. maybe its a sin what I'm doing but I do not think it is because I am content about it and I'm looking forward to beam with Mick and Alice again and my wee sister too.
> I want to thank yous for all the help you give me over the years, espessly after

Mick died, because it was hard for me. But you know in the past three weeks it got harder and I think maybe I can't fine a womin because I'm not so good at all that.

And anyway I niver wanted a wife, just maybe a womin friend, because I had a lot of bother when I was a wee one with the things they did to me but that's the way it was and I cant forget it no matter what I do. It was a silly thing for me to think that any womin would bother with me to start with anyway.

Anyway I don't want yous to be worring about me because I'm going to a better place alright.

So many doors in Jamie's mind kept opening and closing as he tried to write. The past and present were showing him so many different versions of himself, but all he knew for certain then was the feel of the pen upon the page and the presence of the noose above his head that would end his plight. He took another bun from the bag, the crumbs dusting the page as he labored on.

I want yous both to have the house and farm and to look after wee Shep it isn't much but its all I have. Theres £3079 and fippence in my post office saveings book that'll put over me funerill and maybe a wee do after at Slopes afterword because I want everbody that knows me to have a wee drink and a dinner on me. With the money left over you could do up the house because its in bad shape and maybe yous would be wanton to sell it.

I want my accordjin to be give to Declan Colt and the silver Bullits as a keepsake because Declan always liked to here me playing and like yourselves he give me a chance. And there wasn't too many in this life that stopped to take notice of me.

I think this is all for now Rose and Paddy bye, bye I'll see yous sometime.

Your good freind

James Kevin Barry Michael McCloone.

P.S. My saveings book is behind the middle plate with the green rim round it at the back of the glesscase.

Jamie took another swig of the whiskey and slowly read over the letter. He hoped he hadn't made any mistakes, because it was hard enough to write and he didn't want to be doing it all again. He laid his hand on the dog's head as he read.

But presently Shep sat up with ears cocked. Jamie stared at him. He knew that a dog could hear thunder from a great distance, and wondered what might have alerted him. He patted Shep's head. There was no time left to ponder such things.

He was pleased with the letter and folded it in two as the dog bounded out of the barn. He placed it carefully in an envelope and sealed it. Shep was barking now and he thought it good that the dog had gone. All he wanted to do was shut the door and get on with it.

He snapped the letter beneath the string of a high bale and went to shut the door.

Rose proudly ushered Lydia into her only-frequented-on-special-occasions parlor.

"Sit yourself down there, Lydeea."

Lydia settled herself in a plump armchair, which, like its twin on the opposite side of a fake-coal fire and the matching sofa before it, was swollen with scatter cushions and crocheted throws, the armrests fattened with embroidered covers.

The room was small and intensely crowded, with examples of Rose's handiwork serving as a backdrop for a mob of cherished but often ill-considered impulse buys.

Many of the objects that populated the mantelshelf, the china cabinet, and the sideboard had been purchased in a hurry at various seaside resorts throughout Ireland; purchased, wrapped and paid for, more often than not whilst the exasperated bus driver sat revving his engine, blasting his horn and threatening to roar off if his excursion ladies didn't get "a bloody move on!" Mrs. Paddy McFadden was usually the last to board the bus, red-faced and breathless, "God-blisses-an-save-us," clutching that must-have souvenir.

Lydia's eyes took in a troupe of plaster fairies dancing in a plaster field, a luminous holy-water font fashioned roughly after a cast of Dürer's praying hands, an image of a glossy Virgin Mary being assumed into heaven on a plastic cloud, a line of somersaulting dwarfs pursuing a fleeing Snow White down a wooden path.

She could not have guessed, however, that the pair of hearthbound frogs (wearing knitted tricolor scarves and matching bootees) who sat staring up at her from big ceramic eyes, had very nearly resulted in Rose being left stranded in a shop on the west coast of Mutton Head Horn Bay one August evening of the previous year, as the heavens opened and darkness fell.

"What a beautiful room!" Lydia enthused.

"Thank you very much, Lydeea, but you know me and my Paddy don't use this room very often, because you know a woman needs to keep one room in her house kinda nice and proper for guests and the like."

"I completely agree, Rose."

"God-blisses-an-save-us, Lydeea, but James will be very happy to see you." Rose stood in front of the simulated fire on the cabbage-green Berber rug. She had swapped the sheep-flocked apron for a housecoat of buttercup yellow. As a point of gaudy interest, over the left breast pocket, she'd appliquéd a velvet sun of crimson above a patch of corduroy clouds.

"Y'know," she continued, "as I sez on the phone to you, he was very disappointed, so he was. Because y'know, Lydeea, he's a kinda soft creatur is James, if you unnerstand me. Now me mother, God rest her soul, was the same. Couldn't look at the crucified Christ in the chapel without startin' to blubber." Rose crossed herself quickly at the thought of her weeping mother and Lydia seized on the precious pause.

"Gosh, Rose, what I have to tell James will make him very happy. I'm certain of it."

Rose beamed, bursting with curiosity. In her head she was already stitching a satin wedding outfit and positioning a lace-rimmed collar, was already beating together the ingredients for a three-tiered wedding cake.

"I unnerstand you completely, Lydeea," she said, "James's ears are the first ears that should hear great news like that." Rose clasped her hands together, hardly able to contain her joy. "Now, Lydeea, a wee drop o' tea an' a bun while we're waitin'? My Paddy's just away there, so him and James should be arrivin' any minute."

At three minutes to seven Paddy's Morris Minor shuddered to a halt by Jamie's front gate. He sounded the horn as usual, but it could not be heard above the racket Shep was making as he circled the car, yelping frantically.

Across the yard, behind the closed door of the barn, Jamie was draining the last of his Black Bush whiskey, mopping up the last of the cake crumbs with a moist finger from the torn paper bag.

Paddy heaved himself out of the car seat. "Now now, wee Shep," he said, bending down to stroke the dog. "God, you're terrible excited this evening, and so will Jamie be when he hears who's waitin' for him at our house."

He secured the door of the Minor with the length of baler twine, as was his custom. He slowly wound it around the trunk handle. On this occasion, however, he exerted more pressure than was necessary.

The twine broke.

In the barn, Jamie smiled and climbed up onto a high bale.

An annoyed Paddy opened the trunk. He had another hank somewhere—but where now, that was the thing?

"Wait tae we see now," he muttered to himself, then began rummaging through the disorder of the cluttered trunk.

A helpless Shep bounded toward the barn door, barking and moaning. He raced back to Paddy, jumping up and whimpering, but Paddy shooed him away and continued with his search.

In the McFadden farmhouse, Lydia accepted from Rose what was to be the first of many cups of tea. In the trunk of the car, Paddy finally found what he'd been looking for. And behind the timbered door of the barn, James Kevin Barry Michael McCloone placed a noose about his neck.

Having finally succeeded in securing the car, Paddy knocked on the cottage door and shuffled inside. In the McFadden parlor, Lydia selected a coconut monkey from Rose's proffered plate. And in the Duntybutt barn, a rafter cracked with loud abandon.

Paddy, having discovered that the cottage was deserted, stood in the yard deciding where Jamie might be. He heard what sounded like a thunderclap. "Ah Jezsis!" a muffled voice was heard to cry. He rushed to the barn door and pulled it open. He was astonished to find his friend sitting in a heap on the floor, nursing a broken rafter attached to a length of twine.

"Christ, Jamie, what happened?"

Jamie, still stunned from the fall, stared at Paddy, wondering if indeed he'd arrived in paradise and, if he had, then what was Paddy McFadden doing in paradise, too?

Reality soon dawned when an excited Shep bounded through the barn door and leapt onto his master.

"Christ, Jamie, what happened?" Paddy tried again.

"There, there, wee Shep." Jamie finally found his voice and hugged the dog.

"I was up…tryin'," Jamie began, "tryin' to fix that bit of a rafter when the damned thing fell on me." He focused on Shep as he spoke, too embarrassed to meet his friend's eye.

Paddy surveyed the scene and tried to make sense of it. He saw the empty whiskey bottle and torn bun bag on a bale. Why, he asked himself, was Jamie having a picnic by himself in the dark shed while tryin' to fix a bit of a rafter?

"God, Jamie, you could a got yourself kilt!"

Jamie made no reply. Then Paddy noticed the letter on the high bale and the length of twine about Jamie's neck—the length of twine that Jamie was now vainly trying to conceal inside the collar of his shirt.

Paddy averted his eyes from his friend, to spare his blushes. He considered the condition of the roof.

"Aye, them oul' rafters is fulla woodworm. Dangerous boys, so they are."

Jamie released Shep and the excited collie bounded over to Paddy. He took him by the collar.

"I'll take the wee dog out, Jamie, and then I'll help ye up."

He led Shep out, thus affording his friend the opportunity of preserving his dignity by discarding in secret the evidence of his attempted suicide.

He returned a few minutes later, and was glad to see Jamie on his feet and the letter gone from the high bale.

"God, Jamie, you'll never believe who's waitin' for you at our house."

"Who?" was all Jamie could manage to say, as he accompanied his friend outside.

"Lydeea, Jamie, Lydeea Devine!"

"Lydeea?"

"Aye, Lydeea…and she sez she's got some great news for you… and she sez she'd like to hear ye playin' so you'd better bring the wee accordjin with you because we're gonna have a party!" Paddy was breathless with excitement.

Jamie stood staring at him, not knowing what to think. Just a few minutes earlier he had had his hand on heaven's doorknob, but for whatever reason, God had seen fit to slap the hand away. A period of readjustment to the earthly plane was necessary.

"Lydeea's waiting for me? With Rose? At your house?" Jamie heard himself ask the questions that seemed just too incredible for words.

"Aye, that's right. So you'd better run in and put your new suit on."

Jamie looked back at the barn, at the necklace of wheeling wood-pigeons that were still circling in the sky above its roof. All at once he was no longer in the drab yard of his homestead. He was in the place he'd yearned toward for so long: "the sunlit clearing." Suddenly all the black thoughts, the ones that had battered and buffeted him all his life, fell away and were replaced by a gleaming glade of joy. At last he understood.

"Heaven's...heaven's not up there," he said at last, pointing toward the pigeons.

"Well, maybe not...I don't know," said Paddy, confused. "But y'know, Rose would always say it was...because she would always say that whenever you see the Blessed Virgin bein' assumpted into heaven, it always shows her standing on a wee cloud when she's goin' up...in the prayer books and the like."

Jamie continued to gaze up at the sky. He seemed not to be listening. Paddy shook his arm.

"Jamie, ye better go in and get your suit on. We don't want Lydeea—I mean *Lily*—to be waitin' too much longer."

"*Who?*"

"Aye. She said her pet name was Lily. She was called that when she was a wee one, so she was."

Jamie stared at Paddy in amazement. He tried to say something but the words simply would not come. He was remembering what he had told himself just a few hours earlier.

This evening I'll be with you Lily, as sure as I'm standing here.

Nothing was making sense today—and everything was making sense.

"I'll turn the car," Paddy said. "Don't forget the accordjin."

Jamie hurried inside and Shep followed him. In the bedroom, he donned the shirt that Rose claimed was not so much "sunshine" but closer to a "custard" yellow. And the suit, that in her considered opinion was not peat, but "more of a gravy brown."

Shep, lying on the bed, watched his master closely as he adjusted his tie, before slipping on his shiny shoes. He reached for his accordion, then straightened to admire himself in the mirror. No, heaven's not up there in the sky, he said to himself. *It's now, begod; it's here. I'm part of it. I'm living it. It's mine.* Shep stood to attention on the bed and emitted a full-throated bark. He sensed a change in his master's routine—and it met with his full canine approval.

Jamie strode proudly from the house into the gilding sunlight, smiling broadly as he went. And as the dog went frantic and Paddy stood amazed, Jamie finally knew what happiness was. The best kind of happiness; that which through years of searching struggle is finally found and realized.

The ten-year-old boy from the orphanage had become a happy man. He belonged. He had leaped across that gorge of emotions and scaled an awesome height.

He sat in the passenger seat, Paddy at the wheel, Shep at his shoulder, and the accordjin on his lap. As the Minor pulled away from the farmhouse, Jamie was scarcely aware that the car was moving. When Paddy chose the wrong gear and the Minor spluttered and lurched as it began its slow labor up the hill, Jamie did not even register the jolting. He was dreaming, seeing only the beauty of the world through the grimy windshield, hearing only the sound of his accordjin music spilling out across the quiet fields.

"God, Jamie, there's another thing I forgot to tell you," Paddy said, careering down the hill and narrowly missing a milk churn. "I was in the post office the other day and Doris Crink told me…well, what she told me to tell you was that…was that she'd like you to call in for a drop o' tea this Sunday."

"Lordy me, is that so?" said Jamie, beaming broadly.

"Aye, she maybe wants to talk to you about your savings account…I don't know what else it could be about…. Maybe she's a wee bit of interest…a wee bit a interest to add on or maybe…"

Paddy continued in his fanciful conjectures, his voice fading away, merging with the rattling of the Minor. Jamie scarcely heard him. He was giving himself fully to the moment, his mind a flurry of memory and speculation. *Lydeea…Lily my wee sister! How can that be? She died as a baby. The nuns said so. But then the nuns said I'd never been given a name. The nuns said lots of things that weren't true. I know that now.*

Then he recalled a remark Rose had made.

"Paddy, didn't Rose say when she saw us in the Royal Neptune Hotel that Lydeea and me had the same noses?"

"She did indeed! She said ye could a been brother and sister, the pair a yous were that alike."

As the Minor rattled into the McFadden yard and Lydeea hurried to greet him, Jamie said goodbye forever to that frightened, ill-favored little boy, to the child who'd answered to the number Eighty-Six, and in whose tortured dreams this sunlit future gleamed.

And he knew at last, as he ran to meet his sister, that life's whole arduous journey had been in preparation for this moment. This perfect moment, free of pain and loneliness, and the memories of cruel people in darkened rooms that had haunted him for so very long.

For, in the tear-stained, heart-stopping warmth of Lily's embrace, James Kevin Barry Michael McCloone understood with the utmost joy that he'd survived it all, and wanted to live.

He wanted to live and sing and dance and play for each and every one of his glorious,

> his precious,
> his God-given,
> love-driven,
> Lily-rescued days.

Special Note

Even though this is a work of fiction, the regimes depicted in those sections set in the orphanage are based on real situations. The activities engaged in by the children, and their deprivation and punishments, are faithful to a great number of accounts related by those who survived such places.

Those institutions—the so-called "industrial schools," orphanages and "Magdalene" laundries—were run by certain religious orders in Ireland for the better part of a century, and were little more than places of slave labor, from which the Roman Catholic Church profited substantially at the expense of orphaned children, or children forcibly removed from single mothers.

The cruelty and inhumanity of such regimes only came to light in the early 1990s. The last such institution was closed in 1996.

Acknowledgments

Grateful thanks go to my agent, Bill Contardi, at Brant & Hochman, NYC, for picking up the novel and believing in it from the beginning. To everyone at Toby Press, most especially Deborah Meghnagi, for her kindness, keen-eyed observations and solid editorial advice. And last but not least to my husband, David, for his never-faltering faith in me.

About the Author

Christina McKenna

Christina McKenna grew up in County Derry, Northern Ireland. She attended the Belfast College of Art, gaining an honors degree in Fine Art, and studied postgraduate English at the University of Ulster. In 1986 she left Northern Ireland and spent ten years teaching both of these subjects abroad. She was, at the same time, pursuing a career as a painter. She mounted several exhibitions of her work—both as a solo artist and in group context—when abroad, but also on her return to Northern Ireland. She has written a memoir, published in 2004, titled *My Mother Wore a Yellow Dress,* and co-authored a book on exorcism, *The Dark Sacrament,* with her husband. *The Misremembered Man* is her first novel. She lives in Rostrevor, County Down.

The fonts used in this book are from the Garamond family